KV-579-246

SPECIAL MESSAGE T

THE ULVERSCROFT FOUN

(registered UK charity number 264873)

was established in 1972 to provide funds for research, diagnosis and treatment of eye diseases. Examples of major projects funded by the Ulverscroft Foundation are:-

- The Children's Eye Unit at Moorfelds Eye Hospital, London
- The Ulverscroft Children's Eye Unit at Great Ormond Street Hospital for Sick Children
- Funding research into eye diseases and treatment at the Department of Ophthalmology, University of Leicester
- The Ulverscroft Vision Research Group, Institute of Child Health
- Twin operating theatres at the Western Ophthalmic Hospital, London
- The Chair of Ophthalmology at the Royal Australian College of Ophthalmologists

You can help further the work of the Foundation by making a donation or leaving a legacy. Every contribution is gratefully received. If you would like to help support the Foundation or require further information, please contact:

THE ULVERSCROFT FOUNDATION
The Green, Bradgate Road, Anstey
Leicester LE7 7FU, England
Tel: (0116) 236 4325

website: www.ulverscroft-foundation.org.uk

740009853956

THE GIRL I LEFT BEHIND

As a young girl, Ella never considered that those around her weren't as they appeared. But when her childhood best friend shows Ella that you can't always believe what you see, Ella finds herself thrown into the world of the German Resistance.

On a dark night in 1941, Claudia is taken by the Gestapo, likely never to be seen again, unless Ella can save her. With the help of the man she loves, Ella must undertake her most dangerous mission yet and infiltrate the Nazi Party.

Selling secrets isn't an easy job. In order to find Claudia, Ella must risk not only her life, but the lives of those she cares about.

Will Ella be able to leave behind the girl of her youth and step into the shoes of another?

ANDIE NEWTON

THE GIRL I LEFT BEHIND

Complete and Unabridged

MAGNA
Leicester

First published in Great Britain in 2019 by
Aria
an imprint of Head of Zeus
London

First Ulverscroft Edition
published 2021
by arrangement with
Head of Zeus Ltd
London

Copyright © 2019 by Andie Newton
All rights reserved

This is a work of fiction. All characters, organisations, and events portrayed in this novel are either products of the author's imagination or are used fictitiously.

A catalogue record for this book is available from the British Library.

ISBN 978–0–7505–4880–9

Published by
Ulverscroft Limited
Anstey, Leicestershire

Printed and bound in Great Britain by
TJ Books Ltd., Padstow, Cornwall

This book is printed on acid-free paper

For Matt, Zane, and Drew

Historical Note

Hidden inside Nazi Germany, deep within the fabric of society, groups of rebels risked their lives defying the laws of the Third Reich. Many were young people, children who grew up in Hitler's Germany where Nazi indoctrination started in kindergarten. As these children reached adulthood, they realized that what they had been taught to admire wasn't worth admiring after all, and they resented the way the Nazi Party tried to control all facets of their life. These non-conformists were the resisters of Nazism, the youth of the German Resistance.

Prologue

1943

Germany

The man was a spy. This much he would have admitted, but only if the ropes had tightened just a hair more around his wrists, or if the water they threw on him had got any colder. There was, after all, only so much torture a man could take in Nazi Germany before his defences would break and his British accent would betray him.

The Gestapo had perfected their torture techniques, and contrary to belief, they liked to use the dullest knives, not the sharpest. The dull ones caused more pain and had been proven to yield much more information. Luckily enough for the man, informants hadn't learned this technique, and while they decided on the best approach for extraction, the man had wiggled out from the ropes that bound him, reached for the dagger he always carried in a sheath above his right ankle, and killed his way out of the Munich storage room where they'd held him captive.

He dared not go home to his flat for fear they'd already discovered where he lived. Instead, he broke for the side exit, shuffling down the long corridor the best he could with an injured leg that caused him to limp.

A trample roared just above him one floor up

and he listened with his eyes to the ceiling, counting the thumps, deciding how many informants were on the verge of discovering he'd got away. He limped on at a galloping rate, knowing his own hobbling could be heard, and burst out the side doors into the dark alley, tripping into some rubbish bins that hadn't been emptied.

A cat screeched from somewhere, and he stumbled forward, rushing toward his contact who'd been waiting for him outside for more than an hour: a girl — a shop girl, she had told him not long ago — who gleamed like a new coin in the night. She waved the bouquet she'd bought earlier, concealing the intelligence tucked inside. 'Where have you been?' she said, and he snatched the flowers from her hands.

His throat was dry, and try as he might, he didn't have the strength to tell her he'd been caught, but he did have the sense to tell her to run, and she took off in the other direction.

The man rounded the corner onto the street, and for a moment breathed a sigh of relief, thinking he'd outsmarted the informants and that his spy was safe. He took a deep breath, but then slumped forward from a surprise, life-ending stab to his abdomen.

The informant yanked the bouquet from the man's hands, laughing as he pulled his knife back, letting the man walk his last humiliating steps into a crowded square where he would die.

And when the man fell onto the cobblestones, people stopped and stared. To his horror, just when he was about to take his last gurgling breath, the girl he'd told to run leaned over his body and looked into his eyes. He saw the shock on her face, and then heard it from the others when English words spilled from his lips.

As she covered her mouth watching him die, his last thought was not one of shame for having been caught, but of guilt, because he'd remembered that hidden under his mattress with his notes, he had scrawled her name on a piece of paper.

1941

1

October

Nuremberg

I hurried through the crowded streets of Nuremberg, checking my watch every few seconds as the hands moved closer and closer to seven o'clock. The League of German Girls didn't wait for late arrivals, and if I missed Frau Dankwart's opening remarks, I'd hear about it from Aunt Bridget, who'd die from embarrassment if I showed up tardy again.

I had one job to do this evening, and that was to close up my aunt's antiques shop in time to make my League meeting. I didn't account for an unexpected customer who couldn't make up her mind, and then having the terrible misfortune of using my aunt's cramped office to change into my League uniform.

I rounded a corner, getting ready to cross the street, but then bumped right into a child, knocking the poor boy to the ground. He lay paralyzed with fear, eyes wide and unblinking, with his little hands clinging to his sides. I went to help him up, and that's when the yellow star sewn on his left breast shone up like a beam of light in the gloaming just before his curfew.

His mother screamed silently, hands to her mouth for the attention he caused, probably wondering if I was going to alert the policeman directing traffic nearby in the square. 'It wasn't his fault,' I said to his mother. I looked back at the policeman who hadn't seen a thing. 'Go!' And they walked into a sea of foot traffic, disappearing between the bodies.

I ran across the street, only that same policeman who'd been directing traffic had blown his whistle. Someone else took his post, and he walked up to me, hand gripping his billy club close to his side. I closed my eyes briefly, mad at myself, knowing I shouldn't have been running.

I smoothed my tie flat.

'Who are you running from?' He reached for my elbow, but I'd unbuttoned my coat just enough to show him my League uniform — thick blue tie and white shirt — which had actually started to dull, much to Auntie's dismay.

'I'm late for my League meeting. I'm sorry.'

Bystanders shot me strange looks, some probably hoping I'd be dragged away, give them a sight to see. He looked at his watch, tapping the crystal. 'At this hour?' He squinted.

I gulped, knowing his questions could go on indefinitely if he wanted. I tried not to sound impatient. 'I work at my aunt's shop. This is the first time I had to close *and* make a League meeting right after.' I hung my head down. 'I should have planned better.'

'What shop?' He tipped his helmet up, looking down the street and past the Nazi flags hanging above shop windows.

I pointed. 'The antiques shop just there. Next to the old beer cellar with the red door — '

'I know of it.' He sounded bored, and then quickly spotted someone else to go after, an old man with a cane on the other side of the street who moved much too fast for his age. 'Be off now,' he said, pulling out his stick and heading across the street.

I turned away, not wanting to see what was about to come next.

I took a deep breath once I'd made it to Frau Dankwart's house. All was quiet. The rest of the girls were already inside. I straightened my jacket and smoothed my hair back, if only to look less hurried. I went to knock on her tall black door and was suddenly thrown back to the first day I'd met her.

My parents had only just died when my aunt told me she'd enrolled me in the League of German Girls — the female branch of the Hitler Youth. She said my mother had broken the law since membership was compulsory. When I told her I wasn't a National Socialist she shushed me. That was five years ago. Now, it was only a matter of weeks before I turned eighteen, and I'd graduate out of the League.

I rapped once and the door flew open. Frau Dankwart's rail-thin body stood like a pole in the doorway, her dark eyes sinking into her face. 'Ella Strauss,' she said. 'Glad you *finally* arrived.' Her voice was stern, and I fully expected her to scold me, but then she threw a wrinkly old finger into the air, pointing at her parlour. 'Get inside. We're reading *Mein Kampf*,' she said, as if I thought we'd be reading something else. 'You almost missed my opening remarks.'

'Yes, ma'am. Sorry. Pardon me . . . ' I said, and

I slipped past her through the door.

Frau Dankwart's sitting parlour had been rearranged to look more like a classroom during League meetings. The most devout League girls sat at the desks. The ones she hadn't made up her mind about sat at the tables off to the side, and the ones she had little hope for sat on the floor way in the back in the draftiest part of the room. I made my way to the back.

I tripped on a ripple in the rug and bumped into a girl's desk. She looked up from her book, sniffling and snivelling, wiping tears from her eyes. 'I'm in love with the Führer,' she gushed.

I patted her arm and continued to the back of the room where my friend, Claudia, sat criss-cross on the floor waiting for me, her auburn hair twisted over one shoulder. I sat down in a hurry, grabbing my copy of *Mein Kampf* from my ruck-sack.

'You're late,' she whispered.

The girl in front of us turned around sharply. 'Shh!'

Claudia held her book up to her face, shoving her nose into it. 'What took you so long?' she whispered. 'I'm about to go out of my mind. Frau Dankwart's in one of her moods.'

I scooted closer to her, looking up over the pages of my book at Frau Dankwart, who was too busy looking at her reflection in a handheld mirror. She smoothed her grey hair back, which had already been pulled into a bun at the base of her neck.

'Sorry,' I said. 'My aunt has me closing the shop now by myself. Still not used to the hours, or how long it takes to walk here.'

Frau Dankwart cleared her throat from the front of the room, eyes scanning, and we pretended to be absorbed in our reading, ducking down just a bit, mouthing the text to ourselves.

Claudia leaned into my ear. 'What are you reading?' She took a quick look at some of the pages, and then we switched books. The book jacket was Hitler's memoir, but we'd changed the books inside months ago.

Frau Dankwart clapped her hands once, and we stood bolt upright. There was a moment of quietness as we looked up at Hitler's portrait on her wall. 'Ready, girls?' She clasped her hands together. 'Begin.'

And all thirteen of us drummed out our pledge. 'I promise always to do my duty in the Hitler Youth, in love and loyalty to the Führer . . . '

Claudia leaned into my ear. 'Can you help me again tonight?' she whispered, and I looked at her. 'Please?'

I glanced at Frau Dankwart to see if she was looking, but her back was to us.

I nodded once, and Claudia smiled.

* * *

I had just blown out the candle on my nightstand and settled deep into the down of my feathered bed, when I heard the tick of a fingernail tapping against my window. I kicked off the sheets and then peered into the dark reflection of the glass. It could have only been one person.

'Claudia.'

She climbed through the window, plopping the burlap bag she had strung over her shoulder onto my bed. I tipped the bag upside down and gave it a stiff shake: a brown mop-topped wig, a sack of hair pins, barbed metal hooks, and a tin of lard to help mould it in place — the makings for a disguise.

Claudia sat on my bed and batted her emerald-green eyes. A row of pin-pricked freckles ran across her crinkled nose as she held the wig close to her face. 'Can you pin this?'

My jaw cracked when I yawned, nodding.

'Thank you for doing this, Ella. I know it's late.' She kissed my cheek before wrapping her arms around my neck.

I cleared a spot on the floor with my foot and then relit the smouldering pillar candle on the nightstand next to my bed. This wasn't the first time she'd asked me to thread her hair. I'd plaited a synthetic wig into it last week. But never had she come to my window so close to midnight.

Claudia situated herself on the floor, talking about how she wanted to use every strand of hair she had brought. 'None of it should be wasted.'

I brushed her hair out before dividing it into sections. Plaiting was meticulous, eye-straining work, but it was the best way to secure pieces of a wig into place. Her scalp still looked tender and raw from the last time. 'Your scalp hasn't healed.'

'Don't worry about that,' she said, flicking her fingers at me. 'Pull it as tight as you can. Even if it hurts.' And I did, pulling and stretching her hair tightly into place, especially behind her ears, using a dab of lard to smooth fly-a-ways before snipping a small lock of hair from the wig.

'I'm getting good at your disguises.' I rubbed a few of the strands in between my fingers; it was silky, not dry and bristly like the last one. 'Is this — '

'Real? You can tell?'

I held it to my nose. There was a delicate scent to it, almost as if she had rinsed the hair in rose water.

Claudia's stomach rumbled. My aunt's room was opposite mine, down a long corridor in the corner of an old, half-timbered house in the Altstadt, Old Town, and even though there was a good distance between our rooms, she had sharp ears. Auntie also had the bladder of a little girl, often getting up in the middle of the night to relieve herself. The sound of splintering floorboards always gave her away. Tonight, those noises would serve as a warning.

Claudia's stomach rumbled again, but this time it sounded like a wrecking ball slamming against her ribs. 'Shh! You'll wake my aunt.'

She winced. 'I didn't have time to eat dinner. I'd stop it if I could — I swear it.'

'I'd get you something from the kitchen, but with my aunt . . . '

'I know,' she said. She turned around unexpectedly, and her soft hair slid down the flank of my hand, unravelling the twisty curl I'd pulled from the wig. 'You're an incredible friend, Ella, always helping me, never asking any questions.' She reached for my face, her fingers feeling unusually icy as they grabbed my lower jaw and aligned my eyes to her own. 'I need another favour. You can say no.'

'What is it?'

'I need you to deliver a key to a man you don't know.'

I scooted up. She'd never asked me to do something so mysterious before, and my heart beat faster. 'Where? And who is he?'

'At the Hauptmarkt near the fountain, before the merchants set up their tents in the morning. His name is Wilhelm.'

The Hauptmarkt was one of the oldest squares in the city, right in the middle of the Altstadt, where merchants sold everything from linens to fruit and vegetables.

'He'll speak French to you. You still know some, right? It's a good idea to speak in another language. In case anyone overhears.'

'Remember?' I said. 'Both my mother and father were fluent. We talked in French all the time before they . . . ' My back got a little straighter. 'Passed away.'

She patted my knee. 'I'm sorry,' she said. 'The anniversary of their car accident is coming up, isn't it?' She got very quiet and reached for my hand. 'Such a shame we had to mourn the deaths of our loved ones together.'

During the same week many years ago, Claudia's older sister, a teacher, had been hung outside her apartment for not aligning her curriculum with Party ideology. Her sister's eight-year-old student had turned her in.

Claudia took a deep breath, then dug into her pocket and fished out a key. 'There's a message too,' she said. 'The key is useless without it.' She pulled a piece of paper out from under her sleeve and unravelled it. 'Here,' she said, showing it to me.

A puff of air escaped from my lips. It was an address — a house she once lived in, now used as one of her father's rentals. I glanced up at her.

'They're sending all the Jews east, Ella. Against their will.' She stared at me while I thought about what she'd been doing. I wasn't that naïve; I knew that, with all of her disguises, she was doing something that could get her arrested. From the beginning, she only told me things I needed to know. It was safer that way. I just didn't realize she was actively hiding them.

'Will you be all right?' she said, and I nodded. 'If it's too much — '

I thought of that little boy I ran into earlier. He looked about ten years old or so. Brown hair and eyes, chubby cheeks, innocent. Scared.

'I'll do it,' I said. 'Deliver a key and an address. I'll go before I head to the shop. But where will you be?' I knew not to ask, but it slipped out. At the very least, I thought she could tell me how she kept her activities from her parents. 'What do you tell your parents?'

'My father's regularly in Frankfurt on business and my mother has her liquor. I'm not missed.'

Claudia let go of my arm and fitted her elbows back into the crook of her knees, leaving a swirl of gritty dust on the floor where she had spun back around.

'And you'll need a scarf,' she said, 'something with a lot of yellow in it. Otherwise you'll blend in with everyone else. He'll be looking for it.'

'In that drawer,' I said, pointing with my head.

She sifted through a mound of scarves and ribbons until she found the solid yellow one my uncle gave me before the Party transferred him to Berlin to develop ciphers.

She bit the tag off with her teeth and tossed the scarf into my lap. 'Don't forget it, and stay until Wilhelm arrives. Don't leave the square with the key still in your pocket.'

I peeked over my bed, reaching for the hooks she had brought with a searching hand. 'I won't,' I said, and the bag flopped to the ground like a fat-bottomed sack of flour with metal barbs sticking from it.

Following Claudia's firm request, I anchored the hooks into the base of each curl. 'You didn't have me do this last time.' I used my grip on her hair to move her head around to look at me.

'Pull my hair nice and tight on the top,' she said, and I did, drawing her temples back with a fine pull. After a few minutes she clawed her way around her scalp, silently memorizing the location of each hook.

An hour of silence passed before I noticed the tips of my fingers were as raw and red as fleshy little tomatoes. They burned with each thread of her hair, but the backs of my hands felt like my knees, cold and numb. As the clock ticked, my shadow on the wall withered smaller and smaller next to hers, like a grape left on the vine, but then I noticed it wasn't me changing.

It was Claudia.

Gone was the anxious girl that slumped between my legs and in her place a stoic, complacent young woman, whose arrow-straight shadow on the wall loomed over mine like a steel beam. Her arms stretched out to feel the warmth of the candle's flame just as I tied the last of her hair up. I broke the silence with a breathy sigh.

'I've never seen a wig made out of real hair before, Claudia.' I sat back, and let my limbs fall where they may. 'This poor woman must be bald!'

A pin fell from my lips. 'She's dead,' Claudia said.

It landed, clear as a bell, and rolled but neither of us moved to stop it.

2

Wagner blared from the front room and my eyes popped open from my bed. A steadfast nationalist, Aunt Bridget only played German composers in the morning, with a nod to the English late in the afternoon, but only when she thought she was by herself.

I lay still, sliding my eyes toward the door, following the sound of Auntie's footsteps as she walked down the corridor. Shadows wrestled with the breaking sunlight under my door as she made one last pass before knocking.

'Good morning,' she said, slightly elevated, careful not to offend the pomp of *Valkyrie* in the background. I pulled the blanket up around my neck, mentally telling her to walk away, but then she called me by my nickname, Sascha, and I knew I'd have to answer.

'I'm up.'

My feet met the floor again, as they had earlier, but this time they were more aware. A pang of loneliness hit me as I looked at the spot where, just hours ago, a crime had been committed. The imprint of my body still pressed into the sheets tried to lure me back, but it was too late. The day had begun.

My door flew open with a bang.

'Ah!' I jumped to a stand, only to slump in place when I saw Auntie's smiling face. 'Auntie, you scared me.'

She threw a fluffy white robe on top of my bed, the warm smell of morning eggs trailing in behind her. 'I thought you heard me.' Her hair was wound up into a braided bun behind her head, and it looked very tight, which made me wonder how long she'd been up. 'You're awake now, that's what matters.' She smiled, patting my shoulder.

I put the robe on, listening to her as she moved about my room and picked magazine clippings off the floor. 'I don't understand today's fashion,' she said, holding up an advertisement for women's trousers. 'What are you going to do with these?' She bundled the clippings into her hands.

'Paste them to my wall. All the girls do it, Auntie.'

'Hmm,' she said, stuffing the clippings into a drawer. 'Girls these days. Well, can you at least keep your room a little cleaner? I feel like I'm always straightening it up.' The pink in her cheeks reddened and lightly blackened lashes fanned out from her eyes as she smoothed her white apron against her waist.

I yawned, nodding. 'Sorry, Auntie. I'm still so tired.'

'Are you? Your eyes look very bright to me.' She swept a lock of hair behind my shoulder, and her hand briefly touched the nape of my neck. Then she paused, and looked into my eyes, deeply, as if she had lost something. 'You know, your mother was my favourite sister, and although she gave birth to you — '

'She was your only sister, Auntie.'

'Be that as it may . . . '

'Yes, yes, I know the whole story. You were the

midwife who delivered me, and your blue eyes were the first I ever saw.'

She moved to the dresser, rearranging my things to look more orderly, and picked up a photograph of my cousins, Joseph and Alex. She got lost for a moment staring at their faces. Both had left for Munich last summer, one for medical school and the other for the Reich, which left only me and Auntie to run her antiques shop. She wrote them every Tuesday, but only Joseph wrote back, and I felt sorry for her, which is why I didn't mind when she made references about me being more like a daughter to her than a niece.

'Everyone is gone now,' she said, wiping a little tear from her eye. 'Your uncle, on business with the Party, and now my children.' She took a deep breath and then smiled, looking at me. 'Except you, my sweet. I'm glad you are here.' She set the frame down. 'Now, come into the kitchen. Breakfast is ready.' Her dampened gaze slid to the ground, noticing the swirl of dust Claudia and I had made on the floor with our bodies. Auntie didn't like Claudia, said a mother who drank more often than she cooked wasn't a true German. I'd get punished for sneaking friends into my bedroom, but it would be double if she knew that friend was Claudia.

My heart sped up the longer she stared at the floor. 'Something wrong?' I moved toward the door, trying to coax her out of my room, smiling nervously, hoping she wouldn't read anything into it.

Auntie swiped the wood planks with her foot. 'No, no. Everything is fine.' And she walked out of my room, only to stop in the corridor and adjust Hitler's portrait hanging on the wall. 'Everything is *perfectly* fine.'

* * *

My stomach was already upset, thinking about Claudia's key, and then as soon as I saw the slivers of meat and yellow cheese Auntie had out for us in the kitchen, my insides twisted into a cluster of mushy knots. I forked a piece of salami, lifting it in the air, examining the multi-coloured sheen glistening on top.

Auntie turned to see her hind-end reflecting in the windows, unaware I was making faces at the meat. A tiny frown questioned the sag in her apron tie, which she tightened with two quick pulls, before running her thumbs in between the apron and her waist. I set the meat down just as she reached for a silver tray that had two hard-boiled eggs on top and the decorative egg cups she rarely used.

'Sorry, Sascha. I forgot the eggs and they cooked a little longer than usual,' Auntie said, wincing. The shells had split and bits of white burst from the cracks. When I didn't reach for an egg, she set one on my plate.

'What's this?' I asked. 'Your special egg cups?' Auntie kept them in a locked glass cabinet with her silver-plated flatware, china and a few crystal goblets.

'I have my reasons. These were your grandmother's.' Her voice lifted as she studied the design on the cup — dull red roses, rimmed in a band of burnished gold. 'Aren't they exquisite?' she said as I gave the top of my egg a good crack with my spoon.

The egg cups were a family heirloom that had been passed down from mother to youngest daughter for the last seventy years. I remembered the day my grandmother gave them to my mother. It was a spring day because roses had started budding in the flower boxes. I was twirling in the parlour, giggling, getting dizzy when someone said that someday they would be mine. The egg cups passed to my aunt after my mother died.

Auntie set a place for herself opposite me, tailings of grease-slicked salami hanging over her plate, and poured herself a cup of hot black tea. 'I'm trying to remember the last time we used these cups. Was it at Easter?' Her eyes drifted to the ceiling, her head tilted in thought. 'Humph!' She shrugged her shoulders and then tucked into her food.

A piece of meat grazed her chin as she manoeuvred it into her mouth, leaving a slimy mark on her skin, which she later wiped off with the back of her thumb.

I smirked sourly, watching her eat. 'Auntie . . .'

'What? A good German always eats her food.' Despite what she ate, Aunt Bridget had the physique and grace of a Grecian statue — a true goddess and a real German beauty with rounded hips and a tiny waist. 'Well, do you remember, Sascha? The last time we used your grandmother's egg cups?'

'I don't know, Christmas, Easter, the Führer's birthday . . .'

'Oh yes, all the wonderful holidays.' She smiled while chewing. 'Well, one day they will be yours.'

I imagined the cups spending an eternity on a dusty attic shelf, wrapped in crinkled newspaper next to the blue chalice she'd bought while on subsidized holiday in the Adriatic. 'Perhaps one of the boys would like them?' As soon as I said the words I wished I hadn't because her eyes crossed.

'You don't want the egg cups? But they're a family heirloom.'

I put my hand on hers. I didn't want to tell her outright that I didn't care about the egg cups, she'd be too hurt by it. 'Egg cups aren't something a girl my age gets excited about, Auntie. Ask me when I'm older.'

Her mouth hung open for a second or two. 'Well, if that's your choice,' she said, reaching for her tea. 'It's all about choices now, isn't it?' She blew steam from her cup, testing the temperature with her tongue, when a squadron of bombers flew over the house, rattling the windows and jingling the empty fruit jars on the shelves. Both of us looked up at the ceiling. 'Must be a clear day out,' she said, finally taking a drink of her tea. 'A good time to fight the enemy. Nice and early.'

'What time is it?'

She looked at her watch. 'Almost eight,' she said, and I thrust my chair backward into the wall.

Wilhelm! My spoon catapulted off the table and careened to the ground, clinging and clanging its way under the buffet as I grappled with my robe tie. 'I have to go! I have to get dressed.'

'Relax,' she said as she chewed. 'There's no shop today.'

My face jumped. 'What?' Auntie only closed the shop for funerals and birthdays.

'It's just for the day.' She fluttered her fingers in the air, then coughed and fiddled with the table setting. Her walnut-shaped eyes sank into tiny round doughnut holes, firm cheeks turned flabby, and her lower lip drooped below her gum line.

'Aren't I . . . aren't I doing a good job?' I had to wonder if I'd made an error in her ledger and she needed a day to sort it out, but I'd been careful. Being a good shop girl seemed to be one of the only things Auntie thought I did well.

'Yes, of course,' she said. 'I thought we could use a break.'

'Oh, all right,' I said, but then I had to think up a lie that was plausible enough to get me out of the house. 'I'm not going to the shop anyway.' My right eye twitched when I lied, but she was too busy making a mess of the table to notice. Forks changed positions with the saucers and glasses made room for relocating egg cups. 'I'm seeing a friend, Greta. We're spending the day together before she leaves for Berlin tonight on the train.'

Auntie stopped. 'Oh! Greta. That nice girl from the League?' A smile streaked across her face and she nestled her body tightly into the cleft of her high-backed chair. The wood spindles cracked against her spine as she pressed her weight against them, using the points of her laced napkin to blot the corners of her mouth.

'Yes, Auntie. From the League.'

'Greta is a sweet girl, a good German. Not like that Claudia you befriended.'

'I really must go . . . '

I said the words, but hesitation weighed heavy in my legs, and I couldn't move until she gave me her blessing. Once she gave me permission to leave the table I felt — in some back-handed sort of way — she was giving me permission to commit treason.

Auntie refolded her napkin, smoothed its creases with a flat hand and gave me a hard wink. 'Sounds like a lovely idea, Sascha. Just don't forget your League meeting tonight at Frau Dankwart's house. Better wear your uniform.' She waved me out of the room like an elegant cat, and I left her in the kitchen sipping her tea, staring contently at the blank space where I had sat.

* * *

I slipped on a pair of old stockings under my skirt and tucked in my white shirt, which hadn't been cleaned or starched. Auntie must have sensed I wasn't put together as well as she would have liked since she stopped me at the door. A dribble of tea stained her apron from jumping out of her chair.

'Halt!' Auntie shuffled toward me, her arms reaching for my neck.

'I have my Youth League uniform on.' I flipped back the lapels on my faded black trench.

'Yes,' she said, 'but your tie is all wrong.' She tucked the tie under my collar, reaching behind my neck. 'If your tie is sloppy your League leader will think *you* are sloppy.' She finished tightening my tie, slowly constricting the knot against my throat.

'Auntie, it's too tight.'

She loosened my tie just a hair so I could breathe.

'I can't wait until New Year's Eve when I turn eighteen and can put this uniform in a drawer.'

'Oh, don't be ridiculous!' She felt the fabric between her fingers. 'This is good quality German wool. What's not to like?'

'It's not that, well, it is partly that, but Auntie, you know my parents weren't National Socialists. They didn't raise me to — '

Auntie closed her eyes. 'Your parents were misguided. We've talked about this a hundred times, really, Sascha.' Her eyes popped open and she finished adjusting my uniform with a pull to my collar. 'And what's this?' She turned my wrist over, revealing the yellow scarf tied there. 'Your uncle would be pleased to know you're wearing the scarf he bought you.'

'Don't worry, Auntie. I'll take it off before the League meeting.'

'Thank you,' she said. 'Frau Dankwart isn't one for flashiness.' She examined a pulled thread where the tag had been. 'Be careful with it, won't you, Sascha? Your uncle doesn't buy cheap things.'

'I will.'

She centred the tie on my neck. 'There. All fixed.'

Auntie took a step back to admire her work, but then frowned at the sight of my dingy white shirt. I pulled the lapels of my coat closed before she could examine it too closely.

'Auntie, I'm going to be late.'

'Yes, of course.' She kissed both my cheeks. 'Have a big time, Sascha.'

I shut the door behind me, feeling the key in my pocket and the stiff, childlike awkwardness of my uniform. I had compromised by adding a silver hairclip behind my right ear and a pair of heels I had been dying to wear. Had Auntie noticed those things instead of my uniform, she might have asked me to take them off.

I went over the details Claudia had given me — the scarf, the key and the location — and then set out for the square, walking through town. The sun was out, and so were the Wehrmacht — new recruits testing out their uniforms, taking their last cigarettes before saying goodbye to their sweethearts. Behind them, work crews were refitting a Jewish school with Nazi emblems and flags. I squeezed the key in my pocket.

My pace quickened when I got to the Pegnitz River and started over the crowded foot bridge, knowing the Hauptmarkt was just on the other side, but then noticed the sputter of white exhaust pooling out of an empty four-door Mercedes 260D. I stopped abruptly.

Only the Gestapo left their engines running when parked.

I knew somewhere up ahead two — possibly even three — Gestapo were looking for someone. I thought about turning around, but people might think that was suspicious after I'd seen the car. So, I walked on, brow furrowed low and eyes heavy to the ground, a jab here, a jab there, poking some in the stomach and others in the back, quickening my pace, almost to the other side. A hand grabbed my shoulder, and I flew forward onto the ground with a yelp. My cheek hit the cold cobblestones, and I lay stunned and unmoving with commuters walking around my head and toes.

A man chuckled over me. 'I didn't mean to startle you!'

I said nothing, nose to the cobblestones, feeling the burn of fresh scrapes on my knees and the coolness of one bare foot without a shoe.

'Ella, it's me,' he said, and I looked up from the ground. 'Herr Coburg.' My aunt's trusted art supplier — the last person I expected to see. He shook my shoulder with the same meaty hand that had grabbed me, his body ballooning as he bent down. 'I thought you saw me.' His breath smelled of sausage, and his cologne stunk like an old man's.

I swallowed, wetting my dry throat. 'Herr Coburg . . . ' I scraped myself off the ground. 'I . . . I fell.' The ox statue marking the entrance to the meat halls towered over us and almost looked alive, the way his tail lay near his feet and his body, chiselled, with eyes that bulged from its face. I felt dizzy staring at it.

'Yes!' He laughed, and the ox's horns seemed to jut straight from his ears. 'You did fall!'

Three Gestapo officers suddenly surrounded us, sharp-brimmed hats, leather shoulder straps, slate-coloured double-breasted trench coats that hung longer than their knees. I lost my balance from standing in one heel and staring at the ox, and fell into the arms of one of the officers. He scowled, dropping his club to catch me, one eye glaring, before tossing me to my feet like a dog.

'Sorry.' I winced, and he straightened his jacket.

A different officer had picked up my detached

heel and juggled it in his hands. Early thirties, razor-sharp jaw, silver eyes that matched the glint on his belt knife. 'Here you are, fräulein. Looks like you dropped this.'

I reached for my heel, but he didn't let go right away. I felt his gaze as I tugged on it, his eyes swooping across my chest like a heavy hand.

'You can call me Muller.'

I gulped. 'Officer Muller, pleasure to meet you.'

He smiled from ear to ear, exposing a disturbing set of blazing white teeth. 'And you dropped this too.' He pulled back the flap of his coat just below his waist. Hooked on a silver buckle, next to a palm-sized bulge in his trousers, was the rest of my shoe. He shifted his hip and it fell off.

They laughed when I went to snatch it from the ground.

'Coburg, you know this girl?' the third officer said, patting his shoulder.

They know each other?

He was a tall but stout man with an egg-shaped belly, hooded eyes, and a weather-beaten face. There was a red band of paper wrapped around his cigar and he played with it like a ring around his finger. The tips of his moustache fluttered in the gentle wind and it reminded me of my uncle, though with his wide, caterpillar brow and imposing stature he looked more like Wilhelm II.

'Yes, Dietrich. I do,' Coburg said through stained, brown teeth. He twirled a cane in the air with his spotted hand. 'Gentleman, this is Ella Von Bruen. She works at one of my antiques shops.'

Of course, it wasn't his shop at all, and Von Bruen was my aunt's surname, not mine. But since he gave my aunt first pick of his inventory, I had to let some things slide.

Dietrich took three short puffs from his cigar and sneered. 'Where exactly were you headed this morning, fräulein?' He stepped closer, exhaling with flared nostrils. I acted as if I didn't hear him and attempted to straighten my coat, my elbow poking him mid-belly where his buttons gaped into diamond-shaped holes.

'Yes,' Muller said. 'Where could such a pretty — ' he cleared his throat ' — girl be off to so early in the morning?' His words felt heavy like syrup, trapping me in place.

Coburg squinted. 'Bridget closed the shop today, Ella. You know that, don't you?' He tugged on my uniform tie, pulling it out from under my coat. 'And League meetings are much later in the day.'

This was the first time I'd been questioned when I actually had something to hide. For a moment I thought ignorance would save me, so I kept messing with my coat. But when I glanced up they were taking notes.

There had been only one other time I felt that way, trapped and cornered. When I was thirteen, Frau Dankwart caught me drawing a picture of Hitler dressed like a little girl — pink ribbon in his hair, a bonnet, and even a dress. She whipped my knuckles in front of the entire Youth League. But that wasn't the unpleasant part: it was feeling trapped under the suspicious eye of Frau Dankwart as she stood over me, questioning me, demanding I explain myself as I tried to hide the drawing under my hand.

I struggled to come up with a story and then coughed to buy some time. Only Muller started patting my back. 'You all right?' His voice sounded concerned, but not genuine. Then he smacked his palm in between my shoulder blades, hard, as if he were used to hitting a woman in such ways. I squeezed my eyes shut, wondering how long I could keep up the coughing charade with him pounding on my back, when a bus lurched to a stop just a few feet away.

My skirt fluttered from a burst of exhaust. Doors flapped open, and people scurried out like ants onto the pavement. Dietrich pointed his cigar at a grey-haired man carrying a black case. Muller dropped his arm, and I slipped away, toddling down the stairs into the meat halls as fast as I could wearing uneven shoes.

I weaved in and out of hanging carcasses, trying to find a safe spot to hide, when a butcher surprised me, coming around the side of a blue-stamped deer. He glanced at my shoes, one with a heel, the other flat, and then to the machete lying on a garnet-stained table before walking away. *The machete.*

My whole body straightened.

Claudia always said that if something doesn't work right, you should change it into something that does. I laid my shoe on the table; I hadn't time to think about it, I simply grabbed the knife, squeezing the handle with ten white knuckles. *Slam!*

The heel snapped free like a bone from its joint, rolled off the table and fell to the ground, but I was already making my way into the square, waving my yellow scarf around as red-and-white striped tents opened with a flap, ready for business.

I wasn't sure what would happen — would Wilhelm walk right up to me? Would he pass a note instead? I sat down on the steps of the Schöner Brunnen, under its Gothic spire, tucked my skirt under my thighs, and waited — waited for Wilhelm, waited for a sign.

Hours passed. Nothing.

Daytime turned into the afternoon, and the sun had disappeared behind a blanket of grey clouds. A raindrop fell on my shoulder — then another and another until it started pouring.

And I realized, something had gone terribly wrong.

3

Claudia told me not to leave the square with the key in my pocket, but there I was, standing in the courtyard of Claudia's old house in the Am Oberg, staring at the back door with my feet sinking into mud. *Maybe the Jews are already gone?* I thumbed through probable scenarios like pages in a book. The more quiet seconds I stood looking at the house, thinking about what to do, the harder my chest pounded. I needed to do this or go home. After all, it was late. I was sure I had missed my League meeting, and my aunt was probably wondering where I was.

My heart moved into my ears, ebbing and thumping, and I slid the key into the lock. Two clinks and a shove later, the door creaked open with a dull moan. I left my shoes in the mud and stepped into the room. When my bare feet hit the wood floor, they stuck to it like a pair of clammy dead fish.

'*Hallo*,' I whispered. 'Claudia sent me.'

A few moments passed before I heard the pop of snapping floorboards. My eyes swung to the ground, searching for the noise. A little old lady hobbled out from the darkness. She had bottle-thick glasses and frizzy, grey hair that hadn't been set in days; some parts lay flat, other parts curled behind her ears. But as she stepped out from behind the velvety blue curtains, it was the relief in her eyes I noticed first, and my heart stopped pounding so much.

She clutched her chest. 'Oh, I thought we were forgotten!'

An old man climbed out from behind the divan. 'Not so fast, Maria.' He shuffled toward me, reaching into the inside pocket of his wool jacket to pull out a pair of round spectacles. Not the type a grandfather would wear, but the type I had seen young aristocrats wear with leather ear wraps. Slicks of silver-streaked hair hung over his eyes as he fitted them to his head. 'Another girl?' He leaned forward, taking a long, scrutinizing look at me.

A young woman slid out from along the baseboards and scurried to his side. 'We're rescued!' She was in her mid-twenties with wavy brown hair pinned behind her ears with gold, glittery clips. I backed up into the crack of the door, feeling every bit of my drab uniform hidden under my coat, thinking if she were in one of my magazines, I'd clip her out and paste her to my wall.

'Don't be afraid,' she said, holding her hand out as if trying to catch a bird. 'We're not going to eat you.'

A man, who I thought might be her father, rested muscular hands on her shoulders. 'Well, not until we know your name at least,' he said.

'Karl!' the old lady snapped. 'Don't tease the poor thing. She's here to help us, after all.'

'Would everyone shut up?' The old man growled as he spoke. 'She hasn't told us why she's here.' He dissected me with his eyes, moving his mouth back-and-forth as if he was chewing on something tough and needed to spit.

'I'm sorry.' I cleared my throat, not sure what to say other than the truth. 'I didn't know what to expect when I got here.'

'Expect?' he said. 'Four people in a house with no lights or food, that's what you can expect!'

I backed up further into the crack.

Karl touched the old man's shoulder. 'Papa, Mama is right,' he said. 'Let's give her a chance to speak.'

Maria gently took my hands and moved me away from the door. 'We're the Kortens, and we've been waiting for you all day.' She gazed into my eyes batting sparse lashes, and I saw my reflection in the lenses of her glasses. 'What's your name, dear?' Her fingers curled around mine.

'I'm . . . Sascha.' I stuttered when I said my name. Only Auntie called me Sascha.

The old man grumbled, 'That's a boy's name.'

Maria put her arm around the girl's shoulders and pulled her forward. 'This is my granddaughter, Elsie. My son Karl is her Papa, and, well, you probably have guessed this old man giving you the treatment is my husband, Bart,' she said, giving him a scowl.

Bart took a step back and his eyes wandered to the ground. 'You understand though, right, fräulein?'

His words sounded like an apology, and I accepted it with a nod.

They talked about freedom and hugged each other, but my thoughts slowly drowned out their voices when I realized I hadn't thought things through. *Where should I take them? They can't stay here. It's not safe. The renters could be here any minute.*

My face hardened and felt as plastic as a cheap doll's frozen in a quizzical expression.

Then something odd happened. A rumble in the distance — akin to a million boulders hurling down the street. Shouting voices zigzagged into a perverse roar. *A raid.* We stood paralyzed like a handful of mice shining in a cat's eye.

Elsie pointed a shaking finger at the wall.

Against the floral wallpaper a silhouetted string of gingerbread-shaped figures marched military-like with what looked like guns jutting from their bodies. A booming kick to the house next door made me jolt, and then the screams from those hiding inside waved like a shiver over us all. Men pleaded for their lives, and women cried for their babies. Crashing glass spraying across the stone step sounded like wet potato strings thrown into hot oil.

Then without warning, it just stopped.

'The Reich!' Elsie cried. 'They're going to get us!'

'They'll kill us before we get out of Nuremberg,' Bart said.

My instinct was to hide, and my aunt's shop wasn't far away.

'There's an antiques shop a block from here. On Obere Schmiedgasse. It will have to work for now. Grab your things,' I said, but everyone had already covered their heads with hoods and scarves before I finished talking.

We gathered quietly by the door, listening, waiting for the right moment to escape, and then snuck out the back.

The castle lights shone over the wall — *too much*

light, I thought, *too much light*.

I slipped backward in my shoes, and Karl hurriedly scraped our footprints away with a rake he'd found propped against the fence. We reached the open street, but once there the sheer darkness of the city made us all stop in our tracks. Black figures scattered like insects, some ran, others hooded themselves with cloaks or ducked into alleyways. Then we heard the terrifying noise of a beating fist.

Boom. Boom. Boom.

Elsie locked arms with me. Screams were everywhere — in the eaves, from the dark windows, and through doors that swung open from broken hinges.

'It's a roundup,' Bart yelped.

A line of Gestapo marched down the road. They banged on doors before barrelling up staircases, all the way into the lofts, and then dragged the people from inside out into the street and into giant armoured trucks. They tore the women's jewels from their necks and took money from the men's pockets.

Karl pushed Elsie and me to keep moving, and we did; Bart and Maria followed just a step behind, through shards of glass that pierced the soles of our shoes.

Herr Rudin's bakery next to Auntie's shop was a sad sight. His front door lay in the street and a dark, cavernous hole marred by broken brick and toppled tables had replaced his display window. Fresh breads and strudel baskets rolled into the street; other bits sucked their way toward the back of his shop like a sinister void — Herr Rudin's wife was a Jew.

My heart sank, thinking the Gestapo had dragged her away, and then raced when I heard them marching back toward us.

I snatched the spare keys from the window well and fumbled my way around the ring with heavy, rapid breaths. Bart and Maria stumbled into my backside, knocking my face into the door and the keys right out of my hand. With a pounding heart I picked them off the ground and started my search all over.

'Hurry,' Karl said, looking over his shoulder. 'Open it!'

Maria and Elsie tapped my shoulders, each saying something different with urgent, almost tearful voices. Bart's breath blew hot on my neck. 'It's that one,' he said, trying to grab the keys.

The deadbolt clicked over and like dominoes we fell into the shop, one on top of the other, while the bell chimed wildly. Someone's knee hit my back, another's elbow jabbed my face. Elsie threw her arms around my neck, and I dragged her body away from a beam of light that shone through the window and streaked across the floor.

A voice yelled just outside the shop. '*Aufhören!* Stop!' Two policemen rushed past the window and tackled someone to the ground, bones and flesh smacking against the pavement. I closed the door from the floor, and we scuttled along the dark wall toward the back of the shop and the basement.

We filed in blind with our hands on each other's shoulders, down three stone steps. I searched desperately for the light cord hanging from the ceiling and then pulled forcefully enough to break it when I found it. The snap of the light echoed off the wall like a struck match: something felt off.

The twinge in my spine twisted me around. The stove-sized cast iron door that led into the abandoned sixteenth-century beer cellar on the other side was cracked open a finger's width from the wall. Its rusted latch had been replaced by a silver pin hook, and the blackhead screws that anchored it into the brick wall looked brand new. The door had been there for years, before I was born, but never in my life had I seen it open, until now.

'That's odd.'

Bart pushed Elsie to the side to get a closer look. 'Odd? What's odd?'

'That door.'

'What about it?' he asked. 'You act as if you didn't know it was there. Didn't you say you've been here before?' Bart sounded condescending.

Maria adjusted her glasses with trembling hands. 'Should we be alarmed, dear?' She looked over the top of her lenses and squinted at the door.

'No. I don't think so.' I pulled the door open and peeked inside but saw only darkness. A quick shiver bumped across my skin when I thought about the rats that lived in there. I clamped the door shut. There was little I could do other than lock it with its pin hook. So that's what I did.

'Is everyone all right?' I said.

'You mean besides our damaged egos?' Bart said. 'I guess we're all right.' He shifted his eyes from wall to wall, rubbing his chin with one hand as if judging the basement's security. Satisfied, he sat down on a bench carved into the wall, brushed the space off next to him with his hand

and motioned for Maria. Their bodies fit snugly together like a puzzle.

There was a loud boom, as if someone had lit a stick of dynamite not far away. The floor shook from the blast. Then all went quiet. Elsie turned her back and covered her mouth with her hand, but I saw her torso bobbing up and down as she silently wept. Karl stood in the middle of the room with muscled arms braced between two wooden beams.

My stomach growled, and I'm sure I heard theirs too. 'I'm going back up to get some food.' I paused, waiting for a response, then Maria's eyes slid upward.

'Maybe you should wait a few minutes, dear. We just got down here. What if the police are still outside?' I had seen the police arrest people before, and they worked fast, but something in her voice made me sit back down.

'All right.' My stomach growled again. 'I'll wait.' My back scraped against the stone wall as I slid into a squat next to a few storage boxes. 'When I go back out, I'm going to check for some blankets too.'

Karl nodded.

I started taking my coat off, pulling it down off my arms. Elsie's glance turned into a stare, and then Karl's and Bart's while Maria blinked behind her large lenses at the sight of my Youth League uniform shining up before them, stiff black tie against my white shirt and the thick belt around my waist.

I put my coat back on, and they slowly looked away.

Bart pulled a white-faced watch from his pocket, the Kaiser's image and the year 1914 engraved in the silver. I recognized it instantly as an award watch given to German officers for bravery. My uncle had one just like it, and I wondered how he'd got one.

'You fought in the war?'

Bart's eyes swung to mine, his jaw tightening, and then Karl answered for him in a heavy tone. 'We are Germans, Sascha. Gentiles of Jewish descent.'

Bart's breathing grew rapid, so much so Maria put a hand on his shoulder; then he stood up. 'I grew up proud of my country after emancipation,' he said. 'Now that iron cross I earned fighting for this country doesn't mean a Goddamn thing.' His voice crumbled, and he sat back down. 'Not the way the country is now.'

Karl uncrossed his arms. 'Papa — '

Bart slammed a closed fist against his knee. 'Damn the Race Laws. Damn them!' Maria cringed from the anger in his voice.

'But if you're Gentiles why — '

'The edict is complicated,' Karl said. 'If you have a Jewish grandparent you're legally defined as a *Mischling*, or mixed blood. It doesn't matter if you're German, if you're a Gentile, or how many medals you earned in the war if you don't follow the Reich's demands and do what they tell you to do.' He ran his fingers through his hair and laced them together at the top of his head. 'It's about genetics.'

'My son and I,' Bart said, pointing to Karl, 'run a very profitable company here in Nuremberg called Maschine Arbeitet. That is, until a few days ago when they came after us.'

'Ach! Do we have to relive this again, Bart?' Maria lifted her hands up in the air and dropped them into her lap. 'I don't want to think about everything we left behind, what we are now.' Her lips quaked as she talked, which made Bart kiss her forehead.

Elsie pounded the fleshy part of her hand into the brick wall. 'What we are?' She swiped her nose with a wet hankie and glared through blotchy, meatball-swelled eyes. 'The Nazis may call us criminals, but that's their term, not ours. I'm not ashamed of the Jewish blood in my veins.'

Karl put his arm around her. 'None of us are.' He looked at me, his eyes heavy, and asked if I had any other questions.

Claudia would be aghast to know how much I had pried into their lives already, reminding me that the less I knew the better. But I couldn't help myself. It was just me and them in the quiet basement, and I wanted to know. He did ask if I had any questions.

'How did it happen?' I said. 'How did you end up in the Am Oberg?'

Karl waved everyone closer, and below the dangling light they recounted their story to me in great detail. They ran a post-war corporation that employed hundreds of people, buying dilapidated industrial parks, restructuring them and turning them into thriving manufacturing centres. Last week Karl received a summons ordering him to sell the company to an Aryan conglomerate. When he didn't, a friend at the documentation office told him that his family's name was on a deportation list for the east, despite his iron cross which he said should have been enough to keep him off the list.

'Deport us east?' Bart breathed heavily, ripping his glasses from his face only to put them back on. 'Never.'

'The same friend got us in contact with someone who brought us here. They said they could get us out of the country,' Karl said. 'It happened so fast, we only had time to grab our coats.'

Elsie blotted her tears away. 'I'll never forget the sound of those Gestapo trucks driving down our road,' she said, sniffing.

'It's not the house I'll miss most,' Maria said. Tears welled in her eyes and she squeezed Bart's knee. 'It's the vase Bart gave me on our wedding day.'

Bart pressed Maria tightly into the crook of his shoulder. 'There will be plenty of vases in our future, darling.'

Maria dried her glistening eyes. 'Sascha, it was the most beautiful thing I had ever seen. It was royal blue with raised flowers and had serpents for handles.' She simulated the vase's design by moving her fingers in an hourglass shape. 'It had a vignette of soldiers on horseback on one side, and flower sprays on the other. It was a Meissen, not sure if you know what that is, dear, but they are very nice.'

'Meissen, yes . . . I know it,' I said. 'Porcelain from Dresden?' It wasn't typical for a girl my age to know such things but working in my aunt's shop afforded me a certain kind of education, one that trained the young where the gold was, and a Meissen was indeed worth its weight in gold.

'Yes!' Her face lit up. 'But *my* vase was made for a king!'

Elsie smiled. 'Grandma, you're telling tales now.'

Karl chuckled. 'Now Elsie, if Mama says her vase was made for a king, then it was,' he said, giving her a wink.

'It was! It was!' Maria yelped. 'You think I am telling a tale here, but I'm not. Every one of you can laugh, but the stamp on its base said so.' She shrugged her shoulders and batted her eyes as if to make light of her own conviction. But I knew Maria was probably right. In the early eighteenth century, King Augustus II of Poland commissioned his own set of Meissen pieces, marked with his initials. I was about to say something, but Maria seemed to enjoy the teasing so I let it be and listened to them carry on while I snuck back into the shop to look for some food.

Thank goodness my aunt hadn't thrown out the kipfels Herr Rubin gave us the day prior; the crust had turned tough, and the bready inside crumbled into flaky bits that flecked to the ground, but I didn't think the Kortens would be picky. I looked over her desk for something else to eat, Hitler's dark-as-tar eyes watching me from the wall where Auntie had hung his portrait. I dug out a handful of caramels from the candy jar, and then went to the closet to get the blankets.

Maria gasped with delight; she thought I'd brought her the store. Bart thanked me with a puff of his chest and a rub of his belly. Elsie clapped when she saw the candy, and then popped a few pieces into her mouth. Karl sat down next to me, in front of the door on the second step, watching them dig into the pile.

'Aren't you hungry?' I said.

'*Nein*,' he said. 'What about you? I heard your stomach growling.'

'They need it more than me.' I took my coat off to use as a cushion and Karl eyed my uniform. Then he asked me the question I was sure had been on everyone's mind.

'Why are you helping us? We're strangers. I'm sure you know the risks.'

I loosened the tie from my neck until it hung down low on my uniform.

'This uniform is my aunt's doing. I wasn't raised to believe in the Reich.' I took a long breath through my nose, reliving my childhood on the outskirts of Nuremberg with my parents. 'I haven't told anyone this story before, but when I was young, I think nine or ten, the Jewish girl across the street told me she couldn't be my friend anymore. When I asked why, she said the Reich wouldn't let her attend school because there were already too many Jews. Each morning I'd see her staring out her front window, hands to her face, watching me leave for the schoolhouse with my other friends. At that moment, with her sad eyes on my back, I told myself that no matter how hard the Reich tried, I'd never become one of them.'

I think Karl was surprised, because he sat for several seconds looking at the ground after I'd told him the story. 'Well, thank God for that little girl. You might have just saved our lives.'

We sat quietly, watching the others divvying up the food. Then Karl put his face in his hands and rubbed his eyes where dark creases had settled into his skin. 'Now what?' he said. 'Where do we go from here?'

'There's someone I need to find.' *Claudia.* 'Because you can't stay here. The shopkeeper, she is . . . not sympathetic.' I stopped short of saying my aunt was a full-blown member of the Party. He didn't need to know, and I didn't want to say it out loud either.

'Don't tell them,' Karl said, glancing at his family. 'I'm not sure my mother can take another move. They thought we were leaving for France today. No need in telling them we're not.'

I slipped back into the shop, locking the door to the basement behind me. My aunt would be opening the shop bright and early tomorrow. I felt sick thinking about it.

I had to find Claudia.

There was only one place I thought to go — the Fountain of Virtues. Another reason why my aunt disliked Claudia; the fountain was the site of our 'episode', as Auntie had called it, the place where we'd publicly disobeyed the Reich.

I just hoped Claudia was there.

4

Sirens wooed outside. Lorries sped down roads. Window curtains opened momentarily only to close once I passed. The square was empty, but lit up by moonlight now that the rain had stopped, which made the Fountain of Virtues look grey and spooky. The water had been emptied for the winter, and I saw a rat rooting around in some leaves that had fallen into its basin — very different than it looked the day of our episode.

A day I would never forget.

We followed our League leader across the square as she escorted a line of girls through busy afternoon foot traffic, barking at us not to stop. But it was hot outside, and our feet ached. Claudia stopped next to the fountain and dipped her hand into its cool flowing water. Her eyes glowed when she read the sign that warned us to keep out. 'Follow me.' Claudia slipped off her shoes and hopped into the fountain.

Her face pruned from the initial chill of the water but quickly changed into a beaming smile. I took my shoes off, draping my socks over the keep-out sign and loosened my tie. Claudia stood under the fountain's water spout, a steady stream drilling the top of her head. 'It's cold,' she said, running her hands through her hair as if she were showering. People stopped to stare, many with their hands over their mouths, gasping.

I waded through the gushing water as Claudia marched defiantly in circles, cupping the water in her hands and throwing it into the air. Frau Dankwart had stopped when she heard the commotion and came charging back. She stood at the edge of the fountain, her grey hair twisted up in a bun and her mouth ajar.

'Git,' she shouted. 'Git! Git!' She flicked her finger at us, her lips pursing in between her words. Claudia kicked her feet up like one of those dancers from Paris, peeling her wet skirt from her body and lifting it in the air, her eyes caught in Frau Dankwart's vengeful glare.

The girls from our League had gathered around in shock and wonder. Some started to take their shoes off, as if they wanted to join us, but then stopped when they saw the police walking toward the fountain. Frau Dankwart waved frantically at them to hurry while still shouting at us to get out.

Claudia scowled, the water streaming down her face. 'I've had enough of you telling me what to do, Frau Dankwart. The Reich!' She undid her tie and then flung it at Frau Dankwart's face, which surprised even me. Then she started to undo her buttons and my mouth dropped. She took off her shirt and waved it at her if she were charming a bull, Frau Dankwart's hands reaching for it every time the tail-end flicked in her direction.

'Ella,' she said, the water spraying over both of us. 'This is our place. If ever we can't find each other.' I held her hand, squeezing, before the police ripped us from each other and pulled us out.

Later, Auntie paced with her hands on her head, out of her mind, spouting like a teapot she was so mad. 'What were you thinking when you took off your socks? Did you even stop to think about how your little episode would affect your uncle and me? Our status in the community?'

'No,' I said, shrinking under the weight of my uniform. 'I didn't think about any of that.' I only wanted to be free of the uniform, if only for a second, forget about the Reich and live free like I had in the country when my parents were alive, but try as I might to tell my aunt this, she never understood.

'You never do think,' she huffed. 'You never do . . .' Uncle tried to calm her with a hug, saying I had got out of the situation unscathed.

Auntie looked at me from over his shoulder. 'Why do girls have to be so hard?'

Claudia disappeared for two weeks after the police took her away. When she came back, she refused to talk about where she'd been, but judging by the bruises on her arms I assumed she had been stashed away someplace horrible. Her father was a nationalist and pushed for her punishment, her mother unable to help. Auntie blamed Claudia for the episode, saying she had forced me to join her, which was enough of an argument to keep the police from arresting me.

'Claudia,' I whispered into the night air, and then listened. A woman shrieked from not that far away and a child cried. Car doors slammed, and windows crashed. My hands shook, alone in the square, and a twisting panic brewed up inside me thinking she'd left or wouldn't come at all, but then a crackling noise came from the alley and out from the shadows Claudia rushed toward me. I almost collapsed with relief when I saw her face, but she grabbed me by the coat sleeve, out of breath and looking down the street, and forced me to walk. 'We're not safe here.'

We walked a few blocks before ducking into a narrow alley between two towering buildings.

'Where have you been?' she said, hugging me. 'I went by your place and got worried when you didn't open the window.'

She waited for me to answer. I was overjoyed to have found her, and yet a little scared. The wig I had pinned to her hair was gone, and she looked very concerned. Then the enormity of the night hit me, and my eyes started to water. She brushed a lock of hair away from my face.

'He never came — Wilhelm. I waited all day just like you said.' I gulped, about to tell her I'd broken her one rule. 'So I left the square and moved the family myself.'

Claudia's head flopped back. 'Ah, thank God.'

'You're not upset?'

'No!' she said. 'You did the right thing.'

'They're at my aunt's shop.' For a second, I thought she might be mad at me for moving them to a place like my aunt's shop, but then she gave me a sympathetic smile.

'I knew I could count on you if things went wrong.' She pulled a hankie from her sock when she heard me sniffling.

'Why didn't Wilhelm meet me?'

'I don't know . . . ' she said, shaking her head.

A loud screech startled us both, followed by a commotion of heated commands. Claudia peered down the alley. 'We should be walking.' I turned and saw five men with long wool coats and knee-high boots enter the adjacent building. Some had guns slung over their shoulders, others held sledgehammers and knocked their way through locked doors.

I gasped. 'The Gestapo!' Screams echoed down

the alley, some high-pitched, some low, painful moans. Chairs crashed through windows; women hopped out, dresses ripped down the middle like robes, their wounds branding the ground with their blood. A man tossed off the fire escape went limp on the stone pavement in his soiled night clothes.

'This way!' Claudia yanked on my arm and we walked the length of the city wall. That was when I noticed a scrape running from her forehead, along her jaw and down to her chin. It looked fresh, with gravel still clinging to the open parts of the wound.

'What happened to your face?'

Claudia paused, looking up at shuttered windows and judging how far away the nearest raid was by listening to the night screams. 'In here . . . ' We ducked into a barrel arch in the city wall where we could hide. 'Listen, I'm involved with something. Something big.' I stared at her, wondering how much bigger it could get than hiding Jews in her father's rental, when she blurted, 'I'm in the resistance.'

I exhaled from having held my breath. I knew, I suppose, that she was in the resistance. It just didn't seem real until she said it out loud.

'We're going to get rid of the Reich.'

'How are you going to do that?'

'We have many plans,' she said. 'Exciting plans, Ella. Ways to disrupt.'

'You believe it's really possible?' I thought about all the times we'd talked about what life would be like in Nuremberg without the Reich. No uniforms, no political parades, nobody telling us what to do and how to think. A day where a girl could run down the street without being stopped. Our Jewish neighbours could come back home. 'I do believe it's possible,' she said. 'Tonight, I held a stick of dynamite in my hand.'

My eyes widened. *Dynamite?*

'There was a rumour the Reich had a torture device in the basement of the Zum Gulden Stern restaurant. They call it the Nazi Clock. I tried to get rid of it.'

I gasped. 'The Zum Gulden Stern? But Auntie takes me there all the time! Did you destroy it?'

She shook her head. 'The police chased me into the Altstadt and jumped me from behind, near your aunt's shop.' She dug her fingers into her shoulder and adjusted the joint with a painful wince. 'It wouldn't have been this bad if it weren't for the glass.'

I looked at her as if she were a ghost. 'Near the shop?'

'They threw me into a police car, but I wiggled out of the cuffs and lit the dynamite in the backseat. There was a lot of screaming and commands shouted at me, but I jumped out of the car as it was rolling and took off running.'

The boom. After learning what Claudia had been through, I couldn't believe she was still alive. I flung my arms around her and my hand snagged on something spiky. 'Ouch!' Barbed silvery points poked out from the fabric of her coat. 'The hooks!'

'Yes, the hooks,' she said, looking down. 'Careful.'

'When did you do this?' I said, remembering every single one of those hooks I'd so carefully hidden in her hair.

Claudia held out her coat sleeve and pushed a few of the barbs back into the fabric. 'In the pews of a church,' she said with a smile. 'You like it? It's my only defence since I got rid of the dynamite.'

'My God.' Claudia was just a girl, only a few weeks older than me, not somebody you'd expect to outwit the Nazis. But as I looked at her with the scrape on her face, the wig gone from her hair, and hearing about the dynamite, I thought maybe she *could* do it. 'What else did you do?' I asked, as if nothing else could surprise me.

'That's it. What about you? What happened here?' she said, picking at my ripped stocking.

I blushed. 'Nothing.' Suddenly my night and the entire day leading up to it paled in comparison. 'Are you worried the police will find you?'

'Remember? They're looking for a dumpy hausfrau with moppy dark hair. They don't know who I really am.' She put her hands on my shoulders. 'Now Ella,' she said. 'That family in your aunt's shop. How can I get inside, and what time does she open up for business?'

'Early. She's there by eight every morning.' I dug into my pocket.

'There's a set of keys in the window well. That will get you in the shop, but they are in the basement,' I said. 'Here's the key.'

She slipped the key into her pocket. 'Where will you take them?' I asked.

'I only have one place,' she said. 'I just hope there's still time — and that I can save them all.' She gave me a hug, kissing my cheek. 'I'll have to hurry.'

* * *

I saw my aunt's head bobbing up and down through the window, behind the Nazi flag hanging over the glass. As I got closer, I saw her back up and pace in a circle with folded arms. I opened the door slowly, peeking in, and Auntie yelped and collapsed to her knees. I jumped from the shrill cry of her voice; I'd never heard her so relieved and frightened at the same time.

'Sascha! Where have you been? It's so late — I was worried sick!' She hugged me at the waist, tugging so hard she nearly brought me to the floor with her. I started to speak, but she'd cut me off. 'Wait, don't answer. I don't care. You're safe . . . you're home. Here, sit.'

She led me to the divan and we sat under her flag which cast a pink hue on us from the lamp shining just under it. Her freshly powdered cheeks stuck to my skin as she pressed them to my forehead, hugging me very tight. 'Were you raped?' she said. 'Wait! I don't want to know. Don't answer.'

My eyes lowered along with my head.

She gasped and shook her fist at the ceiling. 'In Christ's name!'

'*Nein!*' I raised my voice so she would hear me. '*Tante* Bridget! I wasn't violated by a man.' I pulled my stockings up at the thighs, now ripped from knee to ankle, and showed off my flat, dirty shoes. 'But I'm sure my appearance says otherwise.'

She covered her mouth and nodded.

'Time ran away from me . . . ' My voice trailed as I remembered the lie I had told her. 'I got stuck at the station after Greta's train left for Berlin.'

She exhaled loudly, cheeks puffing, after noticing my tattered scarf. 'Oh no,' she said, reaching for it. 'It's got a hole!'

There was a slight tear in the fabric next to the pulled thread Claudia had made with her teeth when she bit the tag off. It could have happened at a number of times, but most likely ripped when Bart tried to grab the shop keys from my hands.

'It's all right. I'll darn it for you. You're home, that's what's important.' She turned me toward the kitchen and I caught a whiff of cooked eggs. 'Now, I made you eggs. You must be starving.'

I imagined Aunt Bridget cooking in her white apron, catching peeks of her reflection in the window and straightening her bow while I hid from the Gestapo. Shouting came from the house over, followed by thumping made from a fist pounding on a door. Auntie took me in her arms and we got real quiet, listening to three men arguing.

'Sounds like Gregor, Frau Schmitz's tenant.' Auntie let go of me when we heard the arguing move into the street. We watched from the window with our hands to our faces, peeping through our finger gaps. The man threw a punch at Gregor's chin and he fell flat backwards on the pavement, bleeding from his nose and ears. The men dragged him away into the dark, while Frau Schmitz wept from her front steps.

'We should go to her,' I said, making a move off the divan, but Auntie closed the curtains with a quick snap.

'We can't, Sascha,' she said, eyes closing. 'We can't.'

The late evening bulletin announced over the

radio. *The Reich continues to destroy Britain with air raids . . .* We listened intently, and I spun the dial on the volume, waiting to hear what the Reich would say about the destruction in the streets and the roundup. *Gestapo have apprehended Communist rebels that violently attacked local German businesses and homes.*

'Oh my,' was all Auntie said.

'Auntie, there were no rebels. It was a Gestapo roundup. I saw it myself. Jews dragged out of their homes, beaten in the streets just like Gregor, only they were hauled away in trucks. Whole families.'

'Evacuation isn't to be frowned upon, Sascha,' she said. 'And it's the Communists causing the violence, not the Reich. You heard it yourself on the radio. And you saw it outside just now. We'll keep our doors locked tonight.'

'But I saw it!' My blood had started to boil, and I could tell my aunt knew it because she took a step back.

'The radio doesn't lie,' she said. 'Everyone knows that.' She tightened her hair bun, and then swiped her hands together, staring at me, blinking her eyes. I thought she expected me to say something, but what could I say? She turned the dial off on the radio and dusted the set, tidying up for the night.

I stood up, not knowing exactly where my place was in this conversation, and then decided there wasn't a place. Fighting with her was useless. She said my parents were the misguided ones, but it was her. It had always been her.

'Oh, good idea, Sascha. You should rest. I'll bring you some eggs in just a moment. You shouldn't go to bed without food in your stomach.'

'No eggs,' I said back to her. I closed my door softly before falling face first onto my bed. Not long after, I heard Aunt Bridget press up against my door.

'I'm glad you're home, Sascha,' she said, voice crackling.

5

We left for the shop early the next morning. Shop girls gripped their bags, popping the collars up on their wool coats, as Auntie and I crested the edge of the small circle waiting for the tram, our breath frosted white. The tram stop wasn't normally that packed, but petrol was expensive, and nobody wanted to take their cars into town.

'Feels unusually cold for an October day,' Auntie said aloud. Just then, old Frau Baer and her daughter Christa walked up from the kerb, wearing new fur coats. Christa sashayed by me, burrowing her way into the warm middle, a sly little smirk on her lips. 'Don't you think, Sascha?' Auntie said, and I turned to her.

'What?' I folded my arms for warmth.

'Cold for October,' she said.

Frau Baer burst in between me and Aunt Bridget, squeezing her way into the pack. Auntie looked aghast at her gall, and then pinched her lips up when she heard someone comment on how beautiful Frau Baer's new coat looked.

'Come by my shop later,' Frau Baer said. 'I have a closet full. Marked down just for my favourite customers.'

Auntie rolled her eyes. 'I can get fur coats too,' she mumbled.

I thought of the record keeping I still had to do that morning, and the items I had to remark for sale, when suddenly there was a slight twist in my stomach. What if the Kortens were still in my aunt's shop? What if Claudia didn't make it? I was still lost in thought when the tram showed up and passengers started embarking up the steps. Auntie pulled on my arm when she noticed I'd lagged behind. 'Are you coming?' she said, and suddenly I couldn't hurry enough.

The shop seemed smaller as we walked up, narrower, as if the buildings on its sides had squeezed it like bookends.

'All right,' I said. 'Open up.'

Auntie looked at me strangely. 'I have to get my keys.'

My body stiffened instantly when I saw the dirty footprints near the door's threshold; two were Maria's, I could tell by the size and width. One was flat and smeared — must be mine — the other looked petite and doll-like, which I thought had to be Elsie's. I looked for Claudia's before swiping them away with my foot, but I couldn't tell if any were hers.

Auntie jammed the key into the lock and her fingernail snagged on the metal faceplate. 'Damn manicure,' she whined.

'Auntie, just open the door.' I wanted to get in, and get in fast, confirm the Kortens were gone. Claudia moved them. I was sure of it — no, now I wasn't sure at all.

She twisted the doorknob, bumping the door with the side of her arm. The door barely moved, so she bumped it again, throwing her shoulder into it until the door flung open. 'There, finally!'

She sighed, ran her fingers over her bound hair, and then walked inside gaily. I sloughed off my coat and walked straight to the basement door, where it was quiet, dead quiet. Auntie followed me after picking up my coat from the floor and hanging it on the metal rack.

'Could you please pick up after yourself?' She put a hand on the basement door and fingered the knob as if she were about to open it. 'I had to pick your coat up off the floor, Sascha — really, it isn't that hard.' She was playing with the knob now, moving it back and forth, her arm stiff, pushing against the door, and I imagined the worst: that the Kortens had spent the night and were now huddled in the corner, Bart's arms wrapped around Maria, Elsie near crying with Karl standing like a wall trying to protect them all from whomever was about to rush in on them, followed by my aunt screaming for the SS, Gestapo or both.

'Of course, Auntie — '

She burst through the door and down into the basement. My words got caught in my throat, leaning into the room, eyes stretching. The room was dark and empty, thank God, except for my aunt and her voice. 'I've got suppliers coming this morning and I want the shop to be tidy,' she said, picking up the small crate Elsie had used near the trapdoor. 'Shut the door for me, please,' she said as she walked back into the shop, pausing to look at my face. My chest was puffed up from holding my breath.

'Everything all right?' she said, her eyes flicking over me, smiling slightly.

A mere moment felt like it had turned into a minute.

'Of course.' And with that, she walked into her

office, talking about how late it was and that customers would be arriving soon.

I reached for the knob, taking a second to feel the emptiness of the room before closing the door. *And breathe.* The Kortens were indeed gone, just as Claudia said they'd be. I had no reason to worry after all; my aunt had no idea they had been there. 'Be safe,' I whispered, before going back to the front of the shop.

Not long after, I heard the hum of a diesel engine rumbling down the road. I peeked outside and saw a green paddy wagon with metal grates tied to its grill and a thick coated arm hanging out the open window. A chubby hand pointed a lit cigar at our door and the wagon screeched to a stop. *Herr Coburg.* The deliveries had arrived, and once again, my aunt was first on his list.

A smile spread across my aunt's face when he came through the door. 'Greetings, Herr Coburg. Come in.'

He coughed, catching his cigar with probing lips. A waft of air blew past him as he closed the door — smoke and the stench of an unwashed body. If I didn't think my aunt would wither with embarrassment, I would have offered him the buttermilk soap we had for sale.

'Why, Bridget, it's good to see you so well, especially after the ruckus of last night. Nice to see the street thugs didn't get your shop before the Reich caught them,' he said, looking around, twirling his cane. 'But who could harm such a charming little shop?'

'Herr Coburg,' she said, blushing, 'you are so kind.'

'Ella!' he said, suddenly. 'You're looking better than the last time I saw you.' He smiled with brown teeth, and I grimaced — my natural reaction.

Auntie glared as nonchalantly as she could, hoping Coburg wouldn't notice, begging me to be polite with her tense face. I smiled big. Coburg looked at my aunt, then back at me, jutting his chin as if he suspected we were up to something.

'Here,' he said, pulling my silver hairclip from his pocket. 'I found this — '

'Thank you,' I said, cutting him off. Auntie would be mortified if she knew I had fallen in front of him and his Gestapo friends on the bridge.

Four men jumped out from the back of the truck and tossed boxes onto the kerb. Some were long and hit the pavement like dead bodies. Others were quad-flapped squares with lumpy middles with edges that bowed and split.

'When did you order new things?' I said.

Auntie looked around for her reading glasses and then discovered they were on top of her head before signing an invoice slip Coburg had given her.

I asked her again. '*Tante* Bridget?'

She slid her glasses up the bridge of her nose, and the one eye that had crossed slightly straightened itself. 'Oh, don't you know? I have a standing order.'

Coburg and my aunt whispered into each other's ears, then she handed him a bulky envelope stuffed with reichsmarks.

'Ladies!' he said, tipping his hat. 'It was nice doing business with you!'

He flipped through the money in the street before hopping into his wagon and speeding away.

'Don't you think he's peculiar?' I shivered.

She patted my shoulder. 'Yes, but he gives us first pick. You'll need to learn how to be nicer to our suppliers if you want to be a good shop girl. I saw that look you gave him.' She waved me away from the window. 'Now, over here. Help me with these boxes, would you please? We've got a lot of things to go through today.'

She sauntered over to the largest box and nudged it with her hip to gauge its weight, before cutting it open, pulling out three fur coats. Her mouth drew open with surprise. 'Will you look at that!' She held one to her face, taking a big sniff. 'And it smells like me! Here, Sascha, smell!'

I took a sniff and nearly gagged, which made Auntie laugh. *4711 Eau de Cologne.* It was the same cologne submariners wore after a month at sea, but my aunt wore it to smell beautiful.

'Take that, Frau Baer,' she said, hanging the coats up on a rack to sell.

A wooden broom hit the front of the building with two quick swats. My aunt jumped. Shards of glass trickled into a tin rubbish bin. It was Herr Rudin from the bakery next door, cleaning up the Gestapo's mess. His usual white apron was smeared with ashy handprints, and it sagged low on his hips as if he had forgotten to tie it. Sad eyes, half-hidden under a brown flap hat, flickered cautiously in our direction.

My aunt gave him a fleeting look and sighed. 'Ugh! I can't look at unpleasant things right now. Poor Herr Rudin and his wife. That's all I can say about that,' she said, turning her eyes away.

'They took her away, Auntie.'

Just then Frau Rudin stepped out from the broken window and onto the pavement. 'No, there she is,' Auntie said.

I watched the Rudins sweep up the glass together. Her marriage to Herr Rudin, an Aryan, must have saved her from going east.

Auntie turned her back to them. 'Don't go over there anymore, Sascha,' she said, and I looked up at her. 'Just . . . don't.'

Frau Rudin wore the dress Auntie sewed up for her just last winter. 'But you're friends,' I said.

Auntie closed her eyes, squeezing them really tight, and after a few silent moments to herself, she went over to one of the boxes. 'I can't believe the deal I got on this order. It's amazing what people will sell in Paris.' She pulled a collection of gilded pâté knives from the box, followed by a pocket watch with a long chain. 'Coburg makes deals every day, ships it back to Germany for a fraction of the cost.' She dusted her items with a plume of violet feathers. 'Frenchmen know nothing about value. Grab a pair of shears, Sascha,' she said, but then handed me her pair. 'What's in that small box over there?'

Herr Rudin and his wife had walked back into their ruined shop, and I took a breath. Auntie pointed to a box by the front door. 'Right there.'

'I got it,' I said, dragging the box across the floor. I cut it open with Auntie's shears, and reached into the middle, plunging my hand through a wadding of newspaper. I grabbed what felt like a handle and then gave it a pull, only to stumble immediately backward with a gasp that I swear had sucked all the air from the room.

A vase — made of dove-white porcelain and glazed in the middle, royal blue, with cream-coloured serpents that coiled at the sides into handles.

The Kortens' vase.

'What do you have there?' Auntie adjusted her glasses, peeking over my shoulder. 'Look at that!' she yelped. 'It's a Meissen. What's the picture on the back?'

I closed my eyes, not wanting to be right. 'It's a vignette of soldiers on horseback.'

'You know this piece?' Auntie pointed to the inscription on its base. 'The mark of King Augustus! This is at least two hundred years old, and it's in perfect condition.' She pulled the vase from my hands, peered into the hollow middle and then held it up to the light. 'Who would get rid of this? You'd have to pull it from my dead hands before I'd sell this vase!'

My eyes shifted to hers. 'They didn't sell it.'

'You mean they gave it away for free?' She laughed. 'You're very amusing, Sascha.'

I sat still and watched her as she eyed her prize. Then her face went blank, as if she had just remembered something. 'Go find my Meissen catalog, will you? I'll need to put a price on it right away.'

'Umm . . . ' My hands started to shake, drawing connections between Coburg's bulging boxes and the roundup last night, looking at all the items Auntie had purchased — these were belongings; not unwanted things people had sold in France. *Auntie believes everything the Reich tells her. Is the watch Karl's? What about the gilded knives? Somebody. They belong to somebody.*

Auntie noticed I was struggling. 'Are you all right?' She let go of the vase long enough to put her palm to my cheek. 'Go relax in my office. You look feverish all of a sudden. I'll finish up here.'

I walked away, feeling my own face, and went straight to the liquor cabinet under her desk where my uncle kept his scotch. He said it was for emergencies, though my aunt and him differed on what kind of emergencies required scotch.

'Sorry,' I said into the air, as if the Kortens could hear me. Two long gulping slugs later, I only felt worse with a knot in my stomach that had turned sour and hot. I sat in her chair, head in my hands.

The front bell chimed, and I heard voices. *Customers.* My head throbbed, thinking of helping a customer in this state.

I expected Auntie to yell for me to come out, help her sell something, but everything was quiet. I sat up, wondering if the customer was someone else. Perhaps one of Auntie's friends? But then suddenly she was walking back to her office, feet pounding, louder and louder and louder as if she were mad.

My stomach sank, thinking for a split second it could be the police. I stood up and she was staring at me from the doorway.

6

Auntie looked at the opened bottle of scotch on her desk, and then to me and my face, which felt red as a cherry. 'What on earth?' Her lips pursed.

'Auntie, I didn't,' I said, putting the bottle away. 'I was just cleaning.'

'You stay here. I'll tell your visitor to go away.'

'Wait!' I said, closing up the liquor cabinet. 'You mean it's not the police?'

'God no, what are you talking about — the police?'

'That's not what I meant.' I shook my head from standing up too quickly. 'Let me catch my thoughts.' But Auntie was already walking away. 'Auntie, stop,' I said, and she did — I can't believe she did — her back to me, not even bothering to turn around. 'Who is it?'

She said nothing, back still turned.

I could hear someone messing with the display near the window. 'Who's out there?'

Auntie finally turned around. '*That girl*, Claudia,' she whispered. 'I should have sent her away.' She tried shooing me back into her office and into her chair, but I ducked under her arm. 'Sascha, I . . . ' she said, following me to the front.

My face instantly lit up seeing Claudia at the door. Her hands were clasped loosely together in front of her with a smile plumped on her cheeks. A twisted curl sparkling in soft light hid the scrape on her face. She winked. I nodded, which I thought was a good sign that the Kortens were safe.

'Claudia! What brings you by?' My head instantly felt better.

She kissed both my cheeks. 'I was a few shops down and I thought I'd call on my dear friend Ella, see how you were doing — '

'We are doing excellently, Claudia,' Auntie said, standing next to me, squaring her arm around my shoulders. 'Ella here is a brilliant shop girl. I couldn't run this business without her.' Her voice changed; it was stern, offensive. She tapped her fingers on my sleeve and then moved her body ever so slightly in between Claudia and myself. 'How's your mother? Relaxing today, perhaps?'

Claudia glanced at me before answering. 'She's wonderful. Thanks for asking.' Claudia's mother was most likely passed out on the divan, which Auntie knew.

'Claudia, would you like to take a walk?' I said.

'Now?' Auntie quipped. 'But we're in the middle of inventory.' Her eyes slanted inward like a *Lustige Blätter* cartoon character.

'Yes, I'd love to,' Claudia said. 'Let's catch up.' She offered me her hand and I took it, but Auntie tightened her grip on my shoulder, digging her fingers into my upper arm.

'I don't like it, Sascha,' she said.

'But . . . ' Auntie moved me away from the door where we could talk privately, leaving Claudia standing by herself. 'I won't be long.'

She leaned in close and whispered. 'After last night? Unless you're going to and from the shop, or to a League meeting for that matter, I don't want you venturing off.' She glanced up at Claudia who was now twiddling her thumbs and looking at the ceiling. 'Besides,' she said, whispering even quieter, 'I don't want you associating with the wrong crowd.'

I looked at Claudia, and then to my aunt, my mouth hung open with words to be said but nothing came out. I wanted to tell Auntie I was lost and alone after my parents died and it was Claudia who reminded me I wasn't. But how could I say such things to my aunt? She wouldn't understand. 'Auntie — '

'I heard on the radio the Reich squashed those rebel Communists last night,' Claudia piped. 'The streets are safe now. Surely the radio wouldn't tell us untruths.'

We both looked at Claudia. Auntie had put her arm around me again, holding me so tightly I could feel my circulation slowing under her fingertips.

'We won't go far, Auntie. Promise.' I smiled. 'Perhaps even up the street to Bergstraße 19 for some lunch?' Auntie let go of my shoulder, and the blood flowed back into my arm. She couldn't deny the radio report — she lived by the news. 'I won't be long,' I said again, grabbing my coat from the rack and rushing out with Claudia.

I glanced back just in time to see my aunt's face droop along with her body, watching us skip off together.

* * *

Claudia led me to the confectionery shop's window where a chocolatier was dipping pretzels into a bowl of melted milk chocolate. The woman smiled and mouthed her hello to us as we stood street side with our noses to the glass where we could talk without looking suspicious.

'I'm sorry about my aunt,' I said, 'asking about your mother like that.'

Claudia pulled her nose away from the window and looked at me, her face suddenly very pale. 'My mother is a drunk because of what happened to my sister. The Reich killed both of them. You don't have to apologize for what your aunt says.' Something else was wrong. I could tell by the way her eyes lingered, staring into mine. I touched her hand and she blurted, 'I have some bad news.'

I put my nose back to the glass. My stomach tightened like it usually did after I'd vomited and there was nothing left in my stomach — I was afraid to ask. Claudia put her nose back to the glass, and we watched the chocolatier lay dipped pretzels onto a marble slab. 'Bart and Maria got caught,' she said, and I closed my eyes briefly from the sharp pang of her news.

'How do you know?' Claudia didn't say anything, and I waited, watching the chocolatier mess with the pretzels.

'I know,' she finally said. 'I only found housing for two. Bart and Maria were caught before dawn hiding in a transport lorry belonging to his company. They might be boarding a train this very minute for the east, I don't know.'

I broke away from the window and we immediately wrapped our arms around each other. 'I did everything I could.' The chocolatier knocked on the glass, holding up her scraped bowl, mouthing for us to come inside for a lick. When we didn't, she looked concerned and put her bowl forcefully down. 'We'll spoil lunch,' Claudia said to her through the glass, and she appeared to understand.

'Let's go to the station. Maybe we can see.' I knew I wouldn't be able to speak with them, but I thought that if I could see them boarding the train together then maybe they'd be all right, that evacuating to the east wasn't as bad as I thought — just like Auntie had been telling me. A sliver of hope to hold onto.

* * *

The lines out of the train station travelled past the loading platforms and coiled into the street like fat braided ropes. Women held their babies close to their breast, walking in a daze, while the Gestapo ordered everyone inside. All the yellow stars in a row.

'There's so many of them.'

We ducked behind a fence, and walked around to the outbound tracks, where weeds and thickets had grown heartily. 'Nobody can see us over here,' she said, and we knelt down in the weeds and peeked through the fence gaps.

'Do you see them?' she said, but everyone looked the same, with drab coats and long faces.

I crouched down further, pressing my eye to the fence. Passengers loaded onto open-aired freight cars, the kind used for transporting grain, not people. Then the Gestapo marched around the corner onto the tracks where the train had started to steam. They pulled people from the line, making every man getting assistance stand without their canes. Wheelchairs were tossed aside, and the train chuffed away. 'What are they doing?' I looked at Claudia for an answer, but she hadn't one.

The Gestapo waved their rifles, and the Jews shakily moved to the edge of the platform at gunpoint. 'No, no, no . . . ' They raised their guns, and my throat closed up. I reached for Claudia, burying my head, just as a squadron of bombers flew over us, their engines rumbling one after the other in waves, drowning out the shots.

My arms were still clutching her tightly minutes later, long after the planes had flown off to the war, and when I pulled away from her, sticky with tears, the station was completely empty. A lone janitor swept the platform of debris, whistling.

I bolted to my feet and started to run, but then stopped after Claudia yelled out for me. Now it was me who walked in a daze. I thought about Maria's big eyes and Bart's wobbling voice, and then closed my eyes, thinking of the train and the people who were now dead.

Claudia took my hand when we reached the antiques shop.

'Ella.' She swallowed. 'Do you want to join?'

My face flattened. 'As in . . . join?' I dared not say the word out loud. *Resistance.*

'The shop. We could use it.' Claudia took my other hand, and Auntie peeked through the window at us. She was pretending to dust, but was staring hard enough. 'Think about it before you agree. This is different than pinning wigs to my hair.'

I nodded.

'Yes?' she said.

'Yes.'

She wrapped her arms around me and whispered in my ear, 'Meet me at the Steichele Hotel tonight at eight o'clock. Back of the dining room. Wear the scarf.' She let go of my hands and pecked my cheek before leaving.

I threw open the shop door, and a new bell tinkled directly above my head. I looked up, trying hard not to place what shop it had come from, and the door swung closed, kicking me in the heels.

Auntie stared at me from a chair just a few feet away, petting the Kortens' vase with tapping fingers. I already knew she'd seen me holding Claudia's hands and fully expected her to question me about it, but she only continued to tap her fingers on the vase in her lap.

'Auntie?'

She shook her head as if she'd just woken up from a nap and realized I was standing in front of her. 'Sascha! You're back.'

'Are you all right, Auntie?'

She nodded. 'Oh yes,' she said, still tapping her fingers on the vase.

I made myself busy with work, trying to get my mind off what I'd seen at the station, and cleaned up the newspaper packing still left on the floor, when an older gentleman and his younger wife came into the shop. He looked around, pointing to the silver pins and watches in Auntie's glass case.

The wife turned her nose up at a small painting

Auntie had been trying to get rid of for months. Nobody seemed to want a painting of a blue rose. The price had been slashed already and it was worth more than the tag hanging from it. I walked up to them as the husband tried to get his wife to like it. As I got closer, I could hear her say the last thing she needed was another painting.

'Can I help you?'

The man turned around. His face was tired, as if he had been shopping for hours. 'I want to buy my wife something special. But she doesn't like anything. No matter what store we go into.'

The wife puckered her lips, pouting. 'I don't want your gift, husband.' Her legs were as stiff as her face and arms, which were tightly folded. The husband huffed.

'I saw you looking at the blue rose.'

The wife's eyes shifted to mine. 'He feels guilty about leaving me again, so he wants to buy me a gift.'

Her husband walked away, his hands in the air as if he didn't want to hear her anymore. 'It's for business,' he said as he picked through items on a table.

'A gift is a gift, is it not?' I smiled. 'And a woman deserves all the gifts in the world. That's what my aunt tells me.'

The woman looked at me blank-faced, before smiling. 'I suppose you're right.'

I pointed to the blue rose. 'Like this painting. Blue roses are very rare. See the streaks of light blue mixed with the ribbons of dark, and a hidden hue of orange?' The woman leaned in to see what I was talking about, but shook her head. 'It's a blue rose of the Orient.'

'I thought blue roses were made using dye?'

'The legend is they exist. Many have searched and still search for such a treasure. It's a mystery. Like a woman. And beautiful.'

She got very close to the canvas and then gasped when she saw a brush of gold folded into the rose's petals. 'I didn't notice the colours when I first looked. It's like an illusion.'

I nodded.

'This would look lovely in my parlour,' she said.

The woman waved to her husband who was very happy to see she had finally agreed on something. 'Thank you,' he said as he took out his billfold. 'I was about to pull my hair out trying to find her something that would make her happy.' He ran a hand over his bald head. 'And as you can see I don't have much hair left!' He laughed, and then took the painting.

I handed my aunt the reichsmarks he'd paid. Her face was full of excitement. 'Sascha, that was amazing work you just did! That woman didn't want anything in this shop. And you sold her something she didn't want.'

I shrugged my shoulders.

'Don't you see? You reinvented that blue rose, gave it a past and a story, and then you made her believe it. Ribbons of colour — hogwash!' She kissed my forehead, mashing her lips against my skin. 'A good shop girl can make a person believe anything.'

The shop had got quiet with just the two of us inside. Auntie had taken me by the shoulders, smiling, and then her face changed, and she looked very serious. She went behind the cash register.

'Now,' she said, and I looked up.

Auntie placed the Kortens' vase on the glass counter.

'We need to talk.'

7

I gulped, thinking she knew the truth about the vase and was about to tell me the Kortens were dead — but how would she know? She took a deep breath, and then smiled, her lipstick nice and smooth on her lips. 'I want to give this to you.'

'What?' I stepped back, shaking my head. 'You can't!'

She looked puzzled. 'Well, why not?'

I swallowed, trying to think of a reason other than the fact that it wasn't her vase to give, but then muttered up something about the value.

'It's too expensive,' I said. 'It's too valuable for a girl my age.'

Auntie hung her head down, and she looked sad all of a sudden. The tear that had snuck out from the corner of her eye surprised me. 'What is it?' I moved closer to her, reaching out for her hand.

'You don't understand, Sascha.' She pressed my hand to her cheek. 'I'm giving you this vase in honour of your mother.' There was a long pause, and I sat down. 'It's the anniversary this week,' she said, 'of their death. You know she used to help me when she was younger — right here in this shop. All before she met your father, got married and moved to the country.' Her lips clamped when she mentioned my father. 'She was my best friend. It's a tragedy what happened to her, leaving a young daughter behind.' She breathed a few breathy sighs, and then handed me the vase. 'It's yours. I want you to have it.'

I took the vase, feeling the cool Dresden porcelain in my hands, thinking of Bart and Maria, and what it must have been like when he gave it to her on their wedding day. They were gone now. The vase was the only thing left to prove they'd had a life in Nuremberg.

I crumbled into my aunt's arms, weeping uncontrollably. 'Thank you, Auntie,' I said, knowing she could have made a lot of money off the Kortens' vase, but instead chose to give it to me.

'Now,' she said, wiping her eyes and mine. 'Don't you have a League meeting tonight?' I got a good dose of the 4711 cologne on her skin before she pulled away.

I shook my head. 'No, but I do have something else.'

'Oh? What's that?'

My palms suddenly got sweaty holding the vase, and it slipped around in my hands, which I didn't expect. I'd lied to my aunt before, but I supposed this was different now — everything seemed different. 'Umm . . . ' She'd followed me into her office where I'd put the vase on her shelf for safekeeping. I ran my palms down my skirt. 'A few girls from the League are meeting for dinner at the Steichele.'

She gave me a disapproving look, one where her eyes hung low with her head, and I thought she could tell I had lied.

'The Steichele's only two long blocks away,' I said. 'You know the restaurant.'

She looked all right now, smiling. 'Yes,' she said,

'I do know that place. Girls from the League? Sounds like a big time.'

'Yes,' was all I could say.

We took the tram home, and she inspected me before I left for the Steichele.

'I see you have your scarf on again.' Auntie pointed. 'I sewed it for you. Can barely see the stitches.' I turned my wrist over. The stitching was thick and uneven, which made me wonder if she used the thread from her midwife's bag. 'No need to thank me.'

Auntie slipped on a silky blue robe, untwisted her hair from its bun and let her braid fall over her shoulders, separating like spun strands of gold. She held the door open with her foot and watched me leave, the side of her face pressed against the door's frame, and her hand in a slow wave. Just as I crested the edge of darkness, she called out to me.

I looked over my shoulder, and her hand froze in the air.

'Claudia isn't going to be there, is she?'

'No, Auntie.' It was the little lies, I'd realized, I had no problem with. 'Claudia won't be there.'

She smiled, and then continued to wave.

* * *

Walking up to the Steichele restaurant I would have thought it had closed; there were no patrons milling about outside, except for a lone soldier smoking next to a Nazi banner on the street. I gave the door a pull, and my feet slipped on the pavement from it not budging one bit. I stepped back, looking at the marquee, making sure I was indeed at the Steichele, and I was. I pulled again, stamping my feet for more leverage, but again, the door didn't move and I thought about leaving.

The soldier stuffed his cigarette into his mouth and then walked up to me in the night. He pulled on the handle and the door opened right up to a bustling restaurant inside. He walked away without so much as a word, and I walked inside.

A hostess tried to take my coat, and then asked how many would be at my table.

'None,' I said, pulling away from her outstretched arm. 'I mean . . . I'm meeting a friend, but she's not here.'

She stared at me for a second or two, but then went to help an old couple with their coats, leaving me alone by the front door, and near a family crammed into a corner booth made from restored wine barrels. I watched servers walk from the dining room to the kitchen, down a long corridor that led all the way to the back of the restaurant, where Claudia had told me to meet her. With the hostess still helping the old couple with their coats, I walked straight back, as if I had a reason to be in the restaurant's kitchen, but the corridor went on and on, the ceiling getting lower and the air cooler until suddenly there was nowhere else to go but down a dark staircase. That's when I saw Claudia.

'Over here,' she whispered, and then walked up a few steps into the light. She touched my arm. 'How are you doing?' she said, before hugging me.

'I'm fine,' I said, and I wondered if she could tell I had been crying earlier.

'Did you have trouble finding me?' she said.

'A little,' I said. 'I thought this place was closed, I almost left.'

'Rule one,' Claudia said, 'don't be fooled by appearances.' She took me by the arm, leading me down a dank and narrow staircase with carved rock walls and a domed ceiling.

She felt me shudder.

'Don't be scared,' Claudia said. At the bottom of the stairs was a wooden door dotted with rusted bolts. A handful of moths flew over a low-burning candle melting in a wall sconce. She rapped three times on the door, and a man with a curly beard and wine-stained overalls opened it up, only to swiftly lock it behind us.

'We're locked in?' I said, glancing back at him as he folded his arms.

'Don't worry,' she said.

A short corridor led into a low-vaulted wine cave filled with fermenting oak barrels that smelled like sour fruit and peat. In the back far corner, the soft glow of candlelight cast shadowed silhouettes onto the ceiling. As we got closer, I heard the hum of voices.

I thought the resistance were men and women — adults — people without homes who spent their lives fighting. But they looked just like me.

Dressed in their League uniforms.

They were talking quietly, whispering as we walked up, smoking and looking over a city map that lay flat on the ground. One by one they broke away, looking at me and then to Claudia. There was a pause. Claudia lifted her chin. 'She's with me.'

The few girls that were there looked tired in their Youth League uniforms. Each of them had yellow scarves bowed around their wrists, and I was glad I'd worn mine. Claudia pointed to a place to sit. 'I'll introduce you in a moment.' I sat down, stuffing my skirt under my legs. I wanted to look around but felt uncomfortable with everyone looking at me.

Claudia pulled a stool up next to me, and then took the hand of a man walking past, their fingers entwining. His cheek was bruised and he had fingernail scratches on his neck from a fight. 'This is Wilhelm,' she said quietly, and he brought over a stool to sit on.

'Wilhelm,' I repeated. 'As in *the* Wilhelm?'

He glanced up at the group, who'd started forming a circle around us, and then paused. 'I was detained,' he said. 'That's why I missed you.'

Claudia shifted her look between me and him to see how I'd react before leaning into my ear, whispering, 'My name's Marta here. I thought we could call you Sascha. A codename. Is that all right?' I nodded, thinking it was ironic the name my aunt — a Nazi — had given me was now my codename. Everyone got seated, and there were calls to start the meeting. She took her hand off my knee. 'Here we go . . . we're starting.'

Wilhelm stood up and rubbed his neck while waiting for the others to quiet. 'Does it still hurt?' someone asked.

'I'll be all right,' he said. 'I'm more bothered by what the police knew about me.' He'd dropped his hand and now everyone was listening to him. 'Things nobody outside this circle should've known.'

A young man named Hans stood up, pointing a stubby finger at a girl named Sarah. 'Ask that one,' he said, and she shot up. His wool jacket looked a size too small, and his tie constricted around his neck, turning his skin the same ginger shade as his hair.

'What are you saying?' Sarah slowly walked over to him, sliding her dark braid through her hands, and stood a quiet breath away from Hans' face.

'I've seen you on the street,' Hans said. 'You didn't know I saw you, but I did.'

'So what?' she scoffed. 'Am I not allowed to walk down a street?'

'That's not what I meant.' Hans sat back down, leaving Sarah standing in the middle of our circle, allowing every one of us to look her up and down and examine the straightness of her Youth League uniform and the whiteness of her shirt.

'You're paranoid!' she finally said. 'All of you.' She flung a finger at us all. 'I've been a part of this group for months. Before this one arrived,' she said, issuing a sharp little chin flick at Hans before sitting back down.

'What I mean is,' Wilhelm said, addressing everyone, 'that we need to be more careful. Burn your notes. Double back on streets. And whatever you do, don't talk about the safehouses we have outside this room.' He pointed to the map on the ground where yellow dots spun out from the city centre and tapped on the location of my aunt's shop. 'We have a new safehouse on Obere Schmiedgasse,' he said, and I sat up tall. 'It's an antiques shop called Alten und Neuen. Old and

New. You can't miss it. Next door is an abandoned beer cellar with a medieval-looking red door and brass-coloured hinges.'

People leaned in, getting a good look at the location. 'I know where that is,' Sarah said, then she sat back and folded her arms. 'If you're so worried about a spy, why are you talking about our safehouses in front of the new girl?' Everyone turned to me, and Claudia leaned forward in her seat. 'Since when do we bring in new members without checking them out first?'

'She is thoroughly checked out,' Claudia said.

Sarah flipped her braid behind her shoulders. 'If I'm questioned — ' she looked at Hans rolling her eyes ' — then let's question everyone.'

A few others piped up in agreement. Wilhelm looked up from the map. 'She's already proved herself,' he said, and that shushed everyone up.

A boy walked in late, sat down next to me, and ran a hand through his pomade-slicked hair before fitting a wool cap over his head. He looked eighteen at best. His smile was sweet, like a puppy, with late-afternoon whiskers budding on his chin. Blue eyes pierced the darkness. Beautiful, like a lake. 'Sorry for being late,' he said to the group. Then he looked at me, and seemed pleasantly surprised. 'What did I miss?'

Sarah pursed her lips and Hans shifted in his seat away from Sarah.

'I was just about to introduce a new member,' Wilhelm said. 'This is . . . ' He looked to me to finish.

'Sascha,' I said, and my voice cracked. 'Sascha,' I said again, after clearing my throat.

'Welcome to the Falcons,' Wilhelm said.

The boy offered me his hand to shake. 'Welcome to the group,' he said, and then smiled. 'Name's Geb.'

I slid my hand into his. 'Hello,' I said, but I wanted to say something else if only to keep my hand in his, as distracting as he was. He rolled his shirt sleeves up and teased my curiosity with the hint of a tattoo on his forearm. I strained to see more of it, but I thought he could tell and looked away.

'Tell us more about the new safehouse,' someone said, and I got nervous thinking about them using my aunt's shop when she might be there.

Claudia stood up. 'There's one thing you should know — '

'The shop is only available from nine at night to sunrise,' I said, having made up the times, knowing my aunt would definitely not be at the shop so early or so late in the evening. 'Anyone left after sunrise will get caught. The owner isn't sympathetic. Sorry,' I said, catching my voice, 'this is how it has to be.'

'The owner doesn't know,' Wilhelm announced to everyone as he dragged a stuffed burlap sack to his feet and wedged it between his knees. 'Be on notice.' He began pulling documents from the bag and passing them out to a horde of outstretched hands.

Claudia put her hand on my shoulder. 'Don't worry about the shop. This group is very discreet. All right?'

Some of the documents spilled out of the bag and onto the floor as Wilhelm dug through them;

one slid near my foot. The picture affixed to its right-hand corner was of a girl, not more than fifteen or so. She had frizzy hair that was similar to mine, but her face was flat and lacked expression. I wondered who she was. The paper called her Anise, but she didn't look like an Anise to me, or from France like the document said. As to why she needed a set of forged papers, there could only be one reason: she was Jewish.

When the meeting was over Claudia pulled me off to the side. 'I saw you looking at Geb.' She smiled.

'I was?' I said, as my eyes trailed back to where Geb was talking.

'He's cute,' Claudia said. 'You like him?'

'I don't even know him,' I said, still looking at him from afar.

Claudia chuckled. 'Sure.' She watched me watch him. 'What do you think his real name is?'

He stood up, looking as if he was about to leave. His trousers were stained with greasy handprints all over his rear-end, and I wondered if he was a mechanic and had had his hands in an engine before he came here. I tried to guess what his real name was, saying different ones in my head, but nothing sounded right.

Geb paused at the stairs before walking up, then looked over his shoulder and smiled as if he had sensed me staring. I looked away, but I knew he'd caught me. Then he was gone.

Claudia grinned. 'You like him.'

I flicked her shoulder. 'Stop.' I was curious about her codename. 'Why'd you pick Marta? I've never heard you use that before.'

'I picked it out of a hat, if you can believe it,' she said.

'That will be hard to get used to. The only Marta I know is the one from Youth League, the one that reads *Mein Kampf* until her eyes bleed.'

Claudia took a foil-wrapped square of chocolate from her pocket, snapped it in half, and then handed me a piece. 'Say it a few times and you'll get used to it.' A chuckle puffed in her cheeks. 'I know it's strange to call me another name, but you only have to call me Marta when others are around.' She chuckled again.

'Why are you laughing?'

'I was just wondering what your codename would be if it wasn't Sascha. Maybe Dankwart? That would be a good name.'

I laughed. 'You're a real tease, you know that?'

'It's good to laugh, isn't it?' she said. 'Sometimes you have to remember to do it. After everything you see, what we saw today.' She touched my arm. 'We can't let the Reich take everything from us. If we do then they've won.' And for the next few moments we ate our chocolate quietly.

'Remember the first day we met?' she said. 'I was huddled in the corner of Dankwart's house complaining about the fit of my League uniform.'

'I remember. It was my first day in the League.'

'I never told you this, but moments before you walked in the door, Dankwart was yelling at me for being a slob. She said I didn't know how to wear my uniform and challenged the other girls not to talk to me until after I had sorted myself out.'

'You were the first person — no — the only girl

I talked to that day.'

'Why did you talk to me?' Claudia said. 'You must have noticed what a mess I was fiddling with my uniform, and how the other girls avoided me.'

'I noticed. And I thought you were the only one that wasn't insane.'

She smiled, tugging on the tips of my scarf. 'I'm glad you're here, Ella.'

'I'm glad too.'

* * *

Claudia walked me back to my aunt's house after the meeting. We lit cigarettes under a burnt-out streetlamp and smoked together, digesting that night's events until my fingers got tingly. 'Do you think I'll see Geb again?'

'Probably.' She smiled and then giggled to herself. 'I knew you were going to like him.'

I shrugged, trying to hide my smile, but she pushed her finger into my cheek. 'And you like Wilhelm,' I said, flicking my cigarette to the ground. 'I saw your fingers touching.'

'Mmm,' she said.

Two boxes filled with junk had been stacked on top of each other near the gutter — not rubbish, but broken household supplies most likely left after the raids. 'Come on,' she said, 'let's climb up.' She reached for my hand after tucking her cigarette into her mouth.

We balanced our weight on top of the highest box, holding onto each other's arms. 'The Reich calls us the Resistance . . . ' she said, whispering. 'But I like to say I'm a jumpbox.' We teetered and swayed catching our balance. 'Because only the brave would jump off the box of lies the Party has made us stand on.'

Jumpbox. The clip of footsteps somewhere in the darkness scared us both, stopping a stone's throw from where we were.

'The streets have ears,' Claudia said. She took one last inhaling puff of her cigarette before flicking it to the ground. 'Come on, let's go.'

And we jumped off the box together.

1942

8
April

As soon as I pushed the divan away from the wall and saw the layer of dust underneath, I knew I had found my shoe. I swore loud enough for Auntie to hear, but she made no mention of it. My aunt's Nazi flag hanging outside the window had been replaced with a much larger one, its black swastika in the middle now like a large eye peeping into the house. I bobbed up from the floor, rear-end high in the air, and watched its tips flail with a whip of wind.

For weeks the neighbourhood had been stringing up posters and banners down our little residential street in preparation for the Führer's birthday. Every year our neighbours tried to out-do their display from previous years. This year, Auntie added a small flag to hang the length of the rear window of her Volkswagen that she had parked out front; the car she got half-price because its cloth interior had been ruined by pet stains and bite marks. Auntie polished its lacquered green exterior every day with a white cloth, and kept the mirrors so clean you could see things that didn't exist.

Auntie had been up since four o'clock in the morning preparing a spread for her after-celebration celebration. Her heels clicked against the wood floor as she pranced between the kitchen and the dining room where she had arranged iced cakes and streusels on a laced tablecloth for that afternoon's tea. Hitler's birthday was a national holiday and she closed the shop for the day; I'd assumed she would, she'd even said she'd open late the day after.

'Make sure you come home right after the parade,' Auntie shouted from the kitchen. When I didn't answer she rushed around the corner. 'Sascha, don't forget my party.' She clutched a chocolate-smeared mixing bowl in one arm and pointed a freshly licked finger at her dessert table. 'I have ladies coming from my Nazi Women's League. Many have sons and grandsons your age.'

'You want to set me up?'

She put down her bowl just long enough to straighten the miniature Nazi flags she had stuck in a vase for a centrepiece. 'Would it hurt to have a boyfriend on the front?'

'What if he got killed, Auntie? Why would I put myself in that position?'

'Very well,' she said. 'I won't try to set you up.' She took hold of her spoon and mixed the chocolate in her bowl. 'But could you wear your uniform today to the parade?'

'My Youth League uniform?' I felt my face scrunch. 'My birthday was on New Year's Eve, Auntie. I graduated out at eighteen. I'd look silly wearing a uniform for someone much younger than I really am.'

'Your birthday wasn't that long ago. Don't be absurd. Besides, it's common for girls to wear their Youth League uniforms on the Führer's birthday. You know that.' She pointed with her head to a hook in the corridor where my uniform was hanging. 'I had it pressed! Of course, I could always buy you a new Bund Deutscher Mädel uniform, if you'd volunteer. The Reich's Belief and Beauty branch of the League is a wonderful opportunity for a young German woman like yourself.'

I never thought I'd see that uniform again, much less looking clean and tidy and ready for me to wear. I felt my throat close up just looking at the tie. 'The girls in the BDM are just like the ones in the League, and they're as ugly as Frau Dankwart.'

'They are not! It's the beauty branch, Sascha.' There was a very long, excruciating pause as Auntie looked down at me. 'Please, Sascha,' she said. 'It's a special day.' She looked at the scarf tied around my wrist. 'You wear the scarf your uncle gave you all the time. Can't you wear this for me, if not for the Führer?'

I took a deep breath, looking at Auntie's sad face. 'All right.'

I went into my bedroom to put it on and realized the shirt had shrunk a full size from having it washed with hot water. I shoved my arms into the sleeves; I had plans to meet Claudia at the Bergstraße 19 before the parade, and I wasn't going to risk being late over an outfit, even if the shirt did fit uncomfortably tight around my chest.

* * *

The streets were busy with people walking here and there, some wearing traditional lederhosen, while others wore Party uniforms, making their way to the parade. A line of marching Wehrmacht soldiers brushed past me holding their flags. 'You're going the wrong way,' one said as I made my way up the street. 'Parade's about to start.'

A woman leaned out her opened window, adjusting a Nazi banner she'd hung on her building, bickering with her husband about the straightness. 'What time is it?' I yelled up to her, and she barked back that we still had an hour before the parade started.

Claudia snuck up behind me. Her hair was much browner than it usually was with a playful yellow flower tucked behind her ear, which I had to admire. She noticed my uniform. 'Nice disguise.'

Before I could tell her Auntie had forced me to wear it, she flipped open her jacket. 'I have mine on too!' She patted a white box she had under her arm. 'I have something for you,' she said, looking through the Bergstraße's windows for a place to sit, but it was full.

'Let's go to the shop,' I said. 'Auntie closed it for the day.' We walked under the Nazi banner the couple had been hanging, which was now perfectly straight, and down the street. Herr Rudin spotted me at a distance from where he'd been sweeping, and then ducked into his bakery. Just when we got to the front of the shop he came out of his front door holding a lumpy brown paper sack.

'I have kipfel for you, Ella.' He nodded once. 'If you want.' Claudia looked at me, knowing my aunt wouldn't let me stop in there anymore, but with my aunt not around Herr Rudin usually sought me out. 'My wife's recipe,' he whispered.

‘Thank you, Herr Rudin,’ I said, taking the sack. ‘I love your wife’s kipfel.’

Claudia and I went into the antiques shop. She handed me the box from under her arm, and I set down the kipfel. ‘Go on.’ She beamed. ‘Open it up.’

A spray of blooming white roses with blue tips.

‘Blue roses? Where’d you get these?’ I dug my nose into one of the buds, taking a sniff. ‘Ah, and they smell heavenly, like summertime near the river. I forgot what that smelled like.’

‘I have my secrets.’ She smiled.

‘I told you about the painting I sold that nobody wanted?’

She looked confused. ‘What painting?’

‘You’re teasing.’

‘Yes,’ Claudia said. ‘I remembered. That’s why I bought these roses over the others.’ We sat down on the small divan in my aunt’s office, which was just big enough for two. The seat cushions were lumpy and soft, which made us sink low to the floor, just under Hitler’s portrait hanging on the wall. We put our feet up and talked about the crowds outside while she rolled us cigarettes with tobacco and paper she had pulled from her pocket.

‘Have you seen Geb lately?’ I asked.

She handed me a cigarette after lighting it with a small metal lighter. ‘That’s interesting. He asked me the same thing about you not that long ago.’

‘He did?’ I puffed on my cigarette and then coughed terribly — it wasn’t just any kind of cigarette. ‘What is this?’ The ember crackled, hissed and sparked. It tasted like mint and sugary tea, but the smoke burned the back of my throat and my lungs felt heavy as tar.

'I put clove in it,' she said as she lit her cigarette. 'Do you like it?'

I examined it cautiously before taking another puff. The smoke warmed me from the inside and I felt calm, but at the same time it made my heart race. When I exhaled, dense, grey smoke filtered slowly from the side of my mouth. I sank further into the divan's cushions. 'I should sell these when I take over the shop after the war,' I said. 'You could make them for me, be my assistant!'

'You're a dreamer, Ella.' Claudia took a long drag from her cigarette. 'Your aunt would never allow that.'

'With the Reich gone, who knows,' I said. 'Maybe she'll be different.'

She patted my hand. 'It is a nice dream.'

My mind travelled to that space where I could dream about the future, the place where Auntie had learned to tolerate Claudia and we didn't have to sneak. I was sorting through all the responsibilities we could share together as shop girls when she sat up suddenly.

'Ella?'

I exhaled, waving the smoke away. 'Yes?'

'Do you remember Anka Zimmerman? Her parents own the Korn und Berg bookstore in the Hauptmarkt.'

'I know of her. Auntie was Frau Zimmerman's midwife. She took me with her to their store a few times.'

'Tell me about the building. What's it like inside — how many floors?'

'It has three levels. The first floor is full of books, of course. There's a staircase that leads to the third floor behind a set of louvered doors in the back. Why?'

Claudia stood up with the flower box in her hands. 'There's something under the roses you need to see.' She scooped up some roses, and then looked for a place to put them, before tossing them in my lap. 'Here!'

I sat fully up with the flowers in my lap as she plopped back down next to me in the cushions. 'Look at these.' She pulled a thick stack of leaflets from the box with a caricaturized image of Hitler on the front. Typed in bold underneath were the words: Failure! Madman!

'There's a drop today.'

I gasped. Leaflet drops were very dangerous because they happened during the day, and not many happened in Nuremberg, but when they did there was always a big stir.

'During the celebration?'

Her eyes glowed. 'Over the Korn und Berg bookstore.'

My mouth gaped open thinking about the location, which was dead centre to the Hauptmarkt, right where the bulk of the parade would be marching. 'You have their permission? Anka's parents are National Socialists.'

'The Zimmermans got in some financial trouble after they were forced to change their windows from flat to round. Hitler himself ordered the change, walked right into their store and spoke to them directly. Now the Zimmermans owe the glassmaker a favour. Those windows were very expensive.'

I got excited thinking she was going to ask me

to join her, and then a little nervous.

'Do you want to come?'

I looked at her, blinking. In the daylight there was nowhere to hide. At least with the basement everything happened under the cover of night.

'It's all right,' she said. 'You don't have to go, but the Zimmermans won't be there, if you're worried.'

I thought about rushing upstairs to the roof of the Korn und Berg with the military parade in full march below, throwing outlawed leaflets with Claudia by my side. 'I want to go.'

'Then it's settled,' she said. 'Wilhelm and Hans are meeting us.' She touched my hand. 'I'm so lucky to have you, Ella. Forever.' She looked at her watch. 'Let's clean these flowers up and go.'

We'd cleaned up the roses, stuffing them back into the box along with the leaflets when we heard the most excruciating noise — a sharp clang that ricocheted off the walls like a dagger trying to find its target.

We froze.

Smoke filtered out of the room and into the corridor as if someone had opened a door. A blank stare washed over Claudia's face, and my hands trembled, suddenly hot and sweaty, holding the box with the leaflets inside. Getting caught for planning was just the same as getting caught for doing.

'What was that?' she mouthed.

I pointed with my head toward the corridor. 'It came from the basement.'

'When was the last time someone stayed here?' Claudia whispered.

'Three days,' I whispered back. 'A couple from Furth. But that's all.'

Claudia peered down the corridor. 'Come on.' She grabbed my hand and we crept toward the basement. A spot of cold air hovered in front of the door. She placed her hand on the knob, wrapping her fingers around it quietly, tightly, before kicking the door open.

Bang!

We both screamed, holding on to each other, looking into the basement, the door swinging back and forth.

Nobody was there.

'Did we imagine it?' Claudia held me back at the waist as I tried to take a step through the door.

'We both heard it,' I said.

'Wait,' she said, and a box in the far corner moved by itself. We looked at each other and then to the box, just as a mouse scurried out from behind and ran across the room. He squeezed his scrawny little body through the dark space between the trapdoor and its latch, his tail flicking the pin hook before vanishing to the other side.

Claudia sighed. 'A mouse.' She dropped her arm, and my body fell against the doorframe.

'All that noise from one little — '

'Come on.' Claudia motioned for me to follow her down the corridor.

'I don't know . . . '

Her hand reached for mine. 'It was a mouse. Let's go.'

I started to close the door, but then stopped, taking one last look at the pin hook that was still swinging.

'We're going to be late,' she said.

And I shut the door.

* * *

Adulation. It's the only word I could use to describe Hitler's birthday parade — jubilant youths crowding the walkways, beer flowing free from the halls and into the streets, mothers jostling their babies, bouncing them like offerings to a god, and banners and flags hanging triumphantly; little Nazi eyes on every building and in every hand.

A squadron of Luftwaffe bombers flew over the city in formation, wing tip to wing tip, with shiny bombs hanging from their bellies. Cheers erupted.

'Don't look back,' Claudia said. 'Run up and run down. That's all you have to do.'

I nodded quickly, looking at the Korn und Berg store.

Hans came up behind us, tapping Claudia's shoulder. He took a hard look at me before turning to Claudia. 'I thought you were coming alone,' he said.

Wilhelm walked up too. 'Does it matter?' Claudia said.

Hans flicked his chin at the flower box Claudia had under her arm.

'Inside,' Claudia said, and we walked into the store, past the closed sign, and to a set of louvered doors in the back.

'Here,' Claudia said, dividing the stacks into fourths. 'Hans, on the roof, go at least five shops down. Me and Wilhelm will be right behind you. And you, Sascha, stay close.' She looked at each of us. 'We throw at the same time.'

The military's rhythmic march outside got louder and closer, and the far window shook from the cadence. Tiny butterflies swirled in my stomach.

'Follow me,' Hans said, and we ran up the stairs.

We staked out our posts on ascending buildings, listening to the Wehrmacht thumping down below in their boots. I saw Claudia let go of her leaflets between two Nazi flags jutting from a rooftop, so I threw mine over. Then I saw her dashing back, mouthing the word 'run.'

Everything happened so fast — I don't remember running down the stairs, or what it felt like tossing the leaflets. One moment I was wedged between the ramparts, and the next I was back inside the Korn und Berg standing behind the louvered doors.

I steadied my breath — it was over — and walked briskly into the store, only I wasn't alone. A Gestapo officer stood at the bookcase thumbing through a copy of *Mein Kampf*, his back turned to the street with the door wide open.

Bile rose in my throat, feeling that awful, shivering feeling of being caught. I closed my eyes, wondering how hard he was going to throw me to the ground.

'Ella!' he said. 'Ella Von Bruen.'

My eyes sprung open.

His smile gleamed white, and I remembered who he was: the Gestapo officer who watched me fall at Coburg's feet. 'It's me, Muller. Remember?' The leaflets fluttered to the ground behind him like soft rain. He had no idea. If he did, I would have been in handcuffs.

He closed Hitler's book and walked away from the bookcase with one hand resting on his billy club, looking surprised to see me in the bookstore.

'Yes,' I said, voice shaking. 'Officer Muller, I remember.'

He took off his hat and got so close I had to step backward to keep him from touching me. 'You're looking good, Ella. Really good.' His voice slapped me like a whip and I flushed deep red, my heart hammering against my chest.

Claudia peeped through the slats of the louvered door. The flower box was on the ground next to her feet, and I saw a forgotten leaflet clinging to the side. Claudia reached down and crumpled it in her hands — Muller's attention on me was the only thing keeping him from noticing her.

I choked, mumbling something about the parade. I pulled on my tie to breathe, and my front button unfastened from wearing a shirt that had shrunk a size too small. Muller's eyes got really wide. I had his attention. Not the kind of attention a student gives her teacher, but more like the wide-eyed concentration a cat has when teased with a fuzzy ball.

Anka walked in from the street with her hands full of Nazi flags, her eyes sliding nervously to mine, and then to the louvered door. She grabbed something from a shelf and her hip bumped into a small display case. Books arranged for purchase tumbled to the ground, but instead of picking them up she broke for the front door.

Muller started to turn to the noise. I panicked, thinking I'd lose him. *Sell him a lie and he'll believe it!*

‘So, what can I do for you, Officer?’ I cocked my hip like I’d seen a prostitute do once near the Pegnitz Bridge, and untied the yellow scarf from my wrist to slide it through my hands. ‘On this day of all days.’

He smiled, and not just any kind of smile, but the sly kind I’d seen Coburg give my aunt hundreds of times before after they’d made a deal. His hand reached up for my face, and another officer rushed through the open door. ‘Kommandant Muller,’ he said, and Muller turned around sharply. ‘We have a problem!’ He shook a twisted leaflet in the air.

Kommandant? My knees buckled.

Muller pounded his knuckles into his open hand. ‘Damn!’ I jerked from his loud voice. Then he stepped backward out the door with a finger pointed at me like a gun. ‘I’ll come back for you later.’ He winked.

The louvered doors flew open and Claudia pulled me into the crowded street behind Wilhelm and Hans, my body still awkwardly posed in a prostitute’s stance.

‘That was — ’

‘Power!’ Claudia said. ‘That was power.’

And I felt a profound shift inside of me.

9

Auntie's Women's League mingled in her parlour for her after-celebration celebration, sipping schnapps and tea, munching down the last of her strawberry kuchen and chocolate candies. She paraded around, kettle in her hand, serving them with small curtsies. I sat on the divan, demitasse held to my lips, tilting back warm spritzer while watching them from the edge of my cup. The mere thought of those leaflets floating in the air was enough to twirl my stomach. A peep of laughter from my lips and Auntie looked at me strangely.

'I couldn't have done anything today without the support of my niece,' she said, pouring a guest a cup of tea. 'She'd make an excellent companion for a young man who wants to write letters.'

I pulled my cup away. 'Auntie!'

The whole room laughed. 'Don't tease the girl, Bridget,' one woman said as Auntie served her a small cake. 'She must have her eye on somebody by the sound of her.'

Auntie glanced up, her smile fading as she wondered whom that somebody might be. I sat up tall.

A little old lady named Gretel Tiefenbrunn sat in a wide-backed chair in the middle of the room and talked about her cousin, Hermann Göring, the Kommandant-in-Chief of the Luftwaffe. Her face folded and flopped as she spoke in a broken southern accent, which she tried to cover up, though her true past as the wife of a peasant farmer was never talked about in closed circles. Her cousin's success in the Reich, rising in rank so quickly, had given her status and prestige.

Gummibär candy stained her wrinkled lips red, and my aunt's herbed tea tarnished the corners of her mouth a light brown.

'The Luftwaffe's new base is quite extraordinary,' Frau Tiefenbrunn said. 'Despite what the resistance has done to our supply shipments. But it's only a matter of days, I'm sure.' She took a small sip from her cup.

'A matter of days?' Auntie said with a squint.

'Before they catch the resisters and hang them.'

Everyone quieted. Ladies who were standing took their seats and listened to her with devoted attention. 'Hermann can't tell me, of course, but he did allude to his sister, Paula, that a reckoning was coming in short order.' She took another sip from her cup. 'A raid of all raids. And rightfully so.'

Our neighbour, Margot Spitz, a widow of only eleven days, smoothed her blue silken skirt over her knees. 'You don't say, Frau Tiefenbrunn.' She dug her elbows into her knees and cradled her head with ring-laden fingers. 'What else can you tell us about The Blue Max?'

Spritzer sprayed from my nose when she called Hermann Göring by his nickname, as if she knew him. A light titter waved across the room, and Auntie put a hand on my knee, shaking her head very discreetly. I cleaned myself up with a napkin, sitting more comfortably now with my feet up on the coffee table.

Auntie mouthed for me to sit normally, and I flopped one foot down at a time. 'What's with you?' she whispered.

'Did I say something wrong?' Margot said, blushing. 'Because I wouldn't want — '

'Of course not, darling,' Frau Tiefenbrunn said.

Margot exhaled, looking very much relieved. She took a long pin out of her bound hair and let her curls bounce off her shoulders, making her look much younger than her real, thirty-something age. 'Do you have his address?' She smiled. 'I'd love to write him a letter.'

'Well, he is terribly busy, of course,' Frau Tiefenbrunn said. Margot's smile vanished. 'Oh. Right.'

Hilde Kappelhoff stood up. She had been in the Youth League with me, but liked to think herself a full twenty years older than she really was, which I never understood. She looked it too, spindly legs and spotted arms, a slick of dyed, greying hair pinned tight behind her ear. She mirrored her husband Friedrich, who was as rich as he was old.

'That would be some kind of raid,' Hilde said. 'I saw the newsreels. Those disgusting Youth members fallen from grace, terrorizing innocent Germans, ambushing our supply shipments, killing armed Wehrmacht.' She reached for the tea kettle Auntie had placed on the table next to her chair. Auntie rose from her seat to serve her, but Hilde waved her back and talked as she poured. 'The resistance are a bunch of savage Indians. I'm sure they come from classless families.'

'That's what I hear,' Frau Tiefenbrunn said. 'Classless.'

A woman sitting in the corner scooted her

bottom to the edge of her seat. She had scraped her plate clean and rested it on a wide knee with the fork pressed between the plate and her thumb. 'Savage,' she said just above a whisper. 'Indians.'

Frau Tiefenbrunn pinched the corner of someone else's cake sitting on the side table. She looked around for her plate, holding the hunk she'd torn off in her hand, but my aunt had already taken it into the kitchen with the other dirty dishes.

'Darling, can you get me another plate?' Frau Tiefenbrunn said to my aunt. 'Someone has taken mine.'

Auntie glanced into her glass cabinet. The only plates she had left were the ceramic dishes she stacked under her china to make it look like she had more to her set then she really did. Her eyes sank with her chest and she stuttered. 'Of . . . course.' She pulled one of the plates out of the cabinet, spun it around and examined the chips along the edge.

'On second thought, darling,' Frau Tiefenbrunn said, licking her fingers clean, 'how about just a napkin.'

Auntie exhaled her relief before handing her a napkin and sitting back down with her legs crossed delicately at the ankle.

Frau Tiefenbrunn looked around the room from her seat. 'Are you out of kuchen already?'

Auntie's eyes grew bigger. Her guests had practically eaten everything she'd made.

'I have something I think you'll like,' I said, and then stood. 'Anyone want some kipfel?'

'I didn't bake kipfel,' Auntie said.

I smiled. 'I bought some today.'

'When did you have time?' she said.

I looked over my shoulder as I turned into the kitchen. 'I had time.' I pulled Herr Rudin's kipfel from the bottom pantry. Moments later Auntie was in the kitchen with me. She set her tea cup down on the counter as I pulled kipfel from the sack.

'What are you doing?' she said in a breathy whisper.

I crumpled the sack into a ball before picking up the tray. 'Getting the kipfel. For your guests.' She put her hand on my arm, looking at the kipfel on the tray I'd arranged. Only Herr Rudin folded his kipfel to look like horseshoes.

'I know where these came from,' she said, squeezing my arm. 'Put them back.' She snatched her tea cup from the counter, and then let out a boisterous laugh as she reentered the parlour, sitting back down in her old seat and picking up her dirty napkin.

I stood in the doorway, half-in half-out of the kitchen, clutching that tray. Frau Tiefenbrunn asked where the kipfel was, and so did Margot. Auntie started to make up a lie about how she didn't have any after all when I burst around the corner.

'Here they are!' I said, smiling, holding the tray out.

Frau Tiefenbrunn looked each one over, her nose to the tray, touching several before deciding on the lightest one. 'I love a good kipfel,' she said.

'Oh yes,' I said. 'Frau Spitz?' I pivoted my tray to Margot, and she eagerly took one too, not wasting a moment before biting into it.

'Mmm . . . this might be the best kipfel I've ever tasted,' she said.

Hilde reached over my shoulder to grab a kipfel for herself before they were all gone. 'Let me try,' she said, and then gobbled hers up.

'Auntie?' I offered her the last of Herr Rudin's kipfel from the tray. Her lips pursed, and she shot a look of anger toward me, before glancing over her guests.

'It's the last one, Bridget,' Frau Tiefenbrunn said. 'You can't leave it.'

Auntie begrudgingly took the last kipfel from the tray. She smiled politely and then laughed when her guests did, but they'd already moved on to talk about the weather.

I walked back into the kitchen, letting out the gulp of air I'd been holding. I'd never done something so brazen in front of my aunt before, and it felt good. Auntie raced into the kitchen and stood behind me with her hands on her hips.

I wiped off the tray. 'It's just kipfel, Auntie.'

There was a knock at the door and Auntie was glad to let me go and answer it. 'Don't hurry back,' she said, as I walked away, knowing she would have words with me later, and answered the door.

It was Claudia, and I quickly stepped outside before my aunt could see who it was. Her clothes hung heavy as though she'd been in the river, and her hair looked more like a sopped-up mop than anything else. 'What are you doing here?' Something had gone wrong; she would have never come to the front door if it hadn't.

'It's Wilhelm,' she sobbed. 'Wilhelm was arrested.'

I gasped. I didn't want her to see the alarm in my face, but there was little I could do to hide my concern. We sat on the wood bench outside away from the light of Auntie's party. 'What for?'

'There can only be one charge.' Her shoulders stiffened as she wrapped her cold, wet fingers around my upper arms. 'There was a leaflet in his pocket. Hans must have planted it after the drop,' she said. 'Sarah saw the whole thing, said she heard Wilhelm curse Hans as the Gestapo took him away.' She shook her head and let out a gut-wrenching groan. 'They've taken him to Verräters Gasse Prison.'

I shivered, repeating the words. 'Traitor's Alley.' It was a dark, cindered palace with a central courtyard we called The Pit. There was only one reason they brought people there: to be shot. Family and friends of those within its walls brought clothes and other items to their loved ones. Only when the guards refused to accept it did they know the person had died.

'Claudia, be strong. He'll get out of it. If anyone can, it's Wilhelm.' I tried to sound hopeful, but I knew deep down Wilhelm was in big trouble.

Her eyes sagged. 'Ella, you don't understand. It's more than that. We're . . . we're to be married.'

I jumped in my seat. 'What?'

'We have plans to marry in secret. My father knows of his politics, how he hates the Reich, their policies, their control over the country. He would never allow us to get married openly. Don't be mad I didn't tell you. I thought it was safer that way.'

We shared a moment of silence. She did the

right thing keeping her marriage plans a secret, even if it was from me. 'Oh, Claudia.' I held her close, crying along with her. 'He's a patriot.'

She sat up with a jerk, using the back of her hand to wipe her face. 'It's of little consolation, Ella . . . if he's dead now, isn't it?' Her gaze hardened along with her voice.

'What are you going to do?'

'I'm going to kill Hans.' Hate twisted in her cheeks. 'A rat always sleeps.' Sarah swooped out of the darkness and knelt at Claudia's feet.

'Where did you come from?' I said. Her eyes darted toward mine but then slid quickly back to Claudia's. She wore a pair of men's trousers, and hid her hair under a grey swindler's cap, which she pulled down low, almost over her eyes.

'I found Hans,' she said to Claudia. 'He's at the Hütt'n. In the dining room.'

Hans is a traitor. Only Nazis frequented the Hütt'n. It was a restaurant where the Party recruited members, a place where the Reich celebrated victories over the resistance. I thought back to when I first met Hans at the Steichele. He and Sarah had never got along. Now I knew why.

Sarah squeezed my knee. 'I need your help. I left a woman in the basement of the antiques shop. She needs help tonight. Bring some food. Geb will transport her in the morning, but she needs you now.' There was a sense of urgency in her voice, and it was the first time I had heard her sound that way.

'Yes. I'll go.' I looked through the window and saw the hazy silhouettes of Auntie's guests through the Nazi flag she had hung in the window. 'I'll leave now.'

Sarah pulled a leather sheath from her back pocket and unveiled a small dagger. Its blade shined like an icicle even in dull light. 'Are you ready?' she said. Claudia's brow furrowed and a slight frown tugged on her lower lip — and I realized Sarah had killed before, and she intended to show Claudia how to do it.

Sarah tucked the dagger into her waistband and walked toward the open road only to stop in the middle of the street. One hand motioned for Claudia.

Claudia looked at me. 'Ella, why did you jump into the fountain with me? All those months ago. Why, when you knew it would shame your family, your aunt?'

'What?'

She squeezed my hand. 'I need to know.'

I swallowed, looking at Sarah's outstretched hand, and then to Claudia's strained face. 'You know my parents didn't raise me to be a National Socialist. They would have wanted me to jump in it.'

She closed her eyes, and I thought she was relieved to hear me say the words out loud. 'Your aunt always blamed me for what we did. I sometimes wonder if you'd be better off without me.'

'That's impossible. We're connected, forever.' I glanced up at Sarah, who was still waiting for Claudia with her hand out. 'But why are you asking me about this now?'

Claudia hugged me unexpectedly. 'In case I never see you again.' She let go as quickly as she had grabbed me and then ran off with Sarah.

10

There's something about an empty shop at night. The silence. The shadows. The black air. When Jews were hidden in the basement these things were amplified, given a life of their own, a heart; the stillness screamed, objects moved on their own, and black spaces solidified.

I should have noticed these differences when I arrived — a loaf of marbled rye tucked tightly under one arm — but my mind was on other things, like Claudia. The straightness of her face when she spoke, the dagger. It still wasn't clear to me how Wilhelm was caught; why would Hans slip a leaflet into his pocket when we were all part of the drop? How did Sarah know Hans was at the Hütt'n? But I knew Claudia would figure it out, or at least, cut it out of Hans. I winced at the thought, but it could have been me or even Claudia sitting in that prison instead of Wilhelm, and I had to remember that.

A long-drawn-out moan came from the basement.

I scurried down the corridor, unlocked the door in a panic and found a very pregnant woman sitting in the corner with her legs spread out, holding her perfectly round belly with both hands.

'What the hell?'

She huffed and snorted from her mouth and nose. 'Quick,' she said in a scratchy, throaty voice. 'Get some towels!'

Her face pulsed purple, and chunks of brown hair that had been hastily tucked behind both ears soaked in her sweat. She moaned again. This time her voice stretched like taffy and filled the entire shop with a laborious groan. A pool of water spilled out from between her legs, and I jumped. The marbled rye I had tucked under my arm slipped from its sack, hit the concrete step, and then rolled across the floor and into the water that flowed out of her.

'Hurry!'

I shook my coat off, unsure what to do, and placed it on the ground like a dog's piddle pad. She stopped panting and gave me a hard, bitter look as she pulled herself back into the corner of the wall. 'It's over now,' she said, looking at her watch. 'We've got a few minutes before it comes again.'

'Before what comes again?'

She cocked her head. 'Aren't you here to help me? Sarah said she was sending someone smart.' She lifted her skirt up and fanned it over her bump.

My face dropped. 'Sorry, I . . . I . . . are you having a baby?'

She laughed.

When I didn't laugh back, a look of dread washed over her face. 'I was only told you needed me.' I looked down at the marbled rye sitting in her waters and moved it to a dry spot, grimacing from the sight of the soggy bread. 'And to bring you some food.'

'Do you know how to deliver a baby?'

Before I could answer she started panting again. 'Here comes another one.'

‘Another what?’ I scooted back, expecting another wave of water to gush out between her legs.

‘Not that! A contraction!’ Her eyes shook with agony, and she screamed, gripping my hand and squeezing my palm in two. After a few seconds, after the pain seemed to ripple through her body, she tossed my hand to the side and closed her eyes as if she were sleeping. At one point I thought she had fallen asleep, looking very rested and peaceful, but then her eyes popped open and she looked at me as if she had just realized I was still there.

‘Can you be in false labour? I’ve heard of that before.’

‘What’s your name?’

I hesitated. ‘Sascha.’

‘Sascha, this baby is coming tonight, and you’re going to have to help me deliver it. You’ll need to get some blankets and a bucket of water. Hot water if you can.’

My neck got increasingly warm as I loosened the tie from my uniform — I knew nothing about birthing babies.

‘It’s all right, honey. What are you, seventeen?’

‘Eighteen,’ I said, lifting my chin. ‘My birthday was on New Year’s Eve.’

She smiled and didn’t seem as irritated with me as she had been. ‘I appreciate you coming here, even if you didn’t know what you were getting into. Otherwise I’d have to go about this alone.’ She rubbed her belly. ‘My son and husband left for France before the Reich stopped the visas. I was left behind. It was only supposed to take a few days to get me out, but now . . . I guess it has been months now, hasn't it?'

I nodded, pretending to listen, but my mind was on the baby, and how exactly I was going to help her deliver it.

She took a deep breath and exhaled. 'By the way, my name is Julia.' She tipped her head back and rested it in the corner of the cold brick wall. 'Maybe you should add pillows to that list as well.'

* * *

Hours passed. Julia's contractions got worse. She barely had a chance to rest before gearing up for another. Fluids from her bottom soiled the only blankets I had. Moans escalated into wails, and even though she said water wasn't going to flow out of her again, I didn't entirely believe her.

She pulled her sopping wet skirt over the top of her belly, and then adjusted the pillow I had given her behind her head. 'Sascha, you're going to have to check me.'

'Check?'

'You need to check for the baby's head. Look in there.'

I started to mumble, not sure if I could go through with it or not. I had never seen another woman's vagina before and I didn't want to.

Her pants sped up with another contraction. 'Now!' she yelled, and I pushed her knees apart and looked deep into the cavern between her legs.

Liquid oozed from a bloodstained, diamond-shaped hole. I covered my nose and my mouth from the smell, then she moaned and a bald head poked out. 'I see it!'

'How big is it?'

'It's a nice head, a small ball!'

I looked again, but it had disappeared back inside of her.

She shook her head from side to side, hissing. '*Nein*!' She dipped her fingers into her crotch and searched her way around the hole, but she couldn't get close enough to touch the space where the baby's head had been. 'How big is the opening?'

I held my hand close to the hole. 'Four fingers wide. Plenty of room for a baby to squeeze out.'

Julia's pants turned into cries. She searched her skirt for a dry edge, and then wiped the tears from her face with the palm of her hand. 'You need to get help. A midwife. Something isn't right. It should be bigger. I feel like I need to push, and at four fingers my baby will die.'

'Die?' Her words hit me like a slug to the chest. 'But I . . . I . . . ' There was only one midwife I knew in Nuremberg — only one.

'You have to,' she said, now weeping.

'You don't understand — '

'Go!' she yelled, and I screamed, bolting from the shop.

* * *

I stole a car to get home, parking a block away and then sprinting down the street. I burst through the front door and landed on my knees, folding my hands near my face. Auntie had been waiting for me on the divan with every light in the house turned on. She crossed her legs tightly at the knees, watching me.

'Auntie!' I used the back of my hand to wipe some slobber from my lower lip. It mixed with a smudge of Julia's blood and I felt it streak across my face.

Aunt Bridget jumped up when she saw the blood. 'What happened?'

She held onto my shoulders, trying to catch my gaze, but I was near delirious. I thought about Julia, alone in the basement, choking on my own words, then in a fraught voice I blurted, 'I need you to deliver a baby.'

Her eyes constricted into small, black holes. 'Whose baby?' she said in a harsh, direct voice. There was only one reason a woman would give birth in secret. If she didn't have a midwife it was because she wasn't supposed to exist: she was Jewish.

My lips trembled along with my hands. 'Please, Auntie. She's in the basement of the shop.' I hung my head low and reached up for her hands. 'Please . . . '

Her body turned stiff as a board. 'What did you get yourself into *this* time?'

When I didn't answer, she pushed my searching hands away, went to the closet and took her dusty old midwife's bag down from the top shelf. She stood for a second and stared at the front door, holding the bag at her side, her grip pulsating around its handle, breathing deeply. I was just about to call out her name when she grabbed me by the ear and dragged me backward out the front door with her.

We drove her Volkswagen to the shop. Neither of us said a word. Auntie marched briskly into the basement with stiff shoulders and a jutted chin, but once she saw Julia on the ground like a barge unable to unload its cargo, she rolled up her sleeves and crouched between Julia's legs.

Julia's moans turned into sharp screams.

'Ella!' Auntie kicked the water bucket. 'Get some fresh water.' Each syllable she spoke had a tone to itself, and when she called me Ella, like she normally did when I was in trouble, it stung like a zap of electricity.

Auntie ripped Julia's skirt down the middle and flipped them out of her way like curtains. 'I'm Bridget. What's your name?' Auntie's voice changed when she talked to Julia. It was calm, sympathetic. 'Relax. I've done this before,' she said with a wink.

'Ju . . . Julia.' She panted, barely able to say her name.

Auntie butterflied Julia's legs open, and then took her feet and placed them on some boxes to push against. 'How long have you been in labour?'

'Hours.' Auntie whipped her head around, her eyes carving into mine.

'Looks it,' she said. 'You're ripping at the sides.'

'I thought the hole was big enough — '

'Hand me my bag!' Auntie said.

I used the side of my foot to slide the midwife's bag closer to my aunt, and then took a step back. Auntie reached in and pulled out something that looked like silver serving tongs, along with some razor blades and two small metal flasks, which she neatly arranged on a sheet of white canvas.

'Get behind Julia, Ella. Put your back in the corner and cradle her in your legs.' Auntie pointed to the wall with her head as she rubbed the tongs with a grey coverlet. I manoeuvred myself into the crook of the wall and let Julia lean into me so that my legs would support her girth.

'What are you going to do with those tongs?'

Auntie looked at me, still rubbing the tongs. 'These are not tongs, Ella. *These* are forceps. We're going to have to pull it out.' Auntie took a ball of cotton from the bag, squeezed liquid from one of the bottles onto it and then tossed it to me. 'When I say so, cover her nose with that cotton.'

With a shaking hand I brushed the hair out of my face, nodding.

Auntie dropped her tense shoulders and sighed. 'Damn it, Sascha.'

'I didn't mean to — '

'Shh. I don't want to hear it,' she said. 'Let's just deliver this baby, shall we?'

'All right, Auntie.' I pulled my uniform tie off and threw it, loosening the collar of my sweat-soaked shirt.

Auntie picked up the other bottle and squirted liquid between Julia's legs, then she reached for a razor blade. 'All right, sweetie, this is going to pinch a little.' Auntie held the blade to Julia's bottom then motioned with two quick swipes. A squirt of blood hit my shoe and Julia whimpered.

'I've got the head!' Auntie shouted.

Julia's whimper escalated into a screaming cry; it curdled and seeped from her pores as if she were being pierced with a jagged knife. I prayed, making promises to Christ I wasn't sure if I could keep. Auntie, on the other hand, rooted as if she was leading a cheer.

'Come on, girl, you've got it. You've got it. Push!'

The basement warmed with a heavy smell of iron as Julia bore down with gritted teeth. Her face ballooned red, and the veins in her eyes spidered into feathered lines. Then she gasped for air as if she'd been drowning.

'Shit!' Auntie looked at the cotton ball cupped in my hand and shouted. 'Now, Sascha!' She grasped the forceps with both hands and dug them deep into Julia's vagina, who turned instantly limp and quiet the moment I put the cotton to her nose.

Auntie's arms disappeared, and her eyes searched the open air. She wiped sweat from her face with her sleeve, and lipstick smeared across her cheek. Then her clip snapped from her head and her braided bun unravelled down her back. She knelt, face puckering, groaning and pulling, before falling backward with a crying baby in her arms.

'It's a girl!'

Auntie's face gleamed as she cradled the baby and gazed deep into her infant eyes, weeping. 'Oh, dear God. Dear, sweet God . . . '

* * *

Auntie swaddled the baby in a thin white blanket she had tucked in her midwife's bag. I put the pillow under Julia's head and laid her gently on the ground.

'Take the baby, Sascha,' Auntie said, resting her in my arms. 'I need to sew Julia up before she wakes.' Blood that had mixed with a strange gelatinous fluid soaked into Auntie's stockings. She handled a bloody balloon that came out of Julia after the baby. 'This is normal.'

'But Auntie . . . your stockings.'

'I'll live,' she said. 'Birthing is a dirty job, Sascha.'

'Yes, it is.' The basement had soured with an odorous smell, and I felt nauseous, wondering why the hell anyone would get pregnant after seeing what it took to bring a baby into the world. 'Will Julia be all right?'

Auntie looked through the eye of a sharp needle and threaded it with a thick string. 'She will be once I'm done with her.' She looked at the baby and smiled upon her as if she were her own. 'You did the right thing, Sascha. That baby would've died if you hadn't got me. Maybe even both of them.'

The midnight hour slipped into morning. Julia had woken up and Auntie helped her latch the baby to her breast. The two shared stories about motherhood and birthing. Auntie talked about my delivery as if I had come out of her, describing the labour my mother went through in great detail. Julia nodded periodically and cuddled her infant tightly in her arms as I mopped the floor. Neither of them saw me gagging into my sleeve when I squeezed the water out, or when I carried the bucket out of the basement.

The stories ended when my aunt asked her where she was headed.

Julia's speech was slow, but smooth. 'To France, the rest of my family is already there.'

Auntie nodded and petted the baby's head, and I wondered if she thought I'd tell Julia she was a member of the Party. But it was hard to tell after the delivery, with the way Auntie smiled at Julia and looked lovingly at her baby.

'I trust you've got her transport all arranged, Sascha?'

'Yes,' I said, setting down the mop.

A second later a loud screech echoed through the basement. The trapdoor that connected the basement to the abandoned beer cellar next door shuddered, and its pin hook swayed. It was the same sound Claudia and I had heard when we saw the mouse, only louder, more ominous — a sound caused by a person.

Auntie's eyes bugged from her head.

'Oh no,' she said. 'Sascha, how long have you been doing this?'

I couldn't take my eyes off the trapdoor. Auntie grabbed my arm and shook it, trying to get me to answer her. 'Since October,' I blurted.

'This is terrible,' Auntie said under the cover of one hand. 'The Kunstbunker, they heard everything.'

Julia looked very worried. She pushed the baby into her chest and attempted to stand, rolling to her side, using a wooden crate for support. My aunt sat with her legs folded underneath her body, staring at the trapdoor and its shaking pin hook.

'*Tante* Bridget?' My voice rattled as I realized she knew something I didn't. I put a hand under her chin and her head swung heavy toward me, her eyes darkening like an old lady's.

Julia scooted along the wall, getting as far away from the trapdoor as she could. The hinges jiggled loose, and then the bolts connecting it to the wall started to unscrew. One of them flopped out of its hole and tinkled its way across the floor.

'In the shop . . . in the shop.' My aunt flicked her fingers toward the basement door. Julia waddled up the steps, a soaked women's napkin bulging between her legs. But I couldn't move. My feet were as heavy as lead weights. 'Now,' Auntie said in a shouted whisper.

I stared wondrously at the trapdoor as it shook free from its bindings. Auntie boxed my shoulders with her hands, turned me around and pushed me up the steps and into the corridor. She shut the basement door, throwing her weight against it as she turned over all three of its steely-barred locks. Then she took two steps back and folded her arms tightly across her chest.

The front door opened, and terror streaked across Auntie's face when she saw Geb walking toward us, a boy she'd never seen. Julia stepped backward, and my aunt held onto her arm, protecting her and the baby.

'Sascha?' he said, and my aunt relaxed into the wall when he said my name.

There was a loud clang, as if the trapdoor had been completely unhinged and thrown to the ground. The knob on the basement door turned back-and-forth. Then loud thuds slammed up against it, the kind of sound only a body can make. My aunt whimpered as she covered her mouth. She reached for me, gripping my arm forcefully, but then an eerie silence followed — whoever was on the other side of that door had left.

Geb pulled me into a dark corner of the shop to talk. 'What's going — '

I threw my arms around his neck without thinking. 'Geb,' I said, 'thank God you're here!' He hugged me back, and I squeezed a little tighter.

'What's going on?' His eyes rolled up and down my aunt from afar, as if he wasn't sure what to make of her, or what had just happened with the pounding door.

I gulped. There was so much to tell him and almost no time. 'You need to go,' I said. 'The girl and her baby.'

'I don't want to leave you,' he said. 'Did you hear about Hans?'

I nodded, closing my eyes briefly. 'I did.'

'Then you must know we aren't safe tonight.'

Julia's baby yelped a hungry cry, and she tried to soothe her with words of hope and love, telling the little one that she was safe in her arms. Auntie dashed into her office and grabbed the sack of clothes she had left near her desk. 'I bought these the other day, you'll shrink into them.' She looked at Julia's birth-stained clothes and pulled out a clean skirt. 'But you should wear this one now.'

'I can't leave,' I said to Geb.

'But — '

'Trust me,' I said. 'I'll be fine here. Take her out the back door into the alley.'

Geb let go of me completely and went to leave with Julia. My aunt paced the corridor, two dark lines carved between her eyebrows, fingers pressed against her lips. The back door swung open and my aunt's hand reached out for the baby's head as Julia and Geb slipped through. 'Be safe,' she said.

I put my back against the wall and slid to the floor. 'What's the Kunstbunker?' My eyes fluttered to a close as I spoke but then sprung back open.

Auntie leaned against the opposite wall, put her hand to her forehead and breathed heavily like she had a fever. Then she flopped to the floor like a half-cooked piece of bacon, one hand holding her bangs back, the other searching the ground, trying to catch her wilting body. The youthful glow she had always maintained faded from her face and gave way to the middle-aged woman she always had been. For once, she actually looked her age.

'They turned the beer cellar next door into an art bunker. That's why I have been closing the shop and opening late. They've been using the passageway. Mayor Liebel, the head of our local Nazi Party, and Herr Coburg came to me last October, asked me to help with the art effort . . . the Kunstbunker. The Führer would never have approved, hiding the city's art in a bunker implies failure, as if we expect to be bombed, so we've been doing it in secret. Paintings from Dürer, sculptures from Veit Stoss . . . all of them . . . all of them are down there.'

'That can't be,' I said. 'That cellar is a dank cave. Abandoned for a reason. The mould on the walls must be centimetres thick, the air, hazardous, the ground, wet!' As I talked I realized what I had been saying. The cellar had a road-facing, larger-than-life medieval red door, with obtrusive claw-like brass hinges you could see from both ends of the street. The location was so obvious and conspicuous, next door to an antiques shop notorious for its art selections and deliveries, it was perfect. Hidden in plain sight.

'It's been redesigned . . . fitted with the latest

technology, venting systems are in place.'

My aunt talked as if she had seen these systems herself. I was just relieved and surprised my Jews were never caught. I shuddered to think how many times I had Jews hidden in the basement with Nazis on the other side of the trapdoor working away in the Kunstbunker. I should have been more careful.

Minutes passed sitting in silence. Then my aunt cried into the crook of her arm, hiding her eyes which were gushing with tears, and the painful realization of what I had to do hit me square in the chest. A deaf man could've heard Julia's screams. As to how many Nazis were in the Kunstbunker at the time, listening, deciphering, and wondering . . . only a fool would stay to find out. Tears welled in my eyes.

'You can go to Munich — '

'And do what, Auntie?' I cried. 'I've only ever been a shop girl.'

Auntie wiped her eyes with the back of her hand. 'The blue rose, Sascha,' she said, and I looked up. 'Remember when you sold that painting? Nobody wanted a blue rose, but you made the woman see the rose for what it wasn't, and she bought it. You'll have to reinvent yourself, create a story that sells — like you did with the blue rose.'

'How?'

She shook her head. 'I don't know — get a job, perhaps university . . . ' She rambled on about all the things I could do on my own. 'A good shop girl can make people believe anything.' She looked at me, her eyes red and swollen. 'One thing is for certain. You'll need some different clothes. That

Youth League uniform doesn't fit you. I'm not sure if it ever did.'

Auntie crawled toward me for a hug: the smell of 4711. Its scent was sweeter on her than it had been in the past, different. I held the odour with a deep breath, my face buried in the hollow of her neck. When I felt her tears fall on my face, I realized how selfish I had been: I had put my aunt's life at risk. The shop was hers; the Gestapo could easily arrest her for what I had done. And for the first time I understood what Claudia meant when she said hiding Jews in the basement was different to pinning wigs into her hair. The dangers — the consequences for what I had done suddenly felt very real.

'I'm sorry, Auntie,' I said, whimpering. 'I should have thought things through. If something happens to you because of what I've done — '

'Don't think about it, Sascha. If you do, you may not survive.'

'How long do you think I'll have to be gone? A week . . . a month?'

Auntie shook her head. 'I don't know — just wait for my word. Don't come back here without it.' I worried about so many things, and now I started to worry about Claudia. She'd come looking for me, and I wouldn't get a chance to say goodbye.

'Will you tell Claudia?'

Auntie sank down low to the floor when I said her name, and I thought if she didn't know Claudia had something to do with the basement she sure as hell knew now.

'Will you tell her where I've gone?' I tugged on

her arm, trying to get her to look at me in the eye. 'I beg you, Auntie. Will you tell her?'

She stared into the air before flicking her eyes downward as if it were a nod.

* * *

I left for Munich at dawn. Auntie took cash from her register and packed me a rucksack. 'Don't stop along the way. Promise me,' she said, and I nodded. 'You can make the seven o'clock train if you head straight there.' She took a book from a secret drawer in her desk, blew on the cover and then stuffed it in my rucksack with a tin of caramel candies for the trip.

'A book . . . candy?' I said. 'Auntie . . . '

'These are things a traveller would have. You don't want to look suspicious.' She handed me a street map of Munich with my cousin's address written in black ink across the front. We hugged again, only this time it was quick, and then she rushed me out the back door into the alley.

The morning sun oozed dully into the street as I left, walking on from Auntie's shop to the train station, hoping to God that the Reich wouldn't make the connection between Wilhelm and Claudia. And then there it was: Verräters Gasse Prison flanking the south tracks as if watching me walk up with my rucksack.

A blast of firing guns erupted from the prison's courtyard. *Pop! Pop!* Pop!

I paused, wiped a gush of tears from my swollen eyes, and then kept walking.

11
June

Munich

Within a week I found a cheap flat in student housing near my oldest cousin, Joseph. I was told I was lucky to have got a place in the Marienplatz, that it was considered the heart of the town. I didn't know anything about that; all I knew was that the Marienplatz was old — hundreds of years by the looks of its cobblestones — and had a turn-of-the-century glockenspiel with forty-three chiming bells.

I was deep in a dream when I heard a knock on my door. Not just any kind of knock, but the thunderous kind made from a closed fist.

Bang, Bang, Bang — I shot straight out of bed, my heart thumping. *Gestapo!* My eyes were still adjusting to the light when I remembered I was safe in Munich.

'It's Alex! Your *cousin.*'

As soon as I heard his voice I collapsed back onto my bed. 'Go away,' I groaned, pulling the sheets over my head.

'It's nearly noon!' he barked.

'So what if it is?'

'Meet me at the Ratskeller in half an hour. I'm demanding it.'

What gall my cousin had, I thought, yelling at

me as if I were a child. 'Maybe if you'd asked me nicely I would.'

The corridor went quiet, and I started to wonder if he had left. I sat up, thinking he really did leave, but then he piped up again.

'Ella.' He was still far too loud, but quiet for him. 'Please meet me at the Ratskeller. I want to talk to you. This is the fifth time I've asked.'

'Fine!' I realized that the only way to get rid of him was to meet him. I wasn't going to dress up. 'I'll meet you, but only since you said please.'

He stomped away, my door rattling from the thud of his feet as he walked back down the corridor.

Ugh!

* * *

The Ratskeller was a fifty-year-old brick beer hall shaped like a fat L. Students sat in the narrow part, their books sprawled out on the tables. Members of the Nazi Party Students' League sat in the back of the building nearest to the taps, but when they felt like it, they sat near the entrance which pushed the students out of their seats to stand along the brick wall.

Alex was waiting for me at a small table near the rose-coloured windows that bordered the square. He wore a Nazi Party uniform, the creases from its packing twine still pressed into the fabric, and a bright red swastika cuffband around his arm. The colour against his skin did nothing for his light complexion. If anything, it made his moles look a little darker.

'Nice outfit,' I said, lifting my eyebrows.

Alex smoothed the brown shirt over his chest, examining how the fabric fit his body, when the barmaid gave him a stein of weissbier. 'For the NSDAP member,' she said.

He shrugged his shoulders at me. 'I didn't even have to order!'

I paused for a moment, looking up at the barmaid, wondering if she'd give me a stein for free too, but all I got was an impatient, hard stare. I sighed, pulled a few reichsmarks from my front pocket and tossed them on the table. '*Dunkel.*'

'Be nice to that one,' Alex said, once she was gone. 'She turned her sister in. Give her the wrong look and she'll turn you in too.'

'Her sister?' The barmaid washed a glass stein behind the counter, working her arm into it. I didn't realize I'd been staring until Alex tapped my hand.

'Stop staring at her,' he said. 'Now listen. You're going to a dance tomorrow to meet some people from the NSDAP. Good men in the Reich.'

'I don't know how to dance.' Leaflets preaching Aryan relations between men and women had been stuffed under my door. The dances were an extension of the leaflets, meant to create marriages, and children. 'And I don't want a husband — '

'Bread!' Alex yelled into the air, 'and napkins!' He licked trails of froth from the side of his stein. 'I love that they topped it off,' he said, 'but it's overflowing.'

I used to hate it when Alex cut me off. Now, it felt like a nice break. I turned my gaze out the window. A little girl standing on the corner, probably no more than six years old or so, sold yellowed drinks out of paper cups. The sign on her cart read: For Deutschland. Her hair waved and bobbed in a breeze, and her smile buttoned with dimpled cheeks.

'What were you saying?' He took a drink, but I was still looking at the little girl. 'Ella . . . ' He hit the table and I jumped. 'What'd you say? You don't want a husband?' He scoffed. 'Then why are you here?'

'Alex,' I said, pointing at the little girl with my eyes, 'remember that summer when you, Joseph and me took all of Auntie's lemon soda and mixed it with Uncle's weissbier in a big bucket and poured it into paper cones?' I smiled, and I hadn't smiled in days — I'd almost forgotten how it felt. 'Biermischgetränk, that's what we called it. Best shandy in the world.' I turned away from the window and his face had flattened like a pancake. 'We spent all day in the hot sun, and Auntie was our only customer — '

'That was years ago.' He took another drink of his beer. 'Ella, you won't fit in here if you talk about such childish things.'

'I miss Nuremberg,' I admitted, remembering my room, Auntie, and Claudia — my life as a Falcon. I wondered if Auntie had taken down the clippings I had stuck to my wall, and if she did, I hoped she saved them for me for when I came home. 'It's a dreamy memory now.'

'Well, if you miss it so much why don't you go back?' he said, patting my hand. 'Nah! I'm glad you're here, but I'm not sure why you avoid me. I know some great people. Up-and-comers. There's this one, Erwin — he's got connections, uncle's a big shot in the Reich, heads up the document department where they keep tabs on resisters, enemies of the state — '

'Resisters?' I took a swig from the stein the barmaid had brought.

'What I'm saying is, know the right kind of people and you could become very popular.' He looked at me strangely now. 'What *are* you doing here, if it's not to get matched?'

I scratched my head, thinking up something to say. 'Change of scenery.' Nobody but Alex would believe a girl like me would travel all the way to Munich for a change of scenery. 'Have you talked to Joseph?'

'*Nein*. And I don't suspect I will. I'm too busy to chase him down,' he said, flicking his hand in the air. 'The medical students are bohemians and they're spoiled lazy.'

I scoffed. 'Joseph might not wear a uniform like you, but he's studying hard and he's still your brother, the only one you have.'

'I know he's my brother!' he said. 'But right now, we're not friends.' He pinched the front pockets of his brown shirt and then pulled, making his chest puff out like a bird by the river. 'The medical students are against the NSDAP. They make stink bombs, and it's unpatriotic.'

I giggled, which Alex didn't like. I remembered the stink bombs the medical students lit in streets, and in the Marienplatz. I thought it was creative, but smelly. 'Alex. I live in student housing, I know all about it. The Party asked that they put down their books for the summer and work in the smelting pits or harvest grain.' I rolled my eyes. 'Sounds tempting if you ask me. I mean, no wonder they lit all those stink bombs.'

He held a flat palm centimetres from my face. 'You don't know what you are talking about.' He snatched a roll out of the basket, ripped into it with his teeth, and talked while he chewed. 'And I don't want to talk about Joseph anymore.'

A girl with wispy brown hair walked in wearing a Youth League uniform. She sat at a table overlooking the Marienplatz, took out a pad of paper from her bag, and a yellow scarf, which she tied loosely around her wrist.

I sat up, smiling, watching her from over my stein. *A Falcon in Munich?*

'You know that one?' Alex snickered, looking over his shoulder.

'I assume you don't. Not your type?'

He coughed into his fist. '*Nein.* Not my type at all.'

I laughed. 'I bet.' I took my eyes off the girl to look at Alex. 'I know your type, you and the rest of your cronies down at the Künstlerhaus.'

His eyes sprung backward.

'And what type is that?'

'Crimson lip stain, rouge-smeared faces, netted stockings and bauble earrings; the type that swarm around handsome young Party officials like decorated bees.'

His gaze hardened. 'Wait a minute, now.'

'Joseph told me about the girls you've been cavorting with at the nightclubs, down on Lenbachplatz, a stone's throw from St. Peter's Church. Auntie would be disgusted.'

His spine straightened and he peered down at me. 'We're here to talk about you. Your future as a woman, your duty to our race.' Foam bubbled at the corners of his mouth as he chewed the last bite of his bread.

'Oh, right. I forgot.'

'You owe it to our country, Ella. At least think about coming tomorrow night, for Christ's sake! We're at war!' He slid his stein across the table, and it smacked against the window, cracking the rose-coloured glass.

'Relax, Alex.'

'I'm trying to help you out,' he said. 'The future of Germany is embedded in the Nazi Party. You could go places. Get to know the right people and we all could.' His eyes rolled over my face, my chest and down my arms. For a moment he looked just like Auntie used to after she'd acquired a piece of art that needed some restoration, wondering what its value would be after she had cleaned it up a bit.

I buried my face into my stein, taking a long frothy drink from the top. He waited for me to catch a breath, say something, but I kept drinking.

He stood up in a huff. 'I'll pick you up tomorrow night at seven o'clock.'

He pinched a clump of my unwashed hair, tugging slightly. 'You'll have to get your hair done,' he said, tone bitter as a salt lick. 'Don't worry, I'll pay for it.' He threw some reichsmarks on the table and then stormed off.

I sank down in my seat after he'd left, focusing on the girl again, watching her as she adjusted her yellow scarf. She held a book close to her nose but looked over the pages and out into the street.

Perhaps, I thought, I could test the waters and talk to her.

I got up and walked over, slowly, watching her carefully, before sliding onto the bench opposite her. There was a moment where nothing happened, as if she didn't know I was there, then her eyes shifted slowly away from the street, and she snapped her book closed. An awkward silence followed before I sat up, and spoke French, the language she'd expect if she was a Falcon.

'Bonne après-midi.'

Her brow furrowed with my words.

I leaned forward over the table. 'I said — '

'I know what you said.' She put the book back up to her nose.

My stomach sank, suddenly thinking maybe the scarf was a trap, looking around the room, beyond the steins and into the eyes of patrons to see if anyone was looking at me.

'That seat is taken. You'll need to leave — ' her eyes flicked to mine over the pages ' — now.'

I bolted from the booth and out the front doors, but was thrown to the ground outside by an arm to my throat, and found myself looking up from the cobblestones.

12

A woman stood over me, murmuring something I couldn't understand. She put a hand to her chest and pointed with the other to the mammoth-sized Nazi flag hanging vertically over my building's entrance. She gawked at the swastika with entranced, almost glazy eyes.

'What?' I said from the ground.

Her head bobbled in my direction and she spoke through a smile that stretched the width of her face. 'Takes your breath away, doesn't it?' A strange laugh followed her words.

I scooted back, only a hand reached out to help me off the ground. 'Joseph!' I smiled. 'God, help me up!'

'I was looking for you earlier.' He laughed. 'But I didn't expect to find you on the ground.'

I dusted off my bottom. 'Well, you found me,' I said, looking back toward the Ratskeller — nobody had come out to chase me, if anything people were rushing in. I took a deep breath, and then looked back at Joseph.

'Can you come by later? I want you to meet my new roommate, a student named Max.'

My face dropped. 'I hope you're not trying to match me. I just met with Alex, and I don't want to hear anything more about my civic duty and a husband.' I shuddered to think what Joseph would sound like saying the things Alex had, especially since he was my favourite.

'You won't hear that from me,' he said, and I smiled. 'Max is new to Munich and I'm helping him get acquainted, inviting a few of my friends over. That's all.'

Joseph had always been sweet, which made me more willing to do what he asked than Alex. 'Do I have to get my hair done?' I smoothed back a lock of un-brushed hair. 'I mean, I know I should, but do I have to?'

'Come as you are.'

I looked at him for a long moment, thinking about his request, before finally agreeing. 'I'll stop by.'

'Excellent!' he said, walking into the Ratskeller. 'See you tonight.'

* * *

Laughter and the clink of steins seeped through the crack of Joseph's door and floated down the corridor of our floor. I ran a hand through my hair, and then decided it was as good as I could make it. I leaned against the wall and rapped three times. There was giggling coming from the other side — a girl's voice I didn't recognize — and then the door opened.

It was *that* girl from the Ratskeller.

I pushed myself away from the wall. 'What are *you* doing here?'

She stared at me, looking confused.

Joseph rushed up behind her, beer in hand, smile plastered on his face. 'Ella! I'm glad you could make it.' His tone led me to believe he didn't think I would. 'Come in, come in.' The girl flattened herself against the wall as Joseph held the door open.

I pointed my finger at her, but talked to Joseph. 'Who is this?'

My gaze drifted down the corridor and into the parlour. A man drinking from a grey stein leaned against the windowsill. The sleeves of his clean white shirt had been rolled up to his biceps, and the tattoo of a falcon fanned across his forearm. A flip of his head and our eyes met.

'Geb?'

He stood up. 'Sascha!'

All of a sudden it was as if someone had opened a window after closing all the doors. I flew down the corridor and flung my arms around his neck. Everything in my body tingled.

Joseph studied us as we hugged. 'Max, you know my cousin?'

We let go. 'Yes,' Max said, smiling. 'I know her, through a friend of a friend . . . from Nuremberg.'

I hadn't heard his real name before. *Max*. It suited him, perfectly. I stood back and took a good look at him. Trimmed hair styled with pomade, shaved close behind the ears, and freshly pressed trousers with a brown leather belt looped around his waist. He was even cuter than the day I met him at the Steichele.

'No soiled Youth League uniform?'

'Nope!' he said. 'I got out of the paper business. I'm a student now.'

'The grease . . . it was ink?'

He laughed. 'You thought it was grease?'

I shook my head. 'I wasn't sure and I wasn't going to ask.' The girl from the Ratskeller nudged him with her hip as if she wanted him to introduce her. It didn't occur to me until that moment they might have been together. I swallowed.

'Is this your girlfriend?'

She giggled, covering her mouth with one hand.

'This is my sister, Sophie. She moved here today from Nuremberg. Joseph picked her up for me since I was stuck in class.'

'Nice to see you, again,' she said.

Max's eyes narrowed. 'You know each other?'

I smiled. 'I was at the Ratskeller today. She had a yellow scarf tied around her wrist.' I paused. 'I thought she was someone else, and said hello.'

'Oh.' Max made an odd face. 'I asked her to wear it since Joe didn't know what she looked like.'

I couldn't wait to get him alone and ask about Claudia. Surely he had some kind of news he could share. He put his stein to his lips and talked from the corner of his mouth. 'Can you talk later?'

'Down the corridor, room nine,' I whispered.

A knock at the door brought in more of Joseph's friends — another medical student and his girlfriend. I scurried into the kitchen, pulled my hair into a tight bun and smoothed my bangs to one side. I asked Joseph for something to pin my hair with. He handed me a pencil; it did just fine. I twisted my skirt around and was tucking in my shirt when I realized Joseph was staring at me.

'What's going on?' Joseph said. 'I haven't seen you move this much since Nuremberg.' He took a few plates out of the cabinet and set them on the counter. 'Is it Max?'

I smiled, shoulders shrugging into my ears. 'Maybe.'

'Now I wish Mum would have sent him here days earlier.'

'What?' I couldn't believe what he said. 'Auntie sent him here?'

'She knew I needed a roommate and arranged the whole thing.' His brow furrowed. 'Is Max an old boyfriend?'

My eyes must have bulged from my head because Joseph started laughing. 'No,' I said.

'Sure,' he said as if he didn't believe me.

I stared off at the ceiling thinking about Auntie helping Max. Maybe she'd come through on her promise about Claudia too. *Maybe Claudia's on a train headed here right now.*

'Ella?'

'Yes?' I smiled, suddenly very present with two feet firmly on the ground.

'Never mind,' he said. 'Just cut the bread.'

I reached for a loaf of sourdough and tipped its paper sack upside down; the bread slid out and onto a plate. 'Ta-da!' I stood in one place but bounced as if I was walking.

He grabbed a hunk of white cheese from the ice-box and looked at me curiously. 'Are you drunk?'

'What?' I chuckled, then caught a glimpse of my reflection in the window and winced at the sight of my dry, drab face. My thick eyelashes were still there, but my eyes had dulled and looked as grey as my skin. I slid my hand down my throat, arched my neck and wished I hadn't let myself go.

Joseph watched me for a second, then loaded the refreshments onto a tray and rejoined his guests. I followed.

* * *

Later that evening, I found myself frantically straightening up my flat before Max arrived, flipping back bed covers, and shoving empty beer bottles under my bed. I'd never had a boy in my room before, other than my cousins.

I heard a knock.

I raced to the door, sliding across the wood floor to let Max in. 'Does Joseph know you're here?' I waved him in.

'*Nein*,' he said. 'I took Sophie home.' A waft of chocolate and tobacco trailed behind him when he walked past me. 'He thinks I'm there.'

An empty bottle rolled out from under my bed when he sat down. I cringed, thinking he felt it hit his heel, but he didn't mention it.

'I can't believe you're here.' A tuft of hair fell near his eyes, which he smoothed back, smiling with his boyish grin. 'That you're Joe's cousin, Ella.'

'Me?' I sat down next to him, our knees touching. 'I can't believe *you're* here!' My cheeks ached from smiling. 'Tell me about Claudia — ' I shook my head, remembering that he didn't know her by that name ' — I mean Marta . . . the Falcons.'

His brow furrowed. 'You don't know?'

My smile vanished, and my stomach sank like a hot stone. 'Know what?'

'She's been arrested. There are no more Falcons.'

I yelped — hand to my mouth. 'It was Hans,' I said, 'he betrayed us all and left us scattered in the wind. He turned Wilhelm in.' When I closed my eyes, I could still hear the shots echoing from The Pit the morning I left Nuremberg. 'Did they take her to Verräters Gasse?'

'No,' he said, and I was surprised. 'It's as if she's been wiped from existence. They've been very secretive about her location, about her.'

'How did you get here? Joseph said my aunt sent you.'

'Your aunt covered for me when the Gestapo showed up, questioning the noises from the basement that night. Her friends in the Reich vouched for her integrity, and they believed what she said. Afterward, she thought it was best I leave the city, and with Falcons disappearing left and right, I thought it was best too.'

'But what about Claudia?' I put my head in my hands. 'What is to become of her now? She was worried we'd never see each other again, hugging me very tightly the night she left with Sarah.'

He shook his head. 'We'll have to wait it out.'

I couldn't bear the thought of waiting. Claudia's father had probably abandoned her and her mother was too drunk to search on her own. I was all she had. 'No,' I said, shaking my head. 'She's like a sister to me, Max.'

'Do you have a choice? It's not safe to go back to Nuremberg.'

I walked to the window and peeked onto the square, tapping my fingers on the sill, thinking about Claudia sitting all alone someplace dark, hoping someone would rescue her. A young couple danced without music not that far away, and when they spun around I saw that it was Alex. I ducked, thinking he'd seen me, and that was the last thing I wanted, but then I threw open the curtains.

I turned to Max, smiling.

'I have an idea.'

13

I pulled my yellow scarf from a wooden box I bought the day I arrived in Munich. It smelled like ash and clove and had started to look more ragged than Auntie ever would have liked. I thought about the night Claudia asked me to wear it, and the request she asked of me. She'd never ask me to do what I thought of next, but she wouldn't stop me either.

'Can you teach me to dance?'

He looked at me strangely, standing up. 'Why?'

'I'm going to get in with the Reich,' I said, and Max helped me loop the scarf around my wrist.

'Then what are you going to do?' We each grabbed an end and slowly tied a knot.

'I'm going to find Claudia.'

'With a dance?' he said.

'Alex invited me to the NSDAP dance tomorrow. It's my best shot. My only shot.' I spun around in place as if dancing, but I hadn't the foggiest idea how to. Max motioned for me to come toward him.

'Let me show you.' He smiled, taking my hand in his, and then slipped his arm around my waist, pulling me in close. 'Now move this leg back,' he said, touching his right knee to my left, 'and move like you're drawing a box with your feet in steps.' He smoothed his hair back with one swipe, and then wrapped his arm back around my waist, his hand a little tighter, fingers gripping. 'Like this.'

We danced to no music, then he twirled me unexpectedly, and I yelped with excitement and let out a little laugh. Next thing I knew we were in each other's arms, ever so close and still. I felt his heart beating in his chest.

He pecked me on the lips and I gasped, delightedly surprised.

'Ella, I didn't mean to — ' He pulled away sharply, looking quite nervous, but I pulled him back, and we looked at each other, not knowing what to say or do, standing in a dance position and not moving.

'Should I put some music on?' I said.

I turned the radio on low to a crackling instrumental melody, and we danced the rest of the night together in my flat, our bodies touching in a very anti-Nazi way.

* * *

The next night was the NSDAP party and, for once, Alex was right. There wasn't a song that went by without a young man taking my hand and leading me out to the dance floor. By the end of the night, I was dizzy and my ankles had blisters from dancing so stiffly, over and over again, stepping the same pattern; no twirls, no dips, and absolutely no swings. When I took my dress off that night, a dark red line appeared on my back where my zipper had chafed my skin.

The next morning, Alex said he had an opportunity for both of us and to meet him at the Ratskeller. I hurried down, on a Sunday. He looked unusually tidy sitting in our regular booth next to the window. He even stood up to greet me. 'Ella,' he said, smiling. 'This is Erwin Hoffmann.'

I tried to hide my disappointment. He was chubby, this Erwin, with speckly arms and wet lips. 'Hello,' I said, and he leaned over the table to shake my hand, which was fleshy-warm.

'I saw you at the dance,' he said. 'I tried to be your partner, but you were always taken.'

He had an awful whine to his voice, and I took a breath, looking up at Alex. 'You boys just out for a drink?' I played dumb.

The barmaid came by with their free beers before asking me what I wanted.

'Alex said you needed a job,' Erwin said.

I sat up tall. 'Oh?'

Alex twiddled his fingers, looking at Erwin look at me. Alex had already benefitted from introducing me to his NSDAP friends. With every dance I gave away, he gained a new friend. And new friends in the NSDAP were a big deal.

'Everyone's talking about the new girl at the dance,' Erwin said, licking beer froth from his upper lip.

'In a good way, I hope,' I said. 'A respectable way.'

'Oh yes,' Alex said, looking at Erwin. 'Of course, of course.'

'A good German,' Erwin said.

'Yes.'

We drank our beers without talking for a minute or so. 'I have a job offer for you,' Erwin finally said. 'A prestigious job.'

'A job? Where is it?'

'It's for my uncle, Friedrich Hoffmann, the

NSDAP Document Director in the Verwaltungsbau building.'

My stomach fluttered with butterflies — Hoffmann was part of the Reich's administration. I tried to hide my smile. 'I know where the V-building is!' I said, but then I didn't want to sound too excited or available. 'But I'm not sure . . . That's a long walk from my building.' I took a drink.

Erwin looked at Alex, a little huff coming from his nose, and Alex piped up, stumbling over some of his words. 'You need a . . . a job!' he said. 'Don't be obtuse. If you're not here for marrying, then you should do your part for the Reich in another way.' He turned to Erwin, but he was looking at me.

'What do I have to do to be considered?' I said.

'You're doing it right now.' Erwin and Alex exchanged laughs.

'Oh.' I took another drink. 'This is an interview?'

'My uncle trusts me,' Erwin said. 'He's too busy to find a secretary of his own. Of course, a good job like this . . . ' My eyes flicked to Alex. 'Well, it would require a few dances at the next party,' Erwin said. 'Long sets, too. Not the tail end of a song.'

I took a drink of my beer, fully ready to tell him I'd accept, but then got distracted by a man walking unassumingly across the square with the Gestapo running up behind him. I rose up in my seat, looking over Erwin's head, eyes widening, as they jumped him from behind and threw him into a car. The woman he was with had chased after them with her arms waving crazily in the air. People on the street walked around her, pretending she didn't exist — just another hysterical woman — as she watched the Gestapo's car exhaust burn off in the street.

'Ella?' Erwin said, before looking over his shoulders. 'What are you looking at?'

Alex waved his hand in my face, but then Erwin stood up sharply from the booth.

'I don't have time for this, Alex. I'm important,' he said, and I was stunned to see how little it took to upset him. 'I'm leaving.'

Alex looked like he was going to vomit. 'Now look what you've done,' he moaned, putting his head in his hands. I chased Erwin into the square the best I could with fresh blisters on my toes. When I grabbed his shoulder, the skin under his shirt was warm and sweaty.

'Erwin,' I said. 'Please, don't misunderstand.'

His shoulders puffed with his chest, and his wetted lips protruded from his face in a pout. 'I was doing something nice for Alex.' He flicked his chin at me. 'And for you. You should be chasing me around, not the other way around. I'm important.'

'I am chasing you,' I said, out of breath from the quick sprint.

Erwin smiled priggishly, and I thought up a lie to tell him, one that he'd believe. 'I only hesitated because I wasn't sure if I'd be good enough. I don't want to embarrass Alex . . . or you.' I looked to the ground, pretending to be shy and unworthy all of a sudden.

His shoulders stopped puffing, and he dropped his folded arms. The Nazi flag hanging from my building waved and flicked behind him. Erwin was right. He was important — important to me. I took a deep breath. 'All right . . . Erwin?'

He held out his hand and I shook it. 'Meet me tomorrow morning in the foyer of the V-building,' he said.

I nodded simply, which he followed up with a reminder about the next NSDAP dance.

'Yes, of course,' I said. 'Looking forward to it.'

* * *

I met Erwin as instructed the next morning. After a quick guard check, he led me into his uncle's office, up two flights of stairs, and through a secretarial space with its own frosted glass door. 'This is the one I told you about, Uncle.'

Hoffmann pushed his chair away from his desk, started to get up, but then sat back down, hand to his head. 'Can you start today?' he said, before flicking his chin at the door. 'Shut the door.'

I looked at Erwin, and Erwin looked at me. I shut the door that separated our offices, and Hoffmann reached under his desk for a bottle of whisky and poured himself a glass. 'Well . . . '

'Yes,' I said. 'I can start now, if you like.'

He slugged back the whisky, and then thanked Erwin for finding me. 'I've interviewed many secretaries, but nobody came with such a glowing recommendation.' He winked at Erwin. 'Why don't you tell Louise Milch I've selected my assistant,' he said to Erwin. 'She's on the third floor.'

Erwin whined, crossing his freckled arms.

'I can do it,' I said.

'I need you here,' Hoffmann said. 'Erwin can do it.'

Erwin left, but not without getting a peck on his plump cheek. 'Thanks again,' I said, 'for the job.'

'Remember,' he said, crinkling his nose, 'you owe me a dance for this.'

I smiled, but inside I was cringing thinking about his sweaty hand in mine, dancing the night away at another stiff NSDAP dance. 'I know.'

With Erwin gone and just me and Hoffmann in his office alone, I wasn't sure what to say or do until he told me. After he poured himself another glass of whisky, he swung around in his chair and pointed to a set of boxes with file folders that needed to be sorted.

'We are the auditor of file folders — all important information, I assure you, but you'll be doing a lot of filing and organizing. Are you sure you're up for this?' He looked me up and down. 'A young woman such as yourself might find it boring.'

'I enjoy organizing,' I said. 'I promise you, I won't get bored.'

'Very well, arrange those alphabetically,' he said, but then his voice trailed off and I heard snoring. His head had slung back, but his drink was still in his hands. Then he snorted loudly and woke himself up. 'Bring me those,' he said about the folders in my hands.

'Not these,' he said, after taking a closer look. 'Louise files these herself.'

The folders were solid grey, different than the Wehrmacht green ones he told me to alphabetize. 'Wait,' he said, as I started putting them back into the box. 'You're my secretary now. You should be in charge of all the document department's files. I'll tell Louise.'

'All right,' I said, flipping them open. 'Are they special?'

He coughed, putting his hand out to stop me from opening them. 'No need to open them. The files under our control contain information on our enemies. It is all right to know this, but it is not all right to read the reports inside. Just file them in the tunnel file cabinets. You'll see where they go. File cabinet fifty-six. It's grey like the folders.'

I put them on the counter with the rest of the folders I was sorting. 'All right.'

Hoffmann had started snoring again. This time I crept over to his chair, where he had tilted back, and looked at his closed eyes. He was passed out, I was sure of it; his breath had more proof in it than his glass.

I had finished organizing the files when there was a rattling knock on my secretarial door. 'Ella, are you in there?' a woman's voice said. By the time I had left Hoffmann's office and reached the door, she had knocked again. 'Ella. It's me, Louise from the third floor.'

I put my hand on the knob, looked back at Hoffmann in his office with his head flopped back, and then opened my door, standing in such a way so she couldn't see into the room. 'Hello, Louise.'

'I'm not intruding on your lunch, am I? It's just,' she said, tapping her watch, 'I don't have much time today, and I need to give you a building tour.' She stroked a single strand of pearls strung tightly around her neck and shifted her weight back and forth between her feet.

'No, of course not,' I said. 'I'd love to go —' I took one more look at Hoffmann who was still out cold ' — but I'm in a meeting. I should be done in a half hour. Can we reschedule?'

She stopped moving and stood very straight. She gave me a moment to reconsider my rejection, and that's when I realized, looking at her thinning lips, that she was used to getting what she wanted. Her cheeks reddened. 'Certainly.' Her high heels clicked all the way back down the corridor with her stockings scratching between her thighs like two strips of sandpaper.

I waited until she had turned to go up to the third floor before flying back into Hoffmann's office, but then skidded to a stop in the doorframe.

He was up and walking around.

He stopped in front of the sorting table, his body swaying side to side. One hand rubbed his eyes, the other rested on his hip, his thumb hooked into his waistband.

'Director Hoffmann, you are . . . '

He flipped through the stacks, saying words, and slurring badly. 'Well, Ellwa,' he slurred, 'looks like youse took care of everythings here.' His eyes wandered to mine. 'I'm glad my nephews Erwin . . . introduced us.'

He took a pair of bent spectacles from his front pocket and held them at a distance, looking through the lenses. It was then that I noticed how old Hoffmann really was, much older than an uncle should be. He rubbed the frame in between his fingers, trying to adjust the bend back into place, breathing with his mouth open. After a few moments, he grumbled and then slid them back into his pocket. 'Take alls this to the tunnel.'

'Where's the tunnel?'

He took a gulping drink of water and then suddenly sounded much better. 'Louise will show you, get you a key.' He scribbled a note to Louise saying I was now in charge of cabinet number fifty-six. 'In case she gives you grief,' he said, handing me the note, 'and she will.' He slung his coat over his arm and headed for the door. 'Have a good night, Ella.'

Night? It was still lunchtime.

I raced to the door ahead of him and snagged his hat off the rack. 'You too, sir,' I said as he took the hat from my hand. I watched him make his way down the corridor. He gripped the railing to hold his gait and walked steadily toward the stairs.

* * *

I sat in a low-legged chair across from Louise's desk with my knees pushed into my chest, waiting for her to finish typing a letter. Her red-painted nails pounded on the keys like a hundred Wehrmacht boots marching up the Königsplatz. When she finished, she ripped the page out of the typewriter, crumpled it into a ball, and then threw it into the rubbish. With a loud, long sigh, she took an emery board out of her desk and filed her pinky nail with a pinched eye. An occasional glance let me know she hadn't forgotten me. I wanted to ask her why she had a tin of coffee on her shelf when she had no percolator to brew it in, and what she was going to do with the stack of *Fraeun Warte* magazines she had stashed under her desk — but when I made a noise, she seemed to go slower. So, I swallowed her bitter pill and remained still, Hoffmann's documents on a dolly next to my feet.

Louise's supervisor was the Director of the Central Office, and even more important than Hoffmann, though much younger and very blond. He stopped just outside her door and talked to a small group of men more than twice his age about something I couldn't make out. Louise dropped the emery board when she heard his voice, and then fiddled with her typewriter as he walked in. He stood next to Louise's desk and stared at me with deep blue, ocean-set eyes. 'Is this Hoffmann's new girl?'

'Umm hum,' Louise said with a high-pitched squeal.

I guessed by his smooth skin he was closer to thirty then he was forty. I stood up and offered my hand. He hesitated, looking at my fingers as if they weren't clean, before giving me a cold, stiff shake. 'Erik Koch,' he said.

He told me his name, but he was all ice to me. I pulled my hand back, rubbing them together for warmth.

Louise read off a laundry list of items she had finished while he was out. As she talked, she sealed an envelope, dusted Hitler's portrait on her wall and stacked papers on her desk. Erik nodded as she spoke, murmuring 'yes' every few seconds as if to hurry her up. When her telephone rang, he walked into his office and shut the door. After a short conversation on the phone, Louise took a deep breath and gave me a white-toothed smile. 'Are you ready?'

Louise got me a building badge before taking me down into the basement to show me where my folders needed to be filed. We took the elevator first, and then passed through three solid steel doors before encountering our first guard.

He brushed his thumb over my badge, tilting it for inspection.

'She's new,' Louise said, curtly. 'Expect her from now on.'

She walked on, and I followed her down a stone corridor, walking as best I could in the clunky work heels I had on, lugging the dolly behind me. 'Don't worry about the guards,' she said as I struggled behind her. 'Treat them like shit and they'll get to know you soon enough.'

We descended down a ramp, going deeper underground. At the bottom, another guard stood at attention. He checked our badges and waved us through the last of the doors. On the other side, a simple table covered with green folders and hastily stacked papers had been shoved against the wall. One bald-headed watchman with a sour eye and no eyebrows sat cross-legged sipping his coffee. He pushed a clipboard at Louise.

'Sign in,' he barked.

He went to pour himself more coffee, but only drips came out.

Louise signed herself in while I took a good look at the tunnel. 'So this is it?' I said, gazing. Oil paintings hung from walls covered in patterned, gold-coloured fabric. Winged statues and glass cases went as far as the eye could see, and cream-coloured carpet covered half the floor.

Louise nodded. 'This tunnel connects to the

building next door, the Führer's offices when he's in Munich — the Führerbau.' She pointed her finger at the clipboard. 'Sign in each and every time you enter the tunnel.' She watched me write my name under hers. 'Ella Strauss,' she said. 'Your name sounds familiar.'

I faked a smile, and Louise cleared her throat.

'Over there are the files your department audits,' she said, waving the butt of the watchman's pen at a set of black metal file cabinets. A white notebook secured by tape and string hung off the last cabinet and dangled at eye level. 'List the files you pull for officers in the logbook. When you file them back, check off the document and date it. I'm sure Director Hoffmann already explained everything to you.' She tapped her watch with the pen. 'Now, I have to go. I have a very important meeting to attend.' She dug two fingers into her lapel pocket and fished out a cabinet key. 'Take care of this,' she said, shoving it into the palm of my hand. 'It's the master key. The only one I have.'

'Oh,' I said, remembering Hoffmann's note in my pocket. 'There's this.'

She read the note, and then looked up at me, eyes glowering. A long pause followed, and I swear I heard her foot tap. Then she took a deep breath. 'I suppose I should be glad. Less work for me now that you're here.' She got out her key ring and unhooked one with the number fifty-six etched into it. 'And this is the — '

'The only one you have. Got it.'

She stuck the watchman's pen in her pocket and left.

I refiled all the folders, except the grey ones

for cabinet number fifty-six. I opened one of the folders, peeking inside, getting a long look at the contents this time, only to close it quickly when I saw the Reich's confidential red stamp on every single page.

I took a slow look over my shoulder at the watchman, who was slurping the last of his coffee from his cup, before moving over to the drawer labelled fifty-six.

I used Louise's key to open the cabinet, and the drawer flew forward with a cranky clicking. Way in the back was a set of special file folders with black stripes on the top. One folder for every major city stamped Nacht und Nebel: Berlin, Munich and then — I looked over my shoulder again, and the watchman was now looking at the door — Nuremberg's file.

My stomach sank, thinking I'd found Claudia, but when I pulled it from the cabinet drawer, it was empty, no papers, no photos — nothing. My stomach sank again, only this time much deeper.

I kicked the file drawer, but then reached for it, catching it before it closed when I noticed something out of place — a prison photo fastened to the outside flap of another file.

My legs nearly collapsed right there next to the filing cabinets when I saw Claudia's face and her stringy hair hanging long and to one side. Her eyes looked vacant, and almost dead. The number six was written on the back along with: Wilhelm, a leader.

I glanced over my shoulder — the watchman had taken up reading a newspaper — and I stuffed the photo down my shirt. My heart beat out of my chest at what I had done as I tried adjusting it to lay flat against my skin. With nobody watching me, nobody to see what I'd done, I rashly snuck two pages from a random folder and stuffed those down my shirt too.

I took a few shallow breaths, kneeling beside the file cabinet, thinking how close the watchman was, and what could have happened if he'd glanced over at the wrong moment.

But he hadn't glanced over. He hadn't seen a thing.

I waited for my heart to stop beating so fast, and then rolled the dolly out. The watchman swivelled around in his chair; brown and yellow spots covered one side of his head, and scars from his youth cratered into his chin. The Reich probably didn't understand how important their tunnel watchman was, and judging by his appearance, I didn't think they ever would. I needed him to like me, trust me.

I played with the small swastika pendant centred on my neck, thinking up something personable to say. 'You must get terribly bored down here in the tunnel all alone,' I said, looking at his cluttered desk, his papers, and then his empty coffee pot, which he had unplugged and set off to the side.

He lowered his newspaper, crinkling it in his hands. Upside-down vees lifted the hairless indentations above his eyes. 'Sometimes.'

I hesitated a moment, looking back at that empty pot and the cord he'd wound up around it, before signing myself out of the tunnel. 'Louise has a tin of coffee in her office. I can bring you some next time.' I pointed with my eyes. 'Looks like you could use some more.'

'Louise has the tin?' He snarled. 'That coffee is reserved for the tunnel guardsmen since we work into the night.'

'Oh,' I said. 'I didn't realize.'

He gritted, mumbling something about Louise. 'She's not nice,' he said, 'thinks she owns this building. She took my pen — doesn't think I noticed, but I did.'

I patted his hand. 'I'll bring the coffee next time.'

He smiled briefly and then his face fell as if he didn't believe me. 'Well, if you forget I won't get mad.'

'I won't forget.' I smiled. 'See you tomorrow . . . '

'Fritz,' he said with a crooked smile. 'Ronald Fritz.'

'See you tomorrow, Ronald.'

Now I had to think of a way to get that tin of coffee from Louise.

* * *

Max had been waiting for me when I got home from work, smoking cigarettes in the corridor between our two flats. He seemed surprised I'd been gone all day.

'I started a new job.' I lugged my heavy work bag over to my bed. 'In the Königsplatz.'

'Oh?' he said, and I nodded.

'I found something about Claudia.'

I motioned with my head to the window, and we climbed outside to sit on the awning that had turned into our rudimentary balcony. The full moon glowed between two black clouds, the light shimmering off the Marienplatz's moist cobbled pavement. In the distance, the purr of car engines and the honk of a few horns. Even with the scent of oil and rain, it was good to get some air.

'Well, what is it?' He took a pack of cigarettes from his pocket, lighting mine with his lighter.

'Her photo in a file folder labeled Nacht und Nebel.' I pulled Claudia's photo from my brassiere.

He tucked his cigarette into his mouth. 'Night and Fog? Haven't heard of it,' he said, motioning for the photo. 'Let me see it.'

I had just finished telling him about the handwritten note connecting Wilhelm to Claudia when he took his cigarette and held it to the photo. An orange and yellow flame sizzled its way up the edge.

I reached for the burning photo but Max blocked me with his arm. 'What are you doing?' I yelled, as Claudia's face bubbled and stretched. He dropped what was left of the photo, and then smashed it with the heel of his boot.

'You can't keep it,' he said. 'You know that.'

I withered against the balcony and looked out onto the square, smoking the last of my cigarette, looking for something to focus on, when I noticed the old couple, Herr and Frau Haas, who owned the wood and hat shop down the way, standing near their window. Someone else, who at a distance looked like a young man dressed in a green recruit uniform, stood next to them with a rucksack slung over his shoulder. After a few seconds all three of them embraced.

I reached into my shirt and pulled the other papers I'd stolen from the files. 'Might as well burn these too.'

Max separated the pages, looking up at me with a surprised look on his face. 'Be careful in there, Ella.' He set them on fire, and I stomped out my cigarette. 'I got a job today too — a guard in the Königsplatz. First thing they told us was to watch out for spies.'

'I will.'

'Ella,' he said, and I looked up. 'I didn't mean to upset you, burning her photo.'

'I know . . . ' Max put his hand on my shoulder, and suddenly I was very aware it was just him and me on the balcony, together. 'I know you'd never . . . that you didn't mean . . . ' I took a deep breath. 'What I mean is . . . it's all right.'

There was a long moment where neither of us said anything, but his smile let me know he understood why I yelled at him the way I did.

'Claudia's lucky to have you,' he said. 'Did you meet in the Falcons?'

'No, a long time ago in the League. She was the only one who wasn't sobbing over Hitler's words in *Mein Kampf*.'

'I had to read it in the Hitler Youth too. But I changed out the book jacket and read other things to fill the time.'

My eyes grew wide. 'We did that!'

Then he asked me the question I didn't want to answer. 'How was the dance?' I thought he'd forgotten about the dance. But how could he? He taught me how to dance.

'Oh, umm . . . ' I said, looking away. 'I did fine.

Thanks for teaching me.'

'I heard talk about a new girl today, and I thought maybe it was you. From what I heard you never had to sit out a song.' I looked at him, worried he might get the wrong idea and think I liked dancing with those other men. 'So, your plan worked.'

'You're the only one I want to dance with,' I said, and I couldn't believe I said it out loud. My chest tingled admitting this to him, and my cheeks ached from an unshakable smile.

Max looked embarrassed too, looking away bashfully, but then he offered me a cigarette from his own mouth before lighting his own, and when he offered it to me, our fingers lingered together. We sat down on some milk crates that were already there and smoked.

'You know I came back for you that night,' he said. 'In Nuremberg.'

'You did?'

'I thought I'd never see you again,' he said.

I'm not sure who turned first, or if there was any thought on my part, but somewhere in between a long exhale and talking about Nuremberg, we kissed, but this time our lips stayed pressed against each other's for many seconds and, truth be known, I counted.

14

July

Erwin checked the freshness of his breath, huffing and puffing into the palm of his hand on the other side of my door. He put his big eye up to the peephole, blinked a few times and then went back to smelling his breath. 'Ella,' he said. 'I know you're home.'

I opened the door with a rush, as if I had dashed across the room and not been watching him. 'Erwin!'

'Hello, Ella.' His cheeks looked warm and red as if he'd been running. 'It's Friday. I came by your office but you'd already left. I hurried after you, called your name.' Patches of sweat soaked his NSDAP uniform, around his collar and under his armpits.

'Erwin, I — '

'You've been promising me a night out for weeks,' he said, crossing his pudgy arms. 'You've cancelled on me enough.'

'Has it been weeks?' I said. 'It's been a long day. Could we — '

'After all I've done for you — I could have recommended any number of girls for that job.' His voice squealed and a blue vein pulsated in his neck.

I grabbed my foot. 'But my feet are throbbing.'

'You promised,' he said, and I sighed.

Joseph had just walked up the stairs and stood by his door. 'Coming tonight?' he said, fiddling with his keys.

My eyes shifted to Joseph and then back to Erwin, smiling, remembering I had plans after all. Joseph had been recruited to go to Berlin to help the medical department there. He didn't want to go, but if he refused the assignment, he risked being sent to the warfront. 'Besides, I have plans,' I said, flicking my chin down the corridor. 'My cousin is leaving for Berlin tomorrow. It's his last night here.'

'Eight o'clock,' Joseph said just before he shut his door, and I winced.

'You'll be back by then,' Erwin said.

I paused, holding back the words I really wanted to say, before turning to get my handbag, grumbling under my breath, which Erwin didn't hear because he was too busy adjusting his belt.

He sniffed his armpit.

'Don't you want to change your clothes?'

'Everyone's wearing their uniform,' he said.

'Fine,' I said, 'but remember, I can't be out late.'

We walked to the Hofbräuhaus, the oldest and most crowded Nazi beer hall in Munich. It wasn't close to my flat, but it wasn't far either. Despite my being tired from working all day, Erwin struggled to keep up; sometimes he was two, even three steps behind.

Erwin led me to a table full of people only he knew, and we squeezed into the packed, crescent-shaped booth. His thick arm swung heavy around the back of my neck, tugging on my hair as he looked out into the crowd, smiling.

Barmaids walked around with trays of steins filled with dark frothy beer, passing them out to mostly drunk NSDAP members, all of them wearing their signature brown uniforms with bright red swastika cuffbands, just like Erwin said. Cigar smoke billowed into the air from all corners of the hall, mixing with the heavy scent of perfumed girls.

Erwin pushed his lips into my ear. 'Isn't this great?'

I nodded.

'What?' he said. 'I can't hear you.'

I smiled. 'I said it's great!' Erwin dug his fat fingers into the fleshy part of my upper arm and pulled me into the sweaty circle of his armpit. A four-piece band playing traditional polka music in the middle of the room got louder and added to the sing-song in my ear.

'I can't stay much longer,' I said, tapping my watch.

Erwin whipped his head around, his baby-blue eyes turning grey as steel. Another person squeezed into the booth, and I got pushed from my seat. I stood before my bottom hit the ground and tried not to act pleased about it. Now I can leave.

'Sit back down,' he said, trying to make a space for me.

I smoothed my skirt. 'There are five girls and four boys at this table as it is. I need to go anyway.'

Before Erwin could respond I felt a flick between my shoulder blades, as if someone had swatted a bug. It was Alex. He had a stein in one hand and now me in the other. 'Where does my dear cousin think she's going?' He gave Erwin a wink. 'It's too early to leave.'

He breathed into my face — the rancid smell of vomit and beer. I put my hand to my nose.

'You're drunk,' I said.

He grinned and took a wobbled step backward. 'I'm not drunk. I'm celebrating! It's Friday.'

I smirked sourly. 'Have you seen your brother lately? They're sending him to Berlin tomorrow. You're coming to say goodbye tonight, aren't you?'

He hiccupped. 'I have a brother?'

Erwin and Alex shared a laugh, Alex's voice a little louder than it should've been.

'I'm leaving,' I said.

'Wait — I want you to meet someone.' Alex pointed to some people on the other side of the building. 'I'll be back,' he said to Erwin, and then he wrenched my hand and walked me away from the booth and into a crowd of people where we disappeared.

He said hello to someone who looked a lot like Eric Koch, but was dressed in tan street clothes and talking to an attractive, almost innocent-looking girl I didn't recognize. A lazy smile bowed on his lips, and he blushed from her stare. He tenderly wiped an eyelash from her cheek. I thought it was sweet, the way he looked at her, until Alex called him 'Koch.'

The man of ice? My lingering glance changed into a stare.

Alex yanked on my shoulder. '*Nein!* Not him. Over there,' he said, pushing me toward a dark-haired man. He wore a NSDAP uniform that fit snug around his chest and shoulders, and an even tighter fitting swastika cuffband around his arm. Common brown eyes and flat cheekbones matched his limp hair; when he brushed it out of his face, he exposed a small scar in the shape of a hook just above his right ear. At my angle, I was the only one who could see it. My mouth drew open and my eyes widened.

I recognized that scar from a tunnel file.

'Ella, this is Christophe. He's new.'

I shook the look from my face. 'Good evening, Christophe.' I sounded much more formal than I meant to.

The photo from his file showed him with blond hair, but I knew his tale well. I'd studied nearly every file in the tunnel since I got my job in documents, before changing some or sneaking out a few pages. He got the scar the night the Gestapo arrested him two years ago, when he went by the name Randolph Xavier. They held a knife to his ear because he heard too much, but he escaped. The Reich had a reason to want him. Christophe was a British spy.

'Do I know you?'

'I don't know,' I said. 'Do you? I work at the V-building, in documents.'

'Haven't been there,' he said. 'I spend most of my time at the Braunes Haus. Heard it's a beautiful building, however.' We stood there looking at each other, uncomfortably, when a man with a perfectly round potbelly walked up like he owned the place and put his arm around Christophe. He wore a dark gentleman's suit, which was too formal for a beer hall, and had a wing-tipped moustache with twisted points that moved when he laughed.

He reached into his front pocket with two fat fingers and pulled out a short cigar that had a ring of red paper wrapped around it. He spun the paper around his cigar as he smoked, over and over again. I'd seen that before. I'd seen him before.

Coburg's friend Dietrich. I gulped. *The Gestapo officer from Nuremberg.*

I turned, bee-lining for the toilets. I heard Alex yell 'Come back!' behind me as I walked.

Anxious women, some half-drunk with crossed legs, others just needing a break, flicked their cigarettes at me as I cut into the front of the line and pushed my way to the mirrored vanities.

I pulled my hair back and stared at my reflection, looking for the fearless jumpbox I had been for so many months, but all I saw was a young girl from Nuremberg. I started to panic, and then pulled myself together the best I could with a cold slap to the face.

The girl beside me had the contents of her makeup bag strewn across the counter, a purple ribbon with hairpins threaded into it coiled like a snake next to the tap.

'I'll pay you for some pins,' I said.

Her eyes jolted more than they did when I slapped my own face. 'For pins?'

I pulled my hand from my pocket and a few coins fell into the sink and settled in a ring of standing water. She picked them up with painted nails and tossed them into one hand.

'I would've just given them to you,' she said, 'but since you offered . . . '

I wetted my hands, slicked back my hair and

tightened it into a bun at the base of my neck. The pins locked it in place. *I have to warn Christophe.* In the corner of the lavatory I scribbled a frantic note on some toilet paper: *Don't trust the moustache.*

I crumpled the note in my hand, wondering if I could really go through with it — slip the note into Christophe's pocket right in front of the Gestapo. I was watching them now at a distance from the line for the toilets as they drank and talked. One of the women I cut in front of earlier pushed me from behind. 'Move on, girl,' she said, walking past with her friend. 'You've had your five minutes.'

My jaw locked. *I can do this.* Hand squeezing, I walked straight toward Christophe.

Alex came at me with hugging, open arms. 'Where did you go?' he said, lunging toward me. I ducked, and with a heavy hand I slipped the note into Christophe's pocket. Alex stumbled forward, and with no one to hold onto he fell to the ground. People scooted back, and then walked over him as if he wasn't there. Dietrich turned around from the noise, scanning the crowd, but I slipped out the side door.

Outside, my whole body fell against the side of a dark building. Instead of feeling relief, I felt a little sick, thinking how I could have been caught if the wrong person read the note or saw me slip it into Christophe's pocket.

My hands shook.

It's done now, I thought, rubbing my hands steady. It's done.

* * *

I pushed my way through Joseph's crowded apartment. Max sat with Sophie on a small bench chatting about something near the window. I felt instantly comforted and slid into the space next to him, exhaling.

'It's been a long night.'

'A long night? It's barely past eight,' Sophie said, giggling.

'The whole day has been long.' I looked around the room for Joseph, hiding my hands which still felt jittery. 'Maybe I just need a beer.'

'I'll get you one,' Max said, standing up.

'No, Max.' He'd had a long day too, going to class and then filling his guard post. I started to get up. 'You've worked just as hard — '

'Ella, sit down,' he said. 'Let me get you a drink.'

He touched my arm and I sat slowly back down. Even Auntie would tell me that if a man offered to get me a drink, to let him. 'All right.'

The door swung open and more people joined the party. Joseph spotted me from across the room and took Max's seat, putting his arm over my shoulders and giving me a squeeze. He glanced at my empty hand. 'Get this girl a stein!' He laughed, and several people cheered.

'You're happier than I thought you'd be.'

He leaned in but talked loud enough for everyone to hear. 'There's nothing I can do about it. Thc Reich was going to get me somehow.' He pulled back. 'Besides, I'll get to see Papa.' I wrapped my arms around him like I did the day he left Nuremberg, and felt very sad at the thought of him moving away again.

'I'll be back, Ella. Don't worry. They can't get rid of all the medical students. Who would make the stink bombs?' When I didn't laugh, he pulled away and looked deeply into my eyes, deeply, the way Auntie used to.

'Joseph,' I said, my voice weakening, 'I feel like I just got here and now you're moving away . . . ' I was suddenly very emotional, my lips near quivering, reminded of when I left Auntie.

He kissed my forehead. 'Don't worry. I know Alex is worthless. But you still have Max.' Joseph became serious. 'He's the one, isn't he?'

I was a little shocked Joseph had said such a thing, but then realized it was getting harder and harder to hide. 'Is it that obvious?' I said.

'Yeah,' he said. 'He's a good one. I approve.'

'Oh, you do?' I said, chuckling away my little sobs. 'Thanks.' Max had come back with my stein, but with Joseph in his seat he stood in the crowd talking with some others. He glanced at me more than once while he talked, looking very handsome with his strong arms, yet sweet with his smile and soft eyes.

'You should find a girlfriend too,' Joseph said. 'Someone your own age, one that doesn't wear so many wool work suits. Who was that one you used to get in so much trouble with back home?' He snapped his fingers as he tried to recall. 'Claudia!'

Hearing her name out loud and with so many people around startled me.

'Maybe I should introduce you to Alice,' he said. 'She just moved into the building.' Joseph pointed to a girl standing in the middle of the room. I could tell she was new by the way she looked — a pinch of rose blushed over taut cheeks — and laughed, nervously, clutching her beer with both hands, bouncing around on her tiptoes. 'She could be your Claudia. Without the troublemaking, of course.'

I watched her join other people's conversations only to give up when she couldn't get a word in. Then she laughed at someone else's joke and I realized she was closer to my age than I'd thought by the sound of her.

Joseph got up, about to call Alice over, when I put my hand on his arm, stopping him. 'No,' I said. 'Not now.'

He looked confused.

'What I mean is, not tonight,' I added. 'I'll meet her later.'

He smiled and then gave me a parting hug before rejoining his guests. I looked back to Alice only she was gone. I was glad she had left, I told myself as I stared at the space where she once was.

Max sat back down, handing me the stein he had poured. 'I was wondering when I'd get my seat back.' He smiled and I caught his eye.

'Thank you,' I said, 'for the beer. And for sitting with me.'

He saw the tears still budding in my eyes from when Joseph was talking to me. 'Is everything all right?' He looked at Joseph across the room and then to me. 'I know you'll miss Joseph, but . . . '

I swallowed. Changing information in the tunnel files was a secret job, shoving a note into Christophe's pocket right in front of Dietrich was out in the open, and it felt different. If Max looked at my hands, he'd see there was still a fluttering tremble to them.

'Ella?'

I looked up. 'Everything's fine.'

* * *

It was close to midnight before I left Joseph's, and I was tired — more tired than I ever thought I could be. I slipped into my flat, yawning, fiddling with the light switch, flicking it on and off, but it wouldn't turn on. That's when I noticed the bulb was missing, and that the shades had been drawn, which were open when I left.

I froze, staring into the darkness because I wasn't sure where else to look, and then my bed-post squeaked as if someone was in the room with me.

'How did you know?' a deep voice bellowed from the shadows.

I slammed my back up against the door, the wood cracking from the thrust of my body as a dark figure rose from my bed and moved toward the sliver of light coming from the window. My hands started shaking again, thinking it was Dietrich, or someone else — someone who saw me.

He struck his metal lighter and sparks sizzled into a flame, moving closer to the cigarette hanging off dark lips. The glow illuminated his face; brown eyes, flat cheeks, and a patch of dark hair that hung over his right ear.

I peeled myself from the door. 'Christophe?'

He took a long-drawn out puff from his cigarette. 'How did you know I was a spy?'

I felt relief it was him and took a breath, taking a moment to dust the fear off my face and from my shaking hands, which had suddenly turned steady.

'I know lots of things.'

I threw open the curtains to get some light. The drawer to my nightstand hung from a broken track and the tray from my desk lay on the ground. Papers from the files I had been memorizing lay all over my bed as if he had gone through them. My mouth had dropped, and then hung wide open when I saw my yellow scarf laced in his fingers.

My back straightened.

'I think we're working for the same side.' He closed the curtains and then rested his back against the window frame. 'You're a wolf that looks like a lamb.'

I scoffed.

'Am I wrong?' he said. 'How did you know about Dietrich?'

Just then air raid sirens revved. We threw open the curtains and heard bombs in the distance — a slight rumbling followed by muffled booms. Then the entire city went dark.

'RAF bombs are brilliantly fierce,' he said. 'As they should be.' He smiled, and then said something in English I didn't fully understand.

'We should hide,' I said.

'No,' he said, looking out the window. 'That sounds eighty kilometres away at least. They haven't reached the city, yet. We're safe here. For now.'

I moved away from the window and he

followed me, nearly stepping on my heels. He'd gone through my mail. I picked up what little I had, flipping through the tenant letters and leaflets. 'What were you hoping to find in my mail?'

'Post from home. But you had none.' He took a long drag from his cigarette. 'I know you're not from Munich since you know Dietrich.'

'You ransacked my flat to find out where I'm from?' I set the mail down. There *was* nothing from home. 'I don't believe that's the only reason.'

'I need to know what the Reich knows. You have access to information the British need. Not only what's in the tunnel files, but the administration meetings.' He pointed his cigarette at me. 'I'm sure you sit in on those and take the minutes.'

'Sometimes I do.' I paused, thinking about his request. Despite my position inside the Reich, I still felt like the young girl from Nuremberg who liked to cut pictures out of magazines. I had to remember, Christophe knew nothing about that girl, and he might be able to help me find Claudia.

'You want me to be your spy?'

'Do I have to say it out loud?'

'I'll get you what you want,' I said, 'but call me Sascha. It's my codename.'

A thin smile wiggled across his lips.

'But I'm also looking for information. A girl from Nuremberg has gone missing. I believe the Reich took her someplace secret. A resister from the Falcons. She went by the name Marta but her real name is Claudia.'

'I'll see what I can find out.'

'Good.'

I eyed my scarf still in his hands and thought up

something tough to say. 'And touching a woman's scarf is like touching her stocking.' I snatched my scarf from his fingers. 'You need permission.'

15

August

Weeks had turned into months working at the V-building for Hoffmann. When I wasn't working to the bone as his secretary, I was hiding in my flat, staying out of Erwin's crosshairs, and making up excuses why I wasn't able to go dancing with him.

Nobody told me Munich summers were so hot, and I all but stripped my wool suit off the moment I walked through the door each night, opened the window, and begged for the wind.

On this particular night, I had poured myself a glass of shandy and sat in the windowsill, gazing across the Marienplatz, watching Herr and Frau Haas working away in their little shop, carving wood and making hats. I wondered where they lived, where they went at night. Sometimes I'd see them sweeping the pavement outside their shop, and it reminded me of Herr Rudin and the little bakery back home.

I got very sad thinking about Auntie alone in our old half-timbered house in the Altstadt, making eggs for one and having nobody to clean up after. I missed her voice, and I missed Claudia coming to my window late at night.

A knock at my door startled me. 'Ella! Open up, it's Max!'

I ran to the door, not sure if he was in trouble

or not by the sound of his voice. He hurried into my flat, urgency creasing in his face.

'I know what Nacht und Nebel means.'

I didn't care that he had caught me half-dressed — he had my attention with his words, and I dared not move.

Max turned on the radio so nobody could hear us. The Nazi anthem, 'Die Fahne Hoch', had just begun and he raised the volume to a medium blare. We stood in the middle of the room, our bodies touching, and he talked into my ear.

'I overheard two kommandants on their way back from the Führerbau. Night and Fog is a secret system for political prisoners, reserved for the most destructive. No trails. No files. Like the prisoner doesn't exist.'

'Did they say anything else?'

'Hinzert. There's some at Hinzert.'

My eyes widened. 'I'm travelling there tomorrow — escorting a set of files to the V-building!'

When Hoffmann initially told me I needed to go to Hinzert I made a half-dozen excuses why I shouldn't have to. It meant a day of travel on one of the hottest days forecasted that year. Now, all I could think about was how lucky I was.

Max wrapped his arms around my waist and spun me around. Then there we were, staring into each other's eyes. A blast of blank noise replaced the stiff anthem. He caressed my cheek and a strange sensation fell over me — I had never been held or touched like that before. I went to say something, but what I didn't know. His hands slid slowly down my back.

Students pounded on the walls, yelling for me

to turn the radio off, as we stood very still, holding each other warmly. And we kissed — a kiss that started out long and slow with hands sliding over each other's bodies, but had turned into a fury of heated moments, with my hands moving down to his waist and finding his belt.

'I have to go,' he said, suddenly.

'What?' My heart thumped out of my chest. 'Why now?'

'I'm sorry. I can't stay because I have a late guard post,' he said, pulling away. 'Tomorrow?'

I nodded, knowing exactly what he meant. 'Tomorrow. After my trip.' He let go of me, his hands sliding down my arms until our fingertips were the last to touch.

He smiled just before he shut the door, and so did I, still tasting him on my lips. Tomorrow.

* * *

The hum of the Mercedes G-4 Wagen turned into a low groan and jerked when the driver down-shifted to turn up the long, dirt road that led to Hinzert Prison. He looked over his shoulder to the back seat and winced his apology.

Built for luxury, the car had a dark-brown leather interior, double-stitched at the seams, and cherry-wood grained floorboards that shined like a polished apple. It had six knobby tyres and enough space for eight passengers.

As we got closer to Hinzert a midday breeze blowing through the Hochwald plateau warmed with the scent of berry, dandelion and purple wildflowers. The Hunsrück mountains bordered the prison at a distance and curved into a dark green line. It was hard to believe I was on my way to a prison with such beauty all around. I closed my eyes, thinking of Max waiting for me back in Munich, and the kiss we shared last night.

'That's where our lumber comes from . . . to build the prison,' the driver said, and my eyes popped open. He pointed a gloved finger through the convertible top and then quickly pulled it back in, wrapping his hand back around the steering wheel. I reached for my yellow scarf and tied it over my head to protect my hair, which had been set and smoothed into perfectly formed neck-length barrel rolls. The driver glanced at me through his rear-view mirror. 'Should I put the top up?'

'*Nein*,' I said, looping the scarf under my chin. 'I'm fine.'

Hinzert's rectangular prison huts rose from the ground like ploughed dirt. At the far end workers laid the foundations for more huts; a shallow fence surrounded each one. Its two-storey high, red-brick command building overlooked it to the west like the manor house on some vast estate. Umbrellas attached to lounge chairs and pots overgrown with mauve and dark pink flowers flanked the sides of the building near the service doors like a mountain retreat.

We lurched to a stop. Gravel sprayed out from under the wheels and fogged the air with caramel-coloured dirt.

Just be yourself, I thought, *sell yourself as one of them and they'll talk*.

Alma Hirsch, the camp secretary, greeted

me at the gate. She had neatly combed strawberry-blonde hair and childlike eyes that she kept half-hidden from the sun under the cover of one hand. When the dust settled, her lightly glossed lips spread into a smile.

'*Willkommen* to Hinzert.' Her hand was soft and it left the scent of rose on my palm after she shook it. She wore a pink suit and two-toned heels; not the harsh black skirt-suit I was told prison secretaries wore. 'Sorry for the dust. We're improving the property with additional huts, and I am afraid the construction is a tad unsightly.'

Wooden planked walkways lined with blue enzian and cloud-shaped yellow flowers curved with a serpentine bend into the prison. 'All I see are flowers,' I said, removing the scarf from my head.

'Come,' she said, smiling. 'This way.'

I tied my scarf to the strap of my leather travel bag before following her past the guard shack and into the command building. Her supervisor, Kommandant Hermann Pister, had been waiting for us inside his office. His jacket was thrown over the back of his chair, and the sleeves on his black collared shirt had been rolled haphazardly to his elbows. Behind him, a large window, half the size of the wall, looked into an empty, light blue room. Ropes hung from the ceiling, knotted every few feet until they hit the floor, where small puddles of water pooled around maroon-stained drains.

'Fräulein Strauss,' he said with a nod. '*Willkommen.*' He shook my hand with a damp, almost wet palm. 'How did you like your ride? It's one of my favourites.'

'Excuse me?' I nonchalantly dried my hand off on my skirt.

'He's an automobile buff,' Alma said.

'Oh, quite nice,' I said, 'interesting tyres.'

He looked at me curiously as if he expected more of a reaction. 'Here are the files. They don't belong here simply because they aren't our prisoners anymore.' He paused. 'Do you get many file transfers to your Munich office?'

I nodded. There had been a few boxes of information transferred to our office from political prisons, but most had been coming from around the Königsplatz. Some departments didn't want the added responsibility of archiving their own files. Others thought it was document control's responsibility all along. Regardless, Hoffmann turned everything away that didn't pertain to enemies of the state, saying it wasn't our problem.

Pister pushed a heavy cardboard box to my feet while Alma placed a release form on his desk. 'You'll need to sign for these, of course.'

'Is there time for a tour of the facility?' I bent down to sign the form and talked as I wrote. 'My train doesn't leave for a few hours, and Director Hoffmann mentioned that if given the chance I should see what changes you've made since the fire a few years back. Said it was impressive.' When I looked up, Alma and Pister had duelling smiles. The prison nearly burnt to the ground once, and Pister had been in charge of its restoration.

'Of course,' he said. 'We're excited to show off our handiwork.'

The three of us walked the prison's paved inner perimeter. The huts housed short-term prisoners, serving less then fourteen days. During the day they laboured on the construction sites that dotted the compound. A wooden fence that lined the forest had been broken in places to bring in supplies; barbed wire was planned as a replacement but hadn't arrived. Pister said the main building had an additional holding facility on the bottom floor, but stopped short of saying what kind of prisoners it kept inside. The flowers, he added, were there to console his staff, who complained about the distance the prison was from Polert village. At the end of the property he had plans for a vegetable garden.

When the tour ended, Alma took me into the lunchroom until it was time to leave for my train. She made a scalding hot pot of herbed tea and served it in a carafe of sterling silver, pouring it into gold-rimmed white china. When I blew on it, the tea's flowery steam permeated from the cup and into my face. Cubes of sugar piled high on a dish too small for anything else melted into spots of white and fizzled when I plopped some into my cup. I stirred my tea slowly and tried to think of a way to bring up Night and Fog. They had to be the prisoners on the bottom floor. I wasn't leaving without knowing if I was right.

Alma brushed her hair behind her shoulders and a pair of diamond-studded earrings sparkled from between the strands. When I complimented her on them, she blushed and spun her hair around her finger until it curled. When I commented on her shoes, her face turned gooey.

'I'm the only woman who works at this prison.' She took a slurped sip of her tea and sighed. 'It's so nice to have this girl-time. Sometimes I feel old out here with all these men. I'm only twenty-two! You're my age, right?'

I nodded. *Eighteen.*

White powder flecked from her forehead and into her eyes. She wiped her brow line with the back of her hand, and it rubbed her makeup off completely, leaving a stripe of pale skin that ran from temple to temple.

'What's the prison like downstairs?' I said, taking a drink.

She hesitated. 'I'm not allowed to talk about it.'

I gently put my hand on top of hers and squeezed. She grinned, and a white-headed pimple surrounded by pink skin burst from the dimple near her mouth like a greasy mole.

'Oh. I understand. It's just . . . you see . . . my first love was the prison system.' I shrugged with a little smile. I had gotten so good at lying, given some time, I might have even believed my own stories. 'But my mother got ill and I had to stay close to home.'

'Poor thing,' Alma said.

There was a moment of silence as I let her absorb the thought. Then her eyes brightened. 'You know, I'm sure a little peek wouldn't hurt anybody. We'll just have to be quiet.' She took another sip of her tea, but this time she left a pink stain in the shape of her lips on its edge. The gloss was gone, and her lips withered with moult just like Frau Dankwart's used to. The thought crossed my mind they could be related.

'What a treat,' I said, 'and who knows, maybe someday I can work here with you . . . if I'm lucky.'

Alma gulped the mouthful of tea in her cheeks, and then nodded as if the thought had already percolated in that strawberry-blonde head of hers. ‘I can’t imagine not being able to work where you want to work.’ She leaned over the table and whispered. ‘We have people imprisoned here for safehousing Jews. Can you believe it? Right here from Polert village.’ A disgusted look took over her face as she stirred her tea. ‘Thank goodness they are in the east now.’ She looked up. ‘Those Jews.’

I tried to look disgusted too, then I thought about what the Reich did to the Kortens, and the Jews they shot at the train station, and my face contorted all right. ‘Awful. And right under good German noses.’

Alma set her spoon down after she’d finished her tea. ‘Shall we go?’ Her eyes lit up.

She led me to a small space in the main building no bigger than a large shower, in-between a lounge with overstuffed divans and fluffed pillows and a pantry filled with strudels, biscuits and cakes the guard’s wives had brought in. The space had a casket-shaped window that overlooked a clay courtyard with a freestanding stone wall. A guard looked out the window and stood with his arms crossed, as if waiting for something to happen.

‘I’m betting on nine,’ the guard said.

‘Nine?’ Alma said. ‘I think it will be prisoner number three.’ A bell rang and I jumped. ‘Relax,’ she whispered. ‘Here they come.’ A slight giggle trailed in her voice.

Seconds later a steel door opened into the courtyard and a guard walked out with nine shoeless inmates holding on to a knotted rope. They had burlap bags over their heads and wore tan prison smocks that hung down to their knees. The guard led them past a set of barred windows that were half-buried in the ground and then faced them toward the stone wall.

It was the first time I had seen a real prisoner before, and the thought of one of them being Claudia made me want to crumple in a fit. I could feel it in my back, which had started to slump, and in my throat, which had balled up.

'See that one in the front,' she said, pointing to one of the prisoners. 'His girlfriend is standing right next to him.' She laughed. 'He doesn't even know she's here.'

'He doesn't?'

'We caught him because of her. Resisters are careless — the boyfriends are easy to catch.' She turned to me. 'You don't have to do the acts to be guilty of them — he knew what she was doing. Crime enough.'

My stomach dropped. *Max.*

Alma said something else but all I could hear were my own thoughts, wondering how careless *I* had been. *How many students have seen us together on the balcony? What about at Joseph's party?*

I reached into my bag and felt around for the one cigarette I had left in my pack, trying to hide the nervous tremble on my lips.

'Dirty little resisters,' Alma said. 'They deserve the heat.'

The prisoners wobbled and swayed, their feet baking on the burnt-orange clay. Then one hopped, alternating his feet on the slab before collapsing to the ground like a limp rag. The guard picked that prisoner to pull the burlap bag from their head.

I held my breath, thinking it could be Claudia under there — but it was a man. He covered his eyes, shrieking, as the guard laughed through gritted teeth. He grabbed the prisoner by the scruff of the neck and hurled him through the air until he hit our window and splattered against the glass.

My cigarette bobbed nervously on my lips as I tried to light it with a sparking lighter, running my thumb over the flint wheel over and over.

Alma put her fists in the air. 'I won!' She was so close to the prisoner they would have touched had the glass not been there.

Patches of hair spotted his scalp. Blood oozed from a wound near his ear and stained the bald spots on his head red. One blue eye — focused to a pinpoint — looked directly at me. His arm swung up to the glass and my cigarette fell from my mouth along with the lighter that was in my hand.

Alma watched me drop to the floor and pick up my things. I could tell by the look on her face she was wondering what had gotten me so shook up, which made me even more nervous.

I pulled myself together the best I could, stood straight and tugged on the lapels of my jacket to keep my back from slumping. I kept my eyes on her, knowing if I looked at the man my legs might buckle or I'd cry out for him myself.

'What did you win, Alma?'

'It's a game we play called Betteln.' The squeal of the man sliding down the glass eclipsed her voice.

'Beg?' I stuck the cigarette into my mouth and lit it, finally, puffing hard to cover the shake in my hands.

She touched my arm. 'It gets boring here in the evenings.' She paused to watch the guard kick the man back to the basement door they had walked out of. 'All of these inmates are from a special holding area below the prison. We bring them to the courtyard for our own amusement and make them stand on the hot clay. If you can predict which prisoner will fall first then you get to pick someone to play Betteln. They have to tell us a good story, beg for our attention, and if we're entertained then we let them have an item from the cloakroom for the night. It's where their belongings are kept. If they don't have anything we sometimes let them root around in the pantry. Pister pretends he doesn't know, we're not supposed to do it, but it's fun for us.'

'All right, Alma,' the guard said. 'Which one is it tonight?'

'You mean the prisoner who fell isn't called in for Betteln?' I said.

'God — no,' Alma said with a laugh. 'If they fell it's because they're useless. You want someone who isn't half-dead.' She smiled. 'Fräulein Strauss, why don't you do the honours? Pick a number between one and nine. That's how many Night and Fogs we have.'

My heart jumped when she admitted the prisoners were Night and Fog. 'Me?' I glanced at the ceiling as if I was mulling over the choices, but if that six on the back of Claudia's photo meant anything, it had to be her inmate number. If she did what they asked, she'd get an item from the cloakroom, if indeed she was still inmate number six. Another prisoner fell to the ground. He crumpled into a ball and the guard kicked him in the ribs as I talked.

'My nephew in Berlin turns six today,' I lied. 'How about number six?'

Alma put a finger to her chin. 'Yes,' she said, slowly. 'Number six.'

* * *

Alma escorted me outside even though she didn't have to. When I saw my car and driver waiting for me at the end of the path, I walked so fast gravel spit out from the bottom of my shoes.

I barked at the driver to put the box Alma was carrying into the trunk, and then get in and start the car. Alma stood next to the door, a sad, pathetic look gleaming in her eyes. 'Maybe you could come back again?'

The heat had liquefied the rest of the makeup from her face, and it slid down her cheeks like warmed icing, leaving a moustache of pink skin under her nose and tan spots of various sizes spackled on her chin. She put her hand on my forearm, stopping me with one foot in the car, and looked out into the distance at the forest. 'So beautiful here, isn't it?'

I smiled. 'It really is.' The driver had got into the car and I shut my door. Alma waved a limp-wristed wave, mouthing her goodbye from the other side of the window.

'Go, driver!' I said.

Remembering the image of that prisoner as he hit the glass made me want to throw up, and I thought that if I vomited, Alma and everyone else would know something wasn't right with me.

The driver shot me a strange look.

'I'm late, fool,' I said. 'If I miss the train you'll be responsible.'

He stepped on the pedal and we sped away, leaving Alma and that disgusting prison in our dusty wake.

* * *

My train arrived back into Munich that evening. A courier picked the documents up and transferred them to my office, but not before I had my eyes on them. There were plenty of files on former prisoners who'd long since moved on to other prisons. Nothing on Night and Fog or Claudia though.

I went up the back stairs to my flat, trying to avoid Max all together, quietly opening my door and sneaking inside. Each of the glockenspiel's forty-three chiming bells competed with a quarrelling couple on the street as smells of beer and leavened bread wafted up from the square, through my window and into my dark room.

I lit a cigarette from a case I found in the foyer. The smoke was brown and thick; the kind that could kill you if you smoked too many in one day. I inhaled deeply and listened to the couple argue down below amid the bells with my eyes closed.

'Ella?'

Max's voice at my door scared me straight from my chair. My heart thumped, thinking about what to do and what to say. Then the shaking started up again. It began in my fingertips and worked its way up my arms like an earthquake. *The boyfriends are easy to catch.*

I tiptoed to the door.

'Ella?' I thought if I didn't make a sound he'd go away, but then he tried the doorknob. 'I heard you come home.'

I gulped, trying to think up a lie to get him to leave and leave quickly — at any given moment a student could walk by and see him at my door. 'I'm ill, Max. You'll have to go.'

Everything got quiet. I felt like I was alone in the woods just after the sun goes down with nobody around. My cigarette burned incredibly close to my fingers as I waited for him to reply.

He let go of the knob. 'All right.' I could tell he was let down by the sound of his voice. 'Get well.'

'I will,' I muttered, my back pressed against the door.

I listened to him walk away, nervous someone had heard us talking.

* * *

I woke the next morning with the memories of Hinzert playing over and over again in my head. By the time I had got to work, my nerves had frayed into fragile split-ends. One look by the wrong person and I was either going to burst into tears or scream madly.

I needed a cigarette, but I had smoked everything I could find, and they had become harder and harder to buy since the Reich linked them with cancer. I opened my desk drawer, searching for the old pack I thought I'd stuffed in there days ago, moving notebooks, pencils and paper clips aside, before finally finding it — crumpled and all the way in the back. But it was empty, and a strange urge to punch something came over me. Then I noticed the most amazing thing, a lone cigarette sticking out from the corner of my desk drawer. *My last cigarette.*

I cradled the precious little thing in my palm, scurried down to the ground floor of the V-building, and out the side service doors to a small patio to smoke in private. But when I swung the door open I saw Erik, dressed in his Nazi Party uniform, and Louise, sitting side-by-side at a picnic table. Her notebook was spread open like a cookbook with notes written in the margins. I turned to go back inside before they saw me, but the doorknob slipped from my hand and the door shut with a loud bang. I struggled to open it back up, and then leaned up against the building in defeat when I realized it had locked.

Off in the distance a cluster of men sat at a similar table under the eaves of the Braunes Haus. They waved with a whistle and laughed, watching me scramble with the door. *Damn NSDAP boys.*

'Look who's here,' Louise chirped.

Erik stood up and adjusted his swastika cuffband on his Party uniform, one of several different uniforms he wore to work. That was the beauty of Nazi Headquarters; all branches and all departments of the Reich had offices around the Königsplatz, so if you didn't wear a suit to work, you could wear one of your uniforms instead.

He nodded once. 'Eva.'

'It's Ella,' I quipped, putting my cigarette in my mouth. He got up from the table and walked off as if he didn't care what my real name was.

I flicked my eyes at Louise, patting my pocket for a light. 'Hello.'

Louise folded a page in her notebook as if to mark something important.

'Well, I trust Hoffmann won't be sending you back to Hinzert anytime soon.'

I lit my cigarette. 'Why not?' Smoke spewed from the corner of my mouth and she fanned it away.

'You didn't hear?'

'What are you talking about, Louise?'

She slowly turned a few pages of her notebook as if they were delicate, museum quality pieces of paper. 'There was an escape after you left. Stripped themselves naked, covered their body in lard and slipped out the barred windows.'

'What?' My cigarette slipped between my fingers and I jumped up when it landed on my skirt. 'An escape?' Claudia kept lard in her rucksack for when I'd plait wigs through her hair; it was the only thing that kept the locks in place.

Louise put her pencil down. 'How interesting you didn't know.'

'Was it a girl?' I sat back down.

'Girl, boy . . . does it matter? They're all criminals.'

Louise glanced at her watch, and then quickly gathered up her belongings as if she was late for something. 'Oh, and this is for you.' She slid an article torn from a *Gesundes Volk* magazine at me. Its title read: The Reich's War on Tobacco. 'The Reich doesn't want women to smoke. It could make you barren. And then what would you do?' She waved her hand near her nose, coughing. 'Well?'

'Well, what?'

Her lips pursed and she tapped the end of her pencil on the table. 'What would you do if the smoke made you barren, Ella?'

'Smoke . . . barren . . . ' I rambled; my mind was on many things, and not one of them involved Louise and her talk about babies. 'I'm young,' I said, smoke filtering through my teeth. 'I don't need to think about that right now.'

Louise looked at me suspiciously before wondering aloud what had got into me. I realized I needed to pull my thoughts, and myself, together. I had to believe it was Claudia and find the proof later. I took a deep breath.

'Louise,' I said, catching her as she tried to leave. 'Have you ever had a best friend?'

'I was in the League of German Girls, Ella. And I was very involved in the Belief and Beauty branch until I was twenty-one. The BDM is full of best friends.'

'I'm not talking about the friends you make in the BDM. I'm talking about a *real* best friend. The kind you never forget, no matter how much time passes. One you'd do anything for because they make you feel alive.'

'Is there a difference?' She rose from the bench, dissecting me with her eyes before turning around and waddling off. Perspiration from sitting outside too long had caused her girdle to rub between her thighs, and it sounded more like she had a fish-bowl wedged between her knees than the usual two pieces of sandpaper.

The boys at the Braunes Haus had gone back inside. Louise had left, and I found myself sitting in a quiet space outside Nazi Headquarters, smiling. I thought about Claudia breaking out of the compound under the cover of night, nude as a newborn babe, slicked with lard and running for the forest. There was only one place she'd go: Nuremberg. And she'd go straight to my aunt's house looking for me.

'Run, girl,' I whispered into the air. 'Run.'

16
October

Christophe hadn't been able to confirm anything about Claudia I didn't already know, and the excitement about the escape had worn off by autumn. Avoiding Max had become a daily routine. I knew his schedule and I planned my own around it, making sure to avoid him in the corridor at all cost. And I waited — waited for a letter to arrive from my aunt, and waited for Christophe to come through.

It was early, and I left my building as usual, tiptoeing my way down the back stairs and onto the Marienplatz. Christophe warned me about the trams, said that informants spent days riding them back and forth just to catch a thief, and I'd be better off walking to the V-building even though on the cooler days I'd much rather have taken the tram.

It had been a year since I left Auntie at the breakfast table with Claudia's key in my pocket. A year. And as I walked on to work in my wool suit, appearing very adult with my hair twisted tightly into a bun at the base of my head, I realized how much I missed the Ella I used to be, the one who sold paintings to women who didn't want them, and clipped fashion advertisements out of magazines.

But as I walked through the Königsplatz, which

was lined with more than a hundred flags, and saw SS guards on my building steps dressed in pressed uniforms, I had to remind myself who I was pretending to be. Because today was a special day.

The Führer was in Munich.

I set the morning meetings up for the administration staff, and then helped Louise orientate the new employees in our building for their first official visit from the Führer: girls in the secretarial pool, special couriers who only transported documents between the Führerbau and the V-building, and a few guards that monitored the front entrance. It was up to Louise and me, since we were senior assistants, to make sure that they respected policy and protocol in both appearance and mannerisms in case Hitler did a walk-through of the V-building, which was expected. Nobody seemed to remember it was my first official visit.

The Führer wanted people at Nazi Headquarters to be working as usual when he arrived. There would be no red carpet or ovation waiting for him at the front entrance like I had thought. Instead, his visit would be more like a factory foreman inspecting his production line; workers would go about their business with zest and exuberance while he looked on with his hands clasped behind his back, nodding. Policy dictated that only after the Führer and his advisors got within a few metres of one's presence were you supposed to salute. Ogling eyes were prohibited, but stiff arms held high in the air and even stiffer smiles were expected.

By midday Hitler hadn't arrived, and I was on

my way to the tunnel for some files. Ronald, the same bald-headed watchman I met on my first day, greeted me at the tunnel door with a clipboard grasped firmly in both hands. He stood with his back against the wall wearing a brand new guard's uniform. Gone was his untidy desk and the dirty coffee pot I had grown accustomed to seeing, and in its place was an arrangement of pencils.

'You look different today, Ronald.'

'It's an important day today, Fräulein Strauss.' His voice was dry, nervous.

I straightened my wool suit jacket. 'My suit is too grey. Maybe I should have put on a tie. Though, I never liked the one I had to wear in the League.' I hesitated, wondering if he was now thinking about how young I was. 'But that was a long time ago . . . the League.'

'I never understood ties for women,' he said, fiddling with his own. 'You're right not to wear one.'

I worked in silence for several minutes, bent over, rummaging through the file cabinets, opening drawers and not bothering to shut them. I wasn't sure how much time had passed before I heard the light swoosh of feet coming down the tunnel corridor, followed by the sharp clip of heels. They stopped right next to me, and there was a pause, my face and both hands deep in the files, before I looked up. Then my stomach sank. *Hitler*.

Ronald started to announce his presence but I cut him off by bolting to a stand. '*Heil Hitler!*' I kicked the file cabinet closest to the floor shut with my foot.

Hitler's gaze skirted over me, a sickly-sweet smile bowing on his lips, before reaching out and shaking my hand. His touch was soft, almost kind, and it sent a chill up my spine. His brown Nazi Party leader uniform was crisp, yet loosely fitted and had a short fat tie of the same colour underneath a leather shoulder strap. He was shorter than I thought — his eyes level with my own — but his receding, pomade-slicked hairline and dark bristly moustache were exactly what I had expected.

Three officers from the Reich flanked his sides, and two others stood behind; all wore similar brown Nazi Party leaders' uniforms with swastikas wrapped around their arms. They nodded, and before I had a chance to process what was really happening — that I was shaking Hitler's hand — they turned like a flock of birds and left.

Ronald, who had been watching diligently from his post, burst out a manly, forceful-toned greeting as they passed, but Hitler and the others walked right out of the tunnel door and into the V-building as if he wasn't there. Only after we heard the sound of their footsteps turn into muffled thumps did we exhale.

'You're lucky, Fräulein Strauss.' There was a hint of resentment in Ronald's voice. 'The Führer. He shook your hand.'

I looked at my palm. Any other person would have kissed their own hand and then pressed it to their face like a pillow. I wanted to wash up. I thought about how close he had been to me, how I could hear him breathing. My heart raced just thinking about it and suddenly I felt overwhelmed with having looked into the eyes of a madman.

My knees buckled and my back slammed into the file cabinets; they clinked and clattered like a chain. Then the wailing started, which caught even me by surprise, and I dropped to the floor, tears pouring from my eyes.

Ronald seemed unaware I was heaving on the ground, probably because he thought I was just like every other girl: in love with Hitler.

'Louise will be jealous,' he said.

I nodded, hand over mouth, sobbing.

* * *

I didn't get home until late that night. There was an eerie silence in the street and the air felt static, like a big storm was brewing, but the skies were clear. Then the air raid sirens went off and the city went dark.

People ran out of the Ratskeller, scattering, hiding in the alleys, others who knew where the shelters were disappeared into hidden doorways. I ran into my building's basement. It wasn't an official shelter, but its wide metal door and thick stone walls made it an ideal place to hide.

As soon as I opened the door I wished I had hid in the alley instead. Sitting against the wall, next to some other people from the building, was Max. His eyes lit up when he saw me, but then turned sad when I didn't sit in the space he had made for me.

There was a lit gas lantern in the middle of the floor next to a small puddle that smelled like piss and days-old standing water. Everyone huddled together like fat cigars in a narrow box, scooting together as more and more bodies entered the room, the sirens ebbing and flowing each time the door swung open. The building shook from the blast of the RAF bombs.

There was a communal sigh when the sirens stopped. Some people chatted and laughed as if they had been on an amusement ride, others walked around like zombies trying to find their way home. I made a dash for the door, but Max grabbed me by the elbow and held me back as the others filed out of the room.

Then we were all alone.

'You've been avoiding me.' He searched my eyes for meaning. 'Did I do something wrong?' When I didn't answer he held me real close and my head tipped back. I wanted him to kiss me like he did before, but I knew it was wrong.

He brushed a lock of hair from my eyes. 'Ella?'

I glanced nervously at the door worried someone might open it and see us together, which he noticed and only made him look more confused. *I have to tell him the truth*, I thought. He deserved to know.

'Why have you been avoiding me?'

'Because nobody can see us together. Not while I work for the Reich.' I closed my eyes briefly because it was too painful to keep looking at his face. 'I saw what they do to the prisoners at Hinzert, Max. Don't you understand? If I get caught, so do you if we're together.'

'But you're the one, Ella.' He cradled my face in his hands. 'We can hide, be together in secret. Nobody has to know. Nobody. Don't let the Reich ruin us . . . '

'I can't,' I kept saying, 'I can't . . . I can't . . .'

'I love you,' he said, and I wiggled out of his arms and ran out the door, a desperate cry escaping from my mouth.

* * *

I dragged myself to work the next morning. Louise was there bright and early, staring at me with her clipboard held close to her chest while I opened my door.

'Did you have a good night?'

I thought she was making a joke at first, but she would never make a joke about a raid.

'Did you find a shelter?' I said. 'Luckily there's one in my building.'

Most shelters were homemade and privately built, only a few had been built by the city. Nobody dared to question why out loud, but if the government built shelters then it meant the Reich expected us to get bombed, and admitting such a thing had consequences that far outweighed the potential of an enemy air strike.

'What are you talking about?' Louise said.

I opened the door, but stopped short from walking in. 'The bombs last night.'

Suddenly Max appeared at the end of the corridor dressed in his guard uniform. I'd never seen him in my building. He looked at me, and I turned away, pretending to fiddle with my office keys.

'I don't know anything about that,' Louise said. 'I did hear some thunder though.'

I took a few breaths, looking at my keys, and

then glanced back up at Louise, and over her shoulder where I'd seen Max. But he was gone.

'That's what I meant,' I said. 'The thunder.'

17

December

I sat in my office's windowsill, head pressed against the glass. Two young girls skipped past down below, dressed in League uniforms, kicking up leaves from the chestnut trees. I sat up, watching them twirl and laugh and flick each other's ties in the air until they were just two figures between the trees, disappearing behind the Nazi flags lining the Königsplatz.

A clopping sound and the swish from a heavy palm sliding along the handrail pulled my eyes away from the street; only Hoffmann sounded that way, but he was in a meeting, had been since I arrived at work that morning. The intensity of the noise, the determination in the step, however, wasn't like Hoffmann at all, so I went to the door and peeked around the corner just as Hoffmann ran into me, chest first, armpits second, the brackish smell of too much cologne fuming from his pores.

My hand went immediately to my nose. 'Sir . . . I didn't mean to . . . '

'They want you at the meeting.' He walked to my desk, took three mints from a dish and shoved them into his mouth; one slipped through his fingers and fell to the ground. 'Now,' he said.

He seemed agitated and a little abrupt. A small part of me thought I was in trouble, that someone had noticed anomalies in the tunnel files. Another part of me thought he was overreacting. He probably needed a drink and was taking it out on me. I reached into my skirt pocket and squeezed my yellow scarf, closing my eyes briefly, before following Hoffmann up the stairs to the third floor.

Hoffmann stopped at the double doors that led into the main meeting room, gripped both doorknobs with his big hands and took a deep breath. 'Let me do the talking,' he said.

'Am I in trouble?' I asked.

He closed his eyes as if he didn't know, turned the knobs with force and opened the doors. A pocket of stone-cold air snapped from the seal, and voices quieted with a rigid shift of eyes. I moved my hands to the middle of my body, clasped them together and followed Hoffmann in with a bit lip.

Officers from all branches of government stared up at me from their comfortable chairs around the conference table, Erik and Louise sitting at the head.

My stomach moved to my throat.

Three were dressed in their menacing black Allgemeine-SS military uniforms with silver shoulder boards. The medals sprayed across their chests wasn't just for knowing how to attack, but when.

I eyed the door at the other end of the room; it was too far to run. If I turned around Hoffmann could grab me. I opened my mouth to say something, but wasn't sure what.

Louise looked at me strangely, and then tapped the empty seat next to her with the end of her pencil. 'Have a seat.' When I didn't move her brow furrowed, and I realized I hadn't been caught — just invited to a meeting.

I sat down while Hoffmann scooted into the chair across from me. Crystal decanters of whisky lined the middle of the table. Hoffmann's glass was filled to the brim with water, like it normally was when people were watching.

'Great,' Erik said. 'Now we can begin.' He sat next to a man with a hat that barely fit the top of his head; the Totenkopf death's head placed above its brim. But it was the red and yellow ribbon tied between his buttonholes that gave his identity away: Reinhard Heydrich, Director of the Reich Main Security Office, the organization that sent my department its Night and Fog files to manage.

Erik cleared his throat and introduced me to the panel as Eva. I held my tongue, but then two others from my floor reminded him my name was Ella. Erik, unshaken by the public misstep, kept talking like it didn't matter that he'd got my name wrong, again, and I started to wonder if he had been doing it on purpose.

'Your supervisor is fighting us on this,' Erik said. 'So, I thought we should talk to you personally.'

My eyes darted to Hoffmann; he sat down with a clenched fist, and the veins in his neck boiled into blue ropes.

'We're reorganizing duties,' Erik said. 'There's too much going on at the Braunes Haus and around the Königsplatz in general. Departments are muddled and efficiency has become a problem.' He glanced at Hoffmann as if he expected him to interrupt at any moment. Then Erik looked directly at me with his sharp eyes. 'We'll need to expand your file audits, but your supervisor is adamant that you are already too busy.'

'I'm — '

'Ella, let me handle this,' Hoffmann interrupted, using his elbow to lean forward on the table. 'The document department at the V-building is already overloaded. Ella here is busy from morning to sunset as it is.' He shook his head. 'The burdens of other departments shouldn't become ours.'

An officer from the NSDAP piped up. 'It's not anything new, Hoffmann. It's still documents.' Men grumbled in agreement at both ends of the table.

'It's twice as much work as she's used to getting from me, and from other prisons that have transferred their documents to us.' Hoffmann had accepted the prison files, like the ones I brought back from Hinzert, but he had always rejected other departments' files from around the Königsplatz. He even pasted a notice to the front of my office door that listed our department's jurisdictions, to keep couriers from dumping files off while we were out.

I pointed a finger in the air while people shouted back and forth at the table. 'Sir . . . if I could . . . a moment . . . '

I knew enough about office management to know that Hoffmann wasn't going to win this battle. I had to accept willingly in order to look good in the eyes of the Reich, but I knew Hoffmann felt threatened by the idea of more work. I had become his cover, he drank what and when he wanted and I did all of his work. I saw his frustration settling as wrinkles around his eyes.

Hoffmann blew from his nose. 'I don't want

your documents — '

Erik slammed his hand flat on the table. 'Enough!' Glasses wobbled and some clinked together. Tired old men jolted from their chairs and the stiff got stiffer. 'There's a war going on. We don't have time to fight over petty matters.' Erik's voice was shrill. Hoffmann didn't budge, and I realized the standoff over my duties must have been going on for quite a while.

'Something has to be done,' Director Heydrich said, and I was surprised to hear a soft voice from him, almost as soft as a woman's. 'We don't have the resources to audit our own files, and they span the Königsplatz.' He tilted his head down and looked at me with rolled eyes as if his department's disorganization was my fault.

'I'll do it.' I smiled.

Erik's shoulders dropped and a thankful smile rested on his lips. 'Finally,' he said glancing around the table. 'We have a resolution here.'

Hoffmann put his hand to his forehead and sank into his chair. Defeat battered on his face and his chin started to quiver. *He really needs a drink.*

'The Verwaltungsbau document control will handle the audits of all document files,' Erik said, 'from all departments around the Königsplatz.'

He glanced at Louise who had been picking at her fingernail. 'That includes administration meeting minutes, equipment and the personnel files under Louise's control.'

Her jaw dropped. 'But — '

Erik tapped the table with one finger. 'Documents shouldn't be part of your duties anyway.

Enough said. This meeting is over.' He paused, and then glanced around the table. 'Heil Hitler!'

'Heil Hitler!' everyone shouted back. People hurriedly got out of their seats and headed for the door, thankful the long meeting and argument about documents had finally been resolved. A few of the elders rubbed their eyes and then slipped out the back door that led to the toilets. Louise slammed her notebook shut, shooting me a heated stare. I had the feeling she wanted me to say something, perhaps apologize, but for what I didn't know — after all, I wasn't the one who took her duties away. Erik did, and like he said, documents were documents, it didn't matter what department they came from, they should have been under my control from the beginning.

Louise walked away; the scratching between her thighs sounded as harsh as nails on a blackboard. Some of the men winced.

Hoffmann patted my shoulder with downcast eyes. 'Sorry, Ella,' he said. 'Appears you didn't have a choice, no matter what I said.' He paused, and I looked up. 'I hope you don't have plans for Christmas, because you'll be spending them here. Filing.'

'No, sir. I'm alone this holiday.' I caught my reflection in a glass decanter and looked into my own eyes. The amount of information I'd potentially be exposed to was unfathomable. I rose from my chair, reached across the table for some whisky and poured it into a fresh highball glass. 'Making sure the Reich has what they need is paramount. And if that means working over Christmas, so be it.' I slid the glass across the table and he caught it with one hand.

'You're a good National Socialist, Ella.' He held the glass up, toasting me.

'Thank you, sir.'

⋆ ⋆ ⋆

I volunteered to organize the NSDAP Christmas dance held in a Party building at the west-end of the Marienplatz. Louise had been on my list of volunteers, but when she saw me with a clipboard in my hand and Nazi banner decorations at my feet, directing girls to the far corners of the room, she sat down in a chair and picked at her nails.

The party was in full swing by a quarter past eight o'clock in the evening, the band playing requests from the musical *Kora Terry*, a film about twin sisters, one a wholesome nationalist, the other a sexy traitor. The air was warm, stuffy and full of sweaty young NSDAP-uniformed men and women who wore satiny dresses and thin ribbons tied in their hair. Some of the girls danced modestly, almost stiffly, while others swung their hips and danced like the sexy traitor from the film, which was strictly forbidden, and I had to reprimand them.

Erwin watched me from the doorway next to a table loaded with cakes and glasses of champagne. His stare made me feel uneasy, and I wished I hadn't worn my blue dancing dress. I kept the clipboard in my hand and thought it would be enough to deter him from asking me to dance, but then I saw him adjust his swastika cuffband and check his breath.

I turned around, walking away, but ploughed right into Louise, her pillowy breasts bumping awkwardly into mine.

'Watch yourself!' She looked at me bitterly.

I glanced over my shoulder; Erwin was getting closer. The last thing I wanted to do was to get trapped in his sweaty grip for the rest of the night. I had to think of something, and I had to think of it quick!

I pulled out what reichsmarks I had in my pocket. 'I'll give you this if you dance with Erwin.' She looked shocked initially, and then glanced over my shoulder.

'Hoffmann's nephew?'

I nodded quick, my head practically bobbing, pushing the money at her. I could feel Erwin behind me, and I imagined he was weaving in and out of people and gaining speed.

She scoffed after studying my face. 'You'll need to do better than that.'

I searched my dress pocket, but it was empty. 'I'll give you double tomorrow.'

She snatched the money from my hand, tucked it into her brassiere and then pushed me out of the way like I was a twig in her path. Erwin seemed annoyed at first to see Louise, but when she ran her fingers loosely over the collar of his NSDAP uniform he softened like a hunk of melted fat.

I watched them dance with both hands wrapped around my clipboard, glad I had avoided him and taken care of her. Then a deep voice whispered in my ear and a heavy hand curled around my waist. 'Dance with me.' It was Christophe. He was dressed in a loose-fitting NSDAP uniform, as if he had worn it all day and hadn't bothered to have it cleaned or pressed. I paused for a second and searched his face for an explanation; he hadn't mentioned he was coming to the dance. 'Now,' he said before I could answer him.

He took the clipboard out of my hands and set it on a nearby table as he walked me out to the dance floor. Just as the band was winding down their set, Christophe pulled me close and talked directly into my ear. 'There's a man near the door dressed plainly in a brown suit. He's from General Halder's office. He's been working in the NSDAP offices upstairs for two days. I need to know what he's been doing.'

I glanced toward the door and saw who he was talking about. He had short dark hair, chiselled cheekbones, and was as attractive as he was tall. I wondered what exactly Christophe had in mind. 'How do you expect me to get into his office?'

'You can find a way.'

My head jerked, and I looked directly into his eyes.

'Don't look at me like that,' he said. 'You look suspicious, dammit. You know how many informants are walking around this city?' He paused. 'A lot. Some are probably here right now.' He sniffed the crook of my neck. 'What's that smell?'

I snarled. 'It's perfume!'

'You'll need to smell good for this one. He's not like the fellows in the NSDAP. You'll have to promise him more than a dance or a kiss to get him to unlock his office.'

The song ended and everyone stopped dancing. 'I don't know about this. Alone with a man in his office . . . '

'You're crafty. Think of a way not to compromise yourself — if it means that much to you.' He tugged on my ear, pushing his lips right into it. 'I have information for you about your friend, Sascha. You help me, and I help you.' He turned to walk away and I grabbed his hand, twisting his fingers back.

'What is it?'

He chuckled slyly. 'We can exchange information after the dance.'

I watched the man drink a glass of champagne as if it were water. I probably could get him drunk enough to take me up to his office. All I had to do was get inside. I took a deep breath. Girls seemed to avoid him, as if they knew he wasn't from around here and not worth their time — the dances were designed to promote marriage, what good was he if he was only visiting?

I walked up to him. 'Hello,' I said. 'You're new, aren't you?'

He offered me a glass of champagne he'd just taken from the tray. 'I am.' His dark hair looked as shiny as his face. 'How can you tell?'

Christophe questioned me from afar with a serious stare, and I took the man's glass and drank what was inside in one gulp. *Flat champagne. Ick.* 'You're cuter than everyone else.' I swallowed hard, tasting every bit of the rancid flavour.

'Do you want to dance?' he said.

He had a nice smile. Watching the other men dance with so many beautiful women while he stood singly must have weighed heavily on his mind, and it occurred to me he might have thought something was wrong with him. *It won't be so bad*, I thought.

The music started up again. 'I'd love to,' I said, and he took my hand.

His name was Michael and we danced the rest of the night together. I made sure that when the music stopped we drank another glass of champagne until he was happily intoxicated. Most of the time I'd turn my back and switch my full glass out for an empty one.

Sometime between our dancing and drinking, Max had walked in. He wore a crisp NSDAP uniform with shiny, knee-high black boots, a polished silver belt buckle and pointed lapels with a brand new swastika cuffband wrapped around his arm. *He's a member of the Party.*

He held his drink casually and swayed and laughed to the chatter of a woman wearing a skimpy, gold-coloured dress. Her face was crudely painted with makeup and every time she laughed her chest bounced as much as her blonde, wavy hair. I wondered where she came from — girls like that didn't come to NSDAP dances. *Did they come together?* She took a long drink of champagne, spilling some of it on her ballooning chest.

When the music stopped, Michael walked up to the band to request a song. I stood alone in the middle of the dance floor and stared at Max. He held my gaze for a moment, then walked straight up to me and asked how I was. He stood so close I could smell the tobacco on his shirt. The room suddenly felt very small, too small for Max and me to be in it at the same time, and I murmured something that sounded like a hello back. Then

Michael barged in between us, grabbed my hand and twirled me around — the tune he requested had started to play, more *Kora Terry*.

I laughed and pretended to enjoy the dance, but my gaze kept shifting toward Max, who was still standing in the middle of the dance floor watching me. The woman, realizing Max had walked away from her, drunkenly shuffled onto the dance floor for a dance. They moved very close to Michael and me. When the moment was right, Max switched partners and I found myself in his arms. He put his cheek to mine and whispered in my ear as we spun away from Michael and the buxom blonde.

'I miss you.'

The music moved as fast as we did, his hand moving up my warm back, our bodies touching, eyes locked on each other.

'You know this is just a uniform,' he said. 'I don't really believe.'

'I know,' I said.

Michael cut back in, ripping me from Max's grasp and we danced away. I watched Max's date bump into him with her chest. She laughed loud, loud enough for me to hear her, before she planted a kiss on his lips. I looked away when they headed for the door, together.

The lingering smell of Max's cologne on my clothes affected me in a way I didn't think was possible, and I had to sit down for a moment before I could continue with Michael. I felt my own arms, thinking about his touch, wishing that damn *Kora Terry* song had lasted longer.

The dance floor had thinned, and guests had gathered around the refreshment tables, but the champagne was nearly gone, and so were the cakes. I felt Christophe's watchful eyes still set on me, telling me to get up and get going.

He must have something good to tell me about Claudia.

I stood up from where I was sitting. 'Michael, is there someplace close by we can go?' I was sure he had drunk at least three bottles of champagne himself. 'Someplace private?'

He hiccupped. 'I have an office upstairs.'

I smiled.

* * *

Michael barely got a foot inside his office before he pushed my face into his and kissed me. I could taste the champagne on his lips and smell it on his breath. He backed me into the wall, trying to pin my wrists with his hands, but he could barely stand and felt really heavy.

'Michael,' I said. 'You're drunk.'

He backed up into the flagpole behind the door, lost his balance and fell violently to the floor with a loud clang. I froze, watching him wrapped up with the Nazi flag, waiting for him to move. Then his head flopped backward and he snored.

I locked the door, and immediately opened up all his desk drawers, but they were completely empty. Aside from a cup of pencils, there was nothing to make me believe the room had ever been used as an office. My heart raced, glancing at Michael's drunken body, feeling the pressure of a ticking clock made worse by not knowing how long he'd be out.

Damn! I had to find something to give to Christophe. I pounded my fist on top of a knee-high filing cabinet behind his desk. The bottom drawer jittered and squeaked; its lock wasn't engaged. I opened it slowly. Inside was a brown leather bag stuffed full of handwritten letters.

Gasp.

I crouched down like a child on the floor behind Michael's desk and read them as fast as I could.

Michael was the personal courier of Franz Halder, Chief of General Wehrmacht Staff. The papers were secret correspondence between Halder and Walther von Brauchitsch, Commander-in-Chief of the Wehrmacht. Halder wanted to form a conspiracy to overthrow Hitler, said they couldn't win a two-front war. Brauchitsch was still undecided.

My eyes rolled over the words so fast it felt like I had inhaled them. When I came to the last page I took a deep breath and tried to absorb what I had just learned. That was when I heard footsteps coming down the corridor. I thought about moving but I was paralyzed, save for my eyes, listening to the clip of heels getting closer and closer until suddenly they stopped just outside the door.

I heard a thud against the frosted glass set in the door, as if someone had pressed their face to it and was trying to get a peek inside. The lock clicked over, and blood pumped in my ears.

'Michael?' The voice was a man's. A voice I didn't recognize. The doorknob turned, and then creaked open. Michael lay motionless on the floor behind the door, still wrapped in the flag. 'Michael,' the voice said again.

Everything got quiet. Even Michael's drunken snore had stopped.

The blurred reflection of the open door glimmered off the metal filing cabinet, and I saw what looked like a hand searching the wall before I heard a palm patting for the switch. The door opened wider and pushed against Michael's foot. I squeezed my eyes shut as if the harder I squeezed them the more invisible I would become. Then the light went out and the door closed just as noisily as it had opened. 'Wasting electricity,' the man mumbled, walking back down the corridor.

I breathed heavily, face buried in my shoulder, thanking God I wasn't caught, until at last I was able to get up and leave.

Christophe was waiting for me across the Marienplatz under a very dark eave. He hooked my arm and we walked down the street as if we were a couple, whispering into each other's ears. I had to tell him my news before he'd tell me his.

'The Hinzert prisoner who escaped was a girl. Number six.'

I put my hand to my mouth, stopping. 'Are you certain?'

He nodded. 'She's still on the run. There were agents in Nuremberg looking for her but now,' he said, pausing, 'they think she's in Munich.'

'Munich?' I turned to him, breathless from this information. 'Did you get a name?' I thought that if he could give me a name that sounded like Claudia or her codename I could be certain.

'A name will be difficult. Night and Fog is the most secret program I've come across. Even those who know about it act as if it doesn't exist.'

'That's all right,' I said, savouring the news he did give me. 'What you've told me is good.'

'It was a good night for both of us, Sascha. This news about Halder could be the shift we've been waiting for.' Christophe let go of my arm and walked away into the night.

The blare of air raid sirens erupted out of nowhere. The heavy hum of multiple RAF bombers rumbled along the city's edge, their bombs dropping willy-nilly and nowhere near the industrial centres or railway lines. *Civilians.* I ran past the wood and hat shop near my building, but then stopped dead. The shop was dark and empty; just a few hats had been left on display in the window along with a handful of wood shavings where the boxes used to be, and a string of silver garland on the floor. Pasted to the front door just above a Merry Christmas greeting, was the death card of a young man dressed in a Wehrmacht uniform — killed in action. His dark hair looked white from weathering and he had vacant, sun-bleached eyes. Below the image was his name — he was eighteen and Herr and Frau Haas' son.

A man knocked my shoulder, shouting something I couldn't hear over the whirring sirens and the blasts of the bombs. I ran away feeling the boy's ghostly stare on my back, but then smiled, not caring so much, because of the news of Claudia and that they were looking for her in Munich.

18

It was the day after Christmas, a Saturday, and I was outside, along with hundreds of other people standing in the winter sun, admiring three of the newest style of Panzer tanks on display in the Marienplatz. The tank's long-gun turned in circles — the heavy clinking noise of its mechanisms locking into position — aiming at the heads of the people who were ahhing and ooing. Wehrmacht soldiers marched in a line, some holding guns, others holding Nazi flags.

A man with one eye and a missing hand watched me from the side of a building where he stood lifeless as a flagpole. When he saw me notice him, he turned on his heel and walked away, dragging a sweeping foot.

'Don't mind the wounded,' a second man with a cane said. 'We want to see the Panzers, but don't want to be seen.' He winked, and then hobbled on after him.

I pulled my collar up, more interested in the crowds than the tanks, when I saw a woman not that far away with auburn hair. I could hear her laughing, saying something about the tanks, as she walked away with another girl on her arm. I followed her, straining to catch a glimpse of her face, reaching out for her shoulder when she turned around — and I saw her brown eyes.

My hand recoiled. 'I thought you were someone else.'

She looked at me strangely, and then snuggled up against her friend and walked away.

I watched her disappear into the crowd with her hair bouncing, deeper and deeper until there was nothing left of her, when suddenly Herr Speer, the building manager, tapped my shoulder. 'Fräulein Strauss!' He wore oversized reading glasses that magnified his eyes to the size of gigantic green apples. 'We have a problem. The flag! Under your window.' He pointed. 'It's crooked — what a disgrace!'

I turned around. 'That is a disgrace.' Max stood behind me with some men I recognized from the NSDAP, admiring the tanks. His hands were in his pockets and he rocked back on his heels, talking, a breath of frosty air floating from his mouth.

Herr Speer tapped my shoulder. 'Fräulein Strauss?' he said, but I was too entranced by Max to answer him. 'The flag.' He tapped me again, only this time his finger felt like a needle. 'Fraulein Strauss — '

'Yes?' Herr Speer adjusted his glasses, looking at me with his big green apple eyeballs.

'The flag,' he said, pointing. 'Under your window.'

'I'll fix it. Absolutely.'

He looked relieved, probably thinking that was one less thing he had to take care of. 'The Reich is lucky to have such a good German working for them. A true National Socialist.'

'Thank you,' I said. 'My aunt said the same thing to me on my first day in the League — '

His mouth gaped open. 'Now!' he barked, and I rushed off.

The foyer of my building was empty, and eerily quiet and still, even the Nazi flags on standing poles didn't flutter when I opened the door. A chill ran up my spine, and I paused for a moment before starting up the stairs, but then stopped cold. The handrail shook. Pounding and trampling boomed from the floors above.

The NSDAP boys wouldn't run like that. And the students were outside, admiring the tanks. Resistance.

A boy flew down the stairs, through the foyer and out the back doors, not even batting an eye in my direction. Trailing behind him was a girl who stopped the instant she recognized me.

Sophie, Max's sister.

Her fingers touched mine on the railing. Three more people ran down the stairs behind her and out the doors shouting for Sophie to follow them, and we stared at each other, waiting for the other to say something until finally I did.

'Run!' I pointed toward the doors. A brief smile lifted her face as she took off.

I burst outside through my building doors and into a snowstorm of papers which had been tossed off nearly every building in the Marienplatz and onto the crowds below. I picked one up: anti-Nazi leaflets from the White Rose, a new underground resistance group based in Munich.

I had heard of the White Rose months ago. Hoffmann found one of their leaflets stuffed in a phonebook outside our building. He thought the administration would feel disgraced, an outlawed paper so close to Nazi Headquarters, so he only showed it to me. The leaflet read like a sermon quoting from the Bible, but its message was simple: freedom from Nazism. Nobody was able to figure out who they were. Nobody knew their names. I suspected it was because the members had aliases, just like the Falcons had in Nuremberg; it would be suicide for somebody in the resistance to use their given name.

Two policemen ran toward me shouting as I held the leaflet between my hands — I swiftly crumpled it up. Their faces puffed red. 'Did you see them?' one said.

I mumbled a number before I shouted out that there was only one. 'A man with grey hair who could run like lightning.'

'Which way?' he said, his eyes darting.

I pointed the opposite direction, and they rushed off.

There wasn't a patch of untouched ground in the Marienplatz. Herr Speer shuffled in circles amongst the people with his hands on his head, intermittingly throwing them into the air and cursing to himself. 'Don't look at them,' he kept saying, stretching his hands out. 'We must burn them!'

Some people did pick up the leaflets, glanced at them, and then wadded them up into balls like I had. Soldiers popped out of their tank hatches to bat the leaflets with the butts of their rifles; others threw them into piles for burning where Heer Speer had swept some up with his feet.

A lone leaflet, a forgotten piece, floated down above my head, waffling like a bird with a broken wing in the breeze. I reached for it mid-air and so did Max. Our bare hands touched in the cold.

Neither of us let go.

'I watch you leave for work every morning,' he said. 'Every morning.'

I inhaled a gulp of air, wanting to say something, but held back. I didn't want to move, not even to talk, for fear he'd pull his hand away. He looked older, distinguished and handsome with his muscly arms. Just a few months ago we were talking about taking down the Reich with the rest of the Falcons at the Steichele, with his ink-stained trousers and unkempt hair. Now he wore a NSDAP uniform and I couldn't even be caught talking to him.

'You have to let go,' he finally said, but I shook my head. 'They'll think we're reading it.' He laid his other hand on mine, and I let go.

I stood for a second by myself, watching him take the leaflet over to the pile Herr Speer had now set to burn, before falling backward into the crowd. The long-gun swung around, clinking and clanking its gears. Max turned around, almost catching me still watching him, and I slipped behind a military lorry.

* * *

By Monday, stories about the White Rose had spread like fire throughout Munich. People wanted to know who they were, where they lived, and most importantly, where they were going to strike next. Sightings of the elusive 'freedom bandits,' as some called them, were as wide as the tales of their origins. Some thought the leaders were gruesome, monster-like creatures the Red

Army had created to poison our minds. Others believed they were probably dissenters from the Hitler Youth. Auntie would have loved the Red Army stories, and she would have believed them because they were repeated on the radio.

I was finishing up some correspondence for Hoffmann when the mail clerk rang. She said she was too sick to continue her route and that if I wanted the mail for the V-building I'd have to deliver it myself. Her voice was weak and shaky, which made me believe she was telling the truth, so I told her I would do it.

The mail stop in my building was a small room off the first-floor foyer where the guard posts were. The door had been taken off months ago and the room was more of an open space than a real room in the conventional sense. The basket she left me was filled with a batch of fifty or so letter-sized envelopes addressed to every person in my building, including myself.

I sorted them, and then started dropping them into pigeonholes when Louise walked in to get her deliveries.

'Hello, Ella.' Her voice was whiney, and it sounded more like Erwin's than her own.

'Louise,' I said, glancing up, stuffing a letter into a hole. 'Been seeing Erwin lately?'

She looked at me oddly, as if they *had* been together and wondered how I could have known.

'What I mean is,' I said, trying not to sound too rude, 'your voice reminded me of him.'

Louise watched me finish sorting the mail, but didn't bother to ask why I was doing the mail clerk's job. 'New Year's Eve is nearly here.' She looked me up and down, and I paused, one hand in a pigeonhole. 'Are you going to the NSDAP party?' she asked.

'You mean did someone ask me?' I said.

'Did someone ask you?' she said.

I went back to stuffing envelopes into boxes. 'I suppose somebody asked you?' I replied. 'Let me guess . . . Erwin?' I gathered up her mail. 'Here.' Then I took the deliveries for me and Hoffmann and left.

Moments later Louise barged into my office, hitting the door with her fist and sending a thunderous boom down the corridor.

'Where did you get these?' She held up the envelope I'd delivered with her name on it, flapping it in the air. Its edge was split from being ripped open with her finger. A loud thump came from Hoffmann's office. He had passed out on the divan an hour earlier and I had shut the frosted glass door between us. The noise, either Louise's fist against my door, or her high-pitched voice, must have woken him.

'Why? What is it?'

Louise wadded her envelope into a tight little ball. 'Leaflets from the White Rose.' She threw it at my chest, her eyes glowing.

'White Rose?' I felt a smile budding on my lips and I tried, with all of my might, to keep it from showing. *The mail clerk knew.*

'I put the envelopes in the mail slots, Louise. I didn't post them, if that's what you're suggesting.' I sifted through the deliveries on my desk, showing her the envelope addressed to me. 'See? I got one too. I'm a victim just like you.'

Her face dropped, as if realizing she had overstepped; implying that I had sent the leaflets was more than a grievance. 'What I meant to ask was . . . ' she started to say.

'Why was I delivering the mail?' I said.

'Yes.'

'The mail clerk got sick.'

Hoffmann's door cracked open, and her eyes darted toward his office.

'I didn't mean what you think I meant, Ella.' She turned on her heel and left just as Hoffmann poked his head out of his office.

'What's the commotion?' he asked.

I tore open my envelope. 'The White Rose sent us leaflets,' I said. 'The whole building. Everyone!'

'Hmm.' Hoffmann glanced at my leaflet, but refused to open his. 'This will not go over lightly with the Reich.' He fell into the door, still wobbly from getting up sooner than he would have liked.

I closed my office door, and then read aloud straight from the page while Hoffmann looked over my shoulder. *'Our present state is the dictatorship of evil . . . why do you allow these men who are in power to rob you step by step, openly and in secret, of one domain of your rights after another, until one day nothing, nothing at all will be left but a mechanized state system presided over by criminals and drunks — '*

'Throw them out,' Hoffmann said.

I finished reading the leaflet quietly to myself. Hoffmann plopped his heavy body back onto the divan, and then rubbed his head and closed his eyes.

19

New Year's Eve had arrived. I watched Christophe mull over the munitions supply routes I had smuggled out of the Königsplatz. A thick Trommler cigarette stuck to his bottom lip, its ash growing, hanging off the end. The burst of a New Year's firework popped behind him, and its purple flash crackled through a split in the curtains. I leaned over to catch a better glimpse, seeing a gathering of people in the square, wondering if Claudia was out there somewhere, watching me, or waiting to make contact. I pulled the curtains open wider and wider, until Christophe reached over and threw them shut.

'Is this everything?' he said.

'*Nein*,' I said. 'I have one more thing.'

I pulled a drawing out from behind my bed. I had worked on it for three days, copying it from an original design. 'It's a rocket.' I dangled the page in the air between two pinched fingers and he snatched it away.

'Unbelievable.' His eyes rolled over the page, swerving, stopping and jolting. 'You've outdone yourself this time.'

'One hundred and ninety-three kilometres. It will reach Britain,' I said. 'Everything you need to know is in the margin. Where they're stored, where the test sites are, where they're made . . . '

He rose slowly from the windowsill with the page still in his hands, spitting his cigarette from his mouth and then stomping it out with his shoe.

'Watch it!' I said. 'This is still my flat, you know.'

'Right.' With his eyes still on the paper, he reached into his coat pocket, took out a pack of cigarettes and shook it at me. 'Do you want one?'

I took the cigarette he offered and put it on my shelf for later. Then I picked his butt off the ground and smeared the ash with my foot until it blended in with the wood. I mumbled to myself about the gall he had to spit his cigarette on my floor as if he were outside.

Christophe pulled his head away from the page. 'What did you say?'

'Nothing.'

He stared at me for a hot moment before folding up the papers I gave him into one tight square. 'What did you do before you were a spy?' he said. 'Surely you did something.'

'I was a shop girl.'

'A shop girl?' He laughed. 'I didn't expect that from you, my dear.'

'Why? A good shop girl can make a person believe anything.'

'You have a point,' he said, searching the ceiling as he stuffed the papers into his pocket. 'Working undercover inside the Reich is a feat. You know that it will be impossible for you to be a shop girl after the war, right?'

'Why?'

'After all you've seen and done, it will be hard to live a normal life. Trust me,' he said. 'I know these things.'

'You don't know anything about me.'

I peeked out from behind the curtains onto the

square again, through a gap just big enough for one round eye. A handful of men with women dressed in long, glittering dresses that hung out from under thick fur coats, ogled at an impromptu dance performance by some students celebrating the end of the year.

'I know you're alone tonight,' Christophe said.

He wasn't dressed up either. 'Aren't we all?'

'It's part of being a spy,' he said.

Christophe went to leave but a knock at the door shoved him into the crack where the door met the wall. He motioned for me not to answer the door and be quiet. But when I heard Erwin's breathy squeals on the other side, I knew I would have to answer it. Christophe shook his head as I put my hand on the knob.

'It's Erwin,' came the voice through the door. Christophe flattened himself against the wall. 'Alex sent me.'

'I have to,' I mouthed.

I opened the door. Erwin held a package under one arm and loosened his bow tie with the other. Students filtered out of their flats wearing party gowns and flower corsages behind him. All were headed into the square, I supposed, for the big night.

'Hello,' I said.

He looked surprised to see me still dressed in my grey work suit. 'Aren't you celebrating? Your whole building is going to the Ratskeller. Special party there tonight.'

Instead of answering I waited for him to tell me what was so important that Alex had to send him over. *It had better not be to ask me out*, I thought.

He offered me the package under his arm. 'This came for you at Alex's address. He said you should have it right away. So here I am.' He tapped his foot and smiled as if he expected something for the delivery. I reached for the package and he pulled it back. 'A kiss for my trouble would be nice.'

I snatched the package from his fat hands and he huffed. 'After all I've done for you, Ella.' He walked off and I said thanks when his back was turned.

I shut my door. 'Erwin,' Christophe breathed. 'Disgusting little fellow.'

'Mmm.'

The package was small and wrapped in worn brown paper. I held it to the light and then gasped when I saw a blue rose drawn in the corner, along with the words 'happy birthday' written so faintly even Erwin probably didn't notice it. Auntie.

I tore it open. Inside, surrounded by a nest of paper confetti, was my aunt's special egg cups and a note. The details of the design were exquisite; delicate ruby-red petals rimmed in gold that shined bright yellow. Not the tarnished, common one I remembered.

'Egg cups? Why would someone send you those?'

I smiled. 'Isn't it obvious? It's my birthday.' I held them in my hands; never did I think I would have wanted to see these things again — now I never wanted to let them go.

Christophe lit a cigarette. 'Egg cups for a birthday gift?' He took a drag from his cigarette and talked as he exhaled. 'Germans are strange.'

'You wouldn't understand,' I said. 'They're

special. Family heirloom.' I imagined Auntie sitting across from me at the breakfast table, eating like a horse and looking beautiful while she did it. Something that was once so annoying was now a warm memory, and I wished I hadn't been so insensitive to her the day she tried to give them to me.

He handed me the note from the box but looked over my shoulder as I unfolded it. I expected a birthday greeting but instead got something that looked like it had come from my uncle's cipher books.

I hope you're enjoying the book about Bavarian birds.

Remember my cologne.

ZMXAB AKTOL NAKQR EXRMZ MMLTD ANZFC

TREMM TJMDA DGNPD RDLEN EBCN WPMN

'Is that code?' Christophe was suddenly very interested in what my aunt had to say. He reached for the note, but I pulled away.

'What's this book she writes about?'

'I don't know.'

I thought for a moment, but I really had no idea. Then I remembered the book she put in my pack when I left for Munich. I raced to the closet and found it behind a blanket I was too lazy to fold up. I ran my fingers over the book jacket, the image of a finch, but no words. I flipped it open, and then gasped when I saw what was inside.

'My uncle's ciphers.' The book slipped from my hand, and I stumbled backward onto the bed. I couldn't believe this whole time I had one of my uncle's cipher books in my closet.

'Your uncle writes ciphers?' He was excited; I could hear it in his voice as he flipped through the pages. 'What's your aunt's cologne?'

'Forty-seven eleven.' The only scent she'd ever worn was 4711 — the original.

He opened the book to page thirteen. 'I just added the numbers.' He motioned for the note. 'Give me the codes.'

I handed him the note, and then listened to his pencil slide across the paper as he decoded my aunt's message.

'Claudia escaped prison. She is here. Come home.'

'Claudia?' I shot straight up. 'Home!'

I raced to the window, my heart thumping, wondering what to do first. Claudia was probably waiting for me at my aunt's house, maybe even in my room. She wouldn't go to the shop — or would she?

I threw open my drawers and stuffed clothes into my rucksack while racing around the room grabbing things here and there. Then I had the most incredible thought — maybe Max would come with me? I flung open the window curtains, thinking he was in the square somewhere, headed to the Ratskeller for the New Year's party like everyone else. I looked for him in a panic, but there was too much to do. 'I need a train schedule.'

I dug through papers trying to find a list of trains.

'What are you doing?'

'What does it look like I'm doing? I'm going home,' I said, breathless. 'To Nuremberg.' I went back to the window, looking for Max. The Marienplatz was so full of people it was hard to distinguish one fancy-dressed person from another. Then I saw him, leaving our building and walking across the square. I started to pant, barely able to control myself, thinking it was all over.

I was going to give Max a big kiss right in the middle of the square where everyone could see us. I ran for the door, flinging my rucksack over my shoulder and clutching a train schedule in my hand.

Christophe yanked me back by the elbow. 'You're not leaving.'

'Why not?' I said, jeering.

'You have to ask why?' He looked like he was going to laugh, but then got very serious when he realized I had no idea what he was talking about. 'Because if you quit someone else will audit your files and you'll get caught. They'll find you in Nuremberg.'

'I'll cover it up,' I said. 'I can fix the files.'

Christophe shook his head, and I shrank from his grip and his wretched gaze. 'Face it, Sascha. You're in too deep. Now you can't get out.'

I felt nauseous and faint. My rucksack slipped off my shoulder and fell to the ground along with the train schedule in my hand. I didn't want to believe him, but he was right and I hated him for it; I had spent months doctoring files and altering reports.

'Pray your country loses this war,' he said. 'Keep passing information to me like you have, and it just might happen.'

I looked back out the window, my heart still pounding. Max was gone.

So was my dream of going home and seeing Claudia.

1943

20
February

Hoffmann sent me to Stadelheim Prison on the outskirts of Munich with a stack of files the Gestapo had ordered from the tunnel. The request: everything and everyone associated with the White Rose resistance group. We didn't have much since the Gestapo's files didn't normally mingle with the ones we had from the Reich Main Security Office, but I went anyway, and with what files I'd been ordered to bring.

I learned that morning that members of the White Rose had been caught distributing anti-Nazi leaflets in the corridors near university lecture rooms. They had already left the building but went back to toss the papers that had got stuck at the bottom of their bags. A janitor who'd been cleaning the men's toilets turned them in. One was a girl named Sophie Scholl — not Max's sister, but initially I thought it was her and my heart sank when I heard her name.

Stadelheim was one of the largest prisons in Germany and known for its use of the guillotine. Made of stone, it reminded me of Traitor's Alley in Nuremberg and just walking the corridors with the files in my arms sent an eerie chill up the back of my neck.

I was escorted into a small room that smelled as sterile as a hospital. It had a large, tinted glass window that looked into another room. Five Gestapo stood around a small table, talking casually as if they had been waiting for me to arrive. Initially they didn't seem pleased to see a woman, rolling their eyes up and down my body, judging my significance. But when I told them who I was, and what I had in my arms, they let up.

'Sit down,' one of the officers said, pointing to a plush, red office chair.

'I'm not staying long,' I said, taking the seat.

He pulled a thick file folder from a bag he had slung over the back of his chair and set it on the table. He looked close to my age, early twenties, and had a square jaw and fascinating, almost tormented steely-grey eyes. 'Let me see what you have there.' He compared the folder I'd brought side-by-side with his own. The Gestapo had always believed their interrogations were more superior than any other department's, and I was sure he was laughing inside over my file's difference in size.

The other officers left us and went into the interrogation room on the other side of the glass, dragging in a metal chair and a young man who looked strikingly similar to the one I saw running down the stairs with Max's sister. One of his eyes had swollen shut and was purple and blue from what looked like many punches to the face. The other eye, only half-open, appeared to have been slathered with some sort of jellied cream. They threw him into the chair, slamming his shoulders back. 'You did it! We have proof!' the guard yelled, and the man's head whipped back and stayed in an arched position as if he hadn't the strength to right it. They barraged him with questions, shouting at him, yet never taking a breath to let him answer.

I leaned toward the glass to get a closer look without even realizing what I was doing.

'They can't see you,' the officer said.

I nodded as if he wasn't telling me something I didn't already know and pulled a release card from my skirt pocket for the files I had brought. 'For our records.'

He looked surprised at the card, but then signed it with a wavy line as if it was his signature. 'How long can we have these here?'

'Two days,' I said. 'But if you need them longer I can extend the loan period. If you make duplicates, you'll need to send a request to Director Hoffmann.'

He took a long look at me with his steely eyes. 'Hmm.'

Another Gestapo officer came into the room and motioned for him to walk into the corridor. 'Wait here,' he said, and I found myself alone, the man being beaten on the other side of the glass screaming out for help, when I noticed what appeared to be the corner of a photo affixed to a piece of paper sticking out of the guard's folder. Sophie could be in that folder, I thought, and I reached for it, just to take a look, but then found myself bending over the table, separating one person's dossier from another, thumbing through the stack.

'You need this room?' the guard shouted from the other side of the closed door. Then I saw her, Sophie — definitely Sophie — staring at me from a black-and-white photo. The doorknob twisted, and I slipped the page from the stack. 'She's leaving,' the guard said, cracking the door open as he talked. I hastily folded the paper up and shoved it under my skirt and into my underwear just as the door opened up wide.

I fell back into my chair, a thin smile on my face.

'Give me a moment and the room's yours,' he said to someone as the door slammed shut behind him.

'Well,' I said, my heart hammering in my chest, 'if that's everything . . . ' I wondered if he could hear the paper rustling under my skirt as I stood up.

He sat down with a thump and grumbled before going back to comparing the files, not pausing for a moment to notice I'd had my hands in them. He waved me out of the room. 'Appears so. You have your release card,' he said, and I left.

I walked briskly back down the corridor, through the security checkpoint, and into the chauffeured car I had arrived in. As my car reached the prison gates, a lorry pulled up and a guard kicked out ten students from the back hatch. Each had their arms tied behind their backs while the Gestapo beat them on the ground with billy clubs.

'Do hurry, driver,' I said, trying to sound calm. 'I have lunch plans.'

'Yes, of course,' he replied.

Only after we drove through the electric gate did I feel myself breathing.

* * *

I hadn't seen Sophie since I caught her throwing leaflets from my building just after Christmas. So, she was surprised when I showed up at her flat with a wad of reichsmarks and a train schedule for all routes out of Munich.

'You need to leave,' I said. 'Now.' Even though I had stolen the sheet the Gestapo had on her, it was still too risky for her to stay in Munich.

I grabbed an empty canvas bag near the foot of her bed and started stuffing clothes from her closet into it. 'Why?' she said as I threw her a coat. 'What's going on?'

I stopped packing. *She doesn't know.*

I remembered the night Max told me about what had happened to the Falcons, and worse, when he told me Claudia was missing. Sophie's face tensed.

I looked around for her radio, but she didn't have one. 'I need noise.'

She pointed to a tiny wall shower. There was no curtain or barrier to keep the water from spraying onto her floor, just a rusty showerhead and a drain. 'Turn it on,' she said, flicking her finger at it.

I turned the lever all the way to the opposite side. The pipes behind the wall growled like the engine from a military lorry as the water blasted out of the showerhead and into the drain.

'The White Rose — ' I peered out the window. I was taking a huge risk showing up at her flat. The Gestapo could be on their way for all I knew. 'They caught them,' I said, and she completely folded to the ground.

'Who?' she said. 'Which ones?'

Something in her voice struck me. It had wavered, and I could tell she was asking a question she didn't want to know the answer to — Sophie was worried about someone in particular, someone she cared about. I closed the curtains so that just a sliver of light shone into the room and then looked directly at her.

'Sophie Scholl?' she asked, and I nodded.

She threw a hand to her mouth, clamping her lips.

It wasn't until that moment I noticed three eggs sitting near the hotplate. She was expecting company, perhaps it was Sophie Scholl and her brother.

'Put your coat on,' I said, and her whole body shook; she could barely shove her arm into her coat. 'But . . . but . . . I have nowhere to go.' I gave her the bag I'd packed, but it slipped through her fingers.

'Sophie . . . Sophie,' I said, but she'd started to weep. 'Sophie!'

Her cry trailed into a whimper, and she looked at me, suddenly listening. 'You have a chance.' There was only one place I knew she could get help. 'Go back to Nuremberg. My aunt owns an antiques shop on Obere Schmiedgasse called Alten und Neuen. She'll know what to do. Tell her Sascha sent you. But be discreet, you'll have to pretend to be a customer, buy something.'

I picked the bag up off the ground and gave it to her again, but this time she grabbed onto it. 'Are you going to tell Max I left?'

'Do you want me to?'

'He'll worry if you don't.' She started to cry

again. 'Oh, I don't want to leave!'

'Be glad you're going home.' I could hear the resentment in my own voice. 'Some of us want to and can't.'

I gave her the reichsmarks I had brought along with the train schedule. Then I turned off the showerhead and the rumble behind the wall gave way to the sound of trickling water. I saw both the sadness and uncertainty in her eyes. I wanted to say something encouraging, but the words never came.

Then we left, both going in opposite directions.

* * *

Late that night, I stopped at Max's door to tell him Sophie had left town. I picked up some common mail left in the foyer and was going to pretend to drop it off in case anyone saw me.

I knocked on his apartment door. Several seconds passed before the door cracked open. Max stuck his foot into the jamb, poking his head out, and stared at me almost as if he was unsure what to say.

'I need to talk to you,' I said. 'It's about . . . '

I was just about to tell him about Sophie when I heard the voice of a woman from inside his apartment. It wasn't the voice of someone my age, but deeper, older, more mature in a sultry sort of way, and she was calling his name.

My tongue got in the way of my words and I stuttered. 'Sorry — I didn't mean to . . . '

I turned to walk down to my flat, but his hand caught mine and he tried to pull me back. 'Wait,' he said. 'I'll tell her to go.' I wiggled from his grip and scurried down the corridor to my flat. I felt him watching me as I nervously struggled to open my door, and after I'd closed it, I still felt him watching me.

* * *

I was sitting alone at the Ratskeller, picking through a basket of tough-skinned bread, sipping a stein of beer, when a crowd of NSDAP dressed in their brown uniforms poured through the doors. The barmaids fell over themselves trying to accommodate such a large group in such a short amount of time. They were louder than normal; laughing, chatting, recounting something I couldn't quite understand. It was as if they had all just got back from a football match and were still very excited about what they'd seen.

'Did you see her limp?' someone said. 'I saw her limping.'

'What about the brother?' another one said. 'The balls of that one.'

The crowd got thicker, and the air warmed with a sweaty odour coming from their unwashed shirts. I was thinking about leaving, even though I hadn't eaten any of my dinner, when I saw my cousin, Alex. His face was full and his eyes were as wide as I had ever seen them.

'I just saw the most amazing thing,' he said, helping himself to the seat opposite me.

'Amazing is a strong word.' I looked up. 'What this time?'

The barmaid ordered everyone to be quiet as

she turned the radio up. The announcement: the leaders of the White Rose were dead. There was a strange murmur of voices as the announcer continued to talk. Then the noise of the crowd returned to where it had been.

'I got to see them die,' Alex said. 'The girl, her brother and another one named Probst. Can you believe I was lucky enough to be invited to their execution? Hell, we all were,' he said, pointing his finger at the NSDAP members he'd walked in with.

I felt ill. I wasn't sure what upset me the most, his excitement about watching someone die, or hearing what had happened to poor Sophie Scholl and the other White Rose leaders. I searched Alex's face, trying to find a hint of compassion — these were people, after all.

'Ah, it was great!' Alex said, reaching into my basket of bread. 'You should have seen it.' Alex used his teeth to tear a roll in half. Then he talked while his jaw worked its way through the leathery skin of the bread. 'I'd never seen a real guillotine before.'

One of the men Alex came in with slid into the seat next to him. His hair was blond and short just like Alex's but he smelled worse, and needed more cologne than he had on. 'That's what happens when you're a resister,' the friend said. 'You die.'

'Indeed!' Alex said as he swallowed a hunk of bread. 'It was like cutting heads off snakes.'

'If only they had quit that White Rose nonsense earlier,' his friend said. 'Can you imagine getting your head chopped off?'

He looked right at me, and the image of being dragged to the guillotine by the Gestapo pushed its way into my thoughts. I swallowed, hard, and felt every bit of my throat.

'No,' I said.

He turned to Alex. 'There's an apartment that's opened up in my building. Yeah, some businessman who was hiding Jews got caught. They sent him east with his parasites. You know . . . ' He sliced his throat with his finger, and then laughed. All I saw was his gums.

I stood to button my coat, my chair screeching against the floor, mumbling to myself only things I could understand.

Alex watched me. 'What's wrong with you?' he said. 'You're not like you used to be.'

'Wrong with me?'

'There's talk at the Braunes Haus that you're as dried up as some men's grandmas.'

Alex's friend laughed.

I gasped. 'Who says this?' I was barely nineteen.

'People.' Alex's eyes shifted to his friend and then to me, as if he had just realized he should have kept that information to himself. 'Well, it's true,' he said. 'A little bit, anyway. You used to goad me every chance you got. Now you're all business, different.'

I stared at them both as they stared at me. 'I'm too busy working.'

Alex nodded once, but I could tell he thought there was something more.

'Good day, gentlemen.'

* * *

Spring had come, but not without a good round of showers which made the grass grow green and the flowers bloom in droves. On this day, the sudden rise in temperature made everyone hot and sweaty. To make it worse, our windows had been painted shut, which made it impossible to catch a cool breath. Hoffmann shuffled in from the corridor, and I swiftly straightened up my desk, hiding the note I'd been drafting to Christophe under my desk mat. 'Why don't you go to the park, Ella.' He wiped his brow with a soiled hanky. 'It's too hot to be in here all day without some fresh air.' He looked at me while he folded up his hanky and then stuck it back into his pocket. 'I'm telling you to go. I'd be a cruel supervisor if I didn't insist.'

'You're dismissing me for the day?' My hand rested on my desk mat, thinking of the note that lay beneath for Christophe that was only half done. 'I don't understand.'

'No,' he said. 'Take a break. Write a letter outside to a friend. Isn't that what young ladies do?' He looked around my office, its bare walls, and the mound of paperwork on the edge of my desk. 'The walls must feel like they're closing in on you. Take advantage of the air outside.'

Louise passed by my office, talking to a young woman. I thought she might be giving her a tour, but by the sound of their voices I guessed they knew each other and it was a personal visit. I watched them pass, leaning back in my chair to get around Hoffmann's body, which blocked a good portion of the door.

'Ella?' Hoffmann looked annoyed. He got out the hanky he had just stuffed in his pocket to wipe his neck. 'Just do something. Go . . . take twenty minutes.'

I took my hand off my desk pad. 'All right.'

Outside, the blue chamomiles had taken over a large spot on the open green where League girls dressed in their athletic uniforms ran drills up and down the Königsplatz. These were the older girls, the Belief and Beauty members who liked to attend the NSDAP dances. It hadn't escaped my attention that the Braunes Haus was within shouting distance and several men had come outside to watch them twirl batons in their thigh-high jumpers.

I sat down at one of two tables in the common area of the Königsplatz with my pad, thinking about who to write a letter to, but I had nobody. Hoffmann didn't know, he thought he was doing me a favour. I had been alone for a long time, and I was good at suppressing my feelings, but nothing made me feel more alone than sitting down to write that letter. Out of nowhere Christophe slid into the seat opposite me. We stared at each other.

'Don't look at me like that,' he said. 'It's suspicious.'

I pushed my pad and pencil to the side. 'What?'

'I need you to find out information on Auschwitz . . . '

'What kind?' I said.

He put his arms on the table and leaned in, smiling, making it appear as if we were having a jolly conversation about the weather by pointing at the clouds. 'There are whisperings about the prisons — ' he looked over his shoulder ' — troubling plans.'

'What are you saying?' I said, and suddenly there was giggling behind me, and Christophe's eyes flicked over my head.

'Blimey,' he said. 'Louise.' He laughed as if I'd just told him a joke. 'Act natural. Here she comes.' He slid out from the seat and walked off.

Moments later I heard the shuffle of Louise's fat feet through the grass. 'Hello, Ella,' she said all cheery. The woman I'd seen her with earlier smiled beside her. They jabbed each other with their elbows as if they'd been talking about me.

'Louise.' I opened up to a blank page in my writing pad and took up my pencil.

'Well,' she said. 'Aren't you going to ask me who my friend is?'

The two of them looked at each other, smirking.

'This is my friend from Belief and Beauty.' Louise squinted her eyes. 'You asked me who my best friend was once. This is her.' I looked back at my paper and she reached over the table and tapped my notebook. 'Don't be rude. Say hello.'

'I thought I did.' I smiled at the friend. 'Hello.'

She looked as homely as Louise did in the warm spring sun with her drab brown hair pinned loose behind her neck. She picked a few of the chamomiles and stuck them into the lapel of her jacket, but being playful didn't suit her. 'So, this is Hoffmann's secretary,' she said. 'The one that delivered the White Rose leaflets to your whole building?'

My eyes jolted. 'I'm not White Rose.'

'You did deliver the leaflets,' Louise corrected.

'By accident.' I scowled. 'I was tricked by the

mail clerk.'

'Of course, that's what I meant,' she said. 'But the truth is you still delivered them.'

'Careful what you say, Louise.' I sat up tall. 'And how you say it.' Bold talk, I thought, even for Louise. 'This isn't the first time you've said nasty things to me.'

'What will you do? Take some of my duties away?' She looked at her nails, which were freshly painted and well filed. 'Shame. I should hope to be less busy.' She looked at my pad of paper. 'What are you doing out here anyway? I'm sure you have lots of work to tend to.'

'It looks like she's going to write a letter,' the friend said.

'To a friend?' Louise cackled. 'I've never seen you with anyone. Only heard you talk of this phantom friend of yours who you'd do anything for. Where's she on this beautiful day?'

Louise turned to the woman, talking loudly. 'She asked me if I had a best friend. I told her I was in the BDM and that I had lots of friends, but she said that's not what she meant.'

Her friend looked confused. 'There's a difference?'

Louise's eyes lit up. 'That's what I said!'

They both laughed, and continued as if I wasn't even there, talking about the League girls twirling their batons in the chamomiles. They must have seen me roll my eyes because they stopped talking abruptly.

'You're right,' Louise's friend said as they walked away. 'There's no way she was in the BDM. She quit after the Youth League.'

I watched them walk off together, arm in arm.

The blank page before me was still a blank page, and out of nowhere a tear spilled over my cheek and ran down my face.

21

August

The moment I ascended the staircase in the V-building I felt Louise's heavy gaze staring down upon me from the second floor. She raised one eyebrow before turning around to lean against the balustrade. Then I saw Erwin peep over her shoulder.

'She's coming,' Louise said, and Erwin's arms crossed.

Louise and Erwin had been openly dating for months. Part of me didn't like them together since Louise already had a sore spot for me, and Erwin had probably worked out I'd used him. The other part of me thought they were both perfect for each other — the scratching noise between Louise's thighs complemented Erwin's piggy squeals in a comical, almost cartoonish way. *And to think I paid her to dance with him at that NSDAP dance.*

'Good morning,' I said as I brushed past them. Erwin's nose flared while Louise watched me with her wide eyes. Neither of them said anything. 'Good morning, Ella,' I said back to myself.

Hoffmann had just returned from a lunch meeting at the Führerbau. It had been three hours since his last real drink, so I poured him some whisky and set it on the glass table next to the leather lounge chair in his office.

Beads of sweat dripped from his scalp into his

ears. He pulled his collar away from his neck, complaining about the warm room, but then lifted the glass by its rim with a shaking hand. 'Thank you for this.'

'Louise is upset at me again,' I said, closing his door. 'Hell.'

He chuckled. 'Careful, Ella. You're starting to sound like the men in the building.'

'She's dating Erwin, and I think he's upset with me too.'

'You don't have to worry about either of them,' Hoffmann said. 'You're the best secretary I've had. Erwin is a spoiled boy, and Louise, well . . . ' He looked over the rims of his glasses. 'We know how she is.'

He pulled a folded piece of paper from his back pocket and flapped it in the air until it was flat. 'I suppose this is why she's upset.' His voice gurgled with wetness. 'The Japanese are coming, and you're the chaperone.'

'What?' I snatched it from his hand: the meeting minutes. Mustard and cigar burns stained the edges, and a coffee ring darkened the middle with two different shades of brown. In the margin I saw Louise's name crossed out and mine written instead.

'But Louise has always been the chaperone.'

He downed the rest of his drink. 'Not anymore.' He motioned for a refill.

'Hiroshi Ōshima, the Japanese Ambassador, is coming with his girlfriend or whatever she is, and she refused to come if Louise was the chaperone. Apparently they had some disagreements last time,' he said, waving his finger at the whisky bottle. 'So I volunteered your services.'

I grabbed the whisky bottle by its neck but my eyes were still on the paper. 'But I don't know Japanese,' I said, pouring him another glass.

'Don't worry about that. They speak some German and you'll know some Japanese.'

'How?'

'Japanese class.'

I sat down. 'To learn Japanese?' I knew that the Reich gave language classes when foreign dignitaries came to Munich. Mostly officers and NSDAP leaders attended.

'I thought you'd be excited,' he said. 'Socializing and entertaining. Not a bad way to spend your weekend hours, is it?'

I rubbed the crook of my neck. I still had several hours of work left, followed by an evening rendezvous with Christophe. 'I have a lot going on, that's all.'

Hoffmann took off his suit jacket and got comfortable in his lounge chair. 'Hard work is what you do best, Ella. Besides, the class won't start up for a while. The entourage isn't expected until autumn.' He kicked off his shoes.

I went to the window to lower the shade; that was when I saw Louise marching up the Königsplatz with stiff determined legs, swinging her hips from left to right.

'I can't wait to try the sake,' he said.

'You're going too?'

'Well, you're *my* secretary,' he scoffed. 'They can't send you and not me, can they?'

I followed Louise with my eyes as she walked toward the Braunes Haus, thinking about Hoffmann's intentions. Why was he happy with me working late and all weekend when he had never been in the past? Then it occurred to me what he would get from his secretary escorting the Japanese — he could drink as much as he wanted, good Japanese sake, a rarity in Munich and only available to those in the entourage. He wouldn't have to worry about being watched since everyone would be under the same drunken spell. I had long since proved my ability to work long hours and multiple jobs for multiple departments. I couldn't blame him, I supposed. I watched Louise open the door of the Braunes Haus and disappear inside.

'Oh . . . now I understand,' I said, turning my back to the window.

'What?'

I flashed him a fake smile. 'Nothing, sir.'

* * *

After weeks of Japanese, I didn't learn much more than how to say and bow a proper hello. And classes were often late and tiring with mostly old men talking about the war rather than how to speak that ridiculous language.

'*Konnichiwa*,' I said, practicing a handshake in the air. No, I'd bow. '*Sayonara*,' I said, more forcefully, walking back to my office.

It was late, and Hoffmann had left, but his mess prevailed; a knocked-over rubbish bin spilled apple cores and cigarette butts onto the floor, and a slew of papers with the imprint of a shoe stamped into them bowed across the floor from his desk to the door.

My knees buckled, and I sat in the gap Hoffmann's body had made in the divan cushions. He must have passed out, then realizing how late it was, made his way home; the whisky evidently still heavy in his system, by the looks of his office. He'd expect me to pick it up. I covered my eyes with the palms of my hands and yawned, listening to the tick from Hoffmann's desk clock.

A few moments passed, and then I heard my door open and the tap of heeled shoes scoot across my office floor.

I stood up with a jolt. It was too early for the janitor and all of the workers had gone home. I went for the door that separated our offices, but tripped over Hoffmann's rubbish bin and it banged against the side of his desk with a loud clang.

I lunged for Hoffman's office door, swinging it open.

Nobody was there.

At first glance, my office looked normal. There hadn't been much time to poke around before I shot up from the divan, unless they had been in my office while I was at Japanese class. I glanced back at Hoffmann's dishevelled office; I was sure he had made most of the mess, but had he made it all?

It was then I smelled something in the air, the scent of someone other than myself hovering over my desk. Then I saw the leather desk mat on my desk pushed back and my heart sank. A list of my uncle's ciphers that had been under there was gone. It was just a list of codes, a key I sometimes used. But it didn't matter, if the ciphers fell into the wrong hands it would be dangerous, very dangerous.

I threw open my office door, frantically looking down both corridors before racing downstairs, past the building guard and out the front doors and into the street, arms pumping. Two officers were about to get into a chauffeured car, nothing out of the ordinary. But the bus? Louise was just boarding it, tucking papers into her canvas shoulder bag.

She walked the length of the bus and sat down in the very back, smiling like a fat-faced cat, patting her bag. As the bus pulled away from the kerb her eyes shifted toward mine.

I gasped.

The bus guzzled away, leaving a grey plume of exhaust that settled like fog.

'That . . . that . . . ' I growled, fists clenched, cursing Louise in my mind.

Then everything grew very quiet in the street outside the V-building . . . static. The officers out front had walked away from their car and stepped onto the pavement, staring, studying, deciphering my actions.

* * *

That night I woke with a jolt, sweating from head to toe and gasping for air. I threw off the covers and sat in the dark, panting, remembering my dream.

Erik sat across from me at the conference table, which had been set for a very large meeting. Louise whispered into his ear and he tipped the table over, screaming madly. Suddenly Hans appeared with a leaflet in his hands. 'I was never a Falcon.' He laughed with Louise, and they pointed at my throat where I'd been stabbed with one of Hoffmann's broken whisky bottles.

'It was just a dream,' I said, clamping my throat. 'A Goddamn dream.'

An orange flame flickered near my window and the outline of Christophe's face greyed with its light. 'Looked like a nightmare to me,' he said.

'Jesus!' I said, shouting into a whisper. 'What the hell are you doing here?'

'You missed the drop. I thought you might be dead.'

I put my hands to my eyes and rubbed them closed. 'That's comforting.'

He walked to the shelf above my desk and flicked the corner of my yellow scarf hanging out of its box.

'I was at Japanese class,' I said.

'Where's the bag?' he asked. 'The papers you promised me?'

I pointed under my bed to a laundry bag filled with men's clothes, the papers stuffed in one of the trouser pockets.

'I asked you months ago about plans for the prisons,' he said. 'Have you heard anything?'

I shook my head, still holding my throat where it was now tingling. 'No,' I said. 'But you're right. Something is going on. I'm dismissed from the administration meetings when the prisons are brought up. There's no meeting minutes.' I swallowed. 'I'll keep trying.'

He tucked his cigarette into his lips, slid the bag out from under my bed and heaved it over one shoulder. I wiped my head and my arms of sweat.

'What's going on with you?' A slick of dark hair fell over his eyes. He brushed it back and I saw his scar.

'My office was ransacked today.' An icy chill bumped up my back, breaking the sweat, and I pulled the covers over my legs. 'Someone's on to me.'

His lit cigarette fell from his lips just as the bag thumped to the floor. He dropped to his knees, squaring his face with mine. 'Did they get anything?' A heavy, natural British accent replaced the German one. Christophe was the only person I spied for; all trails led to him. We both knew this, but the tone in his voice made me think he had never thought it could actually happen until then.

I jabbed him hard in the soft part of his chest. 'Back off!' I snarled. 'Jesus.' I had never talked to him with such veracity before.

He paused, waiting for the story. 'Well?'

I picked his cigarette off the floor, pinched the part his mouth had sucked on and puffed on it until it glowed. 'Erik's secretary hates me, Louise, you know her. She went through my desk. She took a list of codes, but that's it.'

A wave of relief washed over his face, then he snatched his cigarette from my mouth. 'You'll have to get her fired.' He glanced at my breasts and his eyes widened. I looked down. Even in dull light their silhouettes under my cream camisole erased all imagination. He flicked his index finger at my chest. 'Shag him and you can have the whole building.'

'Ugh!' I pulled the covers up to my chest. 'Are

all Brits this vulgar or just you?'

He paced around the room thinking, saying things in English before getting in my face. 'Look, if you pissed her off, all right. But if she suspects you of being a resister, or worse, a spy for the British, then we have a problem. Either way, you need to get rid of her and get on with it. If not through Erik, then with a knife.'

'I am not killing anyone!' Louise probably had been searching my office for something to embarrass me with or get me fired. She resented the superiority I had at Nazi Headquarters; I had taken her spot in many ways. Becoming the Japanese chaperone, which had always been her job in the past, was most likely the last straw. Finding the codes might have confused her, but if I gave her some time, she'd just dig deeper.

'I guess you have your answer then,' he said.

I shook my head. 'It's not that easy.'

'I've seen you work, Sascha. That night at the dance with Halder's assistant — you're no shrinking violet.'

'With this one I am,' I said. 'He doesn't even know my name, calls me Eva. He's not the type that can be charmed with champagne, or just a dance — God!' I put my hand to my forehead.

'I can tell you're worried,' he said.

I glared at him for interrupting my thoughts.

'Time to put your big-girl knickers on and do what's necessary — not all of it will be pleasant. Understand?'

'If you knew how old I was, you wouldn't talk to me like that,' I said.

'If you knew how old I was we wouldn't be

alone in your room together! Just remember, if your cover gets blown so does mine, and a whole bunch of other people I can't tell you about.'

'Big-girl knickers? And when am I supposed to do this?'

Christophe shrugged. 'Find a way to get rid of her — take her job if you have to. You do most of it already.'

Erik planned to accompany the Japanese entourage too. Louise wouldn't be around to sabotage me, and if the sake was as good as I'd heard, it might be my best chance to cosy up to him.

The morning sunlight dawned on the Marienplatz and a soft orange glow filtered through my window. They day had begun, and I had to get to work.

'You need to go,' I said, waving him out of the room, 'and I need to think.'

22

October

The Japanese had arrived. A bright Nazi-red carpet, specially rolled out for Ambassador Ōshima, ran from the double glass doors of the Regina Palast Hotel and into the street. Hoffmann and I stood at the end, sandwiched between the gutter and four toadies from the Wehrmacht with body-sized flags projecting from metal poles; the Nazi Cross in one hand, Japan's Imperial Rising Sun in the other. Across the carpet, men from all departments, military brass to straight-faced officers of the Reich, lined the edge with the tips of their shoes touching the carpet.

Weathered leaves fell from the trees and into the street. A few of them tumbled down the carpet toward the road; shifting eyes followed them, afraid to move out of formation. Hoffmann leaned into my ear. 'Remember, treat her like a princess.'

I took a deep breath. 'I will.' My mind was on Erik, and how I was going to get him alone, hopefully, and talk about firing Louise. I hadn't thought about my actual job of escorting the little Japanese princess, even though Hoffmann reminded me every chance he got.

'Thank God there's a bombing reprieve,' Hoffmann said, pointing to the rain-swelled sky. 'The weather came just in time.'

'Yes,' I said, turning to him. 'Thank God.'

And we waited, waited for the rain, and waited for the Japanese, near shivering. Then a black Mercedes 240D crept up out of nowhere and from the opposite direction. Officers and dignitaries shifted around, not sure what to make of the vehicle coming to a screaming halt next to the kerb.

The driver opened the door and we all leaned forward to get a glimpse of the Japanese inside. Then long legs pivoted from the backseat to the kerb.

'I thought the Japanese were short,' I whispered from the corner of my mouth.

Hoffmann tilted his head near mine. 'I thought so too.'

Erik leapt to the front of the carpet to greet Ambassador Ōshima, stepping on my foot to get in close. I yelped with a hop, but he looked at Hoffmann and apologized.

Hoffmann patted my shoulder, and I put on a smile amidst throbbing toe pain.

Erik shook the ambassador's long-wristed hand, but then all attention turned to the white umbrella that had poked out from the car door.

I heard someone whistle low, then the umbrella sprung open with a fluttered snap. Iridescent blue and green birds ran along the edges of the umbrella. In the middle, and offset like a pair of eyes, were two giant, double-stitched dark brown almonds.

Hoffmann elbowed me. *The girlfriend.*

She held the umbrella in such a way that it shielded her face. Three black barrel-rolls of hair lined the top rim. She spun the umbrella clockwise and the birds appeared to fly, yet the almonds never changed and still looked very much like eyes. The umbrella stopped spinning, and Hoffmann elbowed me again. Two satin red shoes popped out from under a long, bluish-grey robe embroidered with violet ribbons that feathered into shades of pink. A tiny, gloved hand reached for the chauffeur's. Her feet scooted across the carpet like a centipede until she stood in front of me and bowed, just slightly, before moving the umbrella away from her face.

'May I present Toyoka,' the chauffeur said.

'*Konnichiwa*, Toyoka. I'm Ella Strauss, your chaperone.'

She straightened from her bow. Rosy cheeks buoyed powdered white skin. Her subtle smile brimmed with confidence. 'Mmm,' she said just above a whisper.

Erik kept trying to lead Ōshima into the hotel, but the ambassador stalled and seemed to be waiting for Toyoka.

I smiled, not sure what Japanese word I should be uttering to get her to move when she turned slowly away from me, first with her body, then with her head, and floated up the carpet like a puff of air behind Erik and the ambassador.

A roll of thunder passed overhead. I took a deep breath, grasping my throat. *This is it.*

Just as I crested the double doors to the foyer of the hotel, rain poured from the dark bulges of the clouds, and it ticked against the pavement with intervals of speed that sounded remarkably like gunfire.

* * *

At five past six in the evening, I arrived at Toyoka's room on the top floor of the Regina Palast Hotel to escort her to the main dining room. I hadn't even knocked on her door before she burst into the corridor and told me I was late.

I apologized with a slight smile, bowing.

Her dinner kimono was scarlet red with thin white ribbons that burst upward from its hem and mushroomed into pools of cream, which made me feel very underdressed in my grey dinner suit. 'You look lovely tonight, Toyoka,' I said in my best Japanese.

She blew onto her shoulder, dusting it with her fingertips. 'Yes,' she said, slowly. 'I do.' She spoke perfect German with a slight Japanese accent, but she didn't sound odd like I had expected. Instead, she sounded exotic.

We walked to the main dining room together, pausing just inside the double doors. Rectangle dinner tables had been arranged in the shape of a giant swastika. Brand new white tablecloths with creases down the middle covered every one. A wheeled metal tray wedged in the corner filled with flutes of champagne and ornate, ceramic steins of beer completed the room.

Ambassador Ōshima and Toyoka had seats reserved in the middle marked by two matching red chair covers. 'Your seat is . . . '

She pointed across the room with a bent wrist and smiled. 'Over there?' Her lips curled at the edges, and for a moment she reminded me of Louise. 'Yes, I can see that.' Before walking over, she turned to me. 'And stop trying to speak my language.' She smiled thinly. 'You're horrible at it.'

Toyoka walked away and I heard Hoffmann's

voice in my head. *Treat her like a princess.* I chased after her.

The chairs closest to Toyoka went first. Metal legs intertwined and clinked together like sharp knives as officers jockeyed for a good seat. A slippery smile smoothed across her face as she watched them fight for her attention.

Platters of roasted pork that fanned out family-style were positioned onto red and black table runners adorned with a thousand miniature swastikas. Ash-coloured china from Dresden rimmed in silver offset crystal goblets filled with the reddest of red wine. Normally this type of set up wouldn't go together, the elegance of formal and the cosiness of family-style, but the Japanese liked it that way, said it was the perfect blend of culture and civility.

Erik sat down directly across from me, next to Ambassador Ōshima, wearing a cunning smile meant for himself. He adjusted his brown NSDAP tie with one hand and leaned onto the table with the other. I didn't have an official plan for that evening, other than for him to take notice of me. I could talk about all the work I'd been doing, most of it Louise's duties, and see where the conversation went. But none of that was going to happen if I couldn't get Erik to talk to me first.

I closed my eyes briefly. Christophe had told me to seduce him.

I gulped my glass of wine down as if it were a shot of whisky, pulled the vee of my blouse forward just a hair and then rubbed my swastika pendant with two fingers.

With a long exhale I lowered my eyes into a

sexy glower, as sexy as I thought sexy could be, and studied Erik through the steaming mound of pork that separated us.

My heart raced as I rose from my seat, bent over the meat and fingered the salt-shaker near his right hand. My chest warmed from the heat of the meat as I paused over the platter and started to sweat.

'Are you using this?'

I rested two limp fingers on the head of the shaker. I waited for Erik's eyes to glance at mine, but he waved me away and turned toward the ambassador. Toyoka shot up from her chair and snapped her fingers for the waiter.

'Sake for the officers!' she said in a forceful, very German tone.

My eyes darted to hers, and her raised eyebrows pushed me back into my chair.

'My Toyoka . . . she thinks of everything,' Ambassador Ōshima cooed.

A cheer erupted in her honour, and glasses clinked in the air as the waiters brought out bottles of Japanese sake. Toyoka giggled and sat on the edge of her seat, a perspiring glass of water clutched in her hand. Erik went behind the ambassador's back, cupped his hand near his mouth, and whispered something into Toyoka's ear that made her smile. When Erik dropped his hand, I heard him say Toyoka's name perfectly.

By the end of the dinner all the men were drunk. Hoffmann waved from the far end of the table, a glazed, placid look hanging on his face. I waved back and he tipped his glass at me. Ambassador Ōshima and Erik smoked cigars and sipped brandy until the dinner had run its course and people started to leave.

I walked Toyoka back to her suite, but when I tried to leave she grabbed my arm and tugged me inside. 'Stay here,' she said, disappearing behind a dressing screen. I glanced at my watch: ten minutes till ten. Erik would probably be taking the ambassador to a beer hall soon, but I didn't know which one. I'd have to leave now if I was going to catch them.

'I'm sorry, I have to go.'

Her stiff finger poked out from behind the dressing screen and pointed at the ground. 'Sit!'

Moments passed, and then her kimono flopped over the top of the screen. I cringed and waited as moments turned into minutes, the irritation of her request turning into something more. I glanced at my watch again: ten o'clock. I huffed loud enough for her to hear me, but then she started to sing. It began as a light hum, then escalated into more of a song. Notes bent with a wavy melody, reminding me of my aunt when she used to sing before my uncle left. If my night had gone better I would have allowed myself to enjoy it.

Toyoka stopped singing mid-note and peeped around the corner. An earthy, olive glow had replaced the white powder from her face. 'A woman should always know how to sing,' she said. 'Can you sing, Fräulein Strauss?'

'*Nein*,' I blurted.

She smiled as if she already knew the answer. 'Of course.'

She walked out from behind the dressing screen. Her kimono was purply-pink, like a bruise, and veined in yellow. With both hands she lifted her garment at the knees, sat on bended feet and lit a fire with a sprig of kindling.

'You can take the pins out of my hair anytime,' she said, with a shake of her head.

'I'm your chaperone, Toyoka. Not your maid.'

She sat silently with her back to me, fanned her fingers out and gazed at her nails. Crackling embers shot from the fireplace and speckled the ground as she shook her head again. She had an egotistic sexuality about her that was somewhat intimidating, and I saw the way she used it, the men melting in her hands. I knew she could make trouble for me if she wanted.

I pulled my skirt up over my knees and knelt down on the ground, picking those pins out, one-by-one.

'Hurry up, secretary.'

Twenty minutes later I was still pulling pins from her head. The fire roared with giant orange flames and my cheeks reddened along with my temper. I wanted to call her a name, something nasty. But Hoffmann's request pulled my voice back, and I spoke it in French.

'*Salope*,' I said, gritting the word through my teeth. *Bitch.*

She put her hands gently in her lap and I swore I heard a light chuckle come from her mouth. Finally, I pulled the last pin out of her hair, flicking it to the ground.

'I don't have time to be your hairdresser.'

I stood up from the floor and she caught my hand. Her dark almond eyes widened to round. 'You should be thanking me for keeping you here so long,' she hissed. 'You made a fool of yourself, hovering over mounds of pork. That is no way to get a man's attention!'

My jaw dropped. 'How did you — '

'Stop!' She jerked on my hand as if her voice wasn't harsh enough. 'Don't insult me. I invented that game.'

'Game?'

Toyoka hopped to her feet to walk to her dresser. She opened a padded, purple satin box that had a golden almond bead for a clasp. Jewellery and coins jangled together as she rummaged through it.

'How do you think I got here? Do you think it luck? Please. A girl makes her own luck. You know that, by now you must.'

My eyes skirted around her room. The door to her wardrobe was open. Kimonos of every colour hung from puffed black hangers. On the floor, six pairs of satin heels, one studded with jewels. A glimpse of her bedroom through a set of pocket doors revealed a crystal decanter on the nightstand half full with water next to a bed sprinkled with pink rose petals.

She plucked a black drawstring bag from the box and dangled it on one finger. 'Why do you think I ordered all that sake? They'll be drunk for hours and I'll be in here enjoying my things.' She waved her hand across the room, a bangle of gold slid from her elbow to her wrist. 'Ambassador Ōshima has his own room and by tomorrow he won't remember if he had me or not. And I prefer it not.'

She snapped the lid on the box and slinked

toward me. Her hair slid off her shoulders and down the middle of her back. It was black as tar but shined silky smooth in the fire's light.

'You can serve your ta-tas on a plate, but you will never get that Erik's attention like you will with this.' She opened the bag and pulled out a men's straight razor with a black grip. Its blade shined like a knife and looked sharp enough to cut a steak. 'Men want what they've never had.' Toyoka slapped the razor into the palm of my hand, and then paused with a sly smile. 'I want to help you because you look like a fool, and I can't have a fool escorting me around and all over the place.'

She pulled on my hand. 'You Europeans are so hairy. Think it is okay to be bushmen. Start at your ankles and go all the way up. Only you can decide when to stop.' My fingers curled around the razor's handle and she let go of my hand. 'Trust me. You will get his attention.'

'All the way up?' Auntie said only prostitutes shaved above their knees.

'Enough!' she yapped, gliding toward her covered balcony. 'If you want to be a little girl about it then continue doing what you're doing. But if you want a chance with this man, you try it my way.' She opened the door to her balcony and the room got cold. 'And the last chaperone that called me a bitch got demoted.' Her eyes lowered to a glare. *She knows French.* 'I'll let that one slide.' She stepped out onto the balcony and then shut the doors behind her.

* * *

I stood outside my building in the pouring rain, staring up at Max's window. The light was on, and I saw the shadow of at least one person through the drawn curtains. I squeezed the razor in my hand, thinking about what tomorrow would bring. I had wasted one day, and I felt time slipping away from me with nothing to show for it. Toyoka was right; I *was* doing it all wrong.

I had never felt so alone and lonely all at one time.

I don't remember walking into my building, or up the stairs. But I do remember standing at my door, thinking about Louise, when I heard Max call my name from his opened door. It had been months since I heard his voice, which made my heart flutter. I knew I shouldn't turn around, but the longing for what was weakened me just enough.

I felt dreadfully ugly dripping in the corridor wet with rain, staring at him.

'What are you doing?' He was half-dressed and bare-chested; he had either just got out of bed or was just getting in it. 'I saw you standing outside for an hour. Are you well?'

My chin quivered, and I swallowed, my eyes flicking behind him, looking for signs that he had another woman in his room. 'Are you . . . alone?'

He searched my face for an explanation before nodding.

Then we hugged very tightly, not saying a word, until all my cold parts had turned warm.

We slipped into his apartment together, and he whispered in my ear. 'It's only been you, Ella, only you.'

And we closed the door behind us.

* * *

I woke up several hours later in Max's bed, believing our night together had been a dream, thinking of his hands sliding down my body, his kisses, and his voice in my ear telling me I was the only one for him. I stretched lazily, thankful for the dream, but then sat bolt upright, looking at him, and then to the window where the sun was breaking, and then to him again.

I slapped my palm to my forehead, squeezing my eyes shut. *What have I done?* My breath picked up and my heart too, wondering if anyone saw me enter his room, when his hand searched the sheets for me, a body part to hold onto.

I slipped away and hurriedly gathered up my clothes from the floor, but then took one last moment to feel the reality of being in his room and hear him slumbering, peacefully, before he realized what I'd done to him. I closed my eyes. *Oh Max.*

I felt the razor in my coat pocket. I glanced at Max to make sure he was still asleep, and then to his vanity and at a tube of shaving cream. Time was running out. I sneaked out backward, out the door and down to my flat with that tube in my pocket.

23

The tang of warmed apples, potato pancakes and savoury sausages hovered over every table in the Regina Palast's breakfast room. I sat dutifully next to Toyoka in a hard wooden chair. A set of double doors that led out to the patio kept opening, and with each waft of air I crossed my shaven legs, which felt naked and awkward — I hadn't found a way to sit comfortably. After the third time, Toyoka snapped me in the shoulder with her paper fan, clenching her jaw.

'Stop it,' she gritted. 'Leave it to me. Sit still and look pretty.'

Erik breezed into the room with his blond hair clumped into slicks of pale yellow, searching the crowd, smoothing the sleeve of his pressed NSDAP uniform. His cool blue eyes skimmed right over me and landed on Toyoka.

Toyoka rose from her seat, touched Erik's swastika cuffband with a flat palm, and pointed to a chair with a white napkin slung over the back of it directly across from me. 'Director Koch.' Erik called for some coffee with a wave of his hand, smiling at Toyoka as she smoothed her jet-black hair back.

A gloved waiter brought plates loaded with food to our table, but Toyoka wouldn't touch her meal until Ambassador Ōshima had arrived. When he did come in, he stood at the entrance, looking long and skinny with a wobble in his knees from too much sake and weiss beer the night before.

Toyoka covered her mouth with her fan. 'When your man bends down, make sure he sees your legs.'

I nodded, eyes looking straight.

'And when you leave, always look back, just at the last minute.'

I looked at her, surprised. 'Why?'

'You ask too many questions,' she snipped.

The ambassador motioned for Toyoka and she bolted from her chair, knocking the table hard with her hip as she rushed to his aid. Erik's fork fell to the ground and vanished under the table. When I felt it hit the tip of my shoe my heart skipped.

Erik flipped the red breakfast linen back, took a quick glance under the table, and then ducked under the leaves to retrieve his fork. I fluffed my skirt up when he lifted it off my shoe — there was a pause — then I felt his breath, warm and blowing in short huffs against my silky shaven leg.

Ambassador Ōshima and Toyoka were standing at our table now, Toyoka subtly holding him by the arm. 'Where's Director Koch?' the ambassador said, looking around the table.

Erik bumped the table from underneath, water pitchers shook from the jolt and milk spilled onto the red linen. His fingers gripped the edge of the table, pulling himself up.

He rubbed his head with one hand and wiped slobber from his lips with the other, looking at me, his face white.

'Drop something, Director?' Toyoka purred.

He held his fork prong side up. 'I found it.'

'Oh, that's good,' she sighed.

The ambassador pulled out Toyoka's chair. She shifted her eyes between Erik and me and smiled to herself as she lowered her bottom into her seat.

Erik leaned forward on the table with one elbow and studied me as if it was the first time he'd ever laid eyes on me. I twisted a lock of loose hair into a ringlet. Another officer talked into Erik's ear; he nodded but I could tell by the light in his eyes all his attention was on me.

'Ella has been the perfect chaperone.' Toyoka's eyes swung to Erik, her face turning porcelain and her eyes sinking with inflection. 'Certainly better than that Louise you stuck me with last time.'

I blushed, swatting my hand. 'Toyoka, it's my pleasure.' I took a short sip of hot tea with my pinky pointed stiffly in the air.

Erik ignored Toyoka, studying me with glowing eyes. 'Ella,' he said, slowly and full of breath. It was the first time I had heard him say my name correctly.

I pushed my plate away, rose from the table and excused myself in a light voice.

I felt Erik's eyes trail me to the exit, and my hips swung from the pressure. A concerned head waiter stopped me at the door with a light touch to my arm. He tried to read my face, worried the food wasn't good enough.

'Fräulein Strauss, you are finished?'

I looked over my shoulder like Toyoka told me to do, and followed my footprints all the way back to Erik's rifled eyes. His hard wink let me know I was in his crosshairs.

I fluffed my hair with one hand, because I wasn't sure what else to do, and looked at the waiter. 'I believe I am.'

* * *

Toyoka ordered lunch brought to her room; a mixture of raw carrots, celery and boiled chicken cut into long strips. Puffed red pillows circled the ground; her stern finger told me where to sit. She slipped on an afternoon robe made of orange satin. It cascaded behind her into a short train of embroidered black lace that rippled across the floor as she floated to her seat on a pillow.

She heaped vegetables into a pile and poured a fishy black liquid over it. Then she spooned it onto crisp cabbage leaves, placed a piece of chicken on top and rolled it into something that resembled a fat cigarette.

'Your food is horrible,' she quipped. 'I thought you should eat something tasteful for a change.'

She handed me a plate with two black sticks she meant for me to eat it with. A gold locket in the shape of an almond dangled from her neck and swung back and forth as she bent forward. I glanced at the pendant and then to her jewellery box as I picked at my cabbage roll. Then I looked at the white umbrella she used on the red carpet leaning against the wall — almonds were everywhere.

The roll sprung open like a bomb and bits of food exploded out of it. I set the sticks down, and the tiny hairs on the back of my neck stood up. *Something isn't right.* I set my plate on the floor just as she took a bite of her cabbage roll.

'*Why* are you helping me?'

She paused, mid-chew and swallowed. 'Help? I told you why already.'

I stared at her, my back straightening.

Toyoka looked at me as if wondering what she should say, but then after a long pause, she sighed heavily and threw her head back. 'I was thrown to the wolves not long ago and my partner was taken from me,' she said. 'I know how hard it is to be by yourself. How hard it is to be a spy.'

My mouth hung open, pushing my plate away. 'Oh my God.'

She hopped to her feet and walked to the balcony. Rain spit on the glass door and clouded into a watery shield. Her body slinked up against the wood moulding, and her eyes stared lazily at the water tracks as if caught in a deep-seeded memory. 'I snaked my way into the pants of this government,' she said, tugging on the locket around her neck. 'It was life or death for me.' There was a long pause, then her hand felt its way down her hip until she found two cigarettes hidden in a lace pocket. She glided back to her pillow, bent to her knees and offered me a smoke with the sway of her gold-bangled wrist. I hesitated.

'How did you know — '

'Please.'

She glanced at the yellow scarf peeking out of my front pocket. Age had separated the threads from its hem. 'Nobody keeps a scarf that ugly,' she said, 'and we have a mutual friend.'

'Christophe — '

'Shh!' She pushed two red-painted fingers against my lips. 'Don't say his name.' She tossed the cigarette onto my lap and then lit her own. After a few puffs, she unclasped the locket from her neck and hooked it around mine. 'Inside is a ground herb,' she said, cigarette dangling from her lips. 'It's Japanese medicine, to help them dream.' Her eyes thinned into tiny slits as she centred the almond into the vee of my blouse. 'It works fast. Imply sex and he'll believe he had it, all the while you could be painting your nails.'

'How am I supposed to do that?'

Toyoka paused, her lips thinning as much as her eyes. 'Now is not the time to be a weakling! I'm putting myself at risk helping you, silly girl. Don't you understand?'

'I'm — '

'Trails are everywhere. If you get caught, and the Gestapo figure out who our friend is, I'm dead too.' Toyoka sat back on her pillow and exhaled. 'I've done my job well, making sure the information I've leaked looks like it came from Ambassador Ōshima, not me — fool that he is. But that can change. It just takes one mistake, from any one of us with ties to our . . . friend.'

'I'm not a weakling,' I said, 'and don't worry.'

Toyoka hopped off the floor and walked to her bedroom, flicking her cigarette into the fireplace as she passed. She paused in the pocket doors that opened into her room and sighed. 'I'll see you tonight.' Then she snapped the doors closed behind her and left me alone in the parlour.

I grabbed a lighter and hastily lit the cigarette she'd given me, sucking most of it away with three long, painful puffs. The almond locket felt heavy on my chest, and between my fingertips when I rubbed it. Tonight.

I threw the butt into the fireplace and left.

* * *

That night I escorted Toyoka to the Hofbräuhaus for the evening cool down; it was what happened after a day of nation building — Germany needed Japan's war in the Pacific to prevail against the Americans, yet flattery and promises were about all Germany could offer. The cool down was a time to relax. Shop-talk was over and officers could talk frankly; they didn't have to portray a sense of equality in the face of the Japanese — a country the Reich believed was inferior in many ways, albeit they were our allies.

Toyoka and I stood inside the foyer of the Hofbräuhaus, in a gap near the hostess' podium and the wide staircase that went to the second-floor restaurant. She smoothed her red, fitted kimono over her hips and straightened its collar. It looked almost like a real dress, hemmed above her ankles with pink chrysanthemums embroidered into the bodice, but it shined like the rubies on her fingers and clung to her skin like wet paint.

She swung her eyes up and down my body. I was wearing an off-white dress with a plunging neckline and the highest of high heels. I had also dusted my eyelids with sparkly blue powder and coated my lashes with thick, black eyelash dye. 'I'm glad you decided to look like a woman tonight. I'm sick of your grey suits.' She pinched the cap sleeve. 'Cream-coloured fabric, tight belt around your waist. This dress *almost* makes you look like a virgin. That is good.'

I rolled my eyes down her dress; the curve of her breasts, the bend of her hips and the slope of her rear looked as taut as the dress itself. Her hair was bound in the back and split into two halves, a red ribbon set deep in the middle.

'You too,' I said.

She laughed, and I smiled, but then rubbed my hands, which had started to shake.

Ambassador Ōshima waved to her from the far side of the room, across a table full of plainly-dressed Party leaders. Erik sat next to him, the only one dressed in his NSDAP uniform, craning his neck around the table to catch a glimpse of who the ambassador was waving to. Toyoka waved her beaded crystal bag in the air. 'There he is.' She looked at my trembling hands, and then scolded me with her face. 'Toss your hair, silly girl. He's watching.'

I flipped my hair from side to side, letting it bounce against my neck.

'Good girl.' She fixed a lock of hair that had slipped from the ivory hairclip above my ear. 'Follow my lead, understand?'

I nodded, but I was still unsure.

'Hard part is over.' She smiled. 'He's interested. Now you need to finish it.' She smiled even more and talked through the thin gap between her lips. 'Because if you don't we're both dead.' She yanked me into the crowd.

The ambassador reached out for her, smiling, but then his face fell.

'You left me waiting at the door!' Toyoka snapped, suddenly looking visibly upset.

'I thought your chaperone was bringing you at eight,' the ambassador stuttered. 'Not seven.' His eyes sparred with mine.

She wiggled from the crook of my arm and sat on his lap, her sparkling jewelled wrist wrapped around his neck. She kissed the top of his bald head with full lips. 'Then let's blame the chaperone,' she said with a choppy laugh. 'I think she's half-French.'

Her voice snipped just one cut away from what the others would think was a fight. Men froze, some with beers held to their lips, shifting their eyes between me and Toyoka. Others collectively groaned, appalled by her insinuation.

It was an aggressive remark, one that couldn't be overlooked. I had to put her in her place. It was a matter of superiority.

'Humph!' I sauntered over to Erik and butted my hip against the table.

His eyes were large and wide, as if wondering how I was going to handle her dig. I had to be tough, yet agreeable. I took the stein from Erik's hands. 'You Japanese have no sense of time.' I took a long gulping drink of beer. 'Rising sun . . . your flag looks like a damn clock.' I slammed the stein on the table, leaving a dark gash carved into the wood. There was a short pause, then a pitched cackle erupted from Toyoka's mouth and she dipped her head as a conciliatory gesture. Every German at the table cheered. The ambassador mumbled and raised his stein in the air, but it tipped over and white bubbles of beer spilled across the table — the cheers got louder.

Toyoka poked Erik's swastika cuffband with the corner of her bag. 'As I said before, this one's better than that Louise.'

The barmaid brought us some steins of beer.

I handed one to Toyoka but she pushed it back. The ambassador pointed to a tall glass of water he had got for her an arm's reach away. She smiled and kissed his liver-spotted cheek.

Erik made three men leave so that I could sit opposite him on the other side of the table. I sat down, back straight as a board, pivoted my legs under the table and locked them at the knees. He leaned forward and rested one elbow on the gash I had made with his stein, excitement pulsing in his lips.

'Your eyes look blue tonight,' he blurted.

A chuckle danced from the corner of my mouth. 'My eyes? When have you looked into my eyes?' I reached deep into my cleavage and pulled out a thinly rolled cigarette that Toyoka had given me earlier. With her eyes set on the ambassador, she slid her golden lighter across the table to me, and I lit the cigarette with strong, heavy puffs. Smokes were nearly outlawed in the Reich buildings, but at the beer halls one could still enjoy its pleasures, though only the brave dared to do it.

'I've seen your eyes,' he said in a sultry, almost syrupy voice.

'Mmm.' I batted my lashes. 'My eyes.' I thought about the times he had called me Eva, or when he'd pass me in the corridor without a glance. That didn't bother me, but when I thought about him stepping on my foot just two days ago, I wanted to blow smoke in his face.

'How long have you worked at the V-building?'

I had a feeling this was Erik's way of making conversation with me, as if he really had noticed me and valued my work.

'A long time,' I said, flicking ash from my cigarette. 'Honestly, I'm not sure why I'm not the only secretary. I've acquired almost all of Louise's job duties. There's no need for her.'

'You have?' Erik looked confused, and I didn't blame him. Louise was very good at looking busy.

'As I recall it was you who passed her duties on to me,' I said. 'I really think I deserve a promotion.'

'You want to be my secretary?'

'That would be your choice to make.' I smiled. 'Now wouldn't it?'

Another officer at our table piped up. 'Louise isn't nice!' he said, taking a drink. 'I wouldn't miss her — don't know anyone who would.'

Toyoka waved down two wandering soldiers and offered them the seats next to me. Their warm thighs squished me on both sides, and we swayed to music, which made Erik fidget in his seat. I laughed loud when they made jokes and listened with a bent neck when they whispered in my ears. When one of them pawed me with heavy, feeling hands, Erik's eyes bulged along with the muscles under his shirt. Then, close to midnight, just when I thought Erik was going to jump right out of his skin, I made my move.

'Toyoka, I'm afraid we need to go.' I looked at my watch. It had stopped working, but I tapped it as if it still worked.

She recovered from a forced laugh and swung a pair of lazy eyes toward me. A slight sneer pulled at her lip. 'I am not leaving.' She scoffed. 'I'm staying here with my man.' She patted the ambassador's hand and arched her back so that her chest moved closer to his mouth.

I got up from the table slowly and let Erik watch me as I smoothed my dress against my thighs. I leaned into Toyoka's ear and whispered, 'Thank you.'

She winked. 'I'll see you later.'

Our eyes connected, and I paused. We both knew she was leaving early in the morning and my duties as her chaperone ended at the Hofbräuhaus. But like her, I nodded as if we really would meet again.

I saw Erik get out of his seat as I slinked my way through the crowd. When I got to the front doors, I turned to confront him. A small crowd of service staff that had gathered in the foyer stood shell-shocked, as if witnessing an arrest.

'You can't leave,' he said.

'Of course I can.'

He put one hand flat on the wall, about neck high to keep me from walking away. 'I mean, you can't go alone,' he said.

'Are you offering me a ride home, Director Koch?'

He smiled with teeth but didn't say anything.

I flicked my head toward the door. 'Let's go.'

* * *

Erik stopped short of my building and the tyres on his 1939 Adler slid across the wet pavement when he pushed on the brakes. I jolted forward, but his thick-coated arm kept me in my seat.

I feared he would move fast once we got into my flat. I thought having a boyfriend would imply

I had other loyalties and he'd have to work to get me into bed, since I needed time to get Toyoka's herb into his body. 'My boyfriend thanks you for driving me home safe.'

His face dropped. 'Your boyfriend?'

'Mmm. In fact, he'd probably appreciate it if you walked me to my flat.' I smiled. 'Perhaps I should offer you some whisky . . . as a thank you for taking me home, of course.'

He tugged on his collar with one hand, loosening it from his neck. 'I have time.' He raced around the car and opened my door. I let him soak in the rain for a moment before I placed my hand in his; it was calloused and burly. Not what I expected from an officer of the Reich.

I tiptoed up the stairs in front of him, but Erik made no excuses for his excitement, planting his feet onto each step with such force, the hanging ceiling light swayed back and forth. Once we were at my door, all I wanted to do was get inside before Max saw us. I jammed the key into the hole and gave it a quick jerk. Then I heard Max's door crack open and my heart moved to my throat.

His door swung open just as mine had. Erik walked into my flat, leaving Max and me staring at each other down the long corridor. He looked confused, and very hurt. I mouthed to him that I was sorry before Erik grabbed me by the hand and yanked me into the room, the door slamming shut behind me.

I felt sick, and then I got angry. I really had hurt Max; I could see it in his eyes. Erik looked around my flat as I tried to collect my thoughts. I needed to pull myself together, and forget about Max or

I could lose everything. I gritted my teeth until I felt them cracking. *Pull it together!*

Students from a nearby apartment plodded heavily down the corridor past my door toward the stairs, yelping about how much beer they could drink.

'What the hell's going on out there?'

Toyoka's voice was in my head, reminding me that I was playing a role. *Just like in the film* Kora Terry. *Be the sexy traitor, Ella. Be her now!*

I turned around and faced him, smiling. 'Oh, you know students,' I said, 'drunk, probably.' I slunk to my nightstand, pulled out a half-empty bottle of Hoffmann's finest whisky from the bottom drawer, and two lowball glasses. 'Turn the radio on, that should take care of it.'

He swaggered toward me. 'Radio? All I want is . . . '

I swung the whisky bottle in the air by its neck, cocked my hip and palmed both glasses in my hand. 'If you want this, you'll turn it on.'

A sly smile curled on his lips. He spun the dial until he found 'Die Fahne Hoch' on the 24-hour channel, lowering the volume as if our nation's anthem was a melody for love. Next, he unscrewed one of the light bulbs in the ceiling so that the room hazed with dull light.

With his back to me, I flipped the almond locket open and dumped Toyoka's powdered herb into his glass. It settled at the bottom and then disappeared when I sloshed whisky on top.

He grabbed the glass from my hand, sniffed it then tilted it in the air for a toast. 'Thousand Year Reich.'

I nodded once. 'Thousand Year Reich.' Our glasses clinked together, and then he gulped his drink in one shot, while I took a sip of mine.

I poured him another. 'Easy, Director Koch.' I giggled. 'Or there won't be any left.'

'Where have you been hiding yourself?' he said, before gulping another.

'I'm not hiding,' I said, drawing the shade on the window. 'Just busy doing Louise's job. You of all people should know that.'

'I should?'

He wrapped his arm around my waist and pulled me into his chest. 'Then why aren't you on the third floor, where I can see you more often?'

'Say the word and it will be done. There should only be one head secretary, and that's me.' A whisky-licked smile lingered on my lips.

'You know,' I said, walking my fingers up his arm, 'if you got rid of Louise, I could sit across from you. And you could drop as many things as you like. All. Day. Long.'

He downed the rest of his drink, threw the glass to the wall and it cracked into three jagged pieces. Then he drank mine and threw it against the wall too.

I gasped in protest. 'Director Koch — '

He kissed me hard, so hard his teeth scraped against mine. Strong fingers gripped the back of my dress and I felt the fabric scrunch in his knuckles as it tightened around my chest.

He pulled away and took a breath as if he had held it the entire time we kissed. 'I like the way you think, Ella.' Whisky glittered in his teeth. Gas crept from the corner of his mouth and he burped into his collar. 'But Louise . . . '

I wiggled out from his hands and pretended to walk away. 'Then I will just stay on the second floor!'

He caught me by both wrists, pulling me back as he twisted them. His neck bowed like an ape's and his lips probed mine. I felt the difference in our size as he groped me. Then his tongue slipped into my mouth and something inside of me clicked. *I'm finished fooling around.* I kissed him hard, forcefully pulling his lips with my teeth. When I stopped and looked at him, his eyes were like moons.

'I'll take care of it,' he said.

I raised one eyebrow.

He nudged me toward the bed, unbuttoning his trousers and his shirt, getting out of his clothes faster than if they had caught fire. His chest bulged with sculpted muscle and it was hard not to notice how attractive he was with his clothes off. Hungry hands clawed their way down my back and he gnawed on my shoulder as if it were food. I felt the weight of his body — he could crush me — and I didn't like feeling helpless. I slapped him across the face, his body swayed, and the medicine glimmered in his eye.

'I'm not your meat,' I said.

He flopped backward onto the bed, a snarled smile dipping low on his lip. '*Nein*?'

I slid the belt from the loops on my dress, held it in the air, and then let it slip through my fingers. 'You're mine.'

He put his hand to his head. Perspiration beaded in his hairline and a woozy groan hummed in his cheeks. I unbuttoned my dress. One jerk of my shoulders and it dropped to my ankles. His blue eyes lowered to a melt, and he teetered forward. Then a slobbered smile skidded off my thigh, and he thumped to the floor like a sack of potatoes.

I cried dryly, dropping to my knees and feeling very numb.

* * *

By the time I woke the next morning Erik had already left. A note on the pillow next to me said to arrive at his office after lunch to start my new job. Toyoka said if I implied sex he'd think we had it, and she was right.

I was relieved. Then I thought about the look on Max's face in the corridor.

And I felt very hollow and sad.

24
December

Erik had sent Louise to Berlin later that morning with a small contingency from the Braunes Haus that already had plans to go there. I heard she protested with an ugly cry that bled makeup down her cheeks, which I was glad to have missed. Now, Hoffmann worried almost every day that I wouldn't have the strength to cover up his drinking and stay on top of the files, but I was doing just fine.

Erik never forgot my name, yet surprisingly, he largely kept to himself, like he had always done before. Though sometimes after the administration meetings, when he'd take his jacket off and loosen his tie, I'd notice a slight change in his demeanour. First, he'd get very talkative, then after a drink to calm his nerves, I'd catch him following me around the office with his eyes.

Then there was Max. I left him notes for several days after he saw me with Erik, apologizing for what I had done, and every day he slipped them back under my door unopened, while I was at work. I was sure he had heard about my new job as Erik's secretary — it was big news around the Königsplatz.

When I moved into Louise's office it was crowded with knickknacks; porcelain kissing birds on top of the filing cabinet, a leafy green plant near the window and a year's worth of *Fraeun Warte* magazines piled under her typewriter desk. Every week Louise sent a letter requesting more of her things, and I accommodated her, but only partially. I drew the line when she asked me to ship her desk; she said she was allergic to anything other than German oak and that she had broken out in hives.

By mid-December I was bored with the game we had been playing and put the rest of her things, things she hadn't even asked for yet, into two medium-sized boxes with fat labels pasted on the front: Berlin. I stood in the middle of the room; just a coat rack, a set of filing cabinets and an L-shaped desk remained, but her smell still lingered like a ghost: a combination of fingernail polish and slept-in sheets.

I pushed the boxes into the corridor and wiped both hands together as if I had just thrown out the last of the rubbish. I had been so absorbed in the cleanup I didn't even hear the panicked pace of a courier's footsteps come up behind me.

'Fräulein Strauss,' he said, almost out of breath. 'A cable from Berlin.'

Erik had been in his office and stood up when he noticed I had a cable in my hands. He read it silently to himself while I rearranged my office. After I had got rid of Louise's things, it felt bigger and I thought I'd play with the position of my desk; maybe move it toward the window like I had it when I worked with Hoffmann.

Erik crumpled the cable into a ball and tossed it in my rubbish bin. 'Louise is dead.'

'What?' I said, sliding my desk toward the

window. His voice was oddly normal, and at first I didn't think I heard him right.

'RAF bombing. The entire detachment from Munich is dead.'

The RAF loved to bomb Berlin, especially since there was nothing left to bomb of Hamburg. 'A raid? Wouldn't they have found a shelter?'

'They died two days ago. Twenty-three hundred pounds of bombs dropped in thirty minutes. Ten thousand people killed in one day.'

I had never heard of such a blitz on a German city. *The RAF are getting stronger*. 'Is there much of the city left?' I wondered if he expected me to lament over Louise. After all, she did go to Berlin because of me. 'Poor Louise,' I added, just to sound concerned.

'That's all the cable says.' He turned to walk back into his office then paused, put a finger to his chin and studied my office, shifting his eyes from wall to wall. 'This is all wrong.' He curled his muscly hands around the corners of my desk and pulled it from the wall, realigning it with the open door that connected my office to his. He flashed a flirty smile, and he slapped my rear-end, hard, which I pretended to like. Then he walked into his office and sat down at his desk as if the news from Berlin was nothing at all.

I walked back into the corridor, crossed out the word Berlin on Louise's box and labelled it for disposal.

* * *

I waited for Christophe in the dark alley next to my building's fire escape with the only thing the florist had left: a droopy purple flower and a bouquet of wilted greenery wrapped in torn brown paper. Stuffed in the middle was a list detailing the newest administration changes in the Reich.

Minutes turned into an hour, and it was already late. I played with the frayed end of my scarf, then a rusted service door from the building across the alley opened with a bang. Christophe tumbled out of it and crashed into some metal rubbish bins, spilling rotten refuse all over the pavement.

He scrambled to his feet and then bolted toward me, snatching the bouquet from my hands and tucking it under his arm.

'Get out of here,' he said, eyes black as marbles, and his face bearded in grey.

'But — ' I thought he'd want to know about Louise.

He looked over his shoulder before he turned the corner. 'Now!'

A cat hissed somewhere nearby, and I trotted as fast as I could down the alley in the opposite direction, along my building's backside, tracing the bricks with my hand in the dark.

I felt some relief when I turned the corner onto Petersplatz and into the light. I searched my pocket for something to smoke. A man walking down the street with his hands stuffed in his pockets and a cigarette in his mouth stopped cold when he saw my face.

'Ella?'

'Max?' I felt a flutter of delight; it pulled me away from the wall and I smiled. *Maybe now he'll talk to me.*

He peered into the dark alley behind me and sneered. 'What are you doing out here?' He took a drag from his cigarette. A live wire strung over our heads sparked blue light, and its glow spread a dead, ashy look across his face. 'You know what? I don't want to know.' He flicked his cigarette to the ground and headed back the way he had come, toward the Marienplatz.

I reached for his arm. Words dripped down my neck and lumped in my throat. 'Max, I need to tell you something.' My fingers touched his coat sleeve, but he pulled away. I stood in a shadowed gap between a parked car and a cobwebbed brick door and watched him disappear into the foggy steam that rose from the gutter. A girl on a small balcony across the street shouted for me to chase him, but I couldn't move.

The look in Max's eyes — the disappointment, the longing — it was too much to think about. The rational part of me knew it was safer for him to hate me. Then I thought, no, he needed to know it was my life I was saving and that I didn't sleep with Erik. I ripped the yellow scarf from my wrist, tucked it deep into my coat pocket, and then hurried after him in a cloppy, clunky run.

I burst into the square looking for him, my breath billowing into frosty white clouds that evaporated into still dark air. A man dragging his girlfriend by the hand shuffled past me and toward a small crowd just a short distance away. I stumbled closer and saw what appeared to be a deer contorted on the ground, but what would a deer be doing in Munich? I found Max buried in the commotion; my arm nudged up against his, my body in a stupor: the deer was Christophe.

Instead of the flowers I gave him, Christophe's hands clutched his stomach, which bled a pool of warmed, dark red blood onto the chilled cobbled stones. Blood spat from his mouth, then he said something in English about his mother. People gasped when they heard his quivering, all too British voice.

I leaned forward, and his head wobbled in my direction before his lazy eyes fixed their gaze on me.

'He's dead,' someone shouted, and a bitter chill blew his hair to the side — his scar uncovered for all to see.

I looked at Max in horror, hand over my mouth, and his face turned pale.

'Ella?' By my reaction, I was sure Max knew I had known the person that just died at our feet. More so, he was British, which meant he was a spy. His fingers searched blindly for mine. When he found them, he gave my palm a squeeze. 'Ella?' he said again, gulping, as if realizing through the face of a dead man that staying mad at me wasn't something he wanted to do.

I broke out in a cold sweat — Max had my hand and people would link us together if they saw. I needed to get out of there, and I needed to get out of there quick.

I pulled my hand away, taking a shakey step backward from the crowd. Brimmed hats and thick-coated elbows dug their way through, people shrieking and whispering at the sight of a dead man. Patrons from the Ratskeller filtered into the street, beers in hand, with the band's tune, 'A Little Hunting Song', bursting intermittingly every time the doors swung open.

I looked at Max, and then to Christophe, with my hand pressed to my mouth, my eyes sliding over the top. I ran away into the dark, my shoes clicking and clacking against the pavement, before being sick not far away in an unlit section of the Marienplatz.

The glass door of a closed shop flew open while I was bent over, and an old woman with wispy silver hair and black eyes loomed over me, holding a stick in her hand.

'Who are you?' she demanded, shaking the stick in the night air, and it was then I realized who she was.

'Frau Haas?'

'How do you know my name?' She stepped forward, gritting her teeth, and I fell backward on the pavement. A new death card had been added to the front of her door: her husband, Herr Haas.

She saw me look at it. 'Who are you?'

I scooted away, feet scraping the cobblestones, scrambling to get up, just as the glockenspiel's forty-three clanging bells erupted wildly throughout the square.

'Go away! Leave me alone!'

And I ran into an alley.

25

For once, I actually thought I could get caught, and not by the Gestapo but by an informant, someone who could stab me in the stomach and leave me to die in the street.

I messengered a note to Erik that I was sick and then hid in my flat, spending Christmas rocking back-and-forth in my chair, knees in my neck and arms wrapped around my legs. By the time I went back to work, fear had turned into restlessness. The bite of winter had settled into the city, nobody seemed to move unless they were running from an air raid, or going to work for the Reich. Everything dripped in grey and had a strange emptiness carved out from the inside: the buildings, the sky, the people — shells of what they used to be. I had just been thinking to myself that I needed to get out of the city, go somewhere where I could forget about the war, forget about the Reich for a while, when Erik strolled into my office. With no administration meetings to attend and his calendar cleared for the day, he'd changed into casual trousers and a collared shirt. I almost didn't recognize him.

'Need to get out of the city?' he said.

'Did I say it out loud?'

He had a winter rose in his hand and a smile that glinted glory. The rose wasn't from a florist, but from the frozen flower boxes outside the V-building, the ones with black petals and gnarled twigs for stems. 'Here.' He shoved the rose into my hand and then waited for me to say thank you. 'What are you doing tomorrow?'

'It's the weekend,' I said. 'New Year's Eve.'

'Yes. I know,' he said, sitting on the corner of my desk. 'I'm going to Schliersee with a few friends from the NSDAP to do a little skiing. Do you want to come?' He tapped his shoe against the side of my desk. *Tap, tap, tap.*

'Schliersee?' I said as if I didn't hear him.

Schliersee was a town Hoffmann talked about on occasion. It was a place where people skied fast during the day, drank beer even faster in the evening and watched the starry winter nights laze into crisp alpine mornings. A place untouched by the Nazi propaganda machine, only a cluster of mom-and-pop pensions along with a few small beer halls populated the town, no real inhabitants except for the tourists — who only cared about skiing.

'Just a little holiday. Two other girls are coming along also — a group of us.'

My pulse revved like an engine when he said 'holiday.' I wanted to get out of Munich, now I had my chance. And a holiday? It meant no work, just play, a day to be myself. No Max, no files, no lies, just Ella. *Tomorrow is my birthday*. 'Sounds perfect.'

He hopped off my desk. 'I'll pick you up in the morning. That is . . . as long as your boyfriend doesn't mind.'

'Boyfriend?' The word took me by surprise. Then I remembered what I had told him in the car the night I drugged him. I wasn't playing hard to get anymore. In fact, I wasn't playing at all. Christophe's death had changed everything. Louise's too. I wanted a fresh start — I wanted to feel something other than loss, anger and duty. 'We broke up.'

He nodded, and I smiled.

* * *

Erik arrived at my door early the next morning. He had a swoosh of blond hair just above his right eye, and the cuffs of his collared shirt flipped up with his cold-weather coat. His cheekbones rounded near his eyes, and he didn't look as tall as he did in the office.

He reached behind me and grabbed my suitcase, the scent of apple Gummibär candy thick in his clothes. I gave him an odd look — something in between a smirk and a grimace. Erik Koch wasn't the type of man I pictured helping a woman with her bags, much less smelling sugary-sweet like a handful of candies. He seemed charming; like any other boy I had met before the war had changed or taken them.

He stood straight with my case gripped tight to his side. 'What?' he said, noticing my look.

'Nothing . . . it's just . . . you look different without your work clothes on,' I said. 'It's as if you're somebody else.'

He dropped my case and stood in the corridor. One hand behind his back, the other held out for me to shake. A slight bow lowered his thick, sandy-lashed eyes to mine. 'Let me introduce myself. I'm Erik Koch. I have one older brother and a younger sister.'

I smiled and shook his hand with a small curtsy.

'And I'm originally from Berlin,' he said, 'but grew up in a small town northeast of Munich.'

'I'm Ella Strauss,' I said, giggling. 'Pleased to meet you.'

We headed outside where a Mercedes G-4 Wagen spewed grey haze into the street; its windows were fogged, and it rocked from the bodies moving around inside. The sound of laughter seeped from a cracked window along with billows of smoke that smelled of filtered cigarettes.

I couldn't help but remember the last time I had ridden in such a car. The hum of the Mercedes' grooved tyres against the pavement and the sway of its chassis when I visited Hinzert. The bitter memory of that prison clung to the corners of my mind and could crack open like a bad egg if I let it. I took a breath. *I'm on holiday now.*

A driver with worn leather boots and a tattered green flap hat hurled my bag onto the roof and tethered it next to some other cases. I tightened my gloves at the wrist, glancing at the ground. Underneath the frosty imprint of my shoes was the dirty stain of Christophe's blood. A sickened roil bubbled inside me, and I grimaced with one hand lightly pressed against my stomach.

Holiday. I'm on holiday. Holiday.

'Are you coming?' Erik said, holding the door open.

The dark upholstered seats looked velvety and warm as he stood there waiting for me to climb in. I dropped my hand. 'Yes,' I said, 'let's get out of here.'

I stepped over an empty beer bottle rolling near the door and slid into the backseat. When I looked up, I heard my name.

'Hello, Cousin!' It was Alex, and at nine o'clock in the morning he was nearly drunk. He slouched in his seat and bowed his legs, one hand gripping a bottle of beer and the other gripping a girl. I guessed she was no more than eighteen with her lollipop lips and auburn hair, some of it pinned into ringlets near her face. She bore a striking and refreshing resemblance to Claudia. I smiled and she smiled back. Next to them both was a dark-headed man I recognized as Erik's friend Paul, and another girl with a plain face.

Alex knew a lot of people around the Königsplatz. He had become a master networker and developed a knack for exchanging favours for relationships in order to get ahead in the Party. So, it didn't surprise me that Alex had been able to weasel an invitation out of Paul. I just couldn't help but wonder if what he had promised Paul in return was the plain-faced girl sitting next to him.

'Alex!' I said. 'You're up early.'

'So,' he said, smug-faced. 'You're the girl Erik enjoys.'

'Enjoys?' Only Alex would use such a word. 'He's my boss.'

Alex laughed me off and pointed the neck of his bottle around the car.

'This is Ingrid, her gal Hannah and my buddy Paul, Koch's friend.' Beer spilled from his bottle onto his knee and shoes.

We said our hellos and Erik slid in next to me, shutting the door. His eyes darted around the car as if he'd missed some incredible joke. Paul counted up the empty bottles on the floor, then smiled at Alex as if expecting him to say something ridiculous. Alex belched into the crook of his arm and flashed me a bright, white smile.

'There it is,' Paul said, pointing at Alex. 'That's what happens when you challenge me.'

Erik scooted to the edge of his seat. 'Did I miss something?'

I shook my head no, but Alex spoke up. 'She's my cousin!' He burped again. This time he took his arm off Ingrid and waved the fumes away with his hand. Ingrid giggled and covered her nose.

'You're related?' Erik said.

I picked up an empty bottle and hid my face behind it. 'Please, don't hold it against me.'

Alex chugged the rest of his beer while Ingrid and Paul cheered him on. When he finished, he growled like a bear and pounded on his chest with his fists.

'*Nein.*' Erik laughed. 'I wouldn't do that.'

Ingrid offered me a cigarette. I reached out without even thinking and then paused, my gloved fingers stuck in mid-air. Although it seemed everyone was smoking, I glanced at Erik as if I had to ask permission; new rules, just two days old, didn't allow for secretaries to smoke. Even when I wasn't working, I had to hide it.

'Relax, we're on holiday,' he said, 'and I'm not your boss this weekend.' He smiled. 'Just Erik, clear?'

The windows had frosted with breathy perspiration and blocked all views of the city. My back unbuttoned along with my coat and my feet warmed with the company. 'Clear.'

I unpinned my hair and let it relax over my shoulders. Ingrid pulled one of her ribbons from her hair. 'Here,' she said. 'I have too many of these. And you don't have any.'

The ribbon was pink. Not the bright kind little girls wear, but soft and whimsically delicate. 'Thank you.' I didn't want to admit how long it had been since I'd worn a ribbon in my hair.

I sank into the seat of the G-4 Wagen; it was cosier and more comfortable than it looked. Erik unfolded a fluffy blue blanket and threw it over both our legs. He held my hand momentarily, giving me a smile. I smiled back.

I needed this trip.

* * *

We arrived in Schliersee just after ten in the morning. The twelve-room pension we lodged in overlooked the town's main street. Our room was on the second floor and had a light green canopy bed, big enough for all of us, centred in the middle of the room, with two smaller trundle beds nestled against the walls. The boys lodged down the corridor from us about six doors down, Erik in a private suite. The Hensels, the old couple that ran the place, lived on the first floor just at the bottom of the stairs where the parlour, kitchen and dining room were.

The French doors in our room opened onto a small balcony overlooking a rushing creek. 'It's so beautiful,' I said to myself. The creek meandered its way through a meadow of untouched snow and whooshed against drifts of ice. It was hard to believe a hollow place like Munich even existed.

Ingrid brought out two flutes filled with bubbling champagne onto the balcony. She'd already changed into black ski pants and wore a knitted snow cap with a fuzzy pink ball sewn on top. 'Too early for a drink?'

Champagne bubbles popped against my nose, and even though I'd had my share of champagne toasts in the Reich, it looked more delicious than anything I'd ever tasted. I sipped it slow with my eyes closed. The champagne slid down my throat and filled my belly with a tingled, warm energy.

'You ready to ski?' she said.

'I'm afraid I'm not much of a skier.' I took another drink and gazed at the winterscape. Icicles hung from pitched eaves and fat, powdery snowflakes fell from a thin, clouded sky.

'Hannah and I have never skied.' Laughter bumped in her voice. Her hand brushed the ringlets from her face, but they sprung back and bounced off her shoulders. 'Oh, I don't care if anyone knows. Truth is we weren't going to turn down a free holiday all because we didn't know how to ski.'

I smiled. 'Me either.'

She smoothed her snow pants against her thighs and angled her boots as if they were heels. 'But I do enjoy the gear. The trunk inside is full of things to wear.'

Our flutes clinked together, and we washed our confessions down with more champagne.

'You're Erik's secretary?' Ingrid said.

'Mm-hmm.' Work was the last thing I wanted to

talk about.

'You must be awfully busy working for the Reich. Do you get enough holidays?'

I pulled the flute from my lips. 'No,' I said. 'I work all the time.'

'Ugh,' she said. 'I can't imagine. I'm not sure what I'd do without time with my friends.' I looked at her from the side of my glass as I tipped the champagne into my mouth. 'I'm glad you were able to come with us. Sounds like you needed a break.'

I set the flute down with a long sigh. I thought about the files, how the walls inside my flat and in my office seemed more like a coffin, and Christophe. 'You have no idea.'

Hannah put her suitcase on one of the trundle beds and unpacked her things, delicately folding five pieces of clothing and carefully putting them into drawers.

'Don't mind her,' Ingrid said in a wet, champagne-coated voice. 'She thinks she's a maid. In fact, if we stay out here long enough I bet she'll put our things away.' I laughed and we clinked our flutes together for a second time.

'I can hear you girls,' Hannah said, smiling. 'And yes, sometimes I think I am the maid.' She kicked her empty suitcase under her bed and joked with her face. 'Can't help it some days.'

All three of us laughed. A pain pulled at my side and I whimpered with an embarrassing cringe. I dug my fingers into it, bending over, but still kept laughing.

'You need to laugh more often.' Ingrid took the champagne bottle and filled my glass up while I was doubled over.

'Or get drunk,' I said.

'That too.' Ingrid laughed. 'That too.'

* * *

After we finished the bottle of champagne, Ingrid cracked open another. Hannah lit the fireplace with the matches left on the mantel, and with the air from a waved book, she fanned flames big enough to warm the palms of our hands. We pushed a few chairs against the hearth and divided up the rest of the ski clothes from the trunk.

Ingrid handed out some cigarettes that seemed unusually thick. I leaned forward, lighting it from her lighter. 'What are these?' As soon as I asked the question, I tasted a sharp tang in the back of my throat. 'Cloves?'

Ingrid smiled. 'All the girls are doing it. Well, not all. But some!'

Hannah sniffed hers before lighting it. 'I'll just have a few puffs.'

'Drink the champagne with it, Hannah.'

Hannah gulped down her champagne, taking puffs in between until her cigarette was nearly gone. 'Or, maybe I'll smoke the whole thing.'

We laughed. 'I used to smoke these back home. My friend, Claudia — she loved them. I haven't seen her in so long.' It was strange to say her name out loud, like a foreign word. I said it again just to hear it. 'Claudia.'

'I'm sorry,' Ingrid said. 'You miss her. I didn't mean to — '

'It's all right.' I grabbed the champagne bottle

by its neck and filled Hannah's glass before taking a swig directly from the bottle. 'You'd like her — she knew how to have fun, and we laughed a lot growing up . . . '

The girls listened to me go on about Claudia. The more I talked about her the more stories I remembered, like how she rolled her own cigarettes and how she could drink a beer faster than anyone else at the table. Keeping her locked up in my mind had hurt more than I realized.

Someone mentioned the boys, and when our glasses went dry we set out to find them. From the second floor we saw Frau Hensel folding a large quilt near the linen closet at the base of the stairs. It was in the same yellow pattern her dirndl was made from and her body blended right into it. Her eyes bulged from their sockets when she saw us traipsing down the stairs with our arms locked together, fumbling our footsteps and catching ourselves on the railing.

Ingrid hiccupped then said, 'Good morning, Frau Hensel.' And we giggled.

Frau Hensel gasped, hand to her chest, and then stuffed the quilt into a drawer. 'It's *noon*, girls.' A thin finger against her lips tried to shush us, but we giggled even more. She took a sharp look down the corridor that led to her husband's office. I saw his feet propped up on some pillows piled high on the divan as if he were taking a nap. She paused, and then pressed her finger even harder against her lips.

'This way,' she said, guiding us into the sitting room in a way similar to how a sheep herder gathers strays on a farm. 'Now, come over here.

Your men have already left for the lifts!' I looked around the parlour. Except for us, there were no other guests around.

Our giggles quieted into a murmur. She pointed to a rack of skis on the wall and sized our feet with her eyes. 'Here, these will fit you,' she said, handing me a pair of skis.

I waved at her to stop. 'I don't ski.'

She tried to give them to Ingrid, who stuck her hands in her pockets. 'Me either.'

When she tried to give the skis to Hannah, laughter shot from our mouths.

Frau Hensel gripped the skis in opposing hands, knuckles whitening, and pounded them on the ground like gavels. *Boom!* A puff of air blew from her lip to her forehead. 'What are you girls doing at a ski pension when you don't know how to ski?'

Hannah hummed her answer — the champagne must have tied up her tongue. I laughed at the sound of her garbled voice, covering my own mouth. But something about trying not to laugh made me laugh even more. Frau Hensel scowled at us and a deep-set scar on her chin bent into a crescent-shaped gash.

'What kind of skills are they teaching girls these days? To get drunk? When I was your age . . . '

Our faces went blank. Her voice pushed us onto an oversized chair under the ski rack, and we sat and listened to her with wide, attentive eyes while she scolded us with a pointed finger. The fire behind her glowed dark orange and smelled of brimstone, which made her seem madder than she really was.

She talked about how she skied before she learned to walk, and about her days in the women's ski corps during the first war. Said getting drunk was for the lazy and the prostitutes. 'Some nights I had to camp in the snow, alone. I didn't know if I would live or die, and not because of the cold. Because of . . . ' She stopped short of finishing and waved her hand in the air. 'Young people these days. Think war is a picnic. A party.'

A photo of a woman with blonde hair, braided at the sides, tilted on the wall behind her. She wore a Red Cross cuff around her right arm and a patch of criss-crossed ski poles. A leather pack tied around her waist balanced off her hip while she faced the snow-capped mountains with dead-set, razor-cutting eyes.

I realized she thought we were a few stupid girls from the city, who probably slept around and drank more than we ought too. I didn't know Ingrid or Hannah's story, but I knew mine.

'Frau Hensel,' I said slowly, trying to control my fat, drunken tongue. 'I'm sorry I'm a little . . . you know . . . ' I stood up, and placed a hand on her shoulder, which I think surprised her. 'I really needed to get out of Munich. It's grey there . . . not beautiful like it is here. I got carried away.'

She stared at me, and then looked at my hands when I held her gaze and all the tension in her body seemed to disappear. Perhaps she knew what I meant about the grey, how depressing it was, and how coming to a place like Schliersee could make you do things you normally wouldn't.

'Girls,' she said, sighing. 'My husband will have words if he finds you drunk.' She paused, put a finger to her chin and rubbed the scar. 'What about the rodel?' Her voice lifted as much as her face. 'You can sled, can't you?'

26

We came back to the pension several hours later, icy-numb yet still laughing. As soon as Frau Hensel saw us she wrapped us up in quilted blankets and sat us on the divan near the fireplace to warm up. Erik and the boys walked through the front doors shortly after.

'Where did you go?' he asked, sitting down next to me. 'I looked for you on the slopes.'

'We went sledding!' I rubbed my hands together and then held them palm side to the fire, giving him a smile.

'I thought you girls wanted to ski?' Erik said.

'We did,' Ingrid said, 'but the skis didn't fit so Frau Hensel suggested the rodels.'

'Oh,' he said, though Paul and Alex didn't seem to care where we'd been or what we did. 'I wish I had known. I would have found some skis for you . . . somewhere.'

'You would have?' It didn't occur to me he cared what we did since they left for the lifts well before we even came out of our room. But the yielding tone in his voice made me question my initial thoughts, and I felt a little bad about not joining him.

Erik sank into the seat cushion, cosying up next to me. 'I'm glad you had a good time though.' He smiled gently, and it reminded me of a boy in Nuremberg, someone whose name I didn't know, but remembered coming into the antiques shop every once in a while. I smiled back.

The salon filled up with skiers returning from the slopes and the hooks near the door got overloaded with wet coats and hats. Scarves fell to the ground and swirled in between clumsy, boot-heavy feet. We scooted closer to the fireplace and made room for the incoming crowd; some sat on the backs of the divans, others sat on the padded parts of the arms.

Paul leaned into the fireplace to spit on the flames. Frau Hensel walked by with a snarl and mumbled to herself when she heard him laughing. Erik told stories about their day, but Alex kept butting in with his own version. Either way, the events were the same: the boys out-skied everyone else on the biggest hill with the most snow. I gazed deep into the fire's flames as they talked — my mind still on the rodels.

The door to the kitchen flapped open, and a waft of fresh bread and broiling sausages filled every corner of the room. For the first time since I can remember, the thought of a plate piled high with wet, sloppy food sounded fantastic. I didn't know why I suddenly felt hungry — really hungry as if I could eat my arm and not care. I only wanted to eat.

'I'm starving!' I announced, throwing the blanket off my legs and heading toward the dining room, but then Frau Hensel announced supper and everyone got up. Three deep-set roasting pans full of cooked onions, potatoes and browned meat had been placed on the buffet next to a black soup-pot stewing with carrots in beer. The cook, who looked just like Frau Hensel only much older, scooped it all onto plates.

I slid into an overly large medieval-looking wooden table with my plate. Platters of blistering pork hocks followed, and the room heated up like a sauna. I pulled a clump of meat from the bone and stuffed it into my full mouth. A spoonful of hot carrots came next. I closed my eyes; suddenly I knew what it meant to indulge, what it felt like to take care of myself, and I was satisfied. When I opened my eyes, everyone was looking at me. Erik nudged a glass of water toward me with his finger; it clinked against my plate and he motioned with his chin for me to take a drink.

'This girl can eat!' Paul said.

A ball of gas built up in my chest. I put my hand to my mouth to stop it from coming out, but it was too late — I belched long and loud. 'Excuse me,' I said with a giggle.

Ingrid laughed, elbowing Hannah in the side. Alex and Paul dug into their meals. Erik wrapped his fingers around my petite wrist. His jaw hung open.

'How do you eat like that and look like this?'

A pained swallow pushed the last of my food down. 'I don't.'

* * *

After dinner we headed to a little beer hall across the street. By Munich standards, the hall was misshapen and divided into three rooms rather than one open rectangle. People crammed in together; arms waved full steins of beer in the air, and froth spilled in spurts onto those underneath. A three-piece band wearing suede lederhosen played polka in the corner and barmaids, not used to a full house, rushed around in traditional green and white servant dirndls.

'Where're we going to sit?' I said.

'Maybe there's another beer hall we can go to?' Ingrid said.

'No, come this way,' Erik said, and we did. 'I have a table for us.' Alex and Paul sat down with a thud next to Ingrid and Hannah. Beer halls rarely saved tables, especially on New Year's Eve.

My mouth hung open. 'You made a reservation?'

Erik helped me take my coat off and then handed it to the barmaid who hung it on the coat hook. 'Yes. Why?'

I smiled. 'No reason.' Erik must have sweet-talked someone, somehow, someway, to get us a table. The Erik Koch I knew from the office would have written me a note to take care of it myself. I thought about how he carried my bag from my flat down to the car, and how he put a blanket over my legs to keep me warm in the Mercedes; it was easy to forget who he was when he acted this way.

Six boot-sized glass steins were brought to our table. The dunkel beer swirled with frothy shades of brown. I took a long slurp. 'That was just what I needed.' Caramel-coloured foam pillowed on my lip.

Erik shook his head in disbelief. 'You sure there's room after that dinner?'

'Oh, there's room.' I pushed the stein into my chest and gave it a hug. 'For this, there's room.'

Alex took three gulps then slammed his stein on the table and blurted, 'No wonder my mother gave you a boy's name. You eat like a man and now you're going to drink like one too?'

'A boy's name?' Erik asked.

I rolled my eyes. 'She likes nicknames.'

Alex bent his head down, slurped the froth off his beer and then blurted again, 'Calls her Sascha!'

Ingrid held her stein in the air. 'Well, here's to drinking like a man!'

Hannah lifted hers with two hands and then we all clinked our steins. *'Prost!'*

We drank and swayed to the band's music until Erik asked me if I wanted to go outside. The room had become so warm, a moment in the cold air sounded exhilaratingly nice. I followed him to the back of the hall and out to a small courtyard with a lit fire pit and an empty two-seater wooden bench. He cleared the snow off using the sleeve from his coat, swiping it side to side and then edging the corners with his cuff. *Who is this man?* There was something charming about this Erik, and I liked him.

The door had closed and the pomp from the polka band reduced to a slight drone. Our arms pressed against each other as we sat down and shared each other's body heat.

'Look at that.' He pointed to a streak of light in the sky — a line of stars that ran from the edge of the universe to the top of our heads. We gazed with our mouths open and our breath made clouds in the air that looked like we were smoking.

'Erik.' He turned, just slightly and looked in my eyes. 'Thanks for bringing me here.'

'Of course.'

'You don't understand,' I said. 'There's something you don't know about me.'

I put my hands to the fire, which roared with flames that sucked the cold right out of the air and spit it back as warm wind.

'You've got a secret?'

I paused, looking him in the eyes. 'It's my birthday.'

'What?' He placed his hand on my knee, and for a moment I held my breath from feeling such a deliberate touch. 'Why didn't you say anything?'

'Nobody asked.' I smiled.

He glanced through the window and pointed at Alex, who had posed in a downhill skiing position on top of the table, circled by half a dozen empty beer bottles. 'Why didn't Alex say anything? He's your cousin. He must know it's your birthday.'

Alex bobbed up and down, pretending to ski, knocking over every bottle on the table as if it were one, which made the barmaid run around in circles with her hands to her cheeks.

I chuckled. 'He doesn't know what day it is most days of the week.'

Erik watched Alex with a disbelieving face. 'You may be right. How old are you?' he asked, and I looked at him with surprise.

'You can't ask a girl her age!' I wasn't sure if I should tell him I was twenty or tell him the age that was on my paperwork at the V-building. 'How old are you?'

'Twenty-eight.' I gave a strange look, and he laughed. 'Did you think I was older?'

'Only by a few years, but that doesn't matter.'

I cleared my throat and got more comfortable in my seat, narrowing the pocket of air between us. He squeezed my knee tenderly and his voice turned buttery. 'Happy Birthday, Ella.' He was sweet, caring and nothing like the Erik Koch I knew at the V-building. I still couldn't believe how different he was, and it showed on my face. 'You've been giving me strange looks all day,' he said. 'Is there something I don't know?'

My whole face scrunched. '*Nein*.'

'You're doing it again.'

I had to tell him what I was thinking. Otherwise, he might have thought I was making fun of him. 'This morning I said you looked different, but you also act different.'

'What do you mean?' His eyes widened, and I realized he had no idea what I was talking about.

'Never mind.' I patted the top of his hand on my knee, and then in a move that surprised even myself, I kept it there, resting on top of his. I didn't want to remind him about all the times he got my name wrong, or how he ignored me when Louise was his secretary. All I wanted to do was enjoy the night, so I decided to change the subject.

'Do you come here often? I mean to this town. Have you been here before?' I looked up into the crystal night sky.

'My family wintered here on holiday when I was a child. My brother, sister, and I would ski in the morning, come back midday hungry, eat pretzels with shandy then go out and ski until dark.'

'You drank shandy?'

He nodded. 'We'd drink it from paper cones.

Tasted like crap, but after skiing all day it didn't matter to us.' He gazed deep into the fire and rubbed his chin. 'Hmm,' he said. 'I haven't thought about that for a long time.'

'I used to sell it on street corners when I was little,' I said, 'and you're right, it does taste like crap.' We shared a laugh that quieted into sighs. His eyes met mine, and then I felt his breath on my cheek. He smelled of Nuremberg before the war, like edelweiss and candy — he wasn't a member of the Party, and definitely not the person I'd seduced with Toyoka's herb. I was wrong about him; I had to be. And then it occurred to me, perhaps, just perhaps, he was a jumpbox, and had fooled everyone this whole time.

Next thing I knew our lips were touching. I heard a relaxing moan but I wasn't entirely sure if it came from me or not. His hand pressed against my back, pulling me in closer, but then the door banged against the wall, scaring us out of each other's arms and out of our seats.

It was Hannah, and her face beet-red and her shoulders puffed. 'I'm going back to the pension!' She dashed into the street, tears spurting from her eyes and bawling like a baby. My lips were still warm and wet from kissing Erik, and my mind reeled from shock. The one car in the village still out motoring on the street almost hit her. 'Hannah!' I yelled, and then left Erik in the courtyard and chased after her.

I managed to grab her coat sleeve and stop her just outside the pension, both of us panting, trying to catch our cold, frosted breath.

'It's Paul,' she sobbed, and then wrapped her

arms around me. 'He cornered me near the toilets — said I owed him.' She pulled back, wiping her tears with the thick part of her palm. 'I guess there's no such thing as a free weekend after all.'

'I'm sorry,' I said. 'Were you starting to like him?'

'I thought I was.' She held her breath until her cry had quieted to a hiccup.

I glanced across the street to the courtyard, but Erik had gone inside. 'Come now, let's get you to bed.'

* * *

I got her a warm washcloth for her face while she changed into her nightclothes. She climbed into the canopy bed and lay with her pillow gripped between both arms and her body bent into a foetal position. I petted her until her hiccups disappeared and her eyes had closed, but then heavy boots pounded up the stairs and stopped right outside our door.

'Hannah,' a voice slurred. The doorknob turned violently in its lock.

'Hannah, where are you . . . ' It was Paul, and by the drawl in his voice I could tell he was drunk.

There was a slight commotion, and I heard Frau Hensel shout, 'This is not proper!' There was a clap, like she had slapped her hands together. 'Get back to your room.'

'But I only want to tell her — '

'Silence! This is not a brothel.' Her voice shouted into a whisper. 'Or a gypsy's fleapit.'

Ingrid and Alex bounded up the stairs seconds

later, drunk and giggling.

'And you, Inid — Ingrid,' Frau Hensel said.

'My name is Ingrid,' she slurred, hiccupping.

'This is your room,' Frau Hensel said.

I heard the rattle of keys followed by the click and twist of my door's lock. *She's opening the door!* I stepped back into the shadow running along the side of the bed. The door cracked open and Frau Hensel pushed Ingrid inside, and she landed on the floor with me as I tried to catch her, our legs tangling on the ground. Paul stood against the wall behind Frau Hensel with one eye comfortably closed, and the other held open by two of his fingers. He moved his head instead of his eye to look around Frau Hensel's body and into our room. A peep of laughter floated from my mouth, and Frau Hensel peered sourly down at us. She clipped a fat ring of keys onto her belt and shut our door.

'Now, you boys . . . get to your room!' she said from the other side of the door.

There was a garbled argument then the slam of a bedroom door at the end of the corridor. I moved Ingrid's head into my lap so that my face was directly above hers.

'Why are you upside down?' she said, and then closed her eyes. 'The room is . . . '

'Spinning?' I said.

I helped her up and she climbed into the canopy bed where Hannah had fallen asleep, pulling bits of clothing off and twisting her body into the bed sheets. The room was quiet now, still.

Erik. I had butterflies thinking of him, and I hadn't felt the tingly sensation of really being alive in I don't know how long. He was tender and thoughtful. And without that uniform on, and away from the V-building, he was just an ordinary man. I regretted walking away from him, especially since Hannah was now safe and sound in the bed.

I wondered if it wasn't too late for us.

There was a creak in the floorboards from the corridor. I looked through the peephole and saw Erik rubbing the back of his neck, walking up to my door, hand poised to knock, only to back away.

I gasped. I'd left him at the beer hall and now he'd come to get me.

I put my forehead to the door, breathing, closing my eyes only to open them right back up, playing with the idea of opening the door. Ingrid was now snoring and Hannah had pulled the covers over her head. I looked again, standing on my tiptoes to get the full view, only this time Erik was gone.

But I had opened the door.

I crept down the corridor after him. Frau Hensel and her cook were in the kitchen preparing for tomorrow's breakfast, murmuring about the best way to cook morning eggs — they had no idea I was up. His room was the last door at the very end of the corridor. I smoothed my hair to one side, straightened my skirt, and decided to knock, but then suddenly wondered what the hell I was doing. I started walking back the way I had come when he opened his door.

My back was to him. 'Ella?' he said, and I froze.

And there was silence in the corridor. Silence while I rethought my intentions, and rethought what I'd decided about him. My heart raced, but not from panic or fear.

I turned around.

'You must have seen me come to your room,' he said, 'I shouldn't have — '

I kissed him, standing on my toes to reach his lips. 'You don't have to apologize,' I said, and he shut the door behind us, and carried me to his bed.

* * *

We sat across from each other at breakfast. Hannah and Ingrid slumped over the table, eating porridge with big spoons. Neither one of them looked well. Hannah was still upset, shooting dagger looks at Paul, who sat down just long enough to eat his eggs and leave. Ingrid wore her winter hat low on her head, almost covering her eyes. She said something about not feeling well, and then left the table holding her stomach. Alex shrugged, because of course, he felt just fine after a night of drinking.

Erik ate his breakfast, glancing up every so often, catching my eye. I couldn't believe I'd just slept with my boss. And not just any boss, with Erik . . . *Erik*? My heart fluttered when he last caught my eye, and I laughed to myself, thinking, of all the people to be wrong about.

'I thought I'd walk around the village this morning,' I said. 'It's so beautiful here . . . '

'Why walk when you can ski?' Alex said. 'Isn't that why we're here, at a ski pension?'

Erik put his fork down. 'I'll go on a walk.'

Alex waved. 'I'm leaving,' he said, and left out

the side door with his skis.

'And then it was just us,' I said, and he leaned back in his chair, smiling.

We walked from the pension into town and stumbled upon an antiques shop. Old skis and boots were on display in the window, and then in the back, it looked like perhaps some paintings. I was instantly struck by the charm of it. And antiques? I couldn't believe the luck.

I read from the sign. 'The Little Shop.' I pressed my face to the glass, peeking in, and Erik opened the door. A little bell tinkled overhead, and a sweet-looking older man walked out from the back, dusting his hands off on his white apron.

'Good morning,' he said, looking over his spectacles. 'Can I help you find anything?'

I walked around the shop, taking my gloves off one at a time while he and Erik struck up a conversation. On a glass shelf I found a figurine of a child dressed in turn-of-the-century Bavarian clothing. By instinct, I turned it over to see what stamp it had on the bottom. It wasn't worth its price tag, a cheap knockoff, but the boy's face was sweet. Painted red lips and blue eyes with bright yellow mittens. I thought maybe that was what Erik looked like when he was a boy before the Reich.

'My parents owned an antiques shop,' he said to the shopkeeper, and I think my mouth dropped a little bit. 'When I was young. I don't remember much about it.' He leaned against the counter, tapping his lips. 'But from what I remember,' he said, glancing over his shoulder and around the shop, 'it looked a lot like this one.'

I walked on, picking up other figurines only to set them back down, pretending to be shopping, just to get a better ear on what they were saying.

'Well, I've had this shop a few years, I have to say.' He took a rag and wiped his counter where it was already clean. 'And every year I think — ' he leaned in close, whispering ' — I don't ever want to leave.'

Erik laughed, pushing back from the counter. 'It is a great place,' Erik said. 'Schliersee. Got a little skiing in yesterday. Wonderful day, the sights . . . ' He looked at me, stopping short from saying anything about how the war hadn't touched the little town, and how it felt like a dream.

'Did your wife go skiing too?' the shopkeeper said, and I burst out laughing from behind the shelves.

'We're not married,' I said. 'In fact, he's my boss.' Erik turned the colour of a tomato.

The shopkeeper looked surprised, eyes lifting into his forehead. 'Your pardon,' he said, and he wiped more of the counter's clean surface.

'Did you find anything?' Erik said.

'I'm not looking for anything in particular,' I said, and then couldn't remember the last time I'd bought myself something. I walked up to the counter and spotted a basket of woollen mittens.

'Look at these.' I sorted through the colours: white, blue and grey — definitely not grey. 'They're made so well.' I held a pair to my face, and they didn't scratch but felt very soft. I slid my hand into one. 'And so warm.' I walked over to the far mirror on the wall, looking at myself with the mittens on, when I heard Erik talk again to the shopkeeper, but this time his voice was lower, quieter.

'I noticed you don't have any Party flags hanging on buildings or in your shops. Does this town not support the Führer?'

The shopkeeper took his time answering, and I glanced up, looking at them both through the mirror. 'I've got some around here somewhere . . . ' He looked over his shoulder as if he was trying to look, but it was very clear to me he didn't care about the flags.

There was an awkward hush, and I slid my hand into the other mitten, still watching them from the mirror.

'We'll take a pair,' Erik said, and he bought me the mittens.

I put the figurine of the little boy on the counter. 'And this too.'

* * *

We walked down the street to a little eatery that made fresh pretzels and sauerkraut soup for lunch, and again he made small talk with the owner. 'What a charming town,' he kept saying.

I ate my soup, and it was the best thing I'd ever tasted. I slurped every last spoonful from my bowl. 'I can't get enough of this! It's not the broth, it's the vegetables, and the — ' I looked up, not wanting to mention how the market shelves were getting thinner and thinner and what selections they did have were already ripened and wilted. I set my spoon down, and Erik smiled. I thought we'd begun to notice our mutual cues, when to change the subject to keep from mentioning the war, and what the Party had done to us.

I set my bowl off to the side. 'What do you want to do?' I said. 'Ski?'

'You pick.'

The day was at my choosing, and it was a beautiful day, with snow hanging heavy on the trees and the sun glistening off drifts that had formed in the night. I tore my pretzel in half, watching the white middle steam.

'How about the rodels?'

Erik laughed. 'Me on a rodel? I'm too big.'

'It will be fun,' I said, suddenly chuckling, thinking about him trying to fit his long legs on a sled. 'Trust me.'

And he did. I couldn't believe he did, because I actually didn't know if he would fit or not. But there we were on top of the hill standing with our sleds. I adjusted my winter hat, playing with the fuzzy ball. Our cheeks were already pink.

'Are you sure?' he said, looking down the steep hill of snow.

I nodded. 'Absolutely.'

He motioned with his chin. 'You go first.'

I dropped my sled in the snow and sat down on the worn, lacquered wood, straddling the sled with my legs while Erik watched me. 'Give me a shove,' I said, and he tapped the back of my sled with his boot. I went slowly at first, gently resting my feet on the steering peg, but then hunkered down, grabbing my ankles, and flew down the hill. A frozen breeze whistled in my ears, twisting my hair behind my neck as I squealed. 'Woohoo!'

When I got to the bottom all I heard was the

pant of my own breath surrounded by the hiss of the crystallized snow. Snowflakes stuck to my eyelashes and melted into a slushy, wintery mix on my face.

I stood and yelled up to the top of the hill 'Come on!' even though Erik couldn't hear me. The tracks of my sled curved down the slope, to the left, to the right and sometimes straight down the middle, which he followed with his own sounds of terror and joy.

Erik's sled swooshed past me. I waited for him to get off, but he didn't move. He turned to me when I laughed. 'Ella Strauss, what did you do to me?'

I balled up some snow and threw it at him, and that got him off the sled. He chased after me as I balled up another snowball in my mitted hands, and he caught me, wrapping his arms around me.

I looked up at him. 'Let's never leave this place.'

I tossed the snowball over my shoulder, and we kissed.

* * *

We drove back to Munich that evening. The girls sat on one side of the car, the boys sat on the other, looking out of their windows, barely speaking. Erik and I sat in the middle and talked the entire way back home about the snow, and where to get the coldest beer in Munich.

Alex looked over at us. 'Sounds like you two really hit it off.' He had a strange look on his face, when normally he would have been beaming from my connections with the Reich.

'It's a new year,' I said. 'Perk up.'

The driver turned the radio on, and through the crackling interference we heard the latest war bulletin. '*The mighty Germans have made a significant effort on the Eastern Front . . .*'

I'd sat in on the last administration meeting long enough to know that the Red Army had used the weather to their advantage. With the RAF on the Western Front, levelling Berlin and now targeting Frankfurt, the Reich was being squeezed on both sides. I could feel the end of my embittered world crumbling like a building under a RAF bomb.

Soon, I thought, this war really will end.

1944

27

January

Despite the winter air, there was a light spring in my step as I walked into work. It followed me all morning like a merry jingle. I had just collected a folder for Erik from a set of files on the main floor and stopped to chitchat with a guard about the snow and rodels. Not long after, Erwin's cake-thick voice snuck up behind me.

'Well, well, if it isn't Ella.'

I rolled my eyes before he could see them. 'Hello, Erwin.'

His body nudged mine. 'Heard about your little trip with Koch.' He whispered into my ear, the stench of sour milk heavy on his breath. 'You just keep getting higher and higher on the food chain now, don't you?'

I had never offered Erwin my condolences after Louise died. I knew he probably missed her, blamed me even, but I hadn't anticipated he'd corner me about it, especially not in the lobby of the V-building. 'I know you're upset about Louise, but . . . '

Erwin left as I was talking, and right out the front doors of the V-building. Even for Erwin our exchange seemed odd. His voice had changed, it didn't squeal like it used to but sounded formulaic and prescribed. The guard watched Erwin leave and then gave me a wondering look. I shrugged my shoulders.

I sat in my office and arranged the things on my desk. Sometime after lunch Erik rushed through the door, opened up the file cabinet near the door and vigorously thumbed through the file folders inside.

'Good morning!' I said, glancing at my watch. 'I mean afternoon.'

The back of his neck was red as if he had been rubbing it. 'Hello,' he said, still thumbing through the file cabinet. He seemed upset about something, but he was fine earlier in the morning when I saw him. *He'll have a drink and then he'll relax.*

I spun my chair around and pointed out the window. Snow had started to fall, and it tapped against the paned glass like tiny pebbles. 'It's snowing,' I said with delight. He gazed hard out the window and swallowed. The sharp angle of his chin matched the crooked cross on his NSDAP cuffband. 'Is everything all right?'

'Anything you want to tell me, Ella?' He glared, and I realized I had done something wrong.

'The folder.' I left it at the bottom of the stairs after I saw Erwin; I was supposed to send it by courier across the Königsplatz. I cursed Erwin for distracting me, and then apologized for leaving the folder downstairs, but Erik walked into his office and slammed the door before I had even finished talking. Hoffmann waved from down the corridor. I wasn't sure he was waving to me, but when I walked toward him it was clear he wanted to talk.

'What are you doing?' I said.

His face was straight, almost scared, and stubbly

from not shaving. He ducked into a cleaning closet and turned off the lights. One hand motioned for me to join him.

'You need to leave.' His breath smelled of whisky. 'Something big is going on. They won't tell me what.'

'Is this about the folder?' A puff of air pushed the closet door away from its casing. I saw my office at a distance. Everything was still, plain, almost sterile; and I realized how empty it was without Louise's things, that I had gone too far stripping it of the necessities and it was hard to tell I had moved in at all.

'Folder?' He shook his head and winced as if I had told him too much. 'Just go home, wait for it to blow over.'

The tone of Erik's voice — he was angry, that much I knew. I must have really messed things up for him in some way. 'You're right, maybe that would be best.'

Hoffmann sat down on a stool in between a broom and a dustpan and wiped his sweaty brow. 'I'm staying in here,' he said.

There was an ominous charge of static hovering in my office. I grabbed my coat and knocked on Erik's door. 'Erik?' I knocked again. 'I've finished up for the day and I'm going home.' I peeked through the frosted glass that separated his office from mine. He stood over his desk with his head down and his arms bracing the top as if he was going to flip it over.

Everything was silent.

* * *

It was nearly three o'clock before I made it to my flat. The buses were full and the tram had broken down so I had to walk, which seemed to happen more often as the war dragged on — the city had given almost all of its working equipment to the war effort, and the trams had to make do with what parts were left behind. Broken couplings and wheels that squealed along rusty tracks had become daily life.

I hadn't even taken my coat off before Max flew through my door. He panted for breath as if he'd been running and pushed his hands against the sides of the doorframe with wild eyes, his face stretching in all directions.

'They know — they know everything!' He lunged at me, grabbing the lapels of my coat. 'They know you're a spy.'

My stomach dropped.

'I overheard a story at the Braunes Haus: a British mole in the NSDAP had information about a contact named Sascha at the V-building — a snake in administration.'

I gasped. 'Christophe.'

'I don't know how they made the connection, but somehow they found out Sascha was you.'

My bones shook, and not from the cold but from fear, the kind a doe feels just before the arrow strikes, and in that millisecond I counted all my mistakes; the obvious ones told in Schliersee. Erik found out about my nickname. He asked some questions, and I told him about my aunt. I told him just enough to get myself caught.

Max shook my shoulders. 'I'll get a car. Meet me in the alley!'

He ran out of my flat and the door swung shut behind him. I stood, paralyzed yet shaking, with my hands in my pockets staring at the closed door. That's when I felt the Bavarian figurine Erik had bought me still in my pocket. His painted yellow mittens, his buttoned red lips, and those mouldable blue eyes. I was still holding it when I heard the Gestapo pound up the stairs, and I braced myself for what was to come.

My aunt's egg cups scooted across the shelf, falling one after the other onto the floor and shattering into a million tiny white pieces. *Boom!* They kicked my door in, and I shrieked. Max fought his way through, pleading, his face red and patched white from the strain of arms holding him back.

'Ella — '

I reached for his hand, screaming his name when something hit my temple — a muffled thump — and everything went black.

* * *

There was a tingle in my ear and the vague sense of the afternoon, but it was the smell I noticed first: like the inside of a rotted peach, sickening sweet, with hints of acid and sulphur. Then the voices came. At first, they were low and deep, blending together like a song on a sluggish turntable; then they turned loud and sharp like a bell ringing in my ear.

'This one is special. Give her everything,' a voice said.

'I planned on it,' another said.

My eyes fluttered open. I lay on a chilled, silver-topped table with wet fleeced straps tied around my wrists and a white sheet with watery-pink stains draped heavily over my body. Above my head, a glass cylinder filled with cloudy liquid that dripped into a thick pointed needle hung from a hook. A woman dressed as a nurse with a flat metal tray laden with sharp, pointed instruments — the kind I thought only dentists used — stood next to my bed humming a nursery rhyme. '*All the pretty flowers open to the sun, clap, clap, clap . . . clap, clap, clap . . .*'

I tried to move my arms, but they were as heavy as tree trunks. When I moved my head my body shuddered with a rolling twitch.

'I see our princess is awake.' Her voice was cheery and as pleasant at the nursery rhyme. She put her hands on her hips and rocked back on her heels. 'How's our little dumpling doing this morning?'

I rasped and wiggled in the straps.

'Oh, don't even try to get up,' she said. 'I'll push you right back down.'

She talked to another woman I couldn't see and they laughed and joked as if they were chatting over a cup of tea. Then their voices quieted, and the air got still. The nurse pulled the sheet off. A sinister grin spread across her face, and she admired my naked body like a fresh fish from the lake. The other woman tapped my shins from the foot of my bed. I squinted, but all I could see was the outline of a pink suit, her sleeves rolled to her elbows.

'You're going to give her everything, right?' the

woman said.

The nurse nodded. 'She'll be here a while.'

'Good,' she said. 'This one deserves it.' There was a long pause, and I felt her hot breath on my cold shins as she leaned over me. 'You're younger than I thought,' she murmured. 'Shame. You're about to be ruined.'

The nurse held a long needle in between her fingers and squirted liquid from its point. 'You didn't tell us you were pregnant.'

My eyes bulged. *Pregnant?* She pushed on my stomach and shooting pains spread like the points of a thousand arrows flying through my body. I squealed in pain. Then it felt like someone was yanking my insides out through my vagina.

The woman in pink laughed. 'Listen to that voice!'

I tried to push my knees together but my ankles were held as tight as my wrists in fleeced straps. Something wet and heavy hit the floor. The nurse leaned in, covered my mouth with her other hand and gritted her teeth.

'Don't worry. We took care of it for you.'

When I realized what she meant my belly jutted into a wave and I flopped up and down on the table. She slammed the needle into my arm, a prickled pain burned its way to my head and the room closed in.

* * *

It seemed like days had passed before they unfastened me from the table. When I was, my legs buckled and I fell to the floor. I lay there until a female guard with whiskers on her chin kicked me into a long corridor.

'Git!' she huffed. 'Git, git!'

I dragged myself away from her boot until I got to a large cemented room, painted dull white, with twelve other women walking slumped over in a circle; a thick rope connected them together at the waist. They wore tan gowns with inverted red triangles sewn at the breast. It was a patch I knew well, studied even; it was the patch of a political prisoner.

They stopped to stare, then they clapped, slowly, one by one, until they'd all gathered enough courage and it echoed into a sort of triumphant song.

'Why are they — '

'Everyone knows who you are,' one guard said.

'We get rats here, but it's not every day we get a snake, especially one so high up in the Reich,' said another.

The guards shouted, threatened to take their food away if they didn't stop. I wondered how they had heard about me, what they had heard. It was the acknowledgement I had never wanted, yet unexpectedly felt I needed.

A tired smile rested on my lips, listening to the clapping.

'All right, lift her up,' the guard bellowed.

Two other guards yanked me up by the armpits and dragged me into a cinderblock room no bigger than a large closet, with a concrete slab protruding from the wall and a tan gown slung on top of it.

I scooted into the corner. The guard with the whiskers threw a soiled rag on the ground. 'For the drips,' she said. 'Makes the cleaning easier.' She turned to leave, the heavy steel door gripped tight in her hand.

'Wait,' I said. 'Where am I?'

She stepped back into the room and smiled, the glint of a silver tooth separating her lips. 'Welcome to Hinzert.'

She poked me in the ribs with her boot and I curled into a ball. Cramps twisted near my bottom and pink liquid oozed out onto the rag she had tossed on the ground. I had become a Night and Fog prisoner, after all. I had vanished, just like Claudia had vanished.

My hands trembled and my chin quaked. I touched my belly, feeling the emptiness of what I hadn't known was inside, and quiet tears burst from my eyes.

28

September

I stood with two other girls, our backs pressed against the corridor's cold stone wall, and waited for orders to move. Depending on if it was night or day shift, the guards were either going to humiliate us or beat us with sticks. I hadn't seen the sky for months; they kept me in a small concrete room tied to a wetted rope that burned like fire, or on the table, as I called it.

We were escorted into a room with a metal desk and a door too small to be anything other than a closet. Out the corner of my eye, I could tell there were three heavyset male guards standing at the end of the desk, and one short guard standing by the door.

'Congratulations, you three,' one of the guards said. 'You've been specially chosen to play a game. But first you have to pass a few tests to prove your worthiness.'

One girl, whose ears had been nibbled on by rats, was slapped immediately across the face. Her limbs crumbled like brittle chicken bones, and she fell to the ground, didn't even try to get back up. A guard pulled her by the scruff of the neck out the door and back down the corridor.

The other girl remained still, but cowered after another guard whipped the back of her shins with a switch he had tucked in his belt.

'She moved,' he said. 'Get her out of here.'

The guard walked past me with the girl's head under his arm, his belly spilling over his belt. She had one eye and yelped like a puppy when his boot hit her, thump after thump back down the corridor.

My back straightened when I realized it was just me and two guards left. I took shallow breaths and looked at a paint-chipped dimple in the wall. *Be strong.* The last of the heavy guards leaned in, got a finger's length away from my right eye and stared, the tang of cooked apples and cabbage wafting from his nose. 'Mmm.' He took my wrist and examined the skin where it was rubbed raw from the table's fleeced straps, and grey with peeling dead skin. 'This one should work.'

I broke my gaze and looked at him dead in the eye. 'What, no whip?' I said. 'You can do better than that.'

Fire burned in his eyes, and he swung his arm back, the power of his muscles behind a flat hand ready to hit me, but the other guard stopped him, grabbing his arm mid-swing. 'Isn't that why we chose her?' he said. 'Only the strongest survive the Nazi Clock.'

My stomach sank with the words Nazi Clock — the machine Claudia tried to destroy all those years ago, the night she asked me to deliver that key. I had spent days on the table, not knowing its real name or why I felt its punch more than anyone else. I asked once. The nurse told me it was because they liked the way I twitched.

'She's perfect for this game,' he said. 'Now let's play. My tea is getting cold.' His voice was familiar, but it wasn't from inside Hinzert — somewhere else. *Munich? Nuremberg?* The bend in my knee curved a little more as I tried to place it, then I looked at him without permission. His hair was thick and wavy now, but there was no mistaking his sour look or the way he wore his clothes; a size too small and buttoned to his neck. I wouldn't dare speak his name, not in front of the other guard, but I said it in my mind. *Hans.* The Falcon from Nuremberg who betrayed Wilhelm and Claudia, along with every single one of us.

'Fine.' The guard threw me into a chair and shoved me into the desk, pinning me between the two. 'This is Betteln.'

Hans sat on the corner of the desk with his arms folded and his cup of tea near his thigh. 'Tell us a good story and plead your case as to why you deserve an item from the cloakroom . . . '

I felt my right eye constrict into a stinky squint. I remembered the game well, the game Alma had told me the guards played, the game Claudia played to win her freedom. 'I know how it's played, and if you think I'm going to give you a laugh — think again.'

Hans tapped his fingers on his forearm. 'Give me some time with this one . . . alone.' We stared at each other and I was sure he knew I had recognized him.

The guard tugged on my hair. 'Yeah, knock some sense into her. The radio isn't working and my foot is tired from the kicking.' He walked out of the room and locked the door behind him.

The room got quiet. Hans rubbed the back of his neck and closed his eyes as if he were thinking about something. I pushed myself back from the desk and braced my feet against the floor like a cat about to pounce. But I knew I didn't have the strength to do much of anything. My words were all I had.

'Damn, Sascha, you're the last one I expected to see in prison.' He opened his eyes and exhaled. 'I thought you'd go all the way.'

His tone confused me. He made it sound like I had let him down, when I expected him to gloat, talk about how he'd fooled Wilhelm and slipped a leaflet in his pocket. 'You seem disappointed.'

'You were the only Falcon I knew was still active.'

I stood and poked my finger into his chest. 'You killed the Falcons.'

'No, no, no. That was your friend, Sarah. *Not me.*' He pushed my finger back, and I sat back down.

'Sarah?' I said. 'You were the one Wilhelm cursed as he was arrested. You were the one cavorting at the Hütt'n. The restaurant only Nazis went to.'

His eyes lowered into a lazy gaze. 'Let me guess, Sarah told you this? Do you think it was a coincidence she sent you to the antiques shop on the very night it got busted? Or that Claudia got nabbed just after Sarah went to fetch her?'

I sank into the chair, my mind racing. *Sarah?*

'I was transferred to Hinzert last week,' he said. 'I've been in Poland working undercover for the British. I thought Claudia might have told you.'

'Claudia? You've talked to her?'

'Not since I helped her escape from this place,' he said.

'That was me, Hans. I helped her escape. I was the one who picked her prison number for Betteln, and she used her prize to escape through the prison bars. Lard, as I recall. She always had some in her rucksack to help with her wigs.'

He chuckled. 'It's one thing to rig the selection for Betteln, but it's quite another to secure an escape route that won't get you shot by the nearest guard on duty.'

My face jolted. 'You saw me when I came to Hinzert, when I worked for the Reich?'

'I was sent to Hinzert for field orientation before the Reich sent me abroad, and I saw you touring the grounds. But I didn't know Claudia was a prisoner until they brought her in for the game.'

A moment of silence passed between us. So much had happened since we were both Falcons in Nuremberg. And to think all this time I thought it was Hans who had tricked us, when really it was Sarah. It blew my mind.

'Have you kept in touch with the other Falcons?' he said. 'What ever happened to Geb?'

Max. I tried to imagine his face, but it was gone, washed away with the rain. 'I don't know where he is.' It sickened me to think Max was anywhere else other than living the life he had created in Munich. The Gestapo fought him back when they arrested me, they didn't know who he really was then, and I never said his name during interrogations, no matter how many times they hit me.

Hans laced his fingers together on top of his head and exhaled. I didn't know what he was thinking, but by the sag in his eyes I was pretty sure he pitied me — he was still undercover, while

I was a scraggly has-been whose own carelessness had got her caught.

'Don't do that,' I said.

'Do what?'

'Feel sorry for me,' I said. 'I'll be fine.'

'No, Sascha. You won't.' He shook his head as if he knew something I didn't. 'The Night and Fog prisoners are being transferred. My guess is they have plans for you, plans more brutal than you've experienced here.'

'They're moving me?' There was a sense of familiarity with Hinzert, I knew the tortures well, and I realized I'd die there. Thinking of dying somewhere else seemed strange.

'Listen,' he said. 'You need to play this game. You'll get to pick something from your property, and the coat you were arrested in is in the cloakroom. Afterwards, the guards want me to chain you up in the courtyard, and with the coat you could hide. Remember the border fence when you visited?'

I thought back to the tour I had with Alma and the camp kommandant. 'I think I do.' I remembered something about a missing section of fence near the forest's edge, a portion you couldn't see from the compound. 'Are you talking about the part that was torn down so they could bring in supplies?'

He nodded. 'Just look out for the dogs. They run loose around the perimeter.'

My heart skipped and then banged against my rib cage when I realized what he was really saying, what I could do when nobody was watching. 'I can escape.'

Heavy footsteps thumped down the corridor. The guard was on his way back. Hans swung his eyes to the door and then back to me. 'First, there's something I need to do.'

He opened the desk's top drawer and pulled out a roll of tape. 'I have to make it look like I did something bad to you.' He tore a short piece of tape from the roll and stuck it over my mouth. 'The shifts change at midnight. You'll know the time because the lights on the outbuildings flicker on the stroke. Head west, it's only a day's walk to Luxembourg. The Allies are making their way there from Belgium. A pocket of freedom.'

The door unlocked and the guard marched in with an agitated look. 'You done yet?'

Hans ripped the tape from my mouth. 'Now I am,' he said, and I closed my eyes from the burn.

The guard sat in a chair on the other side of the desk next to the closet door. He adjusted his belt with one hand. 'Well . . . get on with it,' he said. 'I've been waiting all day, and my wife's expecting a good story when I get home.'

I coughed up some blood from my fragile lungs and spat it on the floor. 'What do you want to hear?'

'You're the spy,' the guard said. 'I'm sure you have something locked away in that head of yours.' Moments passed, but I couldn't think of anything, and the guard became impatient, thumping his feet on the floor and barking at Hans. 'I thought you said she'd play?'

Hans lunged at me with his hand raised high in the air.

'All right, all right,' I said with a wince. 'I'll talk.'

Hans rested his hip on the side of the desk and folded his arms while I gazed directly into the guard's eyes. My hair had been lopped off months ago, and cut close to my head, but I swear I could feel my old frizzy locks brushing against my shoulders as I flipped my head from side to side and sat up tall.

I talked about Louise's girdle, how it squeaked like a child's toy. I told them about Hoffmann's drinking, and made up a story about how I peed in his whisky bottle, but nothing I said got a reaction. When the guard clenched his fist and studied the white of his knuckles, I knew I had to dig deep.

'But you want to know how I really got to the top? I shaved all the hair from my body down below and didn't wear underwear for a week.'

He gulped, but Hans smiled, looking very proud.

'My wife's going to love that one,' the guard said. He opened the closet door with a punch from the side of his fist; brown bags labelled with numbers were stacked as high as the ceiling. My coat, visible, and folded on the shelf.

He waved a finger at Hans. 'Tie her up outside.'

* * *

Hans chained me up by one wrist to an iron post in the far corner of the clay courtyard. It was tight enough to fool the guard who accompanied us outside, but loose enough to fit through as long as I could crack a bone to do it. So many times I was made to stand in the clay courtyard — the same courtyard I saw Claudia in — guards wielding whips at my back or hunks of wood with nails bored into the end. But my mind was on something else. I looked beyond the huts, where the broken, rain-swept night sky met the pitch-black gash of the forest and thought: freedom.

Hans put a pie tin filled with cold porridge onto the clay ground — a prisoner's dinner. The mush slopped over the sides and looked more like vomit than a meal. 'Remember the dogs,' Hans whispered as he left. I scooped handfuls of it into my coat pocket for later and lapped the rain that pooled in the tile's divots. Then I tightened my prison sandals, and waited on bended foot for the right moment to run.

The lights flickered on the outbuildings. I squeezed my hand through the chain, tugging, gritting, pulling, glancing up at the guard tower, anticipating signs of life, pointing rifles, until I heard a loud crack in my thumb, and the chain slipped off.

I escaped across the soggy field, wheezing from failing lungs, with my eyes set on two fence posts with nothing but the night and forest between them. My legs felt like gelatine, wobbly and soft, as if my bones had liquefied.

Out of nowhere a racing growl came up behind me. I turned around in the dark, shaking and scared. 'Here, boys,' I said, weakly, scooping the mush from my pocket. 'Here . . . 'The dogs' snarls turned into whines. One dog licked the mush from my hand and my broken thumb dangled in its mouth.

When they finished eating, they simply trotted off.

I tore the red triangle patch off my chest. *I'm not your prisoner.* A pang of guilt hit me as I stole one last glimpse of the prison huts glimmering in the distance, thinking of all the others left behind — the girl with the nibbled ears and the one with the missing eye — before ducking into the forest, dark-blind, and heavy.

I went as far as I could until my legs gave out, buckling like snapped twigs, then I started to crawl, the thrust of my hips and the withered strength of my forearms, pushing through the rich, peaty ground. It wasn't uncommon to hear the rumble of tanks coming from the woods, and if there were tanks, there were troops. I would have to keep my head down when the sun came up.

By midday, the arms of my coat were riddled with gaping holes and my elbows looked as raw as boiled ox tail. My legs had turned purple, stunk of diseased meat and had tiny iridescent ants swarming in the cuts.

I came to a wide clearing dotted with stumps and burnt trees that crisscrossed each other. In the middle, a bottomless sinkhole swirled like a vat of quicksand with the tail of a plane sticking out of it; the charred image of a swastika painted on its side. Pieces of the plane's cockpit, wings and the propeller circled around it in chunked-up bits. No signs of the pilot.

I didn't think I had the strength to walk around it, the clearing stretched for kilometres in both directions — I had to go through it.

I waited for a sound, any kind of movement to give me warning, but I heard nothing that resembled the rumble of a tank. A woodpecker chipped at a tree trunk in the far distance, the hush of a soft wind blew through the pine trees, and I limped, one bloody stump of a foot dragging behind the other. Halfway through, a handful of black birds burst from the trees, their chirps turning into caws. The ground shook, vibrated almost, and the air hummed with the sound of Panzers.

I limped faster and faster — it was too late to go back — as three tanks broke into the clearing and down a rustic road that disappeared into the forest behind me, hurdling small earthen mounds like giant, skipping rocks.

My limp turned into a desperate, painful gallop, and they fired; the hiss and sneer of their bullets marked by bursts of kindling on the ground in front of me. I tripped and fell into a rise of jagged shrapnel that sliced my shin and cut my lip — my body too numb to feel the pain. Two holes made from something incredibly sharp poking out of the ground, appeared in the centres of my palms. I collapsed, the hum of the tanks fading into the background. I didn't think I could go on and thought about dying. Then I saw something sticking out of my pocket, something I hadn't seen in months: my yellow scarf. I gave it a light tug, pulling it from my pocket and held it in my hand.

I swallowed the only drop of saliva I had left on my tongue and it lumped in my throat like a rock. *I'm too exhausted to go on.* My heart began to slow, so much so I could feel the stillness between each thump. My face sank into a patch of soft black dirt, and I felt my skin melt into the ground like a candle waxing in its dish. But then I heard a voice and felt hands on my shoulders trying to jostle me back to life. 'Ella,' she said. 'Ella . . .'

Claudia.

I could barely make out her eyes, which grew with her smile. 'Roll over,' she said. 'They're coming.' Soft lips pressed against my cheek, and like a bolt my conscious had slammed back into my body. My chest filled with air and I rolled over, gasping as if I had been underwater.

Tyres rumbling in the near distance screeched to a stop near my head. Shuffled feet scurried in all directions, one pair of dusty boots stood next to my head. Through dried mud and the blare of the sun, I saw the shadowed outline of a man staring down at me.

'*Mademoiselle,*' he said in a broken French accent. '*Mademoiselle.*'

He bent to his knees, and a coarse hand swiped dirt from my face. The lines near his eyes multiplied with his smile. Dark eyebrows grew over deep-set hazel eyes with thick lashes. A beard of dust shadowed his jaw line, which made him look distinguished rather than gritty. But it was the roundness of his face and the sweetness of his voice that confused me . . . he wasn't German, British or French.

I traced the rim of his helmet with my finger. It was weather-beaten green with torn netting across the top with an unfastened chinstrap dangling from one side. My arm went limp. He caught it by the wrist and held it gently in his hand. 'I'm an American soldier. I'll save you,' he said in English. He spun a finger in the air and shouted at someone I couldn't see. 'We're packing her up, getting out of here.' He plucked the scarf from my other hand, shook it out and then tucked it into a small pocket hidden in his faded green uniform.

I didn't understand everything he said, but I picked out the American part and that we were leaving. It had been years since I studied English, before the Reich took it out of the schools, and Christophe rarely used it around me. But it wasn't much different than French and I could speak a little of it if I had to, if I needed to.

I wasn't sure how the Americans would treat a German. Would they think I was a scout? Play off their sympathies and report back to the Reich what I had seen? I thought my chances of survival were better if I pretended to be from Luxembourg and spoke the language he'd expect: French.

'*Américaine?*' I said.

He nodded.

'Est-ce le Luxembourg?'

'*Oui*, Luxembourg,' he said. 'Liberation day.'

Liberation. I smiled, closing my eyes, a faint laugh gurgled in my throat. *I made it.*

He scooped me in his arms, lifting me from the ground, and my bones felt as if they had been recalled from some faraway place to join with the rest of my body.

'Wait,' I said, grappling for strength. 'My friend, Claudia . . . ' I pointed back to where I'd been lying, lifting my head up, but saw only the mud outline of my body.

He turned around. 'Who?'

And I realized I'd imagined her and sunk back into his arms.

He carried me to the bed of a green military

truck that had metal casings rolling around in the rippled grooves of its tail-end. He laid me next to a man with a bloody wound cut into his thigh, his body jittering like an engine, shell-shocked and weary. His shirt was torn, but I recognized the coat of arms pin on his right breast: Luxembourg Resistance.

The soldier's arms slipped away as he laid me down and the strangest sensation befell over me, one of falling off a high cliff with nothing below but some jagged rocks and a shallow stream. I was alone, more alone than I had ever been before. I pulled him back with my good hand, clenched his uniform by the buttons and dug my fingers desperately into the holes.

'S'il vous plait . . . ne me quitte pas, ma famille est morte.'

His forehead wrinkled. 'I only speak a little . . . '

Someone shouted at a near distance, 'She wants you to stay with her. Family's dead.'

He cradled my head in his hands and spoke loud and slow, 'Don't worry, you're in the hands of the United States 5th Armoured Division.' His smile was dingy yellow, but his words were like a song.

A medic swooped in out of nowhere and opened a small metal box filled with bandages. Then something poked me, and my body warmed as if I had drank an entire glass of brandy in one shot.

'For the pain,' the medic said in French.

'*Merci*,' I slurred. My eyes drooped to a close. I felt a lethargic smile tug on my lips. '*Merci* . . . '

29

After a brief stay in a makeshift hospital set up for those wounded during the liberation, I was moved in the middle of the night by a convoy of sisters to the nave of Saint Michael's Church in Luxembourg City. I assumed the hospital had become too crowded and they took me in, like the true orphan I was. One of them shushed me, told me not to talk until I was strong. I nodded, fell asleep and took her advice literally, feeling safer with the silence.

I lay there for weeks on a metal-framed bed with a thin mattress and an even thinner, almost see-through white curtain strung between my bed and one other that was empty. The sisters put me in a ruffled blue sleeping gown and bowed fresh bandages around my knees and elbows like ribbons. Sometimes I heard onlookers, who occasionally stood on the other side of the veil, wondering who I was, what village in Luxembourg I had come from.

I spent my days staring at the stained-glass windows set high in the church's stone walls. When the sun crept in, I gazed at beams of coloured light that danced under the ceiling's shallow coffered arches. Often, the shadows of Allied bomber planes streaked across the stones. The rumbling from their engines shook my bed and my bones they were so close.

Three times a day the sisters walked in single

file from the narthex into the nave with a low-burning white candle cupped between their hands. The hems of their black habits swooshed against their feet as they walked and the candles spread a peaceful, yet ghostlike glow onto their faces, which were flush against the black veils that covered their heads and cascaded down their shoulders like hair.

They stood at the foot of my bed and prayed silently. After a few minutes, they bent to their knees, rubbed scentless oil into the palms of my hands, kissed my wrists, and then walked out the same way they came in.

One morning I woke to find a girl lying in the next bed to me. Her face was sickly white, with grey lips and droopy blue eyes that stared right into mine. A long, frizzy braid of blonde hair lay against her neck and disappeared into the white sheets.

She rested on her side with her left hand draped over her waist and the other flattened near her face. Sometimes her arms tightened and her chest constricted. I pulled our beds closer using her rail. A tired smile hung on her lips, and I thought she was glad I had done it. Then she went to sleep.

That night I had a dream, and it was the first dream I could remember since I'd been arrested.

I walked barefoot in a garden of root vegetables that had ripened to the point of spoiling. In the distance a range of purple mountains with white peaks pointed to a halo of orange sunlight. A sister from the church, the one who most often prayed beside my bedside, walked with me, her hands clasped loosely behind her back. Instead of her habit, she wore black trousers and a fitted men's shirt that buttoned up the front. Dark hair flowed like a chocolatey river down her back, and grey, almost crystalline eyes watched me as we walked.

I pointed to the brown and mushy spots on the vegetables. 'There's so much food going to waste.'

Her mouth never opened when she talked. 'Look beyond the vegetables to the far side of the garden, where the field had been harvested weeks prior and think about the crops that had made it into the mouths of the hungry.'

'But why were these crops neglected?'

'What makes you think they were?' she said. 'Do they not supply nourishment to the creatures of the soil or fatten the earth for the next harvest?'

Before I could answer, she asked me what I thought of the mountains, said sometimes the only way to reach new heights was to start at the bottom. I stopped walking and stared at the mountains' white snow-caps. Then images of my aunt, smiling, baking desserts in the kitchen of our half-timbered house in Nuremberg reeled in my mind like a movie projector. Her hair had more grey than blonde in it and her lips were paler than they ought to be. I knew she missed me, yet I also had the overwhelming feeling that she knew I was alive, and that I was safe.

The sister smiled. 'I know what you saw.'

'What about Claudia? And Max?' I asked. 'Both of them have their own paths. Their own destinies.' Suddenly there was a blue rose in her hand, which she handed to me.

'I've seen this before.'

'In a painting,' she said, smiling. 'You must become the blue rose again, Ella. If you want to survive . . . '

I woke up some time in the middle of the night

thinking about the mountain peaks, and how they looked like whipped cream against the clear blue sky.

White pillar candles had been placed at a distance near the high altar and dulled the air with light shadow. I stretched in my bed. The dream had revived me in a way I couldn't explain. A slight groan seeped from the corner of my mouth. I pulled the bandages from my arms and legs. My joints didn't hurt like they had before and the wounds around my knees and elbows had completely healed. Even the grey rings the Nazi Clock had left around my wrists had faded.

The new girl watched me with sagging, nearly closed eyes. 'You're getting better,' she said in French, but her accent was unexpectedly flat. Her hand flopped against the metal frame of my bed and opened like a flower.

'Did they put oil in your palm?'

'*Oui*,' I said.

She closed her eyes as if it was a nod.

'Why do they do that?' I said, continuing our conversation in French.

Her throat sputtered with a moaned laugh, and the darkened hollows under her cheek bones sank into her face. '*Vous ne savez pas?*'

'*Non*,' I said. 'Should I know?'

Her arms tightened and her hands curled into fists. Usually she let the spasms pass without so much as a whimper, but this time her face winced with pain.

'What's happening to you?' I said.

'The Nazis poisoned me,' she said. 'The sisters think they can save me, but I feel dead already.'

'Do you have family?'

She lifted her head just a hair and closed her eyes. 'What's that accent I hear?'

I bit my lip and said nothing. She was nice, and I felt sorry for her, but I didn't feel comfortable enough to tell her my true identity: that I was not Luxembourgian, but one of the enemies of this war. I was German.

'Don't worry,' she said. 'You can hide your German accent just like I hid my American one from the Nazis that took over my village.'

She knows. I scooted up. 'I'm just trying to survive,' I said, defensively.

'I know,' she said. 'I can tell you're different. You wouldn't be here if you weren't.'

I was relieved she didn't judge me cruelly, and I thought it best not to press the subject. But I did wonder how an American had ended up living in Luxembourg. 'American? What is an American girl doing in Luxembourg?'

'I was born there, but I've lived in Luxembourg since I was a child.' She patted her chest and moved something hidden under her dress. 'I've got the documents to prove it.' Her eyes drooped to a close and her voice trailed into a whisper. 'Hold my hand.' She offered me her palm.

She fell asleep again, and I watched her for many hours with her eyes closed. Then sometime just after dawn, her hand went limp and her pulse turned into a calm chill. An odd smile gaped in her mouth. She's dead.

A small brown booklet slipped into the vee of her collar, and I sat up with a jolt. *Become the blue rose.* My eyes shifted to the narthex, then back to her limp, war-thin body. *The war has dragged on for years, and it could drag on for even more. What if the Reich takes Luxembourg again? If they don't kill me on the spot, they'll send me back to prison — which is just as good as dying.*

I pulled the booklet slowly from her dress and tucked it into mine. Then I slipped off the side of my bed, my feet searching the unfamiliar ground for support. My legs wobbled like noodles under the weight of my body. A wooden door set into the stone wall on the other side of the nave called out to me as if I was in a dream, and I took a step, and then another, until I made it to the other side of the church, and snuck out of the door with the dead girl's documents poking out of my brassiere.

⋆ ⋆ ⋆

The sun had risen and streaks of yellow light filtered through the buildings and onto the street like warm rays of gold. I walked slowly to the end of a cobblestoned courtyard near the city's edge and sat on a low stone wall that overlooked a field that swayed with tall green grasses. On the other side, the Americans had set up a base camp that bustled like a small city; smoking barrels lined the perimeter, armoured vehicles rumbled in and out. Some soldiers relaxed in netted beds strung between vehicles while others sunned themselves on the tops of tanks, smoking and joking. If it hadn't been for the distant boom of mortar fire in the north, one would have thought they were camping, perhaps even on a retreat.

I arched my neck to catch the sun on my face,

dangled my feet on the other side of the wall, and let the warm sunlight absorb into my skin. A small market with tattered tents of various colours assembled behind me. Little old ladies with their grey hair twisted into buns pinned tight behind their heads, sold meagre items, mostly wax, nuts and things the Nazis left behind. I pulled the girl's brown booklet from my brassiere and brushed my thumb over the faded black lettering on the front: United States Passport. Inside was a visa from Luxembourg dated 1920. An old photo of a girl about five years old or so stuck to the right corner; she had poufy blonde hair and an innocent smile that tethered chunky cheeks. The paper called her Anna.

I tucked it back into the top of my gown and gazed at the soldiers on the other side of the field behind the barbed wire fence. One sat on the front wing of a dusty green jeep with a white star painted on its door. A guitar rested on his knee. His calf-length boot, coated in European dirt, used the jeep's metal bumper as a foot stand. He watched his own fingers as he strummed the strings on his guitar and played a song I could barely hear.

A withered old lady with worn pointed heels, and a dirty white kerchief tied under her chin, stepped out from behind a merchant's tent, shaking her bony index finger at my hands. '*Les marques de Jésus-Christ*,' she said in a voice too agitated for me to figure out if she was scared or excited.

'What?' I said, and then noticed the splotches of blood my hands had made on the stone wall, which alarmed me at first as much as they did her. She ducked back behind the tent, anchored her eye in a thumb-sized tear in its canvas fabric and watched me inspect the wounds centred in my palms.

Is this why I was taken to the church?

I wanted to say they were escape wounds, long since healed over, but the words never came. I looked back at her, and her one big eye peeping through the canvas. Suddenly every note coming from the soldier's guitar turned crystal clear, and I thought, whatever the reasons were for the wounds, if they were an anomaly or if they were in fact divinely bestowed, one thing was for sure: if I hadn't been brought to that church I wouldn't have ended up with Anna's documents in my brassiere.

Just then, the barbed wire that bordered the far end of the field was rolled back, and opened like a gate that led right to the soldier on the jeep.

I stepped down off the stone wall.

My legs felt strong, sturdier then they had before, and I walked, slowly at first, through the field toward the gap in the fence, the grasses getting taller, greener and more lustrous the closer I got to the soldier. He lifted his head; deep-set hazel eyes watched me from under thick lashes. 'Hey, I remember you.' He smiled, reached into a small pocket hidden in his faded green uniform and pulled out a very tattered yellow scarf.

I stopped, disbelieving, and studied his face. He was all cleaned up now, and suddenly completely recognizable: the soldier that rescued me all those weeks ago. His voice was as reassuring as the day he pulled me out of the mud.

He waved the scarf at me, smiling. 'I was hoping

I'd see you again,' he said in English.

I gently pushed his hand back. I didn't want the scarf anymore. I wasn't a jumpbox; I wasn't a resister or a spy. I reached into the top of my gown, pulled the passport from my brassiere and remembered Anna's flat American accent.

There was a shift — the memory of my aunt, Claudia, and Max silenced like characters in a closed book as I felt Anna's gaunt face and body veil my own.

A good shop girl can make a person believe anything.

The dull roar of an American transport plane rumbled in the distance. I thought about what it would be like to be on it and move far away from here — as far away as I could get — as I answered him back in my best French-somewhat-American-accent.

'Me too.' I handed him the passport.

Acknowledgments

There are so many people to thank. Firstly, this book would not be in print today if it wasn't for the passion and drive of my fabulous editor, Hannah Smith. Her ideas and suggestions turned my manuscript into a book and I'm eternally grateful. She also made my dream come true, and that's an amazing thing! I also want to thank the entire team at Aria Fiction for all of the behind-the-scenes work they did to bring this novel to life. Thank you to my agent, Kate Nash, for her expert advice and for answering every single question I had (and I had a lot). Kate, her clients, and her team have been especially supportive of me, and at times I've had to pinch myself.

Thank you to my husband, Matt, and my two kids, Zane and Drew, for their encouragement, unrelenting support, and for listening to me talk about 'my book' for ten long years. Thank you to my sister, Lori Burns, and my parents. They never once stopped believing in my book, even while I was swimming in a sea of rejection.

This book started with an idea, but as I worked my way through the first draft, I quickly became overwhelmed and I thought I should just give up. If it wasn't for the early reads from Katie Flanagan and Rebecca Wedberg I just might have. Along the way I met Paula Butterfield, an incredible writer who was literally the only person I could talk shop with. She helped me with plot ideas, gave me advice, and read every single word I pushed at her, even when she was knee-deep in her own edits.

Lastly, thank you to the Pacific Northwest Writers Association for the writing award I received many years ago. It was the boost I needed at just the right time.

Author's Note

This book is a work of fiction, however, the backdrop and setting are based and inspired by real events, people, and places. I would love to go through every page and tell you what inspired me and what I fictionalized to craft this story, but since I can't, I'd like to tell you a few interesting facts.

First and foremost, the Nuremberg Kunstbunker was indeed a real thing, although the date of construction happened a little earlier than it does in this story. Many years ago, I caught a documentary on the History Channel about the art bunker (and the little antiques shop next door.) With my background in history, I was aware there were youth in the German Resistance, but it wasn't until after I saw the documentary that I started researching who exactly these youths were and what they did. This is when the pieces for *The Girl I Left Behind* came together.

The Falcons were inspired by many resistance groups. The Swing Kids was a group (and a movement) who openly resisted the confines of Nazi behavior. They listened to banned music and essentially behaved like American teens, which was absolutely scandalous and an arrestable offense. The Edelweiss Pirates and Leipzig Meuten were much different, most remembered for their violent street thug behavior and clashes with the Hitler Youth. Other groups were more organized; they printed phony identification papers and provided safe houses for Jews. Then there were the special sects: renegades — some of them female — who sabotaged patrols, schemed to assassinate Hitler, and infiltrated the Reich to spy for the British. It was upon learning this that the idea to have *The Girl I Left Behind* play out as a female-driven spy novel became too good to resist.

Many emails were exchanged with various places in Munich and Nuremberg to confirm or shed light on information I had researched. Some got back to me; some did not. The Korn und Berg bookstore was one that wrote back. It was through this exchange I learned about the windows, and how Hitler himself had ordered the shopkeeper to change the shape.

Hinzert prison was a political prison that also kept Night and Fog prisoners. The flowerbeds and gardens were real; only a true monster could create this place. The Königsplatz was a unique area because it was where all sorts of different departments within the Reich came together. When I learned this, I had to place Ella there to give her maximum opportunity. Toyoka is a work of fiction, but Hiroshi Oshima, the Japanese Ambassador, was real. I read that he was extremely careless with his communications and the Allies gleaned a lot of information from him. I thought it was an interesting twist to rewrite history and give him a beautiful Japanese girlfriend who was actually a British spy. Yes, he was careless and ignorant, but it seemed much more interesting to me if the intelligence the Allies received was actually a calculated effort by a woman.

Sophie Scholl and the White Rose were indeed real; I couldn't write a book about the German Resistance and not include the White Rose in it. They were notoriously passive, yet provocative with their anti-Nazi leaflets, and incredibly brave.

Writing *The Girl I Left Behind* was my way of exploring this time in history. What was it like to be a young woman in the resistance, and how far would she go in the name of freedom? Most importantly, what would make her break? Sure, history can tell us these things, but through fiction we can feel them.

I hope you enjoyed my book. Thanks for reading!

We do hope that you have enjoyed reading this large print book.

Did you know that all of our titles are available for purchase?

We publish a wide range of high quality large print books including:
Romances, Mysteries, Classics
General Fiction
Non Fiction and Westerns

Special interest titles available in large print are:
The Little Oxford Dictionary
Music Book, Song Book
Hymn Book, Service Book

Also available from us courtesy of Oxford University Press:
Young Readers' Dictionary
(large print edition)
Young Readers' Thesaurus
(large print edition)

For further information or a free brochure, please contact us at:
Ulverscroft Large Print Books Ltd.,
The Green, Bradgate Road, Anstey,
Leicester, LE7 7FU, England.
Tel: (00 44) **0116 236 4325**
Fax: (00 44) **0116 234 0205**

Other titles published by Ulverscroft:

A WIDOW'S VOW

Rachel Brimble

1851. After her merchant husband saved her from a life of prostitution, Louisa Hill was briefly happy as a housewife in Bristol. But then, her husband is found hanged in a Bath hotel room, a note and a key to a property in Bath the only things she has left of him. And now the debt collectors will come calling.

Left with no means of income, Louisa knows she has nothing to turn to but her old way of life. But this time, she'll do it on her own terms — by turning her home into a brothel for upper class gentlemen.

Enlisting the help of Jacob Jackson, a quiet but feared boxer, to watch over the house, Louisa is about to embark on a life she never envisaged. Can she find the courage to forge this new path?

THE WOMEN OF WATERLOO BRIDGE

Jan Casey

London, 1940. After her fiancé breaks off their engagement, Evelyn decides to do her part for the war effort by signing up for construction work on Waterloo Bridge. She begins to realise that there could be so much more to her life than anything she'd ever dared to dream of.

Grieving after her little boy dies in an air raid, Gwen is completely lost when her husband sends their younger children to the countryside for safety. Enlisting as a construction worker, she is partnered with cheerful Evelyn. The two women strike up a heartwarming friendship.

Musical prodigy Joan's life has always been dictated by her controlling mother. When an affair nearly ends in scandal, Joan finally takes her life into her own hands. She soon finds work at Waterloo Bridge. Yet there are other troubles for her to overcome . . .

THE RELUCTANT HEIRESS

Dilly Court

East-End London, 1858. In London's twisting streets, it's hard to tell friend from foe. And for Katherine Martin, arriving back in London after years away, the city is far crueller than she remembers. Her eyes opened to the plight of London's poor, Kate is determined to do what she can to help — even if it means defying her parents. In secret, she opens a soup kitchen. But there is a world of criminals within London's poorest alleys. Catching the notice of Harry Trader and his gang, Kate is out of her depth. Until she begins to discover that her true enemies might not be who she thought . . .